CRY OF DECAY

CRY OF DECAY

BOOK TWO OF THE NECROMANCER SAGA

PAUL BARRETT

Charlotte, NC

FALSTAFF
BOOKS
WWW.FALSTAFFBOOKS.COM

This book is for Aunt Liz, who has always been there when I needed her, and on many occasions when I didn't deserve her.

1

And so it was that the Covenant sundered the Gods, sowing division between Alaisanatha and her siblings; she departed the Heaven of Caros and vowed to never again sully herself with its presence.
  -Tanaran Rown, *Stories of the Gods*

A shiver of dread crawled over Erick's spine. It had nothing to do with the chill air of the dim cavern where he stood and everything to do with the pronouncement his spectral fore-bears had just delivered.

You are the only Necromancer left, Erick Darvaul.

Erick stared at the ten ghosts before him, spirits dead almost a millennium past. Their solid forms, surrounded by a dim glow of white light, stood before him, tiny figures in the amber sheen of the vast chamber.

"The only Necromancer left?" Erick asked, voice cracking as if he were an untried child and not a man of seventeen. He glanced at the quintet of younger traveling companions who stood motionless behind him. He wondered if the statement terrified them as much as it did him. "How is that possible?"

The shades regarded each other as if deciding who among them should answer. Ten people who had been a cadre in life, now forever bound in death to this chamber, where they defeated two of the *Inconnu* and banished the third.

Erick was supposed to have met a similar coterie of living Necromancers here to again battle Eligos, the Master of Shadows. Instead, his predecessors had informed him three of his would-be allies had been killed, and two joined to the cause of the enemy.

The mental conversation passing between the ghosts tickled at the edges of Erick's brain, annoying him like an itch between the shoulder blades, insubstantial as fog. Fear of what he might learn kept him from intruding into their discussion.

Eventually, they turned back to him. Eight of the figures gave him a solemn nod and then faded away. Two remained: Erick's great grandfather many times over, and a stern-faced woman with deep green eyes that, even in spectral form, felt as if they drilled through Erick's soul. Erick watched as their forms, already near solid, grew more so, and they looked nearly alive. The white halo around them brightened as if the disappearance of the others gave them extra energy.

Perhaps it does, Erick thought. They had shared the power of *elonsha* in life to defeat the Master of Shadows. It stood to reason they could also share it in death. He gave another glance back to his friends, trying to gauge their thoughts. Elissia, the girl he loved, looked as pale as her olive skin would allow, her almond-shaped eyes wide. Marcus, her twin brother, stood beside Corby, their cousin. Corby had his head cocked inquisitively, curious at all that happened, as was the scholar's wont. Marcus, used to danger in his profession as a thief, straddled the middle, eyes bright with interest but body tense, ready to flee or fight as necessary. Gabrielle, the group's healer, offered no expression. But then, her enthusiasm for anything had been missing in the past weeks.

Or it could just be exhaustion, Blink, Erick's gargoyle-like familiar, thought to him. *Everyone's worn out.*

Erick couldn't argue with that. He turned his head back and found the man and woman patiently waiting for his attention.

"I am Dendrick, the father of your father, many generations past,"

2

the man said. "This is Janella. Her descendant was one of those killed trying to reach this place. We shall speak for all those who remain here."

"What happened?" Erick asked.

Dendrick, the brown in his curly hair now almost as vibrant as Erick's despite his ghostly nature, answered. "As soon as Eligos resurrected, he sent forth a cry to the Fist, and they dispatched *Eligoi*. They killed Janas as she traveled here."

Erick shuddered at the mention of the fanatical assassins whose only purpose in life was to kill for their dark master. Erick's encounter with these murderers ended with a narrow escape as his home burned to the ground.

The woman's eyes softened. "She is in the Heaven of Caros, for she died performing her solemn duty."

Dendrick continued. "When we felt the power of Eligos returned to the world, we sent out our warning. We bade all to flee and make for *Twr Krinnik*. Only you were successful."

"The only warning I received was three assassins," Erick said, his voice bitter. *"Eligoi* attacked me in my house, and I almost died."

He didn't want to consider the ruin wrought by his compassion in letting one of the *Eligoi* live. Eligos had killed that assassin and turned the body into his *talba*, a vessel to contain his malevolent essence. This entity had tracked Erick to the town of Prospector's Camp, destroyed it, and nearly killed him and his companions.

"Your father should have heard our call. Did he not warn you?"

"I have to assume he died before he could tell me." Erick didn't want to explain that his father's meddling with an ancient tome had brought about the Master of Shadows's resurrection.

"This is a fine wake up," Marcus said. The Procurer, as his guild of thieves was known, had saved Erick's life by killing the *Inconnu's talba*. Before Eligos fled the dying vessel, he had branded Marcus with a *morazol*, a death mark. "What in the Seven Hells do we do now?"

"We do not blaspheme in this chamber." The stern-faced woman turned her pale, penetrating eyes toward Marcus. "The Demon Lords did not deign to involve themselves in the *Inconnu* War, and for that, we thank the Gods. By invoking their realms, you call their attention,

3

and that you do not want. Just as you want no notice taken of you by the Insane Ones."

Erick's breath caught. He knew the Hells existed, as surely as he knew the Gods existed. Alakaneth judged those who died and shepherded their souls to the afterlife that befitted their deeds in life. When Erick called a long-departed soul to inhabit his creations, they always came from the Heaven of Caros. There were certain lesser creatures that could be created using the souls of those from the Hells, but Erick would not use them. He didn't want to deal with such evil.

The Gods, powerful as they were, had never directly intervened in the *Inconnu* War. *Was it possible for the Demon Lords to do so?*

The woman's sharp, grass-green eyes turned to Erick as if she could read his thoughts. "Your task is difficult enough without other powers interfering."

"And what exactly is my task now?" Erick asked. "I was supposed to come here and find Necromancers. Six of us to face Eligos and banish him again. That's not going to happen. So, what possible task could I have, other than to face him alone and die?"

Elissia stepped up and took his hand. A wave of affection flooded through him at the touch. "You wouldn't be facing him alone," she said. He noticed the waxiness in her bronze skin—another consequence of Erick letting the *Inconnu* assassin live. The man had subverted Fathen, the only priest in Erick's town. When Fathen tried to stab Erick in the back with a poisoned dagger, Elissia had blocked the blade and received a gash in her leg. Things had gone poorly for the priest after that. At his direction, Erick's undead servants had seen to it. A ritual performed by the spectral Necromancers stunted the poison's effects. Stunted, but not eliminated.

Erick didn't remark on how cold Elissia's hand felt.

"We'll help anyway we can," Corby said. He was Erick's first—and still staunchest—friend, despite Erick's recent mistreatment of him. Corby offered a wan smile and ran his hand over his hair; its sideshaved scholar's cut gone shaggy and unkempt from their month of travel.

Gabrielle, apart from the others, remained quiet, her eyes on the floor.

"That's right." Marcus scratched at the death mark: three dots curved above a circle burned into his forehead. "We kicked his ass once. We'll do it again."

"You did no such thing," Erick's ancient grandfather said. Erick saw his reflection, aged forty years, in the ghost's round face and blue eyes. "You only destroyed the vessel that held his essence, and only accomplished that because he was weak and underestimated your resolve. He will not make the same mistake again. He will return somehow and continue to grow stronger."

"You saved my life," Erick said, as the small thief bristled at the phantasm's words. "But my ancestor is right. Only Necromancers can exile or kill the *Inconnu*."

"And that is still your task," Janella said. "It is the main task for the Necromancers; the only reason we were allowed to exist after the *Inconnu* War."

"How am I supposed to do it as the only one left alive?" Erick asked. "It took ten of you to do it last time, and four died in the attempt."

The two Necromancers looked at each other. Something passed in their gazes, and they raised their arms. The other eight specters reappeared in a circle, and the ten ghosts stared toward its center. Erick again felt the tingling nag at the edge of his awareness. A soft glow formed above the assembly's heads.

"What are they doing?" Elissia asked.

"Discussing something, but I have no idea what."

"Probably figuring out the best way to break it to you that you're screwed," Marcus muttered.

Are you getting anything from them? Erick asked Blink, using the mental connection they shared.

If I were, you'd be the first to know, the bat-winged, gray-skinned homunculus replied.

As Erick waited, shifting on his feet, the disappointment he had held back crashed in on him. It wasn't fair to come this far and be thwarted by circumstances he couldn't control. He was old enough to know life wasn't always fair; he'd seen enough of that. It wasn't fair his family had been forced to live isolated because of a feud between his father and the priest Fathen. It wasn't fair his father had hidden the *Teloc Sapah*, a book of evil written by the hand of Eligos, and subsequently been consumed by it.

But this went beyond unfair, into the realm of unjust cruelty. Erick had done as instructed. He had fought numerous foes on his trek to Prospector's Camp only to find captivity and betrayal waiting for him. He had escaped and, against a horde of undead, survived to reach Broken Mountain. They had even stopped Eligos, if only temporarily.

He had held up his end of the Covenant with small help from the Gods. Why didn't they help keep the other Necromancers alive? Why didn't they give the two that had turned away and joined Eligos the strength to resist?

Perhaps you've answered the question. Sadness tinged Blink's thought. *If they gave you little help, why would they help the others?*

Perhaps, Erick thought back. It wasn't right, though. A covenant was a pact between two parties, and he had upheld his end of the bargain. Why weren't the Gods upholding theirs?

Movement broke into his melancholy. The cadre of Necromancers faced him as his grandfather approached.

"You and your companions should retire," the spirit said. "There is a small chamber over there."

He pointed behind Erick, to the wall two hundred feet away. Despite the crystalline amber glow throughout the large room, Erick saw nothing to indicate a break in the rock face of the cavern.

"Why?" Erick asked. "What's going on?"

"We will be several hours in meditation and ritual. As we cannot leave this chamber to aid you, we must call the holy powers and remind them of the Covenant. If they are pleased, they will heed our summons and aid us."

~

The chamber was roomy, if uncomfortable. There were no chairs or furniture of any sort, the floor was uneven, and stones of various sizes lay scattered about as if the room had been a work in progress when the inhabitants left.

"Guess they never really planned for company," Marcus said as he entered.

The indistinct yellow illumination that emanated from the walls filled this room as well. It gave everyone a warm, cheery appearance. Even though the mountain's interior wasn't as cold as Erick expected, it wasn't as cozy as the light made it seem. And his mood was anything but jovial.

Corby, his ragged, dark brown hair plastered to his head, studied the glowing walls. Ever curious, he tapped a finger against the stone and then scratched at it. Dust gathered to his finger and ceased to glow. In his left hand, he held the black dagger with the poisoned blade that had almost ended Elissia's life.

"Will you look at that?" Erick asked Gabrielle as he pointed at the weapon.

The plain-faced healer nodded. Despite their long travels, she appeared the least road-worn of any of them. Erick thought she looked better than when he first saw her back in the warehouse in Kalador, her face marked with bumps, her red-brown hair greasy and uncombed. Then, she had been apprenticed to a monstrous, over-bearing woman who treated her as little more than a pack mule. Escaping her mistress to join them and leaving behind the sewers where the Procurers lived allowed the healer to flourish. Her skin cleared and her slump-shouldered bearing straightened. Though still quiet, she was far more confident than a month ago. Travel agreed with her, although Erick had no idea how she stayed so clean in their trek through the mountainous Ruins.

She walked over to Corby, who held the dagger by the top of the handle, giving her room to grab it without touching the blade. She took the weapon, stepped away, and sat on the floor with her back against the wall.

"I need to sit down," Elissia said in a soft voice, drawing Erick's attention from Gabrielle. She placed her hand against the wall, and Erick helped her lower herself to the floor. He sat beside her and crossed his legs.

"Are you okay?" he asked.

"As okay as anyone who's been poisoned," she said and offered a

7

faint smile. "In truth, I'm feeling better. Just tired and thirsty. I could really use some water."

"I'm sorry; we don't have any."

"We can get some," Corby said. "I saw a small fall five hundred feet back in the tunnels."

"That's great," Marcus said. "But we don't have anything to carry it in." All their equipment had been confiscated when the magistrate of Prospector's Camp had arrested them. Their ensuing escape and Erick's battle with Eligos during the town's destruction did not allow them time to gather supplies.

"We'll use my shirt," Corby said, indicating his once cream-colored garment, now dirt-crusted and muted brown. "I'll clean it as best as possible and soak it with as much water as it can carry. It's not much, but it's better than nothing."

"I can walk to it," Elissia said, and started to stand.

"You need to rest," Erick told her.

"I'm—" she stopped halfway up the wall and plopped back down on the floor. "Going to sit here and rest."

"We'll bring back what we can," Marcus said. "I'll clean my shirt, too."

Erick doubted the thief's shirt, coated with splashes of blood, would clean so easily. "You can take mine," Erick told him. It wasn't much better than Corby's, but less blood-stained than Marcus's. He pulled it over his head and tossed it to Corby. The chain shirt his captors had inexplicably left on him rattled as he shifted. He considered removing it to take the weight off his shoulders but didn't have the energy.

"I'll go with you," Blink said.

"We're fine," Marcus told him.

"I can see in the dark better than you. I'll help you find it."

"I remember where it is," Corby said, standing beside Marcus.

"And I'd challenge who can see better in the dark," Marcus said.

"Let them go," Elissia told Blink. "They'll be okay." She nudged Erick.

Erick looked at the thief and the scholar standing beside each other. He had learned on their journey that the two of them cared for each other in the same way he cared for Elissia. Despite his assertion to the contrary, he honestly didn't understand how such a thing was possible. Though he tried his best not to judge, since it wasn't his place, he couldn't make himself approve. The laws of Caros and Calea declared it a sin, and he liked them enough that he wanted Alakaneth to judge them worthy of the Heaven of Caros.

But they had both risked their lives to help him get here. As he remembered Corby's willingness to befriend him in Draymed, when he was the Necromancer on the hill no one dared approach, Erick decided he wouldn't begrudge them anything that was within his power. And what they wanted was time alone. "Stay here, Blink. They can take care of themselves."

"Fine, but don't come grumbling to me to find them when they get lost," Blink said.

"You'll let me know all about the poison when I get back?" Corby asked Gabrielle.

She glanced up from her study of the knife, offered a curt nod, and went back to her examination. Corby frowned, as did Erick. Gabrielle also didn't like their relationship because she felt cut out of it and wanted Marcus for herself. Her reticent manner worried Erick.

"Come on," Marcus said.

Erick rubbed his head, bristly from a month's growth after being shaved bald to disguise himself as an acolyte to Krinnik, the Earth God. His face also itched from the stubble that poked out of his chin and under his lip. "What am I going to do?" he asked the air.

"Save the world, somehow," Elissia said, her eyes closed, her breathing more ragged than Erick liked.

"How?" he asked in anguish. "I couldn't even keep you safe. You're poisoned. Some protector I am."

She grabbed his chin with her chilled hand and turned him to face her. The amber illumination of the walls highlighted the angry fire in her blue eyes. "Let's get one thing straight. No one asked you to protect us. We came on this journey to help *you*, fully aware of the danger. And if we all survive this madness and that undead bastard doesn't take over the world, then you'll help Marcus and me claim our due. We all watch out for each other. We're in this together. I love you, but I don't need you to be my cavalier. Okay?"

Erick sucked in a breath. It was only the second time she had said she loved him, and it rattled through him with as much force as the first time. "I love you, too," he said, "and because of that, I *want* to be your cavalier."

He held up a hand to stop her protest. "But more, I want to do what makes you happy. So, we'll protect each other, we'll get you cured, I'll save the world, and we'll depose your father and make your brother the king of the thieves. How does that sound?"

"That's all a girl can ask," Elissia said. She smiled, then leaned in and kissed him.

Despite the coldness of her lips, the kiss jolted Erick. Sensations of bliss rolled through his body, bounced like a ball in an empty keg, and settled below his stomach. He wanted the kiss not to end. He wanted—

Gabrielle's soft voice interrupted his thoughts. "I wish I had my kit to be sure, but I think I know what the poison is."

~

Corby was glad Marcus had come with him, for several reasons. For one, Marcus could see amazingly well in the dark. Corby's eidetic memory helped him recall every step in retracing the path to the waterfall, but it wouldn't tell him where boulders crowded the trail, or an errant rock stuck out from the wall. Wending through the mountain to reach the chamber, they'd had Blink's keen vision to advise them of such perils. Now Marcus acted as guide.

Marcus also helped keep Corby alert. The awe of seeing the original Necromancers had eased Corby's fatigue. He longed to question them if ever given the opportunity. But now, the weariness returned, and the lack of sleep and hours-long trek through the mountain bore down on him. He wanted nothing more than to sleep. Marcus kept him moving because Corby needed to prove himself worthy of the other young man's admiration.

Gods help him, Corby admired Marcus. More than admired, if he was truthful. Murrough, the sailor Corby had met on their voyage from Keystone Island to the mainland, had shown him many amazing, sinful things. But he had been a rough, uncouth man, and Corby had known their friendship would extend no further than the voyage they shared. The sailor would find some other to occupy him. Corby would be nothing more than a memory of cargo hold trysts.

Marcus was something different. A thief, yes. Sarcastic, certainly. But a noble heart hid under his caustic wit. He cared about people. He certainly doted on his sister and had undertaken this insane journey to help Erick for her alone. That made him more than worthy in Corby's journal.

Above that, his bravery, skill, and willingness to do what was necessary made him an example Corby would gladly emulate. He had not yet done with Marcus the things he had done with Murrough. Corby had every expectation that if it happened, and he longed for it to happen, it would not be sinful and dirty. It would be love, pure and blessed. Surely Caros and Calea would see the emotion behind the act and not condemn him.

Corby didn't know what scared him more; the depth of his feelings, which he usually held so tight, or that those feelings might condemn his soul, despite what Elissia said. His parents had told him Caros and Calea hated what he was. Elissia told him the Gods didn't care. Who was right?

"Why so quiet?" Marcus asked. "I would have expected at least an essay on the formation of this mountain or the history of the battle between the Three and the Ten."

Corby smiled. Marcus could tease him. Instead of being mean-spirited like those in Draymed who belittled him, it sounded gentle and caring.

"I'm fatigued almost beyond rational thought," he lied. The fatigue was real. His other feelings he couldn't share yet. He had to wait until he was more alert, when he could speak without making a fool of himself. "I can only imagine you must be even more consumed with exhaustion. You helped carry Elissia all that way."

"And I'd have gone twice as far if I had to. But yeah, I'm pretty damn beat. Once we get this water and get back, a nap will be the next thing I'll want."

"That makes two of us. I wouldn't be surprised if the others were asleep when we returned."

"Is Elissia going to be okay?" Marcus asked. The depth of concern in his cousin's voice wrenched at Corby.

"Until I know what the poison is, I can't say with any certainty. Even then, Gabrielle will be better able to answer. Poisons were never my specialty. I hear the water."

Another ten paces brought them to the waterfall, little more than a small stream running down the cavern wall, spilling over a lip to splash on the floor and disappear into a crevice.

"I'll take a drink first, in case there's something wrong with it," Marcus said.

Before Corby could object, he sensed Marcus move. The sound of the water changed as the other boy stuck his mouth into the flow. He remained there for several seconds and then stepped back.

"I wish you hadn't done that."

"Someone had to," Marcus said. "Live in a city long enough, and you learn what tainted water tastes like. You also build up some immunity. There is nothing wrong with this. Damn refreshing, actually. Drink what you want, and then we'll take some back. Be careful; it's cold."

Corby leaned down and gulped a mouthful of water. The chill shocked him, but he didn't care. Until the water touched his lips, Corby hadn't realized the extent of his thirst. He swallowed and put his mouth against the stream, pulling in more of the liquid. It was the best drink he had ever consumed, crisp and invigorating. It poured down his throat, easing the dryness.

Something touched his lips. Startled, he backed away and swallowed, almost choking. "What was that?"

Movement, and it touched his lips again—arms wrapped around his body.

It was Marcus. Marcus was kissing him.

Corby froze. Though he and Murrough had done many things, they had never kissed. Even Quinn, the first boy he had sinned with until Quinn's parents had caught them and thrown the wrath of damnation upon them, didn't kiss him. Both claimed kissing wasn't manly. Though Corby never understood the logic, he hadn't fought it.

Now, unsure how to respond, he froze.

After several heartbeats in which Corby couldn't think, Marcus drew back. His hands slid off Corby's back. Corby immediately missed the contact.

"I'm sorry," Marcus said. His tone came out as defensive, not conciliatory. "I thought you would like that."

"I—" Corby paused. "I don't—" he paused again. He didn't know how to feel. It had been so unexpected. His usually quick mind clogged like cold ink. Then his scholar's training took over, and he did what he did when a passage of text didn't make sense, or an experiment didn't work correctly. "Can you do it again?"

Marcus stepped in and once more pressed his lips against Corby's. Arms wrapped around and entwined Corby's back. This time, Marcus pulled himself closer, so their chests touched.

Uncertain what to do, Corby copied Marcus and wrapped his arms around, clasping his hands behind Marcus's. Though Corby was a few inches taller, his movement nonetheless brought the lower part of their bodies in contact. Corby's knees almost buckled at the sensation, which roiled from the base of his spine and flowed through his scalp before ending at his closed mouth. The intensity brought a gasp from him. His mouth opened, and Marcus's tongue slid in, sending unbridled euphoria bounding through Corby's body. He leaned into the kiss, his tongue touching Marcus's. His hands clutched low on Marcus's back, pulling his hips closer. Corby moaned as their balance shifted. Caught off guard, he fell back and slammed into the wall.

Frigid water soaked his shirt. With a shout, he leapt forward, pushing Marcus back. Their contact broke as Marcus stumbled, leaving Corby disappointed, dizzy, and flushed.

"What happened?" Marcus asked as he regained his balance.

"Cold water on the back. Shocked me."

Marcus laughed. "Nothing like a splash of icy water to ruin a nice erection."

Though it hadn't done that, Corby's face heated at Marcus's crude statement. "We should probably do what we came to do," Corby said. "I'm sure everyone else is thirsty."

"We should," Marcus agreed, all humor gone. "But you liked the kiss."

Corby didn't think his face could get any warmer. Though it wasn't a question, he answered, his voice barely above a whisper. "I did."

Marcus walked up and put his mouth beside Corby's ear. "It's nothing to be ashamed of. Amare says all love is sacred. Once we can be alone again, I want to kiss you all night." He gave Corby's ear a quick brush with his lips, then stepped back. "Now, let's get these shirts clean and see what we can do."

Corby removed and washed his shirt, more confused. Even the eight Sane Gods differed on what they thought of his actions. Though he was a scholar and smarter than almost anyone he knew, how did he stand a chance to ever understand what was right?

2

All Necromancers are an affront and deserve to die.
   -Graffiti discovered in The Beggared Pony Tavern in Kalador

Erick and Elissia waited for Gabrielle to continue. The healer sat against the wall, dagger in hand, thin brows bunched in concentration. When she saw her declaration had gotten their attention, she said, "Based on smell, appearance, and the gritty texture of the paste, which I determined by rubbing it against the wall, not touching it, I believe the knife is coated with *vikrin*."

"Is that bad?" Elissia asked. She shivered, and Erick wrapped an arm around her.

"You should have been dead within the first five minutes," Gabrielle stated in the same tone she might use to tell someone she wanted a cup of tea. "Praise to Calea that you aren't."

Erick stared at Gabrielle in dismay. *What have I done?* He thought to Blink.

What you had to do, Blink thought back.

I should have insisted she and Corby not come.

It wouldn't have mattered.

Blink was right. When Elissia and Corby stood beside Erick's

15

burned manor house with him and said they would accompany him on his journey, he tried to convince them to remain behind. They had refused, and Erick hadn't pressed. He should have. Had they stayed, none of this would have happened.

Had they not come, Blink told him, *we would most likely be dead. And they might be burned with the rest of Draymed.*

That didn't make him feel any better.

"Since I survived, I'm going to get better, right?" Elissia asked. The pleading in her voice made Erick want to scream.

Gabrielle shook her head. "Erick's ancestors have kept you alive and delayed the poison, though how is a mystery to me, without the blessings of—" she stopped and frowned. "It doesn't matter right now. They have helped. But the poison is still in you. There will be great pain if it isn't removed. It will eventually kill you."

An irrational urge to punch the healer came over Erick. How could she speak so calmly about this?

"This gives us hope," she continued, though Erick didn't share her optimism. "If we can find vervain or skullcap, and linden flower, I can keep the pain manageable and slow the poison. Any apothecary will have ingredients for an antidote, but we must get it soon. The longer we wait, the more damage will remain after the poison is removed."

"What sort of damage?" Elissia asked.

Erick wanted to cover his ears to avoid hearing what Gabrielle was about to say. But he couldn't. He was responsible.

Stop it, Blink told him.

"The poison damages your nerves," Gabrielle said. "It could cripple you, cause irregular spasms that never go away, or even destroy part of your brain." She took Elissia's hand, and a trace of warmth finally seeped into her voice. "I wish I could tell you for certain, but nerve poisons are unpredictable. You survived, so it's equally possible you won't suffer any ill effects before we get the antidote."

"We can't count on that," Elissia said. "We need to do something as soon as we can."

"Yes," Gabrielle agreed. "But right now, rest is the best thing for you. We are all too fatigued to accomplish anything strenuous. Sleep.

When Marcus and Corby return, I'll make sure they give you some water."

"Thank you," Elissia said, her voice sluggish with exhaustion. She closed her eyes. Within seconds, her breathing evened, and she dropped into sleep.

Erick gently pulled his arm from beneath her. She muttered a moment and slumped against the wall.

"She's going to die, isn't she?" Erick's voice broke.

Gabrielle stood and took his hand. On shaky legs, he followed her out of the chamber, Blink behind them.

Erick glanced toward the center of the large tunnel. The ten Necromancers stood there, unmoving and silent, like spectral statues. Erick only knew they spoke to the Gods because his ancestor told him they would. Erick hoped the Gods answered. Even more, he hoped they offered something useful.

Gabrielle took both of Erick's hands and locked her wide brown eyes with his. "There is a possibility she will die. *But,*" she paused to make sure she had his full attention. "I'm going to do everything by the power of Krinnik, Talan, and Caros, from whom my powers come, to make sure that doesn't happen. She is strong, and—" Gabrielle paused again, frowned, and then continued. "It's entirely possible that being with you saved her life."

"What?" Erick had no idea what the healer meant, though the sudden chill in her voice startled him.

Gabrielle swallowed. "If I understand it right from my reading, the power of *elonsha* is a poison that affects the soul, much as regular venom affects the body. Her exposure to it, when she helped create your doppelgänger, may have inured her in some way to more mundane poisons."

Is that possible? Erick wondered. To throw Eligos off his trail, Erick had created a doppelgänger, which had been "killed" in a confrontation between Erick's companions and the thieves' organization led by Elissia and Marcus's father. At her insistence, Elissia had assisted him in the hours-long process.

Maybe, Blink thought, although his uncertainty leaked through.

"*Elonsha* isn't really a poison," Erick said. "It's evil, pure and simple.

17

You know that. It's the reason healers refuse to help us, right?" Erick tried to keep the bitterness out of his voice but had no idea if he succeeded.

"Poison is evil, too," Gabrielle said. Her eyes dropped to the floor. Erick noted her avoidance of his question. "It's only a theory. Perhaps her inherent fortitude kept her alive. Whatever it was, she survived the initial shock. With luck and her strength, whatever its source, I can keep her alive until we reach a city and get her cured. The first thing I want to do is scour Prospector's Camp and see if I can find any of the herbs I need. Without them, the pain will weaken her, and her chances lessen."

She had regained her calm, detached manner and discussed Elissia's condition as if she spoke about last night's dinner.

Erick wiped at his wet eyes. Sheer willpower kept his voice even. "Is there anything we can do right now?"

"Let her rest. If she remains calm, the poison will stay sluggish. Food would be good, but that's another thing we'll have to see if we can find in town."

Any optimism left Erick. The town had been engulfed in flames when they fled into the mountain. Even if the fire had died out, any food, and certainly any herbs, would have been destroyed. He had no idea what he was going to do.

Movement caught his eye. Corby and Marcus crossed the cavern floor, water-dripping tunics wadded in hand. Corby's pants were also soaked, as if he had gone swimming.

"She's asleep," Gabrielle told them when they drew close. "Give her as much water as she wants and then let her return to slumber. I would advise we all rest. We can do little until we have a plan, and planning is useless until we know our options."

Erick nodded, though he knew sleep, or even relaxation, would elude him. Too many concerns and unanswered questions assailed him.

As a group, they returned to the small chamber. Marcus walked over to his sister, knelt beside her, and gave her a gentle shake. Her eyes opened to slits, and she let out a soft groan.

"It's water," Marcus said, his voice gentle as he held Erick's tunic to her lips.

"Here," Corby said, offering his tunic, which had regained some of its original clean color, to Erick. Erick took it, put it to his mouth, and slurped. A faint taste of sweat, though nowhere near as brackish as Erick feared. He sucked the fabric until he slaked the bulk of his thirst, then he offered it to Blink.

"I'm okay," Blink said. "Sorry, but that's just gross."

"The things you've seen me do, and this is gross?" Erick said.

"Those things are gross, too. But they're private, so I try not to pay attention when you—"

"I was talking about my Necromancy," Erick said. Despite his fears and concerns, he couldn't help but smile at Blink's teasing.

"Oh, that. That's kind of why I exist, so I accept it as part of the job. I'm not that thirsty. I can wait until we find a well. Wish we had some food, though."

Erick handed the shirt back to Corby. "Thank you."

Corby took it and nodded. A smile broke over his face. "Marcus kissed me," he whispered. Then his forehead and cheeks turned bright orange under the amber light as if he had been caught stealing a cookie. "I mean, you're welcome." He turned to Gabrielle and offered her the shirt, not looking at Erick.

That wasn't what I expected him to say, Blink thought.

Me either, Erick thought back. *Let's try and get some rest.*

Despite Erick's concerns, sleep pummeled him as soon as he sat on the floor beside Elissia and leaned against the rough cavern wall. A pleasant dream of happy times with his parents flitted through his mind. Laughter and music filled the vision. His mother played the lute, and his father sang in a pleasant, low voice. Though Erick never developed musical talent, he enjoyed listening to their songs: lays of ancient battles from wars long before the *Inconnu* troubled the world of Krinnik, or airs of heroes rescuing their one true love.

He would listen and dream he might one day do such brave things. For a time, when his parents sang, he could forget he was a Necromancer, secluded from the town that thrived in the valley below his manor and destined never to have friends.

"Erick, wake up," Blink said, shaking him with a taloned hand. "Your ghosts want to talk to you."

Erick opened his eyes, and the dream faded. His groggy mind mused about the differences between his childish speculations and his life now. He had friends he never expected, though it took the loss of his parents and the destruction of his home to get them. While destiny put him on the path to be a hero, he had only stumbled and accomplished almost nothing so far.

Blink awakened Corby, while Gabrielle shook Marcus. Both had put their shirts back on.

Picking up his wadded tunic from where it lay against the wall, Erick turned to Elissia. His heart sank at the sallow hue of her face and the circles under her eyes. She looked so much older than her sixteen years. He refused to let the guilt knock him down. She was strong, so he would be too. Though he wanted to let her sleep, she would be angry with him if he didn't wake her to hear what his ancestors told them.

He leaned over and kissed her cheek. Her chilled skin on his lips frightened him. "Elissia," he said close to her ear, keeping the fear out of his voice. "Wake up."

She stirred and moaned. Erick kissed her again. Her eyes opened, and she turned to face him, the blue in her eyes glazed like thin ice over a pond. "Is it time to leave already?" she asked, her brow furrowed.

"Not yet," Erick said. "The Necromancers want to speak with us. Hopefully we can figure out what to do now."

Erick wanted nothing more than to run to Kalador, get the antidote, and run back, to prove his love for her meant more than dragging her into danger. He wanted to heal her and then take all of them someplace safe. Let some other hero save the world.

But there was no other hero. Eligos had seen to that.

Elissia offered a weak smile and said, "Then let's go listen and get on the road."

Elissia squinted as she walked into the larger cavern. The light hurt her eyes, just another among the multitude of pains wracking her body. She struggled to walk straight, not wanting Erick to know how much she hurt. The water had helped, lessening the scratch of her throat, but it did nothing to abate the headache. Her short sleep had been fitful, haunted by a dream of flashing red and black lightning, a sense of foreboding unleashed with every forked bolt that danced behind her eyes.

The closer she got to the ghosts that stared at them, the more her head pounded. She wanted to flee back to the chamber and hide from their glowering.

Erick took her hand.

To her surprise, the pain decreased. The light became bearable, and she could open her eyes fully. Though her head still hurt, it turned into a dull ache and didn't throb with every heartbeat. The lethargy in her joints eased, and she could walk without striving to conceal discomfort.

She didn't like this chamber. The golden light galled her, and the radiance of the specters felt like a smug affirmation of their superiority, the knowledge they were somehow better than the living beings in the room. Their condescension reminded her of her father's arrogance, his surety that all he did was right, and other opinions carried little validity if they didn't agree with his. She wanted nothing more than to be away from these glorious beings and their smothering righteousness.

An unknown voice whispered in her mind like a wisp of spider web. *I will join my brother soon, and all will sicken and die.* She blinked and stumbled, thrown off by the presence that had been there and then vanished like the lightning from her dream.

"Are you okay?" Erick asked, the concern in his voice almost painful.

"Yes," she lied. "Still not awake. Just hold my hand, and I'll be fine."

But she wondered. She could almost feel the poison running through her like a living thing, weakening her body. She would fight it as long as she could, but what if she couldn't fight whatever had sent her its errant thought? And what did the thought mean?

The dead Necromancers stared at her. She could feel it, and she stared back. Had they sensed the fleeting other?

More than simple poison inhabited her, and she feared what it might be. She pressed herself against Erick, hoping the long-gone Necromancers could help him, even as she loathed being in their presence.

~

E rick looked at Dendrick and waited for the ghost to speak. He feared what the grim faces of the other nine Necromancers portended, although he took some hope when his ancestor smiled.

"The Gods have answered, and though what they offer is encouraging, it will be difficult."

"Why should anything be different now?" Erick asked before he could stop himself.

"A fair question," Dendrick said as his spectral face bunched into a frown. "What did your parents teach you about how we destroyed the *Inconnu*?"

"They said you destroyed Bolfri and Saburoc, but only managed to banish Eligos to the *aesir*." Erick didn't mention his disappointment in their failure. Had they completed their task, his father would never have been tempted by the *Teloc Sapah*, the book of dark magic that lured him to summon Eligos.

Had they destroyed all three, you probably would never have been born, Blink told him.

Erick hadn't considered that. He bitterly wondered if that would have been better.

A discussion for some other time, Blink said.

"Did he tell you how we accomplished this feat?"

"Yes," Erick answered. "You formulated a Ritual to reach into the *aesir*, combine it with *elonsha*, and form an undead giant to battle the three *Inconnu*. The blood needed to power the Ritual required three of you to sacrifice yourselves. The force of the battle destroyed the

22

mountain, and the strain of wielding the creature killed another one of you outright."

"That is the brief way of it. And did your father teach you the Ritual?"

"He did," Erick said. It was early in his education, and he remembered it well, as it was the most complicated formula he ever learned, requiring massive resources of both herbs and blood. After reciting his section of the Ritual, his part was to drink the mixture he created and offer himself as a blood sacrifice, giving his life to save every other person on Krinnik. It wasn't a role he relished. He never mustered the nerve to ask his father how his family had been chosen for that burden. If the time had come, he would have performed the task required. At least, he liked to believe he would have the courage.

"You must again summon such a creature to defeat Eligos."

"Are you insane?" Elissia shouted before Erick could speak. "It took ten of you to do it, and four of you died. How is Erick supposed to do everything by himself?"

"I only learned my part of the Ritual," Erick said. "I have no idea how to do the others, even if I could manage it on my own."

Dendrick did not seem perturbed by their outbursts. "We fought three of them; you need only fight one. If you can find him in a weakened state, before he rallies too many to his cause and obtains power from their sacrifices, he will be easier to defeat. A person with the power to assist you has been made known to us. With her aid, you will need little blood for the Ritual, and will not have to sacrifice yourself."

Elissia's hand tightened on his, and he winced. Not from pain, but that she had discovered his required part in the Ritual. He could feel her glare boring into him.

"Seek her out," Dendrick continued, "and persuade her to aid you in this task."

"Persuade?" Erick asked. "Why do I need to persuade her? Why did her ancestors not assist in your battle, so none of you had to sacrifice yourselves?"

Dendrick didn't speak for several moments. The other specters glanced among themselves in discomfort.

Finally, Dendrick said, "The Gods did not offer this information to us, so I cannot answer. What I can tell you is she is a *wicaesir*, one who can manipulate the *aesir* to her will. She is the last of her kind, and though there is no certainty she will pay heed to your cause, she is the only possibility. Without her aid, the world will eventually fall to Eligos."

A battering ram punched Erick in the stomach. Desperation had nearly undone him when he heard he was the last Necromancer, only to have hope renewed when Dendrick said he and his companions would speak with the Gods.

Now, his heart brimmed over with bitter disappointment as the full hopelessness of the situation slammed him. Somehow, he had unrealistically expected the original Necromancers to have a wise solution. And if not them, then surely—

"This is what your time with the Gods has produced?" Erick couldn't keep the anger from his voice. "First, they couldn't protect the other Necromancers, and now they offer an uncertain alliance with a person that may not even be alive."

"Don't speak like that," Corby said, fearful. "You blaspheme."

"I *will* speak like that," Erick said. "I've earned the right. I've upheld my part of the Covenant and lost everything doing so. Was ready to do more to succeed. And what have they done?"

"Allowed you to exist!" Dendrick thundered.

Erick stepped back as the imperious glares of the Ten bore down on him. His companions, likewise, retreated.

"The Covenant lets Necromancy remain as a force of magic," Dendrick said, his ire matching Erick's, "and keeps *elonsha* from infesting the world despite our need for it. But they do that to protect their followers, not for any love of us. That is all the Covenant allows. It does not require the Gods to aid or protect us or do anything other than leave us be."

"Then it was a poorly struck bargain," Erick said in a low voice.

"That is enough." Janella floated forward and upward until she towered over Erick. She pointed at Elissia. "The Gods also healed that child, when they did not have to. For that, you may thank me, who was a healer before *elonsha* tainted the world."

Gabrielle gasped. "How is that possible?"

The woman continued to scowl at Erick. "They have helped you in other ways. Denech, especially, has favored you, or do you forget?"

Erick's hand drifted to the gold amulet he wore. Eight interlocking circles pierced by an arrow. The symbol of Denech, the god of luck. He remembered the times it flashed or grew heavy, times when something unexpected happened to aid him.

"The Gods help when and how they wish. Or they do not, as they wish. Cease your childish whining and blasphemous speech. It is not your place to question but to do what you can to protect what has been given to us. Seek out this *wicaesir* and entice her to help you with what must be done."

Erick wanted to scream at the old, dead woman. He wanted to cry, or run away, or anything other than what she insisted he must do.

"Do the Gods not care about us?" Corby asked in a soft voice. "Do they wish to see Krinnik consumed by this evil force?"

Glances passed among the ten Necromancers. Uncertainty played over their faces. Erick felt the touch of their passing thoughts. He tried to reach out to their minds, though he had little idea how. With Blink, it happened without effort. He stared at Dendrick and saw himself in the other's mind.

To his surprise, he caught a word. *Powerful.* Then Dendrick turned his periwinkle eyes on Erick, who reeled from a forceful blow to his mind.

"Prying in someone's thoughts is rude," Dendrick said.

"What the Gods do or do not wish is beyond our ken," Janella told Corby. "We live among them, but they do not hold us in their counsel." She turned back to Erick. "Will you do what the Covenant requires?"

What the Covenant requires seems malleable based on whims, Erick thought.

Probably not the best answer, Blink cautioned.

"I will," Erick said, knowing the futility of any other reply. He barely kept the bitterness from his voice. "But what if she's already dead? And where do I look for her? I could spend my life trying to find her, and I'm sure we don't have that kind of time."

"She is alive," Dendrick said. "You will find her in the Viramoren, the swamps of Starrasen, to the west. Below the Surris, where the Upper Serpent River becomes the Lower."

"That narrows it down," Corby said, "but that's almost fifty-two thousand square miles of bog and marsh."

"Ask in the village of Fissis for Alais. It lies at the base of the falls. There you should find those who can tell you where she resides."

Erick wanted to ask why Caros, or any of the other Gods, could not tell them directly, but he was tired of asking questions that received evasive answers. He hated to think it, but he suspected his ancestor was not totally forthcoming, that all the Necromancers hid something. Though he had no evidence and didn't want to believe it, he couldn't deny his gut feeling.

"So that's it, then," he said. "A trek across the continent on a hunt for someone who may not want to be found and may not help even if I do find her."

"When you put it like that," Marcus said, "it sounds like a hell of a grand time."

3

People like to call us parasites and criminals, but I think of us more as civil servants and economic motivators. The rich have everything, and if they didn't occasionally have some of it taken from them, what would be their impetus to buy more?

-Mundar Prolin, Head of the Dorfork Procurer's Guild

Once the Necromancers delivered their pronouncements, they offered wishes for strength of Caros and luck of Denech—blessings that didn't mean as much to Erick as they had recently. He and his companions gathered back in the smaller chamber, preferring it to the vast emptiness of the larger cavern.

"I can't believe you didn't tell me you would have to kill yourself," Elissia said. She sat with her back against the wall. Erick sat beside her, holding her cold hand.

"I didn't want to think about it," Erick told her. "I was so focused on getting here that I hadn't considered the next step. Besides, telling you would have done nothing but worry you." He smiled. Eyes closed, she didn't return it. "Now, I don't have to, so I would have upset you for nothing."

"Yes, the situation we're in now is *much* better," Marcus said.

Erick studied his dirty, bedraggled friends. He knew his appearance was as bad or worse. Tired and hungry, Erick wanted nothing more than to be at an inn, sleeping in a large bed. His companions doubtless felt much the same.

"The situation is bad," Erick said, "and certainly not what I hoped. But it's *my* situation. You got me here, and I can't ever repay any of you for it, but now—"

Elissia opened her eyes. "Don't say it. Don't try to get noble. We're going with you."

"But—"

Marcus, seated with Corby on his right side and Gabrielle on his left, said, "Do you remember what you promised me?"

"Yes," Erick said. "I said if you got me here, I would return and help you get rid of your father when I could."

Corby spoke up. "Actually, Marcus told Elissia, 'I'll go with you and take this idiot to his big mountain' and then told you 'But once you're done saving the world, you have to come back and help save my guild. Agreed?' and then you said, 'Agreed.'"

"You know that's unnatural, right?" Marcus said.

"It is not," Corby said. "I can't help it. It's a talent I have, like your talent for stealing things."

Marcus shrugged. "I had to train years to hone that talent, but point taken. Erick, the condition was when you save the world, you go back with us. I know Lissa is going to be stupid enough to follow you, so I need to make sure you get this thing finished."

"And I have a book to write, so I need to see how it ends," Corby said. He frowned. "Although they took my notes, so I'll have to rewrite them from memory."

"Your memory is a book, so that shouldn't be a problem," Marcus said.

Erick's throat tightened. He recalled a time, less than a year ago, when he never thought he would have friends. Now, he had friends he wasn't sure he deserved. "What about you?" he asked Gabrielle.

"I go where he...they...go," she said, pointing at the two beside her without looking at them.

Erick suspected she meant Marcus more than Corby.

"Thank you," Erick said. "All of you. Now we have to figure out the best way to go about it."

Gabrielle spoke up. "I want to check out the town, as we discussed."

"That's a good idea for all of us," Marcus said. "Salvage what we can; see if we can find food and supplies. Maybe some money, so we can buy whatever we need in the next village or town. I'll steal if I have to, but it's easier if I don't."

"I'd like to procure another staff," Corby said as he hefted the crossbow and quiver of bolts that had seen him through last night's battle.

Erick nodded. "We all need better weapons." Thanks to Elissia, he had become proficient with a dagger. It surprised him how much he missed having one on his belt. "We'll search the town. But then, Blink and I need to go to Kalaser or Kalawen, find what Gabrielle needs to cure Elissia, and get it back here."

"Don't be stupid," Elissia said. "That's almost six hundred miles there and back. I'll go with you."

"I don't want you to do that," Erick said.

She opened her eyes. Despite the circles that made them deep pits, Erick saw the spark of anger. "Since when has that ever stopped me?" she snapped, yanking her hand from his.

Erick gaped. He had expected her to disagree, but her vehemence shocked him. The others looked equally stunned.

Elissia blinked and frowned as if she had surprised herself. Her eyes dulled. "I'm sorry. It's just my head hurts so much. I don't like it here, and I want to get out. I can travel."

"Can she?" Erick asked Gabrielle.

"Don't ask her, ask me," Elissia said.

"We already know what you think," Marcus told her. "But you're as stubborn as Father, and you're not a healer." He turned to Gabrielle.

"She shouldn't, but she can. It may be very painful," she informed Elissia.

"Not any more painful than sitting here or in a destroyed town doing nothing." Her eyes turned to Erick. "I know you want to protect me, and I appreciate it, even if it irritates me. But I need to get out of here."

Erick saw the determination in her face and knew more arguing would accomplish nothing. Maybe once they left this cavern, he could make her accept reason. With the Necromancers gone, the cave felt lifeless. More than lifeless. The residual *elonsha* from the ancient battle pulled at him, draining his strength, working its dark fingers at the edges of his mind. They all needed sunlight and fresh air.

"We may not have to go far," Corby said. "The next sizable town is Dorfork, which is only three days' travel. Maybe an apothecary there will have what Elissia needs."

"Maybe," Gabrielle said.

"We can discuss it later," Erick said. "For now, I think getting out of this dreary cave will make us all happier."

"I kind of like it," Marcus said. "Nice and closed in, no open sky. It's perfect."

"Only you would want to live in a cave," Elissia said.

I t was tough going for Elissia, but the further they withdrew from the Necromancer's chamber, the better she felt. Her head still hurt, but her vision cleared. The bone-deep throb in her joints disappeared, replaced with the fatigue of wearied muscles. Though almost as painful, the muscle aches felt somehow cleaner, more natural. By the time they reached the mountain's exit hours later and stepped into the morning light, she almost felt normal.

"You sure we have to come back out here?" Marcus asked as he stared at the destroyed town.

"Haven't you gotten over that yet?" Elissia asked. Her brother's fear of open spaces had begun to annoy her, and she wanted him to stop whining about it.

Marcus looked aside at her. "I'll be okay in a little while. I just need to get used to it again. What the hell is wrong with you?"

What is *wrong with me?* she wondered. Marcus was the one person in the world who never truly upset her. Whether because they were twins or had a hatred of their father to bind them, they never suffered the petty disagreements that plagued other siblings.

"I don't know," she confessed. "Can this poison be affecting my brain?" she asked Gabrielle. That would explain the headaches.

"Not that I've read. However, it is a nerve poison, and some Masters believe the brain is nothing but a congealed mass of nerves, so I guess it's possible. How do you feel?"

"My head is pounding. I'm hungry and tired, but I imagine we all are."

"Yes, we are," Marcus said. "Let's get down there and see what we can find."

"We need a systematic way to do this," Corby said, "or we could spend hours looking in useless places. Gabrielle, where are the most likely best places to find the herbs you need?"

"An apothecary would be the best."

"I suspect a settlement of this size will lack something that specific. We'll search for one, nonetheless. Alternatives?"

"An herbalist is the next best. A greengrocer might offer some medicinals. A midwife may have one or two of them. After that would be individual homes."

"Then that's the order we follow," Corby said. "The town square will be the ideal location for an herbalist if one existed and the fire hasn't destroyed it. Homes should be our last resort, as they will take the most time."

"There was food in the merchant carts," Marcus said.

Elissia recalled seeing the overturned carts of food as people fled the undead. The thought of the fruits in the stalls made her mouth water. She remembered thinking it strange how the fire raging through town avoided the square, leaving it little touched.

Corby nodded. "Herbalists first, then general merchants, then homes if necessary."

"Seems like a good plan," Erick said. Elissia had to agree. But she wouldn't expect anything less from her genius cousin.

Marcus took the lead, walking down the mountain path toward town. Erick followed, and Elissia stepped behind him. Corby, Gabrielle, and Blink took up the rear. The morning sun barely crested the horizon and highlighted the town's devastation. Though the flames had died out, smoke still wafted from many of the buildings. Elissa saw few bodies but knew many would lay in the square. The same square where a knife wielded by that bastard priest Fathen, a knife meant for Erick, had sliced her and almost killed her.

She shivered, and a wave of nausea passed over her, followed by faintness. She willed herself not to swoon and wondered, despite her assurances to Erick, if she really would have the strength to travel.

~

They reached the town square, and Erick marveled that they had survived to see the day. Undead sprawled across the dirt. Ghouls, wights, and death hounds of Eligos lay strewn among Erick's *vohquana*, the undead warriors he summoned during their weeks-long trek over The Ruins. The more powerful Eligos had badly outnumbered Erick's forces. Only Marcus's bravery in planting three daggers in the *Inconnu* saved them. No one had yet asked about the strange blemish—the *morazol*—burned into the thief's forehead, and Erick dreaded telling them what it meant.

The gallows stood before them. Erick shivered at the body on the raised platform, a dead man once possessed by Eligos and used like a puppet. Erick almost died when facing Eligos alone. How would he ever survive with the Master of Shadows backed by the two Necromancers who refused their duty and joined the cause of the *Inconnu*?

Marcus ran up the gallows stairs.

"What are you doing?" Erick asked.

In answer, Marcus leaned over the body and pulled two daggers from the corpse's back. He sheathed them in his belt holders, rolled the body over, and removed his prized knife from the sternum. The weapon's silvered blade gleamed in the morning sun, and the dark green emerald set in the hilt flashed.

"I believe these belong to me." Marcus kicked the body and descended the stairs.

"Feel better?" Corby asked.

"I feel complete." He twirled the silver blade around his fingers and slipped it into its sheath.

"How did you kill him?" Corby asked.

Marcus frowned. "You were there. I put two daggers in his back and one in his chest. That usually does the trick."

"That's not what I meant." He turned to Erick. "According to all the texts, and what we witnessed here, the living can't kill a Necromancer's creations. So how did Marcus kill the undead that held Eligos?"

"He wasn't undead," Erick said. "He was a *talba*, a vessel for Eligos to use. A *talba* is like," Erick paused to consider a suitable analogy, "clothing, I guess, horrible as that sounds. When Marcus stabbed it, he made the body no longer usable. When you get a rent in your tunic, you sew it or discard it. Since the body couldn't sustain life anymore, and Eligos had no opportunity to mend it, he had to flee it."

Corby scratched his dirty head. "So Eligos isn't undead?"

Erick shook his head. "He can create undead, but he isn't one himself."

"Then what is he?"

Erick frowned. "I don't know," he said. "No one does."

Much as they tried, the Necromancers could never determine the origin or true nature of Eligos or his brothers. They named Bolfri and Saburoc as his siblings, though, in truth, they had no idea if the three beings were related other than in their goals.

Something Eligos said before the battle came back to Erick. The *Inconnu* had made a comment about remaking the world for his people. Did that mean there were more like him? The idea was too horrible to contemplate. Where did they come from? How did they get here?

And most important, was it possible more would come?

That was a prospect Erick didn't want to consider. If he thought about the possibility, it might paralyze him. "Let's talk about this later," he told Corby. "When we're far from here."

They continued their search. The merchant stalls, mostly untouched by fire, had nonetheless been stripped of food and goods. Taken by fleeing townspeople, Erick reasoned.

They found no herbalist in the square, or any place that looked like a midwife's, and Erick despaired that they would have to spend precious hours searching every house in town for the herbs the healer needed.

Off the square, they discovered an inn and a tavern on opposite sides of the road. Both stone buildings had severe damage, their wooden roofs collapsed and burned away, furniture turned to ash and char. The smell of burnt wood and baked rock hung thick in the air.

Careful foraging through the inn offered nothing but broken crockery and half-burned barrels. The larder door was charred cinders, the food within destroyed. Marcus managed to find a few bronze coins that had not melted under a cracked clay bowl. But nothing else useful could be salvaged.

The tavern turned out to be the best thing their small group had experienced since arriving in Prospector's Camp the previous day. The ravaging flames had spared an iron-bound chest behind the scorched bar. Within the strongbox, they found enough bronze *teres* to fill three pouches, and even a small handful of silver *ceres*.

Marcus found the real wealth, a discovery that delighted them all. A door in the floor led to a cool, earthen-walled cellar, where the tavern owner kept extra provisions and crafted his own ales and herbal remedies. Three undamaged casks of water lined one side of the wall, and a shelf held loaves of bread, rinds of cheese, and a slab of salted beef.

Another wall offered an ample storage space with two sets of labeled wooden drawers. Grain, barley, and a variety of spices filled one set. The other held anything a junior herbalist or Necromancer might desire, including the ingredients Gabrielle needed to stave off the effects of Elissia's poison. Erick thought the healer might cry as she exclaimed over each find. Relieved and encouraged for the first time since speaking with the Necromancers, Erick did shed tears.

"Stop that," Elissia said as her own eyes welled. "I'm going to be fine. You've got too much to do, and you'll never get it done without my help."

He hugged her. "I don't know that I'd even want to try."

"Quit talking stupid. You'll do what you must, whether I'm here or not. But I don't plan on being anywhere else."

"I don't want to know what this man's beers tasted like," Marcus said as he sniffed one of the acrid green powders.

"He didn't use that for making—" Gabrielle stopped when she saw the wide grin on Marcus's face.

While Marcus and Corby cleaned their knives and cut slices of meat, bread, and cheese, Gabrielle broke two of the purple skullcap flowers from their stems. She tore a vervain leaf into two pieces and crushed three pale linden flower petals into powder with a dagger hilt. "I wish I had a mortar and pestle."

She put all the ingredients into a scavenged square of cheesecloth and doused the cloth in a wooden bowl of water. As the mixture soaked, she held her hands over the bowl and spoke in a quiet voice. When she finished, she handed the bowl to Elissia.

"Drink this. It would be better with heated water, but this should help."

Elissia downed the mixture in one smooth gulp. She grimaced, but the color in her face almost immediately improved. She sighed and closed her eyes. When she opened them, the dullness had left. "That is wonderful," she said.

"I'll have to prepare some for you every few hours," Gabrielle said. "And it will lose its efficacy, but it will help for a while."

"Thank you," Elissia said.

Erick managed to find a stash of small burlap bags, the right size to carry fist-sized portions of the various herbs and spices. With Blink's aid, he took what he could use to create undead, thankful they had discovered this treasure-filled cache. They spotted several bottles of already prepared items, but Erick couldn't decipher the barkeep's labeling system, and careful sniffing told him nothing but the key ingredients, so he decided to leave them behind.

When he finished gathering and sorting anything useful, he stuffed the small bags in a larger bag. It wasn't Gabrielle's herb kit, which had first been taken by the men who jailed them and then scavenged by the townspeople, but it would do until he could find something better.

They sat and ate, all of them ravenous. No one spoke as they filled

PAUL BARRETT

themselves with bread and meat and cheese. Marcus broached a keg of ale, and they drank from the wooden mixing bowls on the table in the room's center. The brew tasted of cinnamon. Erick didn't much like the spice. He found this drink less enjoyable than the nutty-flavored ale he had in the inn at Firstlast, before they discovered Fathen beaten on the road and regrettably took him into their company.

"I could sleep for days," Marcus said after they reached the point where they picked at crumbs on their plate. "Not really an option, is it?"

Erick shook his head. "I have no idea how long it will take Eligos to recover from what you did to him, but time is not on our side. Hopefully, the Fist will have no idea where we're going, so no more ambushes, but—" He stopped.

"But what?"

Erick shook his head again. "Nothing."

You need to tell them, Blink thought. *You want to keep them out of danger, so they need to know what the danger is.*

Erick sighed. "There's something about the mark on your forehead you need to know. It—"

"What mark?" Corby asked as Marcus lifted his hand to touch his forehead.

Erick frowned. "You don't see it?"

The others all looked at Marcus, who dropped his hand and stared back at them. "I don't feel anything," he said.

"There's nothing there," Elissia said.

"It's there," Erick said, "you just can't see it. Eligos gave it to you after you stabbed him. It's called a *morazol*, a death mark."

"It doesn't mean you're going to die," he continued, addressing the concern on Marcus's face, an expression reflected like a mirror in his other companions. "But it means any undead will be attracted to you."

Relief smoothed Marcus's brow. "That's not a problem, then. It's not like there's a village of them waiting to be recruited."

"No," Erick said, "but the mark also gives Eligos access to you. And I honestly don't know the extent of what that means. My father never told me."

No one spoke for a moment as they digested the news. Finally, Marcus said, "We'll deal with whatever comes. It's all we *can* do."

Erick nodded. "I want you to tell me if anything strange happens to you. Whispers in your head, unusual urges. Anything not normal."

Beside him, Elissia shifted, as if the ground had become uncomfortable, then stood up. "We should go so that we can travel as far as possible before dark."

Surprised by the sudden declaration, Erick stood. "Are you sure you're—"

She put a finger to his lips. "Yes. The medicine has helped me. And the sooner we go, the sooner I get cured. We won't make it to Dorfork for two or three days, but there must be smaller settlements between here and there. Maybe we'll find a village large enough to have an inn so we can bathe and sleep in a bed. If we're fortunate, maybe there will be a shop to buy fresh clothing, since we're suddenly rich."

Erick smiled. Though they were far from rich, the money they found would provide the comforts Elissia mentioned. Erick would give almost anything to lie in a soft bed with thick blankets and a feather pillow. He had grown weary of sleeping on the ground.

The others stood. "Let's pack some food for the road," Marcus said. As he grabbed a sack and began loading bread and cheese, he added. "We need to get another mule."

"If we can afford it," Elissia said, "we're going to buy at least a couple of horses. I'm tired of walking."

"We're not going to get any with the money we found here," Marcus said. "But once we get to Dorfork, give me an hour, and I'll make sure we have enough."

They left the tavern and headed west, the sun shining at their backs. Erick agreed with Elissia's opinion of walking, especially the several hundred miles to Starrasen, but the idea of utilizing horses terrified him. They were large, frightening animals, and he had no concept of how to ride one. He could only hope he wouldn't fall or look like an idiot.

Why? Blink asked with humor in his thought. *Wouldn't be the first time for either.*

Shut up, Erick thought back, but smiled as he did it.

The promise of a sunny, warm day put him in mind of when he set out from his destroyed home to travel here. Only a little over a month ago, it seemed like years had passed. So much loss and so many changes, all for nothing. And now there was the prospect of more loss, more hardship. It was almost enough to paralyze him.

But what choice did he have? He couldn't just stop at the next town, take up farming, and pass his responsibility on to someone else. There was no one else. He was no longer a Necromancer; he was *the* Necromancer.

The only one willing to stand against Eligos, anyway, Blink thought.

Yes, Erick thought back. Blink's comment reminded him that two of his kind had turned against him and joined forces with the *Inconnu.* How would he survive to reach the swamps and find some mysterious woman he knew nothing about? His father had never mentioned anyone known as a *wicaesir,* or a woman named Alais. Erick had always thought of the Covenant as a mutual pact: the Necromancers agreed to use the power of *elonsha* to protect Krinnik against the *Inconnu,* should they ever return, and the Gods both let *elonsha* remain in the world, and made harming Necromancers a blasphemous offense. It was an agreement based on mutual understanding.

Now Erick saw it was nothing of the sort. It was more like a farmer keeping a rabid dog to guard his chickens. He did it only if he had no other dogs and was too lazy to defend them himself. The Gods had the Necromancers because the Gods wouldn't bother to preserve their creation. They wouldn't even take the time to care for their guard dogs.

Erick, taught from birth to revere the Gods because they revered him, found himself wondering if they truly deserved veneration.

The medallion around his neck tingled. A voice, gentle but with an edge of mischief, said, *you are watched.*

He touched his mother's talisman, the eight-circled arrow of Denech, the god of fate. Warmth stole over him, and some peace came to his mind. He relaxed, comforted that at least one of the eight paid attention. Even then, part of his mind nagged at him. Denech was a capricious god, his aid uncertain. Uncertain help might be worse than no help. At least you could depend on no help.

"I'll be damned."

Erick looked up at the sound of Marcus's voice. The donkey that had traveled with them from Kalador stood in the center of the road. It had picked up an apple from those scattered on the ground and chewed as if it had no cares.

"You're kidding me," Elissia said. "I thought for certain he'd be a zombie dinner."

Erick smiled and touched the medallion. *Thanks,* he thought. The aid might be sporadic, but now, it was most welcome.

They corralled the mule, who seemed less than pleased to see them. He brayed in annoyance as they loaded him with their small amount of scavenged provisions.

"Hush," Marcus chided. "Be glad you still have all your legs."

"Since we have the extra carrying capacity, we should load up on wood for fires," Corby said. "There are no true woods between here and Dorfork."

They spent another half-hour scavenging wood from partially burned shelving and furniture found inside the stone buildings. They tied them in bundles and strapped them to the increasingly irritable pack animal.

"That's probably enough," Erick said once they had five clusters attached to the mule. "Any more, and he'll look like a house."

"Not once we put these on him," Marcus said as he walked out of a building that had been a supply depot. He held a handful of gray wool blankets. "There are tents in there, too. We're going to be almost as good as before we got here."

They added more to the mule's burden. The beast appeared ready to bite or kick them if they came near him with anything else.

"You're right, Marcus," Erick said. "Almost as good as when we left."

"We're much better than I would have ever hoped last night," Elissia said. Erick hated hearing how tired she sounded. They all sounded tired. Hopefully, they could rest in a bed at an inn tonight.

"Sooner started, sooner finished," Marcus said.

They continued west down the road.

As they neared the town's edge, a group of six men dressed in rough, dirt-covered clothing rounded the corner. Each one had a mattock perched upon his shoulders. Two men led them. One was stocky with cropped brown hair and a large nose. He wore a taupe and gray soldier's uniform, his gold captain's epaulets torn and dirty. The other man, lean and balding, had more gray-brown hair in his beard than on his head. Streaks of soot and black-edged holes marred his burgundy robe.

"Bastards," Erick snarled. His companions tensed.

The newcomers started at his words. The bald magistrate straightened in arrogant dignity though he no longer wore his purple cloak of office. "Captain, seize them. You men, assist the captain."

Captain Ceran stepped forward and drew his sword.

Marcus and Elissia put themselves in front of Erick, daggers ready. Blink jumped into the air, dust and ash stirred by his flapping wings. Erick's memory flashed back to his first fight, on the road to Firstlast. Like then, his body tingled with fear and excitement.

The miners exchanged uncertain glances.

The magistrate turned to them. "This is the Necromancer who wrought destruction on our town and sent his foul creatures to kill your families. Seize him."

Corby stepped up, crossbow in hand but not aimed. "That is a lie," he thundered. The strength of voice that came from the usually timid scholar astounded Erick.

The miners stared at him.

Corby continued, his voice ringing with conviction. "This is Erick Darvaul, who traveled through flame and treachery to Twr Krinnik, to take up his preordained place in the battle to once again save our world from the depredations of Eligos, the Master of Shadows. We are his stalwart companions, who have journeyed with him from the beginning and shed blood and tears to ensure he arrived to fulfill his destiny. Did we sneak into town under cover of night, intent on assassination and chicanery?"

Chicanery? Blink thought as he settled back to the ground.

He's a scholar, Erick thought back.

"No," Corby continued, "we strolled into your town in the light of day, prepared to announce our intentions to any who would listen. We hoped to seek aid to enter the mountain and solicit information to discover the vaunted chamber where the Ten Necromancers, blessed by the Eight True Gods, destroyed and exiled the foul *Inconnu*. But before we could utter voice to our desires, this man—" Corby pointed the loaded crossbow at Ceran, who stepped back, a glint of fear in his dark eyes. "Without provocation and only on the hearsay of another, illegally detained all of us for Necromancy, a magic only one of us can perform, and a magic that is *not a crime* under the Queen's Law.

"Erick Darvaul's power is sanctioned by the Gods and accepted across the whole of Krinnik. And what transpired while we sat in a jail cell? Another summoned forth the undead that plagued your town, ignited the flames that burned your homes, and killed your families. That culprit was none other than a shard of Eligos himself, in the guise of a man. Eligos, a being to whom these two—" he swung the crossbow to include the magistrate. The man did not flinch, only stared at Corby as if the scholar's words were wind that stirred no emotions. "—sold their allegiance for a promise of power when Eligos reestablished his vile reign."

"These are outrageous fabrications," the magistrate blustered. "You seek to save your own lives with false words, but you will not sway the true hearts of the men of Prospector's Camp. Go ahead and shoot me. Seal your fate."

Corby looked at the crossbow. He pulled the bolt from it and dropped both weapon and missile. "I will not." His gaze went to the miners. "Erick did not summon these creatures. He fought to destroy them. The one responsible lies dead on the gallows. Gallows fashioned for the neck of the very man who fought to save you. If we are so evil, why does the fearsome Necromancer not call forth creatures to wreak havoc upon you all? We wish for nothing but to leave in peace and continue our quest, for it is far from complete. Your true malefactors are the men who attempt to detain us. They are the ones you should seize."

"Enough of this," Ceran waved a hand at the miners. "Assist me in arresting these people."

The miners did not move. Three of them looked to another, who appeared the oldest by at least a decade, his hair thin and gray, his face square. He shook his head.

"Do as I say, or I will have you up on charges of insubordination," Ceran told them.

"We're not soldiers," the miner said, his large hands shifting on the mattock's handle. "We think the lad be telling true."

"Nonsense," the magistrate sputtered, all sense of dignity gone. "They are murderers who deal with dark forces, and they cast aspersions on me, a rightfully-appointed official. To go against my word is to go against the Queen."

Corby said, "The word of a traitor isn't worth the breath to say it."

The magistrate's round face flushed. "Captain, end their miserable lives."

"Hold, Captain," the miner said as Ceran stepped forward.

To Erick's surprise, Ceran paused and regarded the miner. The set of his jaw and tilt of his head spoke of disbelief that the miner would dare such presumption.

The miner looked at Corby. "You speak fair, but you also make serious accusations without proof."

"We just assumed that's the way things were done around here," Marcus said.

"That doesn't facilitate our chances of departure unmolested," Corby muttered to Marcus. "The proof is all around you, in the clasp of undead that fought other undead. Those are Erick's manifestations that he called forth to fight the creatures of Eligos."

The magistrate rounded on the miner. "I've about had enough—"

"Show them your mark," Erick shouted over the magistrate.

"What?"

Erick addressed the lead miner. "All who fall under the sway of Eligos receive a mark, usually on the cheek or forearm. It will look like a tattoo. If these men have it, then they have done what I said. If not, you can do what you want with me."

Are you sure about this? Blink asked.

As sure as I am about anything anymore.

The miner gave a questioning glance at his comrades. They nodded. "Show us your arms," he commanded the magistrate.

It happened before Erick could do anything to stop it. Ceran launched himself forward, sword raised. Elissia let her dagger fly. It caught the captain in his sword arm and threw off his aim. The blow fell wide of Erick.

Marcus thrust upward and buried his blade into Ceran's throat. He yanked the dagger out. Blood gurgled from the wound as the captain's hands tried to stem the flow. He collapsed to his knees with eyes wide.

With a cry of fear, the magistrate turned to run. The miner took one step.

"No," Erick shouted, the word escaping even though he knew it was too late.

The miner's arms swung, burying the mattock in the magistrate's back with a thud that echoed through Erick's mind. He dropped like a felled tree.

For a moment, no one moved.

Ceran let out a last wheeze and fell over, his hands coated with blood. Corby's face paled. He ran a few steps away and became violently sick.

The miner let go of his ax and stepped back. He stared at his shaking hands, as if uncertain what he had done.

One of the other miners, shorter and stockier than his leader, walked to the magistrate. He pulled the mattock from the dead man's back, and Erick winced at the wet grating sound made by the tool-turned-weapon. The man dropped it and turned the magistrate over.

Blood trickled from the official's mouth. His glazed eyes stared at the sky. The miner knelt and rolled up the sleeves of the body's dark robe.

Erick swallowed, fearful of what might be revealed. What if he were wrong? Two more men dead for no reason.

They threw us in a cell and almost got us killed, Blink reminded him.

Erick nodded in acknowledgment, though he didn't know if that warranted their deaths. He held his breath.

The sleeve peeled back to reveal a black symbol like ink pressed

43

into the skin. A thick black line ran from just shy of the wrist to the crook of the elbow. An inch-wide circle of bare skin broke through the darkness at regular spacings, three in total—a representation of the three *Inconnu*.

Erick let out his breath. Unlike Corby's death mark, invisible to all but Erick, these tattoos proved these men chose to become servants to Eligos. They were badges, marks of status as clear as the captain's torn epaulets. These deaths now weighed far less on his conscience.

"Check the captain," the miner on his knees said, his voice gravelly. The leader stared at his hands, unmoving, so the other miner stepped over to Ceran.

Marcus withdrew a few paces, knife at the ready.

The miner deftly pulled up the captain's sleeves to reveal another of the marks of Eligos, this one two small black circles with a ragged slash beneath them. An irregular line wrapped around the symbols. It reminded Erick of a skull. A shiver of dread surprised him.

"So, they got what they deserved," Elissia said.

"Yes, they did," Erick said.

Corby walked back over. "Does anyone really deserve that?" He pointed at the large hole in the magistrate's back.

"That was a far quicker death than any of us would have received at the hands or teeth of Eligos's *gateloah*," Erick said.

"Maybe," Corby said. "But..." He shook his head.

"Thank you," Erick said. "I think your speech saved us."

Corby shrugged. "I only spoke the truth."

"Aye," the miner leader pulled his eyes away from his hands and back to them. "That you did. And glad I am that we listened and did not jump to the captain's orders, as soldiers would have done. To think we might have done you ill, and let these vermin live." His gaze went to the magistrate's body, and he paled.

"It gets easier," Marcus said, wiping the blood off his knife.

"I hope not," the miner replied. "What will you do now?"

"We'll leave," Erick told him. "Your town will be left in peace. What will you do?"

"Those of us who survived will rebuild," the miner said. "We'll bring our families back and send to the Queen for aid. She will allow it, for the mine makes wealth for her. We'll attend to our dead and recover. It will take time and work, but someday the town will be as it ever was."

Erick admired the man's spirit. He didn't know if he would be so optimistic had he been dealt the same blows by fate.

You already have been and are, Blink thought.

Not true, Erick thought. *I'm not optimistic about our chances at all. If someone else could do it, I would go back to Draymed without a second thought. But that choice isn't available. So, I'll do what I must.*

They gave their farewells to the miners and continued west. As the ruined town fell behind them, Erick was as uncertain of what might happen as he had ever been.

4

Aye, they opened across the battlefield, dark as if the night sky had come to the ground. But the beasts that poured out of those rents will haunt my dreams the rest of my days.

-Eyewitness account of portals at the Siege of Rambaris

Keven sat on his small roan and surveyed the destruction of Prospector's Camp, smoke drifting into the afternoon sky. Despite pushing their mounts almost to the point of death, they had arrived too late for the battle. But had Eligos or the Necromancer won?

Beside Keven, NalTalva sat on his froth-mouthed Palomino. He wore a wide-brimmed, green hat to protect his skin, the color of cooked fish, from the sun. "Our master informs me his *talba* has been destroyed, and the priest killed."

Keven shuddered at the man's seeming ability to both read his mind and receive messages from the Master of Shadows. Then, the man's words registered. "Fathen is dead?"

NalTalva nodded, his broad face impassive.

Numb shock froze Keven and twisted his stomach. The man he had considered his true father for all these years was dead? He wanted to weep at the news, but he wouldn't cry in front of this grim warrior. "How did it happen?"

The Sterran warrior shrugged. "I know not. I know only that he is."

They had traveled together for eight days, over ocean and road, and Keven knew almost nothing about the stern-faced man. They had travelled from Keven's village of Draymed, which NalTalva had destroyed with poison, blade, and fire, a task he accomplished with Keven's unwilling assistance. Reluctant aid gained by the warrior's invocation that Fathen wished it and an unspoken promise of death should Keven refuse. Other than threats and commands, the warrior spoke little.

"Then we've wasted our time," Keven said, bitterness replacing his desire to cry. The Sterran despised weakness. He permitted Keven to show none; a slap to the face or fist to the stomach was the reward for any perceived lapse in fortitude.

It's like father all over again, Keven thought. He felt no loss when that man fell beneath the Sterran's knife. He hated NalTalva, too, and longed to see him die a painful death.

But he had endured the arduous five-day journey over the World's Circle ocean, had accepted the punishing rides on stolen horses, had said nothing when NalTalva killed the ostler and his apprentice to take the mounts. They stopped only when it became apparent the horses could go no further without dying. They rested long enough to water and feed the beasts, take a bite themselves, and sleep a few hours.

"We have wasted nothing," NalTalva said. "I will find the master's *talba*, and we will learn what happened."

Keven had tolerated this journey because he knew Fathen would be waiting at the end. Fathen would chastise NalTalva for his treatment of Keven, just as the priest punished Keven's father, threatening physical beatings and spiritual banishment from the light of Caros.

Keven would forever cherish the delight in seeing his father, a broad-shouldered man with land and status, cower before the taller, thinner priest. After that, though Keven's father refused to speak to him unless necessary, he never again raised a hand to his son.

Fathen earned Keven's heart that day with his kind action; had shown himself as the father Keven felt he deserved. Keven became an Initiate to Caros on his twelfth birthday, as soon as he could. He took his place by the priest's side and had been there for the past five years. It had hurt deeply when Fathen left Draymed without taking him.

That bitterness dissolved when NalTalva brought word of his master's whereabouts and mission. Keven relished the prospect of reuniting with Fathen and destroying the Necromancer Erick, the curly-haired abomination who had stolen Elissia, the woman Keven *knew* he deserved.

But his master was dead, which meant the Necromancer probably still lived.

Keven gritted his teeth to keep from screaming, crying, or both. "So, we learn what happened. What good will that do?"

NalTalva did not answer. Another annoying habit, as if Keven didn't merit consideration. Instead, the warrior kicked his horse's side. With an exhausted whinny, the Palomino clopped forward.

The destruction of Draymed came to Keven's mind as they walked down Routh Krinnik, the road from Kalador, into the heart of the town. The orange stone buildings still lined the road on either side. Cracked, soot-blackened walls and charred, collapsed roofs testified to the conflagration that had swept through. Bodies lay across the road, some in awkward heaps, others as if they had merely stopped for a nap. All bore the marks of violence, the rending of claws and teeth. Some had been so ravaged they registered not as people but as chunks of torn flesh held together by shreds of cloth. The sweet smell of seared bodies and harsh scent of burned wood mingled in the still air. Keven held back his rising gorge. If he vomited, no doubt NalTalva would see that as weakness, too.

They reached the town square, where evidence of a desperate fight lay all about. Corpses sprawled everywhere, the remains of scores of undead locked in a deadly embrace. The reek of it all but overwhelmed him, and it pleased Keven to see NalTalva's pale face crinkle in disgust.

Gallows stood in the center of the square, the rope still hanging on the crossbeam. The entire structure was somehow untouched by the fire that blasted through town. Keven could make out a vague black lump atop the platform, ten feet off the ground.

They drew closer to the gallows, and NalTalva dismounted. His horse wheezed, and Keven feared the beast would drop, but it only wandered a few paces and then lowered its head.

Keven slid off his mount and stretched to work the kinks from his back. The hard riding over the past several days caused his muscles to ache constantly. He petted the roan's neck. "I'll get you some food and water soon as I can," he whispered to the beast. Its ears flickered as if acknowledging his promise.

NalTalva walked up the gallows stairs, and Keven followed since his companion had not forbidden it. He wanted to stay close; the deathly stillness of the town unnerved him, though he would admit it to no one.

He stopped on the top step while NalTalva walked across the platform.

The Sterran knelt beside the figure that lay on its back, a slender body with the face of a man that could have been a shopkeeper or a noble.

Keven envied that ordinary face. He had been a handsome child, or so many told him. His warm brown eyes matched his chestnut hair. With a firm chin, sharp cheeks, and a nose that could cut diamonds, he resembled his father in miniature. Keven touched the scar that now ran from his right eye to his upper lip. That same father had ruined his son's features in a fit of anger. It felt as ugly as he knew it to be.

He watched as NalTalva examined the body. Though the black clothing made it difficult to see, a puncture, either from a dagger or sword, pierced the chest. Keven had no idea who the man had been. The deep frown on the usually expressionless Sterran revealed his disturbance at the death.

Again, as if he had read Keven's thoughts, NalTalva said, "This is our master's *talba*, which is now nothing but rotting meat."

Your master, not mine, Keven thought, and then he hoped the man couldn't truly read his mind. "What do we do now?"

NalTalva removed his green hat. His alabaster skin gleamed in the early autumn sun while his black hair absorbed the light. He turned to

PAUL BARRETT

the sky, eyes closed, and said what sounded to Keven like *"camlix de orz."* Then he replaced the hat, returning his face to shadow, and put his hand on the dead man's chest.

Though nothing changed around him, the darkness on NalTalva's face deepened, as if the sun had disappeared behind the clouds. His skin turned the leaden gray of a stormy sky as his eyes all but vanished in the hat's shadow. Standing out against this dimness was the red scar that puckered like a brand on NalTalva's cheek. It reminded Keven of a blood-colored skull, a wavy line surrounding two circles with a slash below them like a mouth ripped from where one had not existed. Keven's stomach clenched as he witnessed the hypnotic pulsing of the blemish cycling from bright crimson to the mottled black of a deep bruise.

Eyes closed, NalTalva's lips moved. The wind stirred. The scent of onions gone to rot chased away the odor of death. Keven shivered despite the day's warmth.

After at least a minute, in which Keven's stomach roiled and twisted, the breeze died, and the sharp smell retreated. Keven never imagined he would feel relief at the scent of dead flesh. Anything was better than whatever malevolent force brought that nauseating onion stench with it.

The shadows retreated from NalTalva's face. His scar ceased its heartbeat color changing. He opened his eyes, turned the body onto its face, and motioned Keven closer. NalTalva pointed at the man's back, where Keven saw two more puncture wounds.

"A cowardly child slew our master," NalTalva said. "Stabbed in the back like a dishonored warrior, then struck in the chest as he tried to defend himself. This body is useless, and the master awaits a new *talba*. We must find one for him and restore him to his place."

"How? We aren't Necromancers."

NalTalva offered a rare twisted grin. The disdain in that leer almost made Keven back up a step. "Eligos is the Master of Shadows. He does not need your meddling Gods' magic to return. He needs only a vessel and sacrificial blood."

Keven nodded, although the words chilled him. "Once he returns, what will your master do?"

"*Our* master," NalTalva said, his voice hard, "has much left to do. But first, as much as I advise against it, he will restore your priest. Though I do not understand the value of one so unable to protect our master, it is not my place to question."

NalTalva's tone told Keven the Sterran did question it, but Keven didn't care. He latched onto the important information. "He will resurrect Fathen?"

NalTalva nodded.

Praise be to Caros, Keven thought. Then he realized his praise was misplaced. Caros would not bring his master back. Eligos would. Keven began to understand the words NalTalva had spoken when they first met, before the warrior opened his rain of destruction on Keven's home. He had presented Fathen's gold chains and said, "Your priest no longer follows his faith. He has found a better path, and desires you remain at his side as his strong arm."

Eligos was that better path.

Keven had known about Fathen's discontent with their deity. They often spoke late into the night of Caros and his indifference. Though Keven found some value to the worship of Caros, their God was a distant, unseen entity. Fathen had been real and true to Keven, had protected him. Keven knew Fathen would never lead him astray. If Fathen said Eligos was the way, then Keven took the words on faith. If Eligos returned his master from the dead, Keven would know his loyalty was well-placed.

From his vantage point, Keven studied the fire-hollowed buildings in the town square. The citizens had deserted their destroyed dwellings. Where would they find a person to be *talba* for Eligos?

A noise from one of the structures drew their attention. Cautiously, a man came through the doorway. Large-bellied, but also muscular and hard-edged of face, he stood straight and glared at them, dignified despite his charred miner's clothing. Behind him, a boy and girl, perhaps both ten years of age, stared fearfully.

"Who are you?" the man asked, the cudgel in his hand ready to offer a rebuttal to a wrong answer.

Keven smiled, hoping his scar did not impede the friendly look he offered. "I am a priest of Caros, newly admitted to the faith."

He revealed the gold chains around his neck: Fathen's gold chains. The chains of a priest of Caros. "My man and I have come to offer succor to the survivors of the Necromancer's destruction. May we aid you?"

The man offered a tentative nod. "That would be most welcome."

Keven's smile broadened as he walked down the stairs. NalTalva followed. Truly, Eligos provided all answers.

5

The Tome of the Father and Mother declares that physical love should transpire only between those for whom spiritual love exists, and only in the interest of increasing the size of the tribe. I declare that if we followed those stipulations, this would be a really boring world.

-Cantaril, High Priest of the Disciples of Amare

Fathen drifted in darkness, a blessed comfort after the pain of rent flesh and torn muscle that took him to his death. The zombies of the Necromancer Erick had destroyed him, ripped apart his body while he flailed and screamed and fought in vain. The agony had been worse than his mind considered possible. Death was a relief.

Now, fear replaced grief. Darkness engulfed Fathen, leaving him only with his thoughts. No reminders of the physical world assailed him. The darkness offered neither hot nor cold. He couldn't touch anything or even form the concept of fingers with which to do so. Though he remembered the idea of his body, the reality of it eluded him. Some form of him existed. He still had memory and emotion. He was aware of how he came to be in this void. Wondering what his fate would be when Alakaneth came to judge him filled him with trepidation.

Caros, forgive me, Fathen's soul thought.

Fathen had betrayed his god. Had cast him aside to follow the dark being Eligos, Master of the *Inconnu*. He had tried to repent at the last, refusing to kill Erick and denying Eligos the energy needed to claim his place at *Twr Krinnik*, the Broken Mountain.

Something had gone wrong.

Furious, Eligos took control of Fathen like a puppeteer with his marionette and forced him to attack the Necromancer. Elissia, the stupid girl who loved Erick, had interfered and been cut. Most likely, she had already succumbed to the dagger's poison and waited, like him, for judgment. Did she float in the void as he did, or was this a prison of his own making?

How long he waited in the nothing, he could not fathom. Time, like physical sensation, lost all meaning.

At some point, the darkness disappeared, and he stood in a room of gray light. His body had returned unbloodied, naked, and bereft of all senses beyond sight. He heard no sound, had no sensation of touch, and no smell came to his nose.

A man in a dark gray robe stood before him. Tall and slender like Fathen, he had curly silver hair, a gray, finger-length beard, and eyes the color of wood smoke. His wrinkled face conveyed wisdom and fairness. Alakaneth.

Fathen's fear grew. He knew deep in his soul he would be condemned to the Hells for his crimes against Caros and his Necromancer. Twenty years of obedience wiped away by his defection to Eligos. His attempted repentance at the end gained him nothing.

Alakaneth opened his mouth to pronounce judgment when another voice spoke, a voice with the whisper of dead leaves on stone.

"You cannot have him, weakling god. He has betrayed me, and he will pay as your Necromancers have. He is mine."

Before Alakaneth offered any response, the gray light disappeared. Sensation returned to Fathen, a sense of being drawn forward, squeezed into too small a space, like air through a reed. Blindness struck him. Voices cried out and screamed in agony, moaning in desperation: the pleas of damned souls. Fathen heard the fate he would one day share.

He feared whatever destiny he now flowed toward would be far worse.

The knowledge of his body returned in pieces. His blindness disappeared, noticeable as a minute lightening in the blackness. His hearing brought him the sound of rushing wind. A compressed sensation bore upon his lungs. Breathing was impossible, but he did not yet need the air of life.

This was not his body, only his remembrance of it, his knowledge of how it functioned. He felt no pain, though he knew it was coming. One did not get torn to pieces by zombies, enduring agony never dreamt, and expect to return to that body without reliving at least a fraction of the torment visited upon it.

Trauma slammed him as he entered his body. He screamed as every nerve, muscle, and sinew announced that he lived. Death would not yet claim him. As the fire of anguish ran through him, he wished it had.

His head throbbed as if his brain wished to escape. Blinding light pierced his eyes. Cloying decay and charred wood wormed into his nose while his tongue tasted the oily feel of burned, greasy meat. Rushing wind threatened to deafen his tender ears. He was a newborn exposed to all of life's sensual experiences in the first moments of awareness. He feared it would drive him mad.

Not soon enough, the overwhelming insanity of sensations abated. Fathen could separate the incoming information and form a coherent thought. Light on his eyelids and warmth on his left arm told him the sun hung low. The roar of wind in his ears fell to a small breeze. Feet shuffled. Excruciating agony lessened to the stiffness of a hard day's work. He groaned, surprised his voice worked.

And so, you have returned to us.

A shivering spasm racked through Fathen at the whispering voice he knew so well. The light on his eyelids dimmed as someone leaned over him. Fathen didn't want to open his eyes. He knew Eligos, in the body he had claimed as his *talba*, looked down on him with expressionless eyes and a disappointed frown.

"*Carobon*, are you there?"

Another voice, one he had never expected to hear again. His eyes opened. He immediately closed them as the sunlight, even though it was low in the sky and dimmed, rammed a spike of pain through his head. Hand over his eyes, he squinted, taking his time to let them adjust.

As he grew accustomed to the brightness, he saw three people standing over him. He did not recognize the man with a face as hard-edged as the mountains, his cliff-like cheeks not softened by his thick brown mustache.

He looked to the others. NalTalva, pale and impassive, his black eyes pits in his face that offered no clue to his thoughts.

"Keven," Fathen said to the third face, its scarring as familiar to Fathen as his hands. "How—" he swallowed, his throat dry as if it was formed of dust. "Water."

"Of course," the young man said as he removed the water skin slung over his shoulder.

A moan escaped Fathen as Keven helped him sit up to drink. The water burned his parched gullet as he sucked it down like a babe gulping mother's milk. Keven pulled it away too soon.

"Slowly, *caroban*. You will sicken yourself."

"I am no longer *caroban*." Fathen dismissed the title Keven used. He had tried at the last to return to Caros, only to have the sun god reject him and leave him to his fate. Judgment he could handle, knowing his sins. Rejection he would not accept. He no longer served as *caroban*, a teacher of the god's way.

But his last gasp denial of Eligos would no doubt merit severe punishment, and he did not know if his dark master would accept him back. Fathen was a priest with no deity.

He swallowed again. The choking dryness in his throat returned as he considered his situation. He wanted more water, but Keven was right. His empty stomach sloshed with the liquid he had already consumed. Any more, and he might bring it back up.

Fathen had been so concerned about the pains that assailed him that he only now realized he lay upon the warm ground naked as he came from his mother's womb. "Where is my clothing?"

"Destroyed, along with your body." NalTalva held out a plain brown bundle. "We scrounged these."

"We'll get you something more suited as soon as we can," Keven assured him.

"Those are more than suitable," the hard-faced man said in a voice that matched his countenance. "They will do until you serve your penance."

Fathen studied the man closer. His large stomach spoke of one well-fed, and his bloodshot eyes and crimson nose told a tale of fondness for drink. He was short but well-muscled.

"Who are you to speak of penance?" Fathen asked, wishing he stood clothed instead of addressing the man from this seated, naked position.

The man's face went stony as he frowned. His eyes turned solid black and danced with red fire. "You know who I am." His voice rasped like knucklebones over tin.

"Master?" His head throbbed as his heartbeat pounded. "Where is Andras?"

The man put his foot on Fathen's chest and shoved him back to the ground. Pain racked through his body.

"That meat is despoiled," Eligos said. "Something that would not have come to pass had you done what you swore. This is my *talba* now, undesirable as it is. You do not have the right to call me master. Your betrayal has stripped you of that honor. You must earn it again."

"What do I call you?"

"This one's name was Min. That will do, but you had best speak little unless I request it."

"I will earn the right to call you master again," Fathen said. "Whatever you wish of me, I will do. There is truly nothing for me with my old god. He allowed me to fail."

"Something I would not have done had you the conviction of your professed faith in me."

"I'm sorry," Fathen said.

"You will be."

"Enough," Keven said. "He has offered his contrition. Will you force him to wallow in it, or are we going after our true enemy?"

The man turned his stormy gaze on Keven. The young man didn't flinch. "You dare to speak to me like that?"

"I do." He pointed at Fathen. "He is my master, not you. I did your bidding at his request, but you do not own me. If you attack him, you attack me. And if the Necromancer could kill you, I suspect I could manage it."

NalTalva tensed, his hand straying to his sword. Min's jaw clenched so tight Fathen expected to hear teeth cracking. Keven made no show of backing down.

Then the man laughed, a harsh, dry sound that grated on Fathen's pounding head.

Min's eyes fell on Fathen. They had lost their sinister darkness and gone the deep brown of rich loam. When he spoke again, it was in the miner's gruff voice. "If you had half the backbone your acolyte has, you would not be in the position you are now."

"If I'm so worthless, why did you bother to return me?"

"Because you wounded the girl and set another plan in motion. Had you not succeeded, I would have left you to your death shepherd."

"What plan?"

"Nothing that needs concern you. Get up and dress. We have much to discuss."

With Keven's assistance, Fathen stood. He placed his hand on the acolyte's shoulder as dizziness struck him. When it passed, he donned the clothing NalTalva offered him. Brown and threadbare, they stank of smoke. The twill pants were loose, so he used a length of rope to tie them off. The high boots crammed against his toes, making him wince in pain. He suspected it would get worse when they started walking.

"When we reach a town, we will dress you in appropriate clothing," Min said. "For now, let this remind you how low you sit in my eyes."

Fathen nodded. Only now, dressed, aching, and famished, did it belatedly dawn on him that he was the product of a miracle. Eligos had done something the Gods themselves, to Fathen's knowledge, had never done.

"How did you do this?" He had vague memories of standing before Alakaneth the Judge, but the fading vision seemed more dream than truth. More lasting, the memory of death's emptiness clung to him like static-bound cloth.

"A simple matter, but one you may come to dislike. Are you hungry?"

"I am."

"Then you should feed." Min pointed behind Fathen.

Fathen turned to find a boy lying on the ground, brown-haired, slight, no more than ten. His hands were trussed behind him and his mouth gagged. He stared with unfocused, glassy eyes. A few feet from him lay a young girl on her back, her chest and torso splayed open, the organs removed. Crusts of blood clung to the desecrated flesh. Fathen gasped. "What is that?"

"That is what returned you to my service, just as this meat was given to return me. If you are hungry, feed."

"On what?"

"On what I offer." Min again gestured at the insensible child.

Fathen looked between the children, living and dead. The resemblance in their sharp faces told him they had been siblings, just as a glance at Min showed he was once their father. "I can't do that."

"Then you will starve and again die, and I will be rid of you. This time, the wretched death scraper god can have you and send you where he will. I think you will not like his judgment."

Fathen walked over to the boy. The child's gaze followed him. Fathen didn't know if the child saw him or locked on a blur of motion. His eyes were red, and the tracks of dried tears ran through the soot on his face.

The face of Calligan, the boy Fathen had refused to kill on Eligos' command, flashed before him. Eligos had ended the young thief's life with a knife across the throat. Where his master's action had once repulsed Fathen, it no longer bothered him. The boy had died, as many others had and would for as long as Krinnik existed.

His stomach rumbled, and his mouth watered. He could hear the child's heartbeat, soft and lumbering. Fear had put him in a senseless stupor. What did this child have to live for? Sister dead. Father dead and serving another. It would be a kindness to end this boy's life.

And he was so damnably hungry.

Fathen knelt and took the child's thin wrist. The vein throbbed with his pulse. Painful longing wracked Fathen, and he knew he must feed or die. This boy would give himself to a higher purpose, as his father and sister had done. Fathen lived again, given a second chance by a being more powerful than anything he had ever known. Who was he to waste this opportunity?

Fathen licked his lips. The last vestige of what he had once been tried to resist, to scream that it was better to die than accept this heinous act. It fought, but it never had a chance.

Fathen opened his mouth and leaned toward the boy's throat.

K even turned away as Fathen bent to feed. He knew it must be done. His master was something different now. Something not human. Eligos, speaking in the voice of Min, explained it. Through the power of *elonsha*, Fathen now existed as a lich. A creature of great power, immune to the weapons of men, imbued with abilities beyond ordinary undead, but forever damned to consume the flesh of the pure.

The child's brief cry turned to gurgling as flesh tore. The choked sound died away, replaced by noisy chewing. Keven's stomach lurched. *I will not be sick*, he told himself. He had not grown ill during the gore-soaked ritual to return his master; he would hold his composure now.

"Do not turn away," Min told him. "Look upon the one you hold dear. If you wish to destroy the Necromancer, witness the price for that dream."

When Keven still did not turn, NalTalva grabbed him by the shoulders and spun him.

Fathen, or the thing that had been Fathen, had removed the child's head and chewed at the ragged strands of neck meat hanging from the severed skull. Blood clung to his chin and cheeks like spilled wine. Ecstasy covered the gaunt face.

What have I done? Keven thought. Was his vengeance against Erick, his need to reclaim Elissia, worth this?

Not for those reasons, he realized. But he would pay any price to have Fathen back to guide him. No matter what Eligos had done, Fathen was still Keven's true father. Keven would destroy any number of villages to help him escape death. That he might also get to kill Erick and claim Elissia made it all the better.

Keven watched Fathen crack open the skull against the hard ground, scoop out chunks of brain, and consume them. *All creatures have to eat,* Keven told himself. *Is this any different than the slaughter of cows or chickens?* His father taught him that the strong made the rules. Fathen reinforced it by showing Keven his father's weakness.

Shame burned his cheeks as he remembered how Erick had cowed him in Draymed, threatening to bring forth undead to kill Keven and the other acolytes. Now Keven had his own undead. He had the Master of Shadows behind him and Fathen to stand beside him. The next time he and Erick met, Keven would be the strong one. He would watch as his two masters crushed Erick, and then he'd slit the Necromancer's throat himself.

Eventually, Fathen finished his gruesome meal. He dropped the empty skull. It thudded on the hard-packed ground, and Keven felt it in his feet. Fathen wiped his mouth, smearing blood across his face.

"Here, *Eliban,*" Keven said, again offering his water skin.

"*Eliban?*" Fathen said as he took the water skin.

Keven nodded. "Just as you taught me the wisdom of Caros, so you will teach me the power of Eligos."

Fathen had flinched at the mention of the Sun God. He smiled, revealing blood and gore-flecked teeth. "I like that."

Min regarded Keven. "May you heed his teachings better than he heeded mine."

Fathen splashed water on his face and rubbed the blood away. So scrubbed, he looked as Keven remembered him, save his waxy skin and tinges of red splotched about his eyes. His long brown hair held no sheen, but Keven suspected the lack of time to bathe might be the culprit. He knew he wanted a chance to wash the grime of travel from himself.

Fathen turned to Min. "I heeded your teaching. Is it my fault you were not as powerful as you claimed, and Caros still had a hold on my thoughts?"

Min strode up to Fathen. Though the priest stood a foot taller than the former miner, Min easily weighed more in sheer bulk. He reached up and slammed a meaty fist against Fathen's head. The priest fell on his backside.

Keven moved to intercept. NalTalva snared his shoulders and stopped him.

"I taught you gently," Min said as Fathen stared up from the ground, "because I thought you would best learn that way. In that, I was remiss and have learned *my* lesson. You will now learn through pain and punishment, as it should have been from the beginning. You, not I, let your bastard god influence you. Never think your flaws are mine. And never think to question me again. I am your superior, and you will give me due respect, or I will destroy you with as much ease as I created you."

Fathen stood and dusted off his brown clothing. "As you say, Master. My—"

Min's fist slammed into Fathen's stomach, and he doubled over with an *oof* as air rushed from his lungs.

"Already, you continue to disappoint me. Did I not just a moment ago say you were not worthy enough to call me master? Nothing has changed between now and then."

"I'm sorry," Fathen said as he straightened. "It won't happen again."

Though the punch didn't seem to have hurt his master, Keven squirmed to see Fathen so humbled. He could do nothing about it. He knew where the real strength lay for now.

"Release me," he snapped as he shook free of NalTalva.

The Sterran stepped back, hands up, a smug smirk on his pale face.

"Now that you have so graciously shown me my place," Fathen said, "may we continue our pursuit of the one who bested you?"

Keven tensed at Fathen's tone even as he admired his master's defiance. So soon after being rebuked, he offered an insult to Eligos. Keven waited for another blow to fall.

Min either did not notice the sarcasm or chose to ignore it. "The Necromancer did not *best* me. Your treachery and my weakness from summoning beings to fight for me made my *talba* an easy target, and a coward exploited that opportunity. I underestimated my enemy. It won't happen again." Min smiled, the expression hardly comforting on his hard-edged face. "But we do not pursue the Necromancer. There are others we will set to that task. We have more pressing business."

"Killing Erick is why I came this far," Keven said. "It's why I helped destroy my home and the people I cared for." He pushed aside the thought that fear of death at NalTalva's hand had also assured his compliance. "I wish to find him and kill him."

"Supposing I let you take up this venture," Min said, "how would you accomplish it? You have no knowledge of where the Necromancer is going. And he has a cadre of at least five others helping him."

"You just said there are others you would put to the task. Those who have tried to stop him so far have not succeeded." He couldn't resist a sidelong glance at NalTalva. "Let me lead five men. I will hunt down Erick and kill him, and the others, for you."

"How will you find him?"

"You know his destination and will tell me." He had no idea if the *Inconnu* had that knowledge, though he suspected the being in Min's body had some method to track those who shared his power.

Min stared at him, a frown on his sharp face. "You would leave your priest so soon after his return?"

It was Keven's turn to frown. "I assumed we would travel together."

"Then you were wrong." Min pointed at the bulk of Broken Mountain, which loomed over them. "Your master's failure kept me from obtaining that as my base. He has made my task more complicated and time-consuming. Why do you think he would receive a second chance to fail? You may travel with him if you go on the task I assign him. Or you may pursue the Necromancer without him. As you said, you are not yet my servant, so you may choose for yourself. Or you may leave and remain free of any allegiance. Should you choose to aid me, I will mark you as a thrall."

Keven considered the options. The idea of being in the service of any man appealed to him not at all. Even as an acolyte to Fathen, his service had been to Caros.

Would this be any different? His loyalty would not be to Min, but Eligos. While not a god, the *Inconnu* was undoubtedly more than a man.

If he left, he had nowhere to go, and no prospects for work, unless he found another Temple of Caros to accept him. He couldn't in good faith say he accepted the sun god. He knew Fathen's misery at pretending to bow to their god for so many years. He didn't want that torment for himself, nor would he stoop to menial labor. He would as soon die as be a dockworker. The shepherd could never descend to be one of the flock.

Hunt down Erick or follow his master? Both spoke to Keven for different reasons, and he had no mind for the decision. As he always had when confronted with difficulty, he turned to Fathen. "What would you have me do?"

Fathen licked his lips. He glared at Min, though he spoke to Keven. "I would go with you to destroy the one who has set us both on this ill course. Since that will not be allowed to me, you must succeed where I failed. I will do what my mas—what Min requires."

Keven nodded. Fathen's decision pleased him, though the dread of leaving his side again raced over his spine.

"I will offer myself to your service," Keven told Eligos, "and I will hunt down and kill Erick, and any others who get in my way." *Except for Elissia*, he thought. Elissia he would take for himself.

"This pleases me," Min said. Keven couldn't help but notice that NalTalva seemed less happy about it. He didn't care. "But you will not kill him."

Keven prepared to protest, but the glare already set on Min's face would brook no resistance.

"What would you have me do?" he asked, hoping he kept the irritation from his voice.

"Capture Erick and return him to me. Then you may speak praise to my name as you drive a knife into his heart so that I receive his *elonsha* to the nourishment of my *ozgah* and open the *ethamz,* the door to my *oali.* Will you do this?"

64

Keven understood almost none of the strange words the *Inconnu* spoke, but he understood a knife in Erick's heart. "I will."

Min offered a grin on his stocky face as red lightning flickered in his eyes. A chill ran up Keven's spine, and he feared he had made a dreadful—

He collapsed to his knees as searing blackness, tinged with flashes of red, danced across his vision and slammed into his head. Burning pain lanced his right cheek. A scream broke from him as a hand of ice reached in and crushed his soul. Sight abandoned him, and he fell to his side.

The pain ebbed. His vision returned. He blinked away tears. Only when a rush of air filled his lungs did he realize he had held his breath. Three faces stared at him: Fathen as a pleased father for an exceptional child, Min nodding in approval, and NalTalva's mouth curled in disgust.

"Rise, Keven of Draymed, as a servant to Eligos. Like your brother NalTalva, you will serve as a sword of Eligos, and destroy my enemies."

I'm not his brother, Keven thought. The deepening of NalTalva's frown told Keven the Sterran felt the same. They were not brothers. They were equals, and the older man could no longer command him as if superior.

Keven stood, wobbling as his legs tried to give out. He touched his sore cheek and felt the puckered skin, the same skull-like lines as those that marked NalTalva. "I will do your bidding, master," he told Eligos. "How may I find Erick?"

"NalTalva, give me your weapon."

The Sterran handed over his simple steel blade. Min took it and walked over to the horses tethered to a charred post. In a swift motion, he drew the sword across the roan's neck, cutting deep. The beast let out a gurgled whinny.

"What are you doing?" Keven shouted in dismay as he ran toward the horse.

"What I must," Min said.

Keven reached the beast. When he tried to approach, it bucked and reared, almost smashing his head with its hooves. He backed up. Blood splashed at his feet.

Blood poured from the gash in the roan's throat, soaking the packed road. The Palomino snorted and backed away, straining against the harness. Keven turned away as tears filled his eyes. Of anything Min could have done, that was the worst.

For far too long, he listened to the roan's grunts and the spill of liquid upon the road. He choked back a sob and ignored NalTalva's disgusted sneer.

When Keven thought he could take it no longer, the horse collapsed. Keven turned, unashamed of the tears on his face. The roan's eyes had gone glassy. Its legs made feeble twitches. Blood dribbled into a black puddle on the dirt.

"Why did you do that?" Keven asked. "That was my horse."

"That was a horse we stole," NalTalva told him. "Stop sniveling."

Keven stormed on the man and stood inches from his face. "I made the horse mine. It was an innocent animal. There was no reason to kill it."

"You had best distance yourself," NalTalva said, his voice low.

"Or what? You'll hit me again?"

"I may."

"I tell you this now," Keven growled. "You won't. We are brothers in Eligos." He grinned, although he wanted nothing more than to pummel the Sterran into unconsciousness. "We're equals. Your days of striking me without reprisal are over."

NalTavla stepped back, never taking his eyes from Keven. They glared at each other.

"What he says is true," Min said. "You shall not hit or punish him anymore. His shame in serving an inferior god is no worse than your shame in being felled by the Necromancer's pet."

What is this? Keven wondered. He focused on Min to keep his eyes from straying to the dead horse. "What do you mean?"

"It is of no consequence," Min said.

Fathen spoke up, and he almost seemed like the master Keven remembered. "NalTalva was in one of the first groups to attack Erick.

He failed. Blink took him down. A pitiful, four-foot-tall creature that weighs no more than a child."

NalTalva strode toward Fathen.

Keven prepared to tackle him.

Fathen bunched his fists.

"Enough," Eligos said, his death-silent whisper coming from Min's mouth. "You are all flawed in my eyes; none of you any more competent than the other. You will cease your squabbles, or I will destroy all of you and start my cadre anew. There is nothing about any of you that I cannot find elsewhere." Min's eyes roiled with scarlet fire.

Keven stepped back as his heart thudded, and prickles of goosebumps covered his arms. Eligos would kill them as easily as he slaughtered the horse. To him, they mattered even less than the animal.

The others must have reached the same conclusion. NalTalva bowed and said, "As you say, Master. My apologies."

It took Fathen longer. The hard edge never left his bloodshot brown eyes, but he inclined his head. "Your will is our will."

Min nodded. Then his dark eyes fell on Keven. "I slew the beast because you need a creature able to follow the *morazol.*"

"I don't understand."

Min held one hand over the dead horse. His other calloused hand he extended toward the Palomino, which had quit straining against its rope and stood shivering at the far reach of the tether.

A chill wind blew up, bringing the rotted onion scent Keven now knew meant the summoning of *elonsha.* A shadow filled with red lightning formed between Min's hand and the dead horse. Another strand of black lanced from his other hand and struck the Palomino in the side. The horse stiffened, and its eyes rolled, showing white.

Keven knew what was going to happen. He had seen it when Eligos resurrected Fathen, had watched as the *Inconnu* drained the life from the dazed child and poured it upon the bloody chunks that remained of the priest, reforming his dead master.

Keven only hoped they didn't have to cut out the horse's heart like they had the girl's. He closed his eyes, not caring what NalTalva thought. He didn't want to see another defenseless creature die.

The wind blew stronger, and Keven shivered as the *elonsha* stench grew near to overpowering. Eligos recited words Keven didn't understand and didn't want to. It hurt his ears to hear them spoken.

The wind swirled around in one last frenzy. A burst of nausea passed through Keven. Another large thud told him the Palomino had given its last. He heard a rapid shuffling sound. Fearful of what he would see, he opened his eyes.

The Palomino lay on its side, dead, its body desiccated as if it had perished months ago. The roan stood, the wound in its neck sealed, blood on its coat the only evidence it had recently suffered a mortal injury, that and the red tinge in its large eyes.

"The coward who killed my other *talba* has been marked with a *morazol*. All creatures who have been returned by my blessing can follow the mark." He looked at Fathen. "Isn't that so?"

Fathen's brown eyebrows bunched in confusion for a few seconds, then they widened. "I can," he said. "Marcus."

"Marcus?" Keven asked. "Who's Marcus?"

"Elissia's twin brother."

Keven started. He didn't know Elissia had any siblings, much less a twin.

"He's off to the west," Fathen said. "Heading for Dorfork, most likely."

Min frowned. "What is he doing?" he asked but seemed to be talking to himself. "The horse will be able to follow the *morazol*," he told Keven. "It will bring you to Erick. Capture him and bring him to me. The others you may deal with as you see fit."

Keven nodded. "Will you provide me with people to help?"

"I will," Min said. "But I must send messages. They will meet you in Dorfork. Find a tavern and wait. They will find you. From there, you may do what you must to gain the Necromancer. Do not kill him before you bring him to me, or I will be most displeased."

"How will I find you again?"

"I will send word. Wait in Dorfork until you hear from me."

"What if I overtake them before Dorfork?" Keven asked. "I doubt they have horses."

"I suggest you don't overtake them," Min said, "unless you feel confident the two of you can kill them and capture Erick alive. Then by the power of *elonsha*, do so."

"The two of us?" Keven asked with a sinking in his gut.

"Yes," Min said. "NalTalva will accompany you."

Fathen watched his acolyte head toward the lowering sun, both men riding the newly raised red horse, NalTalva in front. Keven had been unhappy at the prospect of traveling with the pale man. It showed in the clench of his scarred jaw and squint of his brown eyes.

Min either didn't notice or, more likely, didn't care. He had handed them a small pouch of coins and reminded them to wait in Dorfork for word from him. How he would get a message to them, Fathen didn't know. His master could speak directly to his mind because of the intimate connection his death and resurrection had created. Min had no such bond with the others.

Fathen wouldn't concern himself. His master had proved resourceful and cunning, despite not having his full power. If he said he would get a message to his followers, Fathen believed him.

He turned back to Min. It felt strange to consider this man as Eligos now. He had gotten used to Andras, the man of plain face and middling build. He had been so bland of features Fathen now had trouble recalling what he looked like.

This man, however, bore the distinctive cast and frame of someone used to hard labor. Arm muscles bulged beneath his dark gray miner's suit, a single piece of rugged cloth pockmarked with black splotches and burn holes. His chest spanned the width to fill a doorway and rested over a stomach that spoke of a prodigious appetite. Thick brown hair sat atop a face as sharp as the chisels the man had used in his former life. He regarded Broken Mountain, the top a mile up, blotting out much of the darkening sky.

"Where do we go?" Fathen asked.

"It should have been mine," Min said as if he hadn't heard. "If we had sacrificed Erick, we would be done now. The Necromancers inside would have been consumed, the portal would have opened, and Krinnik could be ours. I will not fail you again."

"What are you talking about?"

Min started, and his dark brown eyes fell on Fathen. "Your fault, and don't forget it. You must do much to regain favor. We are returning to Kalador."

"Why there?"

"We must prepare the way for when Erick is captured. He is powerful but not powerful enough. We will need more. Our chance here is gone."

"You're not making any sense," Fathen said.

A flash of lightning coursed through Min's pupils. "Because you are too pitiful to understand. You only need know enough to do your task. We return to Kalador because the thieves made interesting remarks about the unrest between the Queen and the merchants. I want to see if we can use this schism to our advantage."

Fathen didn't like thinking about the time in the Procurers' Lair, the den of thieves that controlled the underworld in Kalador. The death of Calligan still haunted him.

"I would also send you to the Temple of Caros."

"What?" Fathen said in surprise. "What possible good could I do there?"

"You will sow fear and awe at the power of the *Inconnu*, by killing the Archbishop and turning him to our cause."

6

Quana: The literal translation of the word is "reclaimed." This is an overall term for the most basic undead (or "gateloah") created by the Necromancer, requiring the least amount of materials.

    -Excerpt from *A Primer on the Necromantic Language* by Corberin of Draymed.

T he sun stood high as Erick and his companions approached the first hamlet on their road west. He resigned himself to finding no inn or apothecary. The settlement consisted of perhaps fifteen houses surrounded by several acres of fenced-in pastures. The fields contained sheep, pigs, and a large number of tall birds Erick had neither seen nor read about in his mother's extensive library. Their legs rose as high as his waist. Their thin necks extended at least three feet from their round, gray plumage covered bodies. Black eyes full of wary suspicion stared past long, flat bills as the group of travelers walked by.

"Ostriches," Corby said.

"What?" Erick said.

"Your expression indicated you weren't familiar with the animals. They're ostriches."

"Why?"

"Why are they ostriches? Because that's what the First People named them."

Erick frowned at Corby's literal mind. "No, I mean, why are they here?"

"They're food," Corby answered. "Central Zakerin is known for fine ostrich meat. It's one of their main exports. I imagine we'll get tired of seeing them by the time we travel across the realm."

Erick watched the birds. Their knees bent backward as they walked, and their small heads bobbed on scrawny necks. They were ridiculous creatures. "Hope they taste better than they look."

They walked through the village, past the single-story wooden buildings with wood-shingled roofs. Small oilskin windows kept the interiors hidden, and nobody emerged from the buildings as they passed. Erick saw a few people in the fields tending their sheep. He suspected most were inside for their noonday meal.

"Guess we hope the next rat hole is bigger," Marcus said, "and close enough to reach by nightfall."

Can you see anything? Erick asked Blink. His familiar flew high above them, having taken off as soon as they saw signs of a settlement. The group had learned the homunculus' gargoyle-like appearance caused either fear or repulsion, so they tried to avoid exposing him to people.

Nothing yet. I can fly ahead if you want.

No, it doesn't matter, Erick told him. They would either find a town where they could stay, or they wouldn't. Much as he hated the thought, sleeping outside one more night wouldn't be the worst thing. The early fall day had been warm and dry, which promised a comfortable evening. "Corby, do you know anything about the *wicaesir* the Necromancers mentioned?"

Corby shook his head. "No, I don't. It surprised me when you weren't aware of it. Your father never said anything?"

"No," Erick said. He realized shortly after leaving home there were many things his father had been remiss in teaching him. Erick suspected it was because of the influence of the *Teloc Sapah*. The book had held sway over his father for most of Erick's life. It may have prevented him from imparting knowledge Erick needed.

Yet, in this case, his father may not have taught him because he didn't know. "Did anyone else think the Necromancers seemed..." Erick paused, uncertain of how to phrase it.

"Cagey and defensive?" Marcus asked. "Like they were hiding something?"

"Yes."

"Oh, they were," Marcus said. "I've dealt with plenty of people like that. Their dissemblance was as transparent as they were."

Corby raised his thick eyebrows. "It astounds me you know such an impressive word."

Marcus gave him a gentle punch on the shoulder. "You don't have to be a scholar to know stuff," he said. "If it has anything to do with lying or trickery, I'm probably familiar with it."

"That's not very comforting," Erick said. "The idea that they would hide something. Or worse, that the Gods would."

"They haven't done much for us so far," Elissia said. "Why start now?"

"That's not true," Gabrielle said, her voice almost choked in horror. Everyone regarded her. She spoke so rarely that it surprised Erick to hear her. "The Gods provided the healing that took care of Erick's injuries. The Gods care for us when we show we are worthy of their consideration."

"Denech has sent me messages before, in the form of dreams," Erick offered. Unfortunately, they made little sense until after the events they represented had passed. He remembered his dream in the Ruins vividly. Two auburn-haired women had changed as he watched, their beauty turning cruel, their eyes black and dancing with flickering crimson. At the time, he had no idea what the dream meant. Now he knew it had to be the two Necromancers who pledged themselves to Eligos. Denech had shown Erick their transformation.

Erick touched his mother's medallion. "And he has blessed us with small favors, as it pleases him."

"Maybe." Doubt drenched Elissia's statement. "But if they only help when it suits them, I'd rather they didn't. Unreliable aid is worse than no aid."

Erick squirmed as he remembered his earlier, similar thought. The idea jarred him when he heard it out loud.

Gabrielle's mouth opened in shock, her puppy dog eyes goggling. Then she pressed her lips tight and narrowed her eyes. "I would appreciate it if you did not blaspheme in my presence."

"I would appreciate it if you would mind your own damn business," Elissia snapped. She stopped walking. Her head whipped from side to side as if looking to see who had said something so rude. She frowned.

"I'm sorry," she told Gabrielle, whose broad shoulders tensed in offense. "I still don't feel myself. It's making me irritable. I didn't mean that. Or course, I'll keep such thoughts to myself."

The healer didn't react for a moment. Then she gave a curt nod, and the group continued walking.

They hadn't walked another thirty feet when Elissia fell to the ground, hands clutched to her head.

~

P ain roiled through Elissia's skull. She grabbed at her temples as she dropped to her knees.

Free me, a voice burbled through her brain, fraught with images of pestilence and decay.

What? she thought, barely able to focus through the agony.

Free me, the voice repeated. For some reason, the color green filled her. Not the lush emerald of grass, but the sickly moss color of wilted lettuce.

She barely felt the hands that grasped her. Voices spoke; she couldn't discern what they said. Images of roaches and worms infested her brain, driving out anything else.

Free me.

I don't know how.

Die.

Something touched her lips. Warm, earthy liquid entered her

mouth. Bitter and sweet on her tongue as the vervain and linden battled. The mixture trickled down her throat.

You cannot escape me. Maggots wriggled through the voice.

More elixir filled her mouth. It almost gagged her. She swallowed to avoid choking. The pain eased, and the voice fled. A flavor of fresh loam remained.

She opened her eyes to find her head on Erick's lap. His hands rested on her shoulders. Concern etched his dirty face. His brown hair stuck out in spiky angles, not yet long enough to be curly. She smiled, relieved the pain had receded. He smiled back.

"Better?" Gabrielle asked.

Elissia had been so concentrated on Erick, she hadn't realized the healer knelt beside her, wooden bowl in her hand. "Better," she said.

"Then thank the Gods, who gave me both the knowledge and power to help you," the healer said stiffly. She stood and walked away.

"You've upset her," Erick said.

"I guess I have," Elissia said, although she couldn't muster the energy to care. "But I can't help the way I feel, and I'm not going to change just to make her happy."

Erick nodded even as he frowned. "I understand," he said.

She knew he didn't, not really. His close relationship with the Gods wouldn't let him. Perhaps the less-than-satisfactory encounter with his fellow Necromancers would change his thoughts.

"Maybe you can not talk about it," he continued. "We don't want a disgruntled healer, and I'm not convinced she's accepted Marcus and Corby."

Elissia nodded and sat up, considering the mess. Gabrielle was infatuated with Marcus, Marcus had fallen for Corby, and Corby reciprocated. The three of them had supposedly come to an agreement in the Ruins, though none of them had revealed any details of their discussion.

Near as Elissia could tell, little had changed except the healer didn't actively snarl at Corby, and no longer ignored him as she had before. Things were better, but Elissia wasn't convinced they were fixed. "You might be right. At some point, I need to make someone tell me what they talked about."

"Are you sure you can keep traveling?" he asked.

"I have to. I'm not going to delay you. The sooner we can get me cured, the sooner—" She stopped. She wanted to say *the sooner the voice will leave me.* The words wouldn't come out. She tried, but her tongue stuck, and pale green tinged the edges of her vision.

No.

Faint as a feather tickle across her brain.

"—the sooner I'll be able to help you," she finished. Her vision cleared. She took a deep breath.

"You're right," Erick said. His head tilted and his blue eyes regarded her as if he knew she hid something.

Poor Erick, she thought. *Everybody is keeping you in the dark.* She didn't want to deceive him. Even as she tried again to talk about the sounds in her head, her tongue wouldn't move. She had thought the voice a hallucination brought on by pain. If it were, she should be able to mention it. What was this poison doing to her?

Erick stood and offered her a hand. She took it and stood beside him.

"I'm okay," she told the others as she saw their pensive faces. Gabrielle stood off to the side, back to the group. "Thank you, Gabrielle. I'm sorry if I offended you. I appreciate what the Gods do."

She ignored Erick's surprised stare. The lie came easily enough. If it soothed the healer's bruised feelings, Elissia had no trouble telling it. "Can *vikrin* cause hallucinations?"

Gabrielle faced her and frowned. "I've never read of that as a symptom, but as I said before, nerve poisons are unpredictable. It's possible. Are you having hallucinations?"

"No," Elissia said, even as she thought *yes*. She tried again. "No." She frowned. *Why can't I say yes?*

Again, the barest hint of another's words drifted through her consciousness. *Because I don't want you to.*

She shuddered and wondered if the venom was going to slowly drive her crazy. "I was just curious."

Gabrielle nodded. "Let me know if you have any so I can pass the knowledge on."

I'd be happy to, Elissia thought, *but they won't let me.* She wanted to laugh and cry at the same time. "Okay," she said, putting false cheer in her voice, "I've delayed us long enough. Let's get moving."

～

The sun began setting on the horizon, shining in their eyes, with no signs of a settlement in sight.

Looks like it's going to be another night under the stars, Blink thought.

Great, Erick thought back. Under the sky wasn't the worst thing, but he had hoped to find better shelter. He wondered if a quicker pace would have brought them to a town before dark. He had deliberately slowed them down, concerned that fast travel would somehow exacerbate the symptoms from Elissia's poison.

Corby kept them entertained with stories and a few songs in his surprisingly rich voice. His usual offerings of facts had dried up, since he admitted his limited study of Zakerin's inner lands. He knew the names of the three *bercs*, the land divisions of the kingdom, and the *Bercliets*, their rulers. He could rattle off the major cities, the three large rivers that crossed the land, and the four forests that provided wood and game. Beyond that, he knew little.

Erick had not paid much attention to any of it. His focus was on Elissia, though he did his best not to make it obvious. She would scold him if she caught him worrying about her.

Her condition troubled him. Something more than the poison was wrong with her. He sensed it at the edge of his awareness, like a creature that lurks just beyond sight. The dagger had belonged to Eligos. Had it been coated with something other than poison? Was that possible? He wished he could call up the ghost of his father and ask him.

Could you? Blink asked.

Erick shook his head. *Father is bound to the manor site because of his suicide. I couldn't summon him here.*

What about your mother?

She wouldn't have any answers. She stayed away from father's studies. Erick didn't think he could handle seeing either of his parent's ghosts. Too many bad memories. Erick had all the questions about their deaths answered when he saw his father in Draymed. He didn't want to relive the pain and anger. *I'll figure it out on my own or find some other way,* he told Blink.

"We should probably stop and set up camp," he said to the group. "We'll get up early tomorrow and hopefully find a larger village, maybe even one with an apothecary."

"Unlikely," Gabrielle said. "Few villages have anything beyond a healer or midwife. An apothecary needs a city to support the expense required for the herbs and binding agents necessary for their mixtures."

"That's our Gaby," Marcus said. "Always the ray of sunshine."

"She's only being truthful," Corby said. "False hope can be as destructive as no hope."

"I'll make you another mixture," Gabrielle told Elissia. "It should get you through the night without any more seizures."

Setting up camp had become routine in The Ruins, so everyone went to their task. Soon, they had a fire going and a warm meal prepared with the wood and food salvaged from Prospector's Camp.

After they ate, Erick lay on his back atop one of the blankets they had found and stared up at Talan's Tears, the stars that occupied the Heaven of Caros. He was thankful for the clear sky and the promise of a mild night. The fall nights would soon grow cooler.

Elissia lay beside him, and they held hands. Her once clammy hand had now become so warm it could almost start a fire. He worried about this odd change. She had only nibbled some meat during their meal, claiming Gabrielle's mixture chased away her appetite. He worried about that too, although he didn't challenge her.

"What do the *Inconnu* want?" Marcus asked Erick.

"What do you mean?" Erick asked back.

"Just what I said. What do the *Inconnu* want?"

"You should know as well as I do by now. They want to take over Krinnik."

"I think the better question," Corby said, "is why? Why do they want to take over Krinnik? What purpose would it serve?"

The scholar and the thief sat beside each other, shoulders touching, the firelight playing over their faces. Gabrielle sat near them, far enough away that Erick still thought they excluded her.

Erick reached back into his half-remembered history lessons. "Why did the Straphs attack Starrasen and take all the lands north of the Inner Sea? Why does Falan-Dar constantly harry the southern border of Makern?"

"The first is for land," Corby answered. "The Straphs and Sterrans fought long before the *Inconnu* War. It's only in the last hundred years that they have reached a compromise. Falan-Dar is a desert, so they attack Makern in attempts to claim better pasturage and water. Basically, another fight for land. You believe the *Inconnu* are here for land?"

"Perhaps," Erick said.

"There are only three of them," Marcus said.

"Were only three of them," Corby corrected him.

"Right," Marcus agreed. "Now there's only one. How much land can one person need?"

Elissia leaned up on her elbow. "Subjugation. Some people like power for power's sake. You and I know that all too well."

Marcus nodded. "So do the rest of you. You've met our father."

"Possibly," Corby conceded. "But how is one person, or even three, supposed to subjugate an entire continent?"

"They were well on their way to doing that until the Necromancers rallied against them," Elissia said.

"True. And perhaps they wanted to do it to have subjects and exert control over them. But it seems to me a thin motivation. The tyrants of the Dark Times exerted control over their populace for money, or land, or exploitable resources. I suspect Uncle Torin does it because the Procurers allow him to live in luxury. The power is secondary to the comfort."

Marcus picked up a splinter of wood and tossed it into the fire. "Father does like his comfort. And he enjoys the thrill of a well-planned theft, being able to prove to others how smart he is."

"So what, besides power, motivates the *Inconnu*?" Corby asked.

Gabrielle picked up her blanket and wrapped it over her shoulders.

"What does it matter? He's trying to take over the world, and Erick's trying to stop him. Is the 'why' relevant?"

"Know an enemy's motives, and you know his weakness," Corby said. "General Arkis of the Makerns said that. If we knew the reasons why Eligos wants Krinnik, we might be able to devise a better stratagem than traipsing across the continent, searching for a witch who may or may not help us."

"I don't think so," Elissia said. "How do you stop someone you can't kill by normal means? Marcus stabbed him three times, and he's still alive. Floating around trying to find another body, I guess. Motives don't mean shit when you have to deal with that."

Corby frowned. "You're probably right."

"When I fought Eligos," Erick told them, "he said something about remaking the world for his people."

"The *Inconnu* are a people?" Corby asked.

"That's what I wondered," Erick said. "My father never mentioned it. Nothing I've ever read said anything about it."

"That's an understandable motivation," Corby said. "It all comes back to land again. But where are they from? Certainly not from the other two continents, or I would have read about them. And if this is an invasion, where is the army?"

All great questions, Erick thought. *And I can't answer any of them.* "I don't know."

"They don't need an army," Elissia said as she lay back down and stared at the sky. "They can create an army with undead."

Corby nodded. "True. But then you'd think they would have sent more than three generals. If three could create as much havoc as they did, imagine what ten could have done."

Erick shivered. "I don't want to imagine that, because I want to be able to sleep tonight."

"Hopefully, the mysterious witch woman will be able to answer some of these questions," Marcus said.

"Hopefully." *If we can find her, and if she'll help.*

Quit being so gloomy, Blink thought. *We got this far against all the odds. No reason to believe we can't get to her. I have every confidence you will convince her to help.*

I'm glad someone does.

"Corby and I will take first watch if the rest of you want to get some sleep."

Sleep sounded like a great idea. Erick hadn't completely recovered from the exertion of the previous night, which already felt like it had happened years ago.

"Let's go to bed," Elissia said, standing. Erick stood, and they walked away from the fire to one of the tents.

As they settled down in their bedrolls, Erick caught a whiff of himself and winced. A month without bath or fresh clothes had done none of them any favors. Elissia curled up beside him, and he slipped his arm over her. He was so tired that the close contact did not stir his passion as it might have in other circumstances.

"We're going to make it," Elissia said, her voice drowsy. "I'm going to get cured, we're going to find the witch, she's going to help us, and you're going to destroy Eligos and the traitors."

"Yes, we are," Erick said, wondering if Elissia doubted it as much as he did. *I don't know if we're going to succeed*, he thought. *But with or without the Gods, we're going to try.*

Corby watched Gabrielle walk into her tent, the flap closing behind her. Despite her assurances that she understood the relationship between him and Marcus and her promise that she accepted it, Corby often felt tied in knots around her. Her inconsistency confounded him. At times she acted as friendly as before she learned of Marcus's disinterest in her. Other times, although she never fell back to the icy hatred she once showed, she barely deigned to speak to him. If she did, her responses came out clipped. Corby wished Marcus cared for her instead of him.

No, that was a lie. Marcus's affection was one of the best things to ever happen to him. He wished they had someone else in their conclave that could be the focus of Gabrielle's attention. He wanted her to be as happy as he was. Until she found someone else, that wouldn't happen.

Blink sat by the road, staring out over the short-grassed hills.

Marcus cleared his throat, and the familiar looked at them.

"Don't you want to go to bed?" Marcus asked.

"Not sleepy," Blink said.

"Then maybe you could scout the area or hunt for some dinner."

"Not hungry. Not much sense in scouting. I can see fine from right here."

Marcus sighed in exasperation. "Are you really that dense, or are you just doing it to mess with us?"

The homunculus cocked his head to the side and stared at them.

Corby smiled at Marcus's frustration. Without Erick to explain things to him, Blink could sometimes be as innocent as a child. "Blink, Marcus and I would like to be alone."

Blink's eyes glanced up and went distant. Corby recognized that the familiar was speaking mentally to Erick. After a few seconds, they focused back on the pair. Blink offered his needle-toothed grin. "Okay, but Erick said to make sure you don't get so distracted you forget to keep watch. I'll go do some scouting."

He leapt into the air, flapped his wings, and flew down the road.

Marcus slipped up behind Corby. "I never thought we'd be alone again," he said as he wrapped his arms around Corby's chest.

Corby leaned back, comforted and thrilled by the closeness. "Erick is right, though. We have to keep watch."

Marcus sighed. "Of course. But we can watch like this." His hands moved down to Corby's stomach and gave it a gentle rub.

Corby shivered as chills ran up his back. "That's incredibly distracting."

"It's meant to be," Marcus said, his mouth by Corby's ear. His hands moved even lower.

Corby grabbed the roaming hands before they reached where he wanted them to go. "Not out here," he said, as every nerve screamed that "out here" was more than acceptable. "Someone might walk out. Gabrielle, or—"

"Who cares?" Marcus grabbed Corby's ear with his teeth.

"I care," Corby said when he could breathe again. He still held Marcus's hands. "I want to, but..."

Marcus suddenly sat back, his mouth and hands retreating. Corby yearned for the lost contact.

"But what?" Marcus said.

Corby hated the flatness in Marcus's voice, the withdrawal it indicated. "I don't want to get caught," he said. "I don't want to be punished again."

"Punished? Who's going to punish you? What are you talking about?"

Despite his intelligence, Corby had no idea how to explain it. Elissia told him the Gods didn't care what he did with others. And yet past events gave a different story. Quinn had been his first and had died along with the rest of Draymed, lost in fire and poison. Corby dared to have feelings for Marcus, and now the thief had been marked by the *Inconnu*, fated to have undead drawn to him. Though nothing had happened to Murrough as far as Corby knew, it wouldn't surprise him to hear the sailor's ship had sunk.

"The Gods," he said. "They take away anyone I dare to care about; anyone I sin with."

Marcus sighed behind him. "The Gods don't care," he said, sounding so much like his sister that Corby almost smiled.

"I want to believe that," Corby said.

"Then do," Marcus leaned into him again, hands on Corby's shoulders. The touch comforted Corby. And yet—

"But if I'm wrong, I'll lose you." Corby could all too easily picture Marcus torn apart by slavering zombies, taken away from him as retribution.

Marcus's hands withdrew again. "I'll say this once. You are a great person. You're smart and handsome, and I want to do things with you. Things that are fun and wonderful, not sinful. But if you want to torture yourself with bullshit beliefs about sin and be a martyr to some misplaced sense of doom, I want no part of it. I'm here, and I'll be here. So, you talk with the Gods or the plants or whatever you have to talk to. Figure out what you want. When you do, let me know."

Corby watched over his shoulder as Marcus walked to the other side of their camp. He sat on the ground and stared across the grassland.

Corby knew what he wanted. He longed to run over to Marcus and tell him. But just because he wanted it didn't make it right. Marcus and Elissia might easily dismiss the Gods. They could claim Amare, the god of love, held greater sway over such matters than Caros, the father of all. Corby could not. The teachings of his mother had been too ingrained to disregard them casually. He had experienced the consequences of disobedient love, had felt the pain of losing his best friend and his family.

When considered with logic, resisting his pull toward Marcus was the best thing for both of them.

Then why did it feel like the worst thing?

Elissia walked across a soupy marsh. Vines slithered over the ground, covered with thorns that dripped green ichor. Pools of black sludge bubbled. A miasma hung in the air, redolent with the scent of disease.

Pale chartreuse light, brighter than the sickly green tint that filtered her vision, drew her across the morass. She walked toward the illumination, repulsed and enchanted by it.

As she moved closer, the luminescence resolved into a person, a man, ancient beyond Elissia's comprehension. He was naked. Where his manhood should be, there hung six pustule-covered tentacles. Boils coated his arms and legs. Oozing scabs splayed across his chest. Only his face appeared normal, though covered in wrinkles and folds. Thin, six-inch-long earthworms writhed on his scalp instead of hair. They hypnotized her.

His eyes fixed on Elissia. Nausea roiled through her at that pus-colored gaze.

"Free me," he said. Flies buzzed from his mouth with each word.

"Who are you?" Elissia asked. An oily film coated her tongue as soon as she spoke. Dizziness blurred her vision.

"My brother calls me, and I would join him. Free me." More flies. They hovered around his head and groin. The worms and tentacles snatched them from the air and devoured them with noisy slurps, like a gaggle of beggars drinking soup.

Elissia didn't want to know but asked anyway. "How do I free you?"

He smiled, his teeth blackened with rot. An odor of decaying vegetation drifted from his mouth. "Destroy yourself."

"I won't do that," Elissia said.

"You will," the man said. "There is no resisting."

She sensed movement behind her. Before she could react, vines grabbed her arms, the thorns digging into her skin. She screamed as pain burned through her. Boils appeared on her arms and burst. Maggots dropped from the wounds.

The vines moved, and her arms moved with them. Like puppet strings, they controlled her motion. She reached down to her boot and withdrew a dagger. In vain, she tried to resist. It was like trying to stop the wind.

"Free me," the man said again. Bile spilled from his mouth.

Steered by the thorny vines, she brought the dagger up in front of her, gripped it with both hands.

"No," she said as the blade hovered over her chest.

She awoke in her tent, next to Erick. Her hands clamped her dagger, and she plunged the sharp point toward her heart.

7

Upon the thunderous plain, the world awash in death
  When the Five faced the One, the world held its breath
  The mighty armies paused, their killing fury held
  When the Five faced the One, the shadow of evil paled.
  -Tarina Flos Alea, Poet, "When the Five Faced the One"

Although Keven hated the deaths of the roan and palomino, neither of which he had the chance to name, he had to grudgingly admit there was an advantage to having an undead horse. Though it went no faster than a canter despite NalTalva's occasional irritated attempt to make it do so, it held the quickened pace far longer than a live horse ever could—longer than the humans riding it could take, especially Keven, who rode behind NalTalva. Without the benefit of a saddle or stirrups, he had no way to post and counter the horse's jolting stride. After well over an hour on the road, the sun touched the horizon, and Keven said. "We need to stop for a rest."

In answer, NalTalva snapped the reins, trying to spur the horse to a longer stride. It was a futile gesture, which they both knew.

"Stop," Keven repeated, almost shouting it in NalTalva's ear. "I can't take the pounding much longer."

It seemed as if NalTalva were going to ignore the request. Keven tensed. As he promised the Sterran back at Prospector's Camp, he would no longer be treated as inferior. He was more than ready to prove the point by throwing the other man off the horse. Perhaps his neck would break, which would trouble Keven far less than what had happened to the horses.

A sense of disappointment brushed him as NalTalva pulled back on the reins, and the horse fell into a trot and then a walk. He had almost hoped the warrior wouldn't acquiesce. The thud of him hitting the ground would have pleased Keven immensely.

NalTalva drew the horse to a stop, and Keven slid off with a groan. His inner thighs vibrated with a dull ache as if he still rode. Walking a few steps away from the horse was a torment. NalTalva sprang from the mount as if they hadn't begun their journey. Despite himself, Keven admired the man's stamina. Even posting in the saddle, he should have shown some stiffness. "How can you be so unfatigued?"

The pale warrior removed his broad-brimmed green hat and offered a small smile, an expression rare as platinum. "I grew up riding the lizards of the Dying Swamp. They jostle as if riding an earthquake. I learned techniques to counter such uneven travel."

Keven considered asking the man to teach him the techniques, but then decided he didn't want to interact with him that much. Instead, he said, "Then you ride behind, and I will take the saddle, so I can ride the way I know."

The Sterran narrowed his dark eyes a moment, then nodded. "If it will keep us from having to stop so soon after starting, I will do this."

Keven gritted his teeth. Now he saw the disadvantage of a dead horse. The necessity of keeping live horses living provided for rests and changes of pace, making riding those animals easier. Without the need for such concerns, undead mounts could travel for extended periods at a bone-jostling speed. And it would, if NalTalva had his way. Keven hadn't ridden horses often. Certainly not often enough to go for long distances without a break. He had little choice though. It was either take the reins and use his scant riding knowledge to provide some comfort or sit behind and be bounced without mercy until they camped for the night. "Agreed," he said. "But we need to stop for sleep."

"We will," the Sterran agreed. "When Talan's Lantern stands at its highest."

Keven looked at the moon, which had just come out and hung low on the horizon. "You mean midnight? That's not for at least another four hours."

"That is when we stop. You may stop sooner if you wish, but you walk from there."

Keven nodded. He decided the warrior might still fall off the horse accidentally at some point—sooner rather than later, if he kept trying to be the one in charge.

As Keven walked off as much of the stiffness as he could, NalTalva took some bread and meat from the saddlebags and offered it.

Keven took it along with a water skin but gave no thanks to the pale man.

The other thing Keven had learned about the horse, although it took him a while to realize it and longer to accept it, was that he could sense the creature's thoughts, or thought, since it only had one at the moment. Marcus stood foremost in its dead brain. The marked one, as Keven interpreted the abstract images. The marked one was ahead of them, not moving. Keven couldn't tell how far, only that he had passed where they stood now.

The strange mental connection disconcerted him, though he couldn't deny its usefulness. He tried to send a thought to the horse. A command to run in a circle. The dead creature didn't respond.

After ten minutes, they remounted, Keven still stiff but ready to continue. He took the saddle. Behind him, NalTalva wrapped his arms around Keven's waist. Keven snapped the reins and the horse lurched into its canter.

They had gone almost another hour when NalTalva hissed in his ear. "Stop."

Keven smiled as he brought the horse to a halt. "Not so easy to ride when you don't have a saddle, is it?"

"I could easily go until morning since I am not weak. Look there."

Keven followed where NalTalva pointed. In the distance, almost too far to be seen, something flickered. As Keven watched, he realized it was a fire. Someone had set up camp beside the road.

"It's a campsite," Keven said. "Why did we stop?"

"It's *their* campsite. Do you not sense it? The marked one is there."

Keven realized he *could* sense it. The horse's thoughts incorporated the glow of the fire. The marked one rested there. And where the marked one rested, so too did the Necromancer. "You can feel the horse's thoughts, too?"

"Of course," NalTalva said. "I was chosen of Eligos while you whimpered in your town for your lost priest."

Keven wanted nothing more than to punch the smug Sterran, a challenging prospect in their current position, and an unwise idea anyway. "Was that before or after the pet beat you?"

"He did not beat me," NalTalva said in a low growl. "He struck from behind like a cur. He will not get another chance."

Keven noticed NalTalva and Eligos both liked to blame their failures on the cowardice and knavery of others when their lack of foresight got them bested. Keven had enough prudence to know that offering this observation would be a bad idea.

"Should we attack?" Keven asked. Maybe NalTalva would get killed in the fight. If not, Keven could still make an accident happen after the melee ended.

NalTalva shook his head. "They outnumber us. Even if we surprise them, the risk is too great. We're not to kill the Necromancer, and it is more difficult to subdue an opponent. We also don't know if he has undead protecting him. We will do as our master bid and wait until we have others to help us."

Much as he hated to agree, Keven couldn't fault the warrior's logic. "We'll make a wide circle around them and come back to the road further up."

"Keep the beast to a walk," NalTalva instructed him, "so the noise does not alert them."

They headed off the road into the countryside. They caused little disturbance as they rode across the flat grassland. Another advantage to their horse: it made none of the huffing and snorting sounds of a living animal.

To be safe, they rode until the fire dwindled to a firefly speck. Then they turned west and continued until NalTalva judged it safe to return to the road. Keven deferred to the Sterran, knowing the warrior had more experience in such things. If the Necromancer and his companions discovered them, Keven didn't want it to be his fault.

The grasslands suddenly gave way to a harvested field. Only stubble remained, which crunched under the horse's hooves, releasing the earthy smell of wheat.

Once back on the road, they soon came upon a hamlet: ten houses and a few other wooden buildings. That explained the field.

"Stop," NalTalva said.

As he reigned in the horse, Keven considered asking the warrior if he planned to burn and poison this thorp too, then decided it best not to provoke him. Keven would never engage the Sterran in a fair fight; he knew the inevitable outcome of such a battle.

"We need to wait and see what happens."

"What happens? What do you—"

The marked one draws this way.

Keven almost fell off the horse as it spoke. No abstract thought; it was actual communication. It unnerved him. Animals shouldn't be able to talk, even in a person's head. Especially in a person's head.

He shook off his misgivings. So much of what he recently experienced was beyond his ken that he felt like a child told to run a kingdom. He must learn to accept it or go mad.

NalTalva slid off the horse. "We will hide and watch. We may be able to ambush them."

Keven looked down at him. "You said an ambush was too dangerous."

"In open ground, it is. Here, we can use the advantage of the buildings. We hide, attack from cover, and then flee using the horse. We don't have to destroy them, only weaken them."

Keven nodded and pulled his aching body off the horse. "Then tell me the best place to hide," he said as he rested his hand on his sword.

8

I vow to use my strength in defense of the weak. I vow to spread the light and destroy the dark. I vow to use my wisdom to guide those who are lost. I vow to bring belief to those who are stricken.
    -Vow of Service sworn by Acolytes of Caros

Almira sat in the living chamber of the small house she shared with her twin sister, Isana. While her younger-by-twenty-minutes sister made dinner in the kitchen, Almira studied their latest acquisition under the light of dual lanterns hung from the low ceiling.

They had taken the book from a madman, a follower of Vidali, the insane god. At first, the deal had been simple: the book for an agreed-upon sum of money. When the man came to their humble home on the western edge of the Lisphin, the forest west of the Lis River, he tried to change the deal. In addition to the negotiated gold, he wanted favors from them. Favors that involved their bodies, a great deal of physical contact, and shared pain.

Favors the sisters had no interest in fulfilling.

A large man, a Makern from deep in the highlands of that harsh land, he had the strength of the mountains and the conviction of his insanity. He could easily overpower them.

He couldn't overpower the two *priquana* that attacked him.

The sisters lived three miles from the nearest village, so none of the lumberjacks and woodworkers of that quaint hamlet heard the man's screams.

Now the sisters had three undead servants, one considerably larger than the other two.

The grimoire had been well worth the trouble. It expanded their already considerable knowledge on their subject of interest. Almira felt they would soon be ready to put the theories into practice.

Isana entered the room, carrying two green ceramic bowls and a plate of bread on a tray. Steam rose from the bowls. Almira caught the savory, meaty smell of the stew. Isana placed the tray on the round table and sat opposite her sister.

"It smells like you've outdone yourself, sister," Almira said.

Isana shook her head in embarrassed pleasure. Her hair, like her sister's, was a lustrous maple brown and fell to her shoulders.

The sisters prided themselves on their ability to deceive people as to which was which. Their eyes were both the green of ripe limes and bright against their tawny skin. Their long faces, unblemished, often held the same half-smile that made people think the women knew something others didn't. They *did* know many things others didn't, Necromancy not the most dangerous of them.

Almira placed her bird feather bookmark into the tome and put it aside. She picked up a bowl with her long-fingered hand, placed it before her, and drew in another smell of the stew, the meat earthy and rich. "Rabbit?"

"Yes," Isana said as she took her bowl, careful not to let the hanging sleeve of her azure dress dip into it. "The snares worked beautifully."

Almira sighed. Rabbit was a fine meat, but a long way from the meals they used to enjoy when they were treated as equals among the powerful of Masca. King Terek often had them to his parties. His pet Necromancers, he would call them. Though neither sister cared for the appellation, they accepted it as the price for dining in the company of royalty and the money offered for their services. For many years, having undead servants created by the twins was a status symbol, a sign of prosperity and favor, for they gave their talents only to those who won their admiration. They had lived the life their parents refused to accept for well over a decade.

Then, Queen Galina fell under the sway of a priest of Alakaneth, forced her beliefs on Terek, and suddenly undead became anathema. The purge happened within a tenday. Almira and Isana were exiled to the wilderness almost before they knew what had happened.

Almira tried to push away the bitterness of the memory as she scooped up the stew and ate. She had no reason to be bitter anymore. After all, now that Eligos was their master, she and her sister would soon rule Straphan. Queen Galina and King Terek would become their pet royalty. They would live only as long as they did what the twins demanded.

"This is delicious," she told her sister.

Isana grabbed a piece of dark bread and dipped it into her bowl. "Thank you. Not what it used to be, though."

Almira nodded with her mouth quirked to one side. In addition to looking alike, she and her sister often shared moods and thoughts.

They ate in silence for a few minutes, enjoying the meal without the need to talk. Alexi, the tabby cat that shared their small home, wandered in and jumped onto the wooden table.

"Bad cat," Almira said. She pulled a piece of rabbit from her bowl, wiped the rich brown gravy from it, and placed it on the table. Alexi purred as he gobbled down the morsel.

Three sharp taps at the door sent the cat scurrying to hide. The sisters looked at each other. They never had company they hadn't invited. They were too far off any path for a traveler to come upon them without deliberately seeking them.

Almira pushed back her chair and stood. "*Quana, niiso.*"

The deceased book trader shuffled from the corner of the room and joined Almira. She opened the door.

A streak of black fluttered by Almira's face. She wheeled around and watched a raven land on the table. A familiar smell hit her nose, stirred from the bird's wings, and she knew the creature no longer lived. Their master had sent it.

The bird's head tilted. Its dark eyes stared first at Almira, then the head turned and regarded Isana. Almira walked over, and the creature turned to her once again. She looked to its legs, seeking an attached note as one might do with a pigeon. Nothing.

The bird opened its ebony beak, and a voice whispered from within the creature. "I will come to you soon," Eligos said.

The pleasure of hearing the master's voice made Almira shiver. At the table, Isana did the same.

The voice continued. "Things move now as I desire, despite the setback imposed by the one who shares your talent, but not your conviction. Your discoveries and suggestions please me. Continue your investigations into this great art. When I come, I will see your progress, and you will show me this thing is possible. Then, we shall work your gift upon it. If all comes to pass as you say, all you desire will be yours. Look for me in the mid-time of Denech."

The raven's beak closed. It gave them a look as it screamed a raucous caw, raising goosebumps on the sisters' arms. Then, it fell over on the table, dead.

Before Elmira or Isana could move, Alexi jumped onto the table and snatched the bird, near as large as him. The tabby leapt off the table, bird in mouth, and ran from the room.

The twins locked eyes. They both grinned.

"I must return to my reading," Almira said. "We'll have to go to Phinsa soon to gather supplies and find a devoted candidate." The lumberjacks in Phinsa were brawny. They would need someone strong. He would have to survive two weeks of brutal torture. The sisters had no intention of failing their master.

When he arrived, they would gift him with the secrets of how to summon a demon and turn it into an undead.

9

Historians *like to attribute complex causes to simple events; to say those who turned to the Inconnu did so because of economic, social, or cultural factors. But the truth is those who went to the Master of Shadows did so because they had gullible leaders, and the common people were gullible enough to accept what those in charge told them.*

-Introduction to *The Second Inconnu War* by Corberin of Draymed.

Shuddering vibrations woke Erick. Next to him, Elissia shook like someone chilled by a high fever. In the dim firelight coming through the tent, he saw she held a blade above her chest, the point inches from her skin.

"Elissia!"

She didn't acknowledge him, though her eyes were open. Her shaking increased, and her teeth gritted. The knife moved closer.

"Elissa," Erick said again. He pushed the blanket aside and grabbed her wrists, tugging, trying to pull the dagger away. He stood a better chance of moving a boulder than budging her locked muscles.

"Corby! Marcus!" he shouted, though he didn't know if they still stood watch. "Gabrielle!" *Blink*, he thought, *help me*.

Noise outside. A cry of concern and the thud of feet on ground.

Erick struggled against Elissia's quivering arms. Her eyes stared at him, but he had no idea if she saw him. Her teeth bared as her jaw clenched. To his horror, the dagger point touched the cloth of her tunic.

The tent flap opened. Marcus ducked in, followed by Corby.

"What the—" Marcus said.

"Help!"

"'Lissi, stop it," Marcus shouted as he dropped beside her and grabbed her arms.

"I...can't..." Elissia gasped through her tight jaw. Tears ran down the sides of her face.

Erick and Marcus tugged at her arms. The knife went no further, but they had no success pulling it away.

"What can I do?" Corby asked.

"Pry the knife away," Marcus told him.

Corby shuffled around the tent, almost tripping over Erick's legs. He knelt above Elissia's head and reached for her hands.

Like a snake, the dagger flicked up. The blade bit the side of Corby's right hand. He jerked back with a cry as blood spilled from the parted flesh. The dagger resumed its deadly aim at Elissia's chest.

Two things happened at once. Gabrielle opened the tent flap, and the tent flew into the air. The canvas flopped to the ground, tossed aside by Blink. Air washed over them all, stirred by the familiar's wings. He dropped, landing beside Erick.

Barb her, Erick thought. *Small hit.*

Blink's scorpion-like tail lashed out and struck Elissia's upper arm. She continued to struggle for several seconds. Then her eyes turned glassy, and her muscles relaxed. Marcus grabbed the dagger as her hands opened.

Elissia's eyes closed. Her face went slack.

Erick sat back, quivering with fear and fatigue. Numbness spread over him. He felt as if he had run miles through the snow.

I feel it too, Blink thought to him. *It's like—*

"What in the Festering Hells just happened?" Marcus asked as he dropped back on his haunches.

"I don't know." Erick put his hands to his temples. He had grown so tired of not understanding things.

"Muscle spasms," Gabrielle said. "An effect of the poison."

"That was more than a muscle spasm," Marcus said. "She was trying to hurt herself. She was trying to—" He stopped.

"It's possible," Gabrielle said, "the poison is affecting her brain. Making her hallucinate. Perhaps she thought she was defending herself against an attack."

Erick shook his head. "I think she was fighting it. Her shaking woke me up. It's like someone else was trying to hurt her. When Marcus told her to stop, she said she couldn't." He stared at Gabrielle. "Could the poison do something like that?"

He suspected he knew the answer. There was more than poison at work here.

Gabrielle shrugged and offered a helpless, doe-eyed look. "Anything is—"

"Yeah, anything is possible with nerve poisons," Marcus snapped. "That's your only answer."

Gabrielle flinched as if hit, then her eyes narrowed. "And you have a better one?"

Marcus cringed at the hard edge to her question. "No, I don't."

"What are we going to do?" Corby said. "We got lucky this time. What if she tries something like this again? I don't believe the herbs are as efficacious as you hoped."

Gabrielle put her back to Marcus. "No, they aren't. Either this is a specialized version of *vikrin*, or my training is inadequate."

"We'll keep her unconscious," Marcus said. "I hate to do it, but it's the safest thing. Blink can keep her knocked out."

"He can't," Erick said. "His venom would build up in her system and end up killing her." It only then occurred to him that Blink's sting might cause an unexpected reaction with the *vikrin*. He said a silent prayer to Denech that it not be so.

"Could Blink fly you to Dorfork and back?" Corby asked. "You could acquire the antidote and return with it."

"No," Erick said. "He can carry someone for short distances, but it would end up being no quicker than walking, after he rested between flights."

"We need horses," Marcus said, "and we need them soon." He stared at the ground for a moment. Then his gaze encompassed them all. Erick could tell he had made up his mind about something.

"Rest while you can," he told them. "Start down the road at first light, and I'll meet you."

"Where are you going?" Corby asked.

"I'm going to the next village and hoping they have horses. Unguarded horses."

"I'll go with you," Corby said.

"No," Marcus told him. "You'll slow me down. I'll be back before you know it."

"You don't know how far it is," Corby said.

"Neither do you. If I don't find it in three hours, I'll come back."

"Do you know how to ride a horse?" Corby asked. "Or even how to put a saddle on them?"

"I don't, but it can't be that difficult."

Corby ignored Marcus. "I do. I rode horses with my father when we traveled. I can help you. You can watch for people and make sure we don't get caught."

"I don't need your help."

"You're going to get it," Corby planted his feet in a determined stance. "I'll follow you, and you can't stop me."

The two young men stared at each other through the darkness.

Erick had never seen Corby so adamant about anything. Marcus was right; they needed a quicker way to get Elissia healed. Corby was also right, though not for the reasons he mentioned. Erick didn't want Marcus traveling by himself with a *morazol* on him. Undead didn't concern Erick as much as Eligos or members of the Fist, the men devoted to the *Inconnu*. Any of them could come upon Marcus alone, and he might be captured or killed. Erick knew Corby could fight if pressed.

Sending Blink with him would leave Erick, Corby, and Gabrielle as Elissia's only protection. Erick had limited combat experience, and Gabrielle none at all, other than tending to the aftermath. Erick would feel better with his familiar at his side. "Let him go with you," he told Marcus. "We need horses, and he knows how to handle them."

Marcus narrowed his eyes, and Erick thought the stubborn thief might refuse. But he finally offered a curt nod. "Let's go. Keep up." He started down the road, his strides long.

Corby gave a brief nod to Erick and followed, snatching up his crossbow and quiver. As Gabrielle watched with an expression Erick couldn't read, the thief and scholar disappeared into the darkness.

"Slow down," Corby said as Marcus ranged fifty feet ahead of him. Corby had followed as quickly as he could for the past half hour, doing everything but running. Still, Marcus remained well ahead of him. Now Corby's breath came in gasps, and his pace faltered. The crossbow he carried weighed heavy as a tree trunk. "Marcus, please slow down."

Marcus stopped and returned to Corby, who paused and panted when he saw his friend coming back.

"This is why I didn't want you coming," Marcus growled in a low voice. "You're slow and loud. How am I supposed to sneak up on anything with you braying like a lost puppy?"

The words slapped at Corby like physical blows. What had happened to the tender person who had been so kind inside the mountain? The one who had—

Corby blushed at the memory, even as the change in Marcus tore his heart. "What did I do wrong?" he asked. "I want to help you. You can't do it alone."

Marcus's voice softened. "I *can* do it alone. I've been doing things on my own long before you came along. You're slowing me down, and you're going to make noise when you shouldn't. You need to be back with Erick, where you can't distract me. Where it's safe."

It suddenly became clear to Corby, and the rip in his heart disappeared. Marcus didn't want him away because he thought he was useless. Marcus was worried. Marcus cared.

"I want to help." Corby reached out to take Marcus's hand but stopped short. "I can be quiet, and I can deal with the horses. Being with Erick isn't any safer than being with you. In fact, it may be less safe. And I'd much prefer being with you."

"Are you sure about that? You sure it's not a sin?"

Corby chose to ignore Marcus's sarcasm. "It may be, and I still don't know if any good can come from it. But I can't help myself."

Corby wished he could return to keeping his emotions in check. He had been able to suppress them so well after he and Quinn had been caught in Draymed. He had managed to hide his feelings for Erick, before he met Marcus, so as to not destroy their budding friendship. His encounters with Murrough on the ship to the mainland had been only physical. He had little love for the rough sailor and knew the man returned none to him.

Even that forlorn intimacy had seen his hometown punished for his sin. Logically, Corby understood that his connection on the ship had nothing to do with his town's destruction. But logic mattered little when it came to Gods. They *might* have ravaged his home to punish him for Murrough and Quinn. Corby didn't want to see the same thing happen to Marcus.

Regardless, he couldn't help what he felt. "Have patience with me," he told Marcus. "I'm trying to sort it out. It's all so new."

Marcus didn't say anything for several seconds, then he nodded. "I'll try. Patience isn't one of my strengths."

He began walking again, slower so that Corby could keep pace.

Another mile down the road brought them to a hamlet. Newly shorn fields of wheat had warned them ten minutes earlier that a settlement or farmhouse sat near. Marcus's sharp eyes spotted the first building in the wan moonlight several hundred feet out. In all his travels, Corby had never taken this branch of the Routh Awen, so he did not know this small cluster of buildings or whether the village had a name.

Marcus slipped to the side of the road, and Corby followed. They had nothing to hide them other than the darkness. Marcus put his lips next to Corby's ear. "Move as quietly as you can."

Corby shuddered at the breath across his ear. Marcus continued.

"We need to see if we can find a stable. If—" he stopped and pulled Corby to the ground.

"What?" Corby said.

"Shh." Marcus, flat on the ground, narrowed his eyes and peered into the darkness.

K even silently cursed the board that creaked as he leaned against the house to watch the marked one and the scholar approach. Even more, he cursed the marked one's hearing. How had he caught such a minute noise from hundreds of feet away? Keven held his breath, waiting to see if they were discovered. A hand gripped his arm, and NalTalva pulled him slowly behind the house. He motioned with his free hand and moved deeper into the shadows behind the building.

When he kept moving, Keven hazarded a whispered question. "What are you doing?"

NalTalva glared at him and continued walking. Keven could do nothing except follow. When they reached the furthest structure, a large storage building, NalTalva stopped. "They have come to look for horses," he told Keven, voice barely audible.

"Did the horse tell you that? If so, I didn't hear it."

The flat stare the small man offered told Keven how stupid the question had been. "It's the smart thing to do."

NalTalva found a small door on the back of the building and opened it. Keven winced, waiting for the door to squeak. Well-tended, it moved silently. They both slipped inside. The smell of harvested wheat almost overwhelmed Keven. Bundles of it occupied the floor at the back of the building, notable only as blotches of black outlined by the minuscule amount of light leaking through gaps in the wall.

NalTalva closed the door and studied it for a moment before he grabbed a nearby board and placed it in the iron holders, barring the entry.

They wound their way through the stacks and found the horses at the front. Four stalls, each with a wooden gate and a horse. The animals whinnied as the men approached.

Ceilings created storage areas above the stalls. The scent of hay mingled with wheat. Keven could barely make out the bales nestled over the stalls.

"There is a ladder here," NalTalva said from Keven's right. "There is probably another on the other side. Climb up, and we will wait for them."

"Good," Keven said. "Two less we'll have to deal with when we attack."

"Strike only to subdue, not kill. If we have both as hostages, the Necromancer will give himself over to protect them. He might not care if we destroy one of his companions, but two will give him pause."

"And if it doesn't?" Keven had asked.

The Sterran shrugged, the motion barely noticeable in the dim building. "Then there will be two fewer enemies to fight."

❧

Marcus remained crouched for a long time. Corby stared into the gloom with his breath held. He spotted nothing unusual. Glancing back, he thought he could see the outline of Broken Mountain in the distance.

After a couple of minutes, the soft whinny of horses reached their ears. That answered one question. Corby counted three more minutes in his head before Marcus eased up from his crouching position.

"I hate being outdoors," he said. When they had first met, Marcus suffered from severe agoraphobia. Though he had adapted quickly to life in the wilderness, Corby knew the thief preferred the inside of buildings, or at least a city with walls and tight alleys.

"What did you see?" Corby asked.

"Apparently nothing but jumping shadows. I thought I heard something squeak. Maybe it was an animal or a building settling. Did you hear the horses?"

Corby nodded.

"At least we know they have a stable. Let's find it. If anyone sees us," Marcus pointed, "run that way into the field while I distract them. I'll escape and find you."

Corby nodded. He would never leave Marcus to fend for himself, but Marcus didn't need to know that right now.

They stuck to the side of the road and moved toward the village. Marcus made no sound in the soft dirt. Corby did his best but occasionally scuffled a foot across the ground. Marcus glared at him, and all Corby could do was offer an apologetic shrug. No lights glowed from any of the buildings, so he hoped everyone was asleep and no one walked patrol. They might be able to explain their night excursion as seeking shelter, but such a ruse would end any chance to obtain horses quickly.

The settlement had ten wooden houses, two large buildings that probably held the harvested crops, and one low, long structure Corby guessed was a boarding house for laborers who assisted during harvest season.

An odor of hay, manure, and sweet grain floated to them, followed by another whinny.

"It's going to be one or both of those two buildings," Corby whispered to Marcus, pointing at the two warehouses. The structures sat opposite each other at the far end of the street, one on either side of the dirt road. Typical Zakerin buildings, they were dull, well-built structures.

Corby's heart pounded as they approached. His throat went dry. If they were going to be caught, it would be in the next few minutes. Once they slipped inside, no explanation would convince a villager they weren't up to mischief.

Before they reached the front doors, Marcus grabbed Corby's hand and pulled him into the space between the warehouse and the house next to it.

"What are you doing?" Corby whispered.

"These buildings usually have a side door. Better chance of sneaking in without being seen." He leaned in and kissed Corby's cheek. "Hopefully, that's not a sin."

Heat came to Corby's face as Marcus moved away. Confusion once again disturbed his mind. To have Marcus kiss him seemed right. How could it possibly be wrong? And why would Marcus do such a thing now, when they needed all their concentration?

Dazed, he followed Marcus as the smaller man moved toward the rear of the building.

"I love you," Corby whispered, his voice rough as the unexpected words spilled out of him.

Marcus paused. He didn't turn around, only stared straight ahead.

After several seconds, he said, "I know you do." Corby could barely hear him. "But you have to get yourself sorted before I can love you back. Once you and the Gods figure it out, let me know."

He kept walking.

Confused and uncertain what to say, Corby followed silently.

They turned the corner and found a door. Marcus grabbed the handle and pulled it. When the door didn't move, he tried again. It gave off soft clacking sounds as he rattled it but didn't open.

"Huh," Marcus grunted. He knelt and studied the handle. "No keyhole. Guess it's barred from the inside. We'll have to try the front."

"What if it's locked?"

"I'll pick it."

"What if you can't?"

Marcus took Corby's chin in his hand. The touch shot arrows of delight across Corby's face. "I'm sure there's a lock out there I can't pick," Marcus said, "but it's not going to be on a barn door."

Corby wondered if—hoped—Marcus would kiss him again.

He didn't. He released Corby's chin and said, "Come on."

They moved to the corner. Marcus stopped and peeked around it to look down the road. Corby did the same, peering over Marcus's shoulder.

One house near the center now showed the dim flicker of a candle behind the oilskin window. Corby watched for movement. A calico cat was the only sign of anything searching the barren street. Intent on its mission, it ignored them. Corby wondered why no dogs ran about. Perhaps their masters kept them inside to protect the cat, he mused.

Corby followed as Marcus slid to the warehouse's front and

crouched before the split in the doors. No lock hindered him, so he gripped a handle in each hand and pulled them open enough to stick his head inside. The soft grind of the doors on their tracks sounded as loud as an alarm bell to Corby. He watched the street, tense, his palms sweating. He expected armed men to burst from one of the houses at any moment. His bladder suddenly felt overfull.

The dry, raw smell of wheat, followed by the scent of horses, came to Corby as Marcus pulled his head back out. The almost pleasant odor reminded him of Draymed and the few horses the town had used for farm work. He ignored the sadness the memory triggered, an unproductive emotion. It was an easier sentiment to squash than his equally useless guilt.

Marcus stood, turned sideways, and slipped his slender body into the gap. Corby followed, and they closed the doors together.

"This smells like everything I hate," Marcus whispered.

Darkness filled the building. The shuffle of horses reached Corby's ears. One of the animals gave a soft snort.

Marcus took Corby's hand, and again, jitters ran up the scholar's arm to his head. "I know you can't see a damn thing yet," Marcus told him, "so stay close."

It was true. Corby could make out almost nothing in the gloomy interior beyond the vaguest shapes. He was more than happy to stay close to Marcus for any number of reasons.

They moved effortlessly across the packed earth floor until they reached a series of wooden gates. A horse let out a low whinny and air moved around Corby as the animal shook its head. His eyes adjusted, and he could see the outline of the massive beast. "How many are there?" he whispered.

"Four."

"Do you see any saddles?"

"Not yet. Let's—"

A rustle from somewhere above attracted Marcus's attention. He turned his head toward the sound. Corby saw the shock in Marcus's almond-shaped eyes before the thief pushed him away and drew a knife. A shadow dropped in behind Marcus.

"Watch—" was all Corby managed before pain across the back of his head sent him into darkness.

Keven stared at Corby, who was unconscious at his feet. The scholar lay sprawled, cheek pressed against the ground. A swirl of dust near Corby's mouth told Keven the bookworm still lived. It wouldn't have bothered him to have accidentally killed Corby. Keven knew little about subduing but had vast experience in bare-knuckle brawling. A surprise drop from behind and a punch to the side of the head had done the trick.

NalTalva had used more finesse, but his results with the black-haired boy had been the same. They now had two captives on the ground. A strange smile played on the Sterran's face, barely noticeable in the dim light.

"What are you grinning about?" Keven asked. He saw nothing amusing about the situation.

"This is the marked one who killed our master's *talba* in such a cowardly manner. I appreciate the symmetry of what I've done to him."

Keven didn't know what the man meant by symmetry and didn't care. "Why don't we kill them? Bash using them as hostages."

"Because I don't kill unnecessarily."

Keven laughed at the absurd statement, although he kept his voice low. It wouldn't do for some wandering townsman to hear them and get curious. "You killed an entire village, yet you balk at killing two enemies." He refused to think about his part in Draymed's destruction.

"I destroyed your village because my master commanded it. They were guilty of defying him. Had he commanded I kill these two, I would do so. He ordered that we capture the Necromancer."

"He also said we could do whatever we wanted with the others."

"And what I see fit to do is use them as pawns to trade. I am a warrior, not an assassin."

Irritation usurped Keven's urge to laugh again. NalTalva balked him at every turn, took none of his suggestions seriously, acted as if he were in charge. *If I rammed my sword into the scholar's chest, what would you do?* Keven wondered. He stared at Corby's still form. He had never liked the little book maggot, with his big words and prissy manner, as if he were a noble. Keven was more noble than this scrawny runt, and certainly wealthier. So, who was Corby to think he was better? Why was the rest of Draymed dead and this limp fish alive? His hand drifted to his sword.

"Fetch a horse," NalTalva snapped.

Keven's eyes wrenched up from Corby to find NalTalva less than five feet away, his pale face glaring. He had approached Keven without a sound. Keven jumped back, unable to stop himself. Then, his ears burned because he had reacted so. He locked eyes with the Sterran.

"Kill him if you wish," the warrior said, his voice barely reaching Keven's ears.

Again, Keven shivered at the man's seeming ability to read his mind.

NalTalva pointed to the black-haired boy at his feet. "But if you do, when we present only this one and the others attack because we killed one of their companions, I will let them destroy you."

"They'll kill you, too."

NalTalva shrugged. "Sangara guides me, and I will join his war host when I leave Krinnik. What God will now claim you, betrayer?"

That gave Keven pause. Eligos was not a god, and Keven no longer had Caros's love, having turned away from him. What would happen when he died? Too late, he realized how Alakaneth would likely judge him. His anger disappeared, replaced with the urge to weep.

He would do no such thing.

Not in front of this warrior. Maybe when he was alone, he would pity himself. For now, he would be strong and stay alive until he could figure out how to save his soul from the Festering Hells.

He walked to one of the stalls, annoyed by NalTalva's smug manner. The horse stood at the back of the stall, ears flat, breathing uneven, upset by the violence.

Standing on the middle slat of the wooden gate, Keven hoisted himself up, grabbing a handful of hay from the tight, small bales stored over the stall. He lowered himself and slipped open the gate. The horse shied back, nickering in fear.

"Here now," he said, holding out his open hand with the hay on it. He made soothing noises as he inched toward the horse. The creature whinnied uncertainly, ears still flat.

"Move quickly," NalTalva said.

The horse's ears flickered, and his head bobbed nervously. Keven held up a hand to silence his companion, though he wanted nothing more than to scream at the Sterran to shut up. Keven took his time, both to calm the animal and irritate NalTalva. The horse caught the scent of the hay, and its nose twitched.

"That's it," Keven crooned. "It's okay." The beast reached out with his firm lips and scooped up the yellow stalks.

As the beast ate, Keven walked back toward the gate. The horse followed, chewing the hay. Keven found a bridle hanging by the stall and slipped the leather over the beast's head, scratching the long twitching ears as he did so. The animal didn't protest as the steel bit slipped into its mouth.

He led the horse out. It was a draft horse, solid and sturdy. It was not meant for riding long distances but was perfect for carrying two unconscious hostages.

Though they were no longer unconscious, Keven realized. They sat against the stable wall, Corby's eyes wet, the marked one glaring. NalTalva had removed a trio of daggers from the lanky, black-haired boy, whose resemblance to Elissia astonished Keven. This had to be Marcus, her twin.

With thick bailing twine, NalTalva had tied their hands and bound their mouths with strips of dark cloth. Keven had enough experience with fighting to realize they had recovered from their pummeling without serious injury. Disappointment washed over him.

Keven looped the reins over a metal hook, and the horse bent its neck to snuffle at scraps of oats on the ground. He walked toward the two hostages with clenched fists. Corby shied back, eyes wide, but the other boy continued to glare in defiance. This time, he would make sure they stayed unconscious much longer. Maybe permanently.

The flat of a sword stopped Keven from advancing further. He turned. NalTalva stood beside him, weapon out and pressed against his chest. "What are you—"

"We will not kill them," NalTalva said in a flat voice.

"I wasn't going to. I was only going to knock them unconscious again."

"Which might kill them."

"So, what are we going to do? Expect them to calmly walk with us and not attempt to escape or raise an alert?"

The Sterran's look of disdain made Keven want to choke the pale man. Instead of answering, NalTalva sheathed his sword and reached into the leather bag at his waist. After a few moments of rummaging, he withdrew what looked like an animal bone with a piece of cloth stuffed into one end. He pulled the fabric and poured something black and powdery onto his hand.

Before Keven could ask what it was, NalTalva knelt before the black-haired boy and blew the powder into his face. The boy shook his head and blinked his eyes, which instantly watered. His head hitched as if he wanted to sneeze but couldn't. This lasted only a short while before the boy slumped over.

Eyes wide, Corby whimpered behind his gag while he saw what happened to his companion.

"He is not dead," NalTalva assured Corby, again to Keven's disappointment. "Remain quiet, or I will keep my promise."

The scholar went as silent as if his throat had been removed. Corby said nothing as his captor poured more of the dark substance into his hand, although Corby did close his eyes as the man moved toward him.

It didn't matter. NalTalva again blew the powder, aiming it more for Corby's nose. Soon the boy was as unconscious as the other.

"What did you promise that made him react like that?" Keven asked.

"I assured them each that if one screamed or made to escape, I would kill the other."

Keven nodded, impressed with the tactic. "And what is that?" He pointed at the tube NalTalva was now recapping and placing back into his bag.

"Something from my homeland. Help me."

Frustrated but knowing he would get no further answer, Keven assisted the man. Together they slung first Marcus and then the other boy over the back of the horse. The docile animal gave a small whinny of protest.

After NalTalva scanned outside to make sure their slight noises had not aroused any villagers, he opened the barn door enough to let them slip through with the animal. The draft horse laid its ears back and shied away from the undead palomino. It pulled on the reins, almost yanking Keven off his feet.

Keven planted his legs wide. "Shh," he whispered as he pulled firmly on the reins. Thankfully the animal hadn't made a protesting snort. They were too close to slipping away unnoticed to have things go wrong now.

Firm, insistent tugging brought the horse's large head close to his. "It's okay, shh." He petted the horse's nose and continued to make soft noises. Though its ears lay flat, the draft beast seemed to calm down.

To NalTalva, Keven said, "Take the roan and ride ahead. I'll follow fifty feet behind."

NalTalva nodded, the expression on his pale face unreadable. He mounted the horse and rode. As the undead beast retreated, Keven's new animal grew less restive. He gave it a final rub on its lone face.

"Come on, boy." He walked, reins in hand, and the horse followed.

10

As far as we know, the Inconnu never bothered with the other two continents. It's possible they never knew of their existence. But, given what we know about them now, I find that difficult to believe.

- Corberin of Draymed, *The Second Inconnu War*

My head hurts," Elissia said in a groggy voice. Beside her, Erick took her hand, relieved to see her waking from the sting Blink had given her.

"Water," she added.

"I'm sorry," Erick said as Gabrielle brought a skin of water to her. "We had to…"

"I know," Elissia started to sit up, winced, and remained lying down. "I know I…I know…" she swallowed.

"Don't speak," Erick told her. "We don't have to talk about it now."

But you will have to talk about it, Blink thought. *This isn't typical venom, and we need to figure out what's in it before she succeeds in—*

Enough, Erick thought back. *We'll discuss it when there's light and warmth. And when she's not muddled from getting hit by you.*

Elissia seemed to have other ideas. "It was horrible. All I could think was that I was a pestilence. I needed to rid you of me. I saw what I was doing and wanted to stop but couldn't." She shuddered, and her hand, cold and dry, clenched tight on Erick's. "What's happening to me?"

"Drink this." Gabrielle held out the water skin. Elissia took three loud gulps from it. Her other hand never loosened on Erick's.

When she finished, she asked, "What are we going to do?"

Erick wrapped his free hand over the one that already held hers. "We sent Corby and Marcus to get horses so we can move quickly. We'll get you to Dorfork and find a cure."

"What if there isn't one?"

It tore at Erick to see Elissia, usually so reliable, rattled by what had happened. It hurt him more that it was his fault. If he had killed the man known as Andras when he and the other assassins attacked the manor, Elissia wouldn't be poisoned, and Marcus wouldn't have a death mark. So much would be different.

And if your father hadn't raised Eligos, we might be at home and your parents alive, Blink thought. *It's useless to wish for things that aren't. All you can do is try to fix it and learn from the mistakes.*

Blink was right. That didn't stop guilt from gnawing at him.

"I can feel it," Elissia said, her voice little more than a whisper. "It's like worms moving through my blood. Everything looks green and sickly. I want to puke."

"Some of that is because of Blink's venom," Erick told her. "The puking, definitely." He offered her a weak grin, and she returned it. "I know eating is probably the last thing you want to do, but it will help."

She shook her head. "I don't think I could. I need to sleep. I want you to tie my hands together."

"Are you sure?"

"It's the only way to be safe."

Erick nodded. He stood to get the rope from the mule when Blink said, "Two people coming with horses."

Erick looked down the road. He could discern only vague outlines in the wan light, so he made the mental connection to Blink. He expected to see Marcus and Corby. Instead, his familiar's superior night vision showed him a short man on a dull yellow horse. His face teased Erick at the edge of familiarity. The other, taller man led another, stockier horse several feet behind the first. Erick recognized him instantly.

"Keven."

"What?" Elissia asked.

"It's Keven and—" he sucked in a breath as he remembered the other man. Yet another enemy Erick had let live. Was he to be forever haunted by his compassion? This man had ravaged the town of Draymed with poison and fire. Another two hundred souls on Erick's conscience. If Keven was here with him, that meant—

"That bastard," Erick said. "He helped destroy Draymed."

Elissia sat up and swallowed. "You're not making any sense."

"It's Keven and another man." He didn't want to reveal the other man's identity yet. He wasn't sure what the shock would do to Elissia. "They can't mean us any good." He considered running, but the steady forward progress of the horses told him the men had spotted their campfire. *If they do anything remotely hostile, please put them down,* he thought to Blink.

Of course.

He released Elissia's hand, stood, and raised his voice to a yell. "Stop where you are."

Both men jumped, no doubt surprised they had been spotted so far away from the meager campfire.

"What do you want?" Erick asked.

"We want to make a trade," the bandit shouted back as if they spoke at a bazaar and not on a road in the dark of night.

"What kind of trade?"

The position of the packhorse had mostly hidden its cargo. Erick saw it only as two lumps, shapeless as saddlebags. The man reached up and grabbed one with each hand. He pulled, and the shapes fell to the ground. Erick gasped.

"Surrender yourself, and your companions can live."

Elissia stood. Erick knew she couldn't see their companions but was smart enough to understand what was happening. She stepped toward the men. Erick recognized the grim set to her face and grabbed her hand.

"Wait," he said beside her ear. "Getting yourself killed won't help."

"But we can't let them take you. You know that's what they want."

He did. "If I come with you, how do I know you'll let them go?" he shouted.

"You have my word as a *Napaei* of Eligos."

Erick considered. Eligos was the epitome of death denied. His power, the power of *elonsha*, was an evil force that sought to turn every creature into an undead fiend. But he did not deceive skillfully. That purview belonged to Bolfri, his brother, who had been destroyed by the Necromancers. Ironically, though this man would happily kill Erick's companions, if he promised not to harm them, he would hold to it.

"And if I come with you? What then?"

"We'll take you to our master, who will do as he pleases."

Erick knew what the pleasure of Eligos would be.

"You can't do it," Elissia said in a trembling voice. "You're the only Necromancer left. If you die, no one can stop Eligos."

Erick couldn't willingly sacrifice his friends. He wouldn't be able to live with himself.

Will you be able to live with knowing you killed the entire world? Blink asked. *More importantly, how do you think the Gods will feel knowing you broke the Covenant? Think Caros will accept you into his Heaven?*

If Eligos absorbs my nanta, Erick thought, referring to the power of his soul, *I don't think it will matter.*

A sudden and almost overwhelming urge to punch something rattled through Erick. He couldn't sacrifice the world, even to save his two friends. If Eligos came to rule, they would die anyway. All his capitulation would manage is a delay of the inevitable.

Or it might give me a chance to escape, he thought. Assuming Keven and this nameless man let Marcus and Corby live, they might be able to affect a rescue. Erick couldn't let them die, not when their capture was his fault.

He released Elissia's hand. "Give me your word you will let all my friends live," he told the captors, "and I will come with you."

"No," Elissia said. "You can't."

"I can't sacrifice your brother and cousin. My friends." He lowered his voice. "I'm counting on all of you to figure out a way to save me."

Elissia's dark brows bunched in confusion. Then a look Erick had never seen took over her features. A greenish cast tinted her blue eyes. Her olive skin went sallow. The dim firelight turned her face sinister as her lip curled up in a cruel smile. "I can save you now," she said, her voice thick and deep with anger. She walked toward the captors.

Erick grabbed at her arm. When he touched her, nausea roiled over him. He recoiled as if he had seized a flaming brand. His head pounded and stomach clenched. It reminded him of the dizzy exhilaration of *elonsha*, threaded with the corruption of a living disease.

She strode toward Keven and the other man. The shorter one drew his sword, and Keven followed suit, his blade at Corby's throat.

"Stop or we kill them," the pale man said.

Erick's heart lurched as Elissia didn't falter. She continued her determined march.

"I said—" the man started.

"Those are my people," Elissia said in a thick, almost masculine voice. "You will not touch them." She raised a hand and held it toward them, fingers spread. *"Yolci raclari!"*

Erick recognized the words. *Erupt with sores.*

Elissia was speaking *lonsh.*

The words worked.

Still looking through Blink's eyes, Erick watched as large blisters formed on the face and hands of both men. They screamed as the pustules burst, releasing viscous fluid. They dropped to their knees. Elissia advanced on them. Keven fell on his side with a pitiful wail as the other man reached up to his face. Dark spots dotted his sleeves where the popped blisters leaked through.

"Quas ialpor cnila," Elissia said.

Die from bursting blood.

Crimson shot from Keven's nose and splattered the ground. It likewise leaked through the other man's fingers and ran down his hands.

"Make her stop," Gabrielle gasped. "She's going to kill them."

"Good," Erick said. His compassion had almost undone him twice. He wouldn't suffer from it again.

A voice issued from Elissia that made Erick's flesh crawl. It sounded like a bubbling swamp, syrupy and thick. "Stop. They are my brothers. I will not let you destroy them."

"They have to die," Elissia said, her voice more normal. It was as if two people spoke from one mouth. "You don't threaten my brother and—"

Her arm fell to her side. Her body spasmed.

Keven and the other man started to pull themselves from the ground.

Fearful they might attack Elissia, Erick shouted for Blink and ran toward them. Blink took to the air.

"No," Elissia said in her voice. Then the bubbling voice snarled as she wheeled toward Erick.

"*Dobix oxic.*"

Erick collapsed as an invisible fist slammed into his stomach. He dropped and retched. Blink landed beside him and writhed.

"Leave them alone," Elissia shouted, wheeling toward the captors.

The nausea lessened, replaced by a pounding headache that kept Erick on his knees.

"Flee," she commanded in the noxious voice, aimed at the two men who stood dazed, faces covered with blood and pus. They stumbled back toward the horses.

Erick tried to stand and fell again as blinding pain darkened his vision. He heard more than saw the men mount and ride away. If they suffered anywhere near the agony he experienced, it amazed him they could move.

"Erick."

Elissia's voice wrenched at his heart. He crawled toward the sound, finding her through the slits his eyes had become. Her olive face twisted with some inner turmoil. He forced himself to stand and go to her. He took her hand, shocked at the heat in it.

Her skin rippled green. Her eyes glistened with a yellow tint the color of rancid butter. She grimaced and shut them.

"Leave me alone," she said through gritted teeth. Though she squeezed Erick's hand hard enough to cause pain, she wasn't speaking to him.

Her eyes opened. They'd returned to their usual blue, but they were dull, lacking the sparkle that so dazzled him the first time he saw her. "Help me."

She collapsed.

He dropped beside her. The motion made his temples thrum. "Elissia."

Gabrielle joined him and pressed two fingers against Elissia's wrist. Erick held his breath as he waited, the fear of losing her twisting his stomach.

"She's alive," Gabrielle said. Erick breathed again.

"What about them?" He pointed toward the still forms of Corby and Marcus. A sudden, delayed dread came over him. What if they were dead already, and the two men had used their bodies as bait? His stomach knotted.

Gabrielle ran to them.

Erick scooped up Elissia, ignoring the screaming kick in his head, and returned to the small fire. Blink recovered and threw some of their scavenged wood on the embers. As the flames rose, they gave false color to Elissia's pale face.

"They're breathing," Gabrielle said from the darkness. "I can't be sure, but I think they were given a soporific. Can you help me with them?"

Though relieved, his anxiety for Elissia stayed foremost in his mind. "Blink?"

The homunculus waddled toward Gabrielle.

Erick studied Elissia. Her breath came shallow. The glow of the flames revealed nothing but the pallor of death. "Caros, what's going on with her?"

The amulet around his neck suddenly grew heavy and warm. It pulled at him as if trying to drag him toward the ground. Startled, he removed it. Its weight increased. The firelight reflected off the metal, giving the necklace a soft glow.

The girl, said a voice in his head, low and soothing. Not the vague, malevolent whisper of *elonsha,* but the warmth of a parent's embrace.

Erick lowered the necklace and placed the amulet on Elissia's chest.

A flare of light knocked him back. A *crack*, like the shattering of rocks, rebounded through his head. Elissia gasped.

Quick as lightning and thunder, the light and sound disappeared. The pain in Erick's head retreated. Elissia's face regained much of its olive color, and her shallow breathing deepened, the sound of deep slumber. The wrinkles that knotted her forehead smoothed.

Erick picked the necklace back up. It felt light, nothing more than his mother's gold amulet, eight circles with an arrow piercing the center.

"Thank you," Erick said, sending the thought to Denech. Having no idea what the luck god had done, he was nonetheless grateful.

"What happened?" Gabrielle and Blink asked simultaneously as they returned carrying Marcus between them.

"I got some help from Denech," Erick told them. He realized his ill feelings had disappeared. A quick mental touch with Blink showed the familiar also no longer suffered any afflictions.

"Then you truly are blessed by the Gods?" Gabrielle asked with amazement.

"I don't know if blessed is the right word," Erick said carefully. "But they have some interest in what happens to me. To all of us." *At least when it's convenient*, he thought.

"So, everything I learned about the Necromancers was wrong."

She's only now figuring that out? Blink thought in irritation. *How long has she been with us?*

It's okay, Erick told him. *She's had as much happen to her as we have.* Erick would be the last to fault Gabrielle for any problems in changing her view of him, considering his issues understanding the relationship Marcus and Corby shared. Now wasn't the time to go into any of it.

"I'll help get Corby." Erick couldn't help but notice she had seen to Marcus first. "See if you can wake him."

Gabrielle nodded and bent over Marcus, concern on her plain face.

Erick walked toward Corby, still trying to figure out what was happening with Elissia. Though the amulet had eased her suffering, it gave him no clue what afflicted her. Eligos had infused some evil on the knife that cut Elissia. Erick didn't know enough to figure it out and had no idea who might be able to help him.

They reached Corby. Erick took his shoulders while Blink grabbed his legs, and they lifted his slight body with ease. Erick realized that not only had his headache and nausea gone away, his fatigue had also left. He felt as refreshed as if he had slept a full night in comfort—another gift from the amulet.

They returned to the fire to find Marcus sitting up and rubbing the back of his head.

"Hit from behind," he muttered as he winced, "then some sleeping powder blown in my face." He reached down to his waist and frowned. "And they took my knives, including my favorite. That's just embarrassing." He watched as they laid Corby on the ground. "Is he okay?"

Gabrielle gave Corby a quick examination. "He's fine," she said. Erick thought he heard a trace of bitterness. Or he could have just been imagining it. "Hit from behind, like you." She wiped at something underneath his eye, then held her hand up and examined it in the firelight.

"Elissia hasn't woken up?" Marcus asked.

"She..." Erick didn't exactly know how to explain it. "What happened?"

"I was going to ask you the same thing," Marcus told him. "We found some horses and were getting ready to acquire them when I got hit. But how did we end up here? Are you going to help him?"

Gabrielle started. With her examination of the powder finished, she had been watching Marcus while Corby lay unconscious. "Of course."

"Two men from Draymed attacked you," Erick told Marcus. "They're servants of Eligos. I can only assume they tracked us through your mark, which is what I warned you about."

"Warning taken," Marcus said as he rubbed the back of his head. "How did you get us back?"

"Ow," Corby said as Gabrielle helped him sit up. "What happened?"

"That seems to be the question of the hour," Marcus said.

"Elissia saved you, but I'm not sure how. They brought you here to trade you for me, and she afflicted them with some power I have never..." Erick stopped as dread crawled from his stomach and seized his heart. He had never seen such power, but he had read about it. "Is that even possible?" he whispered.

Considering what we heard and saw, more than possible, Blink thought.

"What?" Marcus asked. "What's wrong?"

"There were three *Inconnu*," Erick said. "Eligos, Bolfri, and Saburoc. Bolfri was the Master of Deceit, and Saburoc was the Master of Disease."

Gabrielle gasped. "The pustules and bleeding."

Erick gave a grim nod. "I think there may have been more to the knife than poison."

"Feel free to make some sense at any time," Marcus said.

"Elissia saved you by making boils erupt on the two men, and blood shoot out of their noses. She would have killed them, but something stopped her. The same entity was responsible for both actions."

"Still not making sense."

"I'm sorry," Erick said. "I don't want to believe it, but it's all that I can think of. When the knife cut Elissia, in addition to poisoning her, it somehow infected her with the spirit of Saburoc."

Though I would have never sided with the Inconnu, *I can see why some of the tribes of Falan-Dar would do so for a chance to live elsewhere. That much sand could drive anyone to desperate actions.*

-Palanad, travelling Zakerin merchant

A moment of stunned silence greeted Erick's pronouncement. Marcus stumbled over to sit beside the sleeping Elissia. Corby joined him. Gabrielle sat where they left her, on the edge of the small fire's light.

Marcus took one of Elissia's hands and clasped it to his chest. "What are we going to do? Is this going to kill her?"

"I don't know," Erick answered. "We have to get her cured soon."

"We know we can cure the poison," Corby said. "Will that also cure this infection?"

"I don't know," Erick repeated. Was he cursed to forever utter those three words?

"Saburoc is dead," Marcus said. His eyes glistened. "Can Eligos do something like that?"

"I think he can," Erick said. "It's no different than bringing up any other dead thing. It *is* a way of doing it I didn't know was possible."

"So, does that make him an undead being, even harder to kill? Is she going to become undead?"

Erick shook his head, wanting to scream in frustration. He had no answers to Marcus's questions and couldn't bring himself to say *I don't know* again. "We have to get to Dorfork. The sooner, the better. How many horses did the village have?"

"Four," Corby told him.

"Keven and the other man had two of them," Erick said. "So, two left."

"Three," Blink said. "One of their horses was a *gateloah*."

"It was?" Erick asked. He had not sensed it. Considering his mental state during the encounter, that didn't surprise him.

"It was," Blink confirmed.

"Three isn't enough. Can horses carry two people?"

Corby nodded. "It's not the most comfortable ride for the person not on the saddle, but horses are more than capable of handling the weight. Especially as none of us is exceptionally large."

"Let's do what we should have done in the first place. We'll all go to the village and use the horses. If we can take them, we will."

"We can't take their last horses," Gabrielle said. "They need them for farming."

"They've already harvested the wheat," Corby said. "They can survive without them."

"And we'll find a way to return them," Erick told her. "I don't want to do it, but we need to get to Dorfork as quickly as possible. How far to the village?"

"An hour, roughly," Marcus said.

"Then let's go. We can have the mule carry Elissia."

"I can walk."

Everyone jumped at the voice that came from the ground. Marcus released her hand as if it had turned into a snake.

Elissia opened her eyes.

Marcus leaned down and kissed her on the forehead. "Lissi. You're okay."

"Hardly. Hopefully, once we get to Dorfork, I will be. But I can walk. I don't want to ride the mule."

"I'd like you to." Erick knew better than to insist on it. "I don't know what will trigger Saburoc to come back. It could be stress or exhaustion or whenever the thing wants to come out. I don't want to take any chances. It's less strenuous if you ride."

"I think he's right. We all know you're as tough as any of us."

"Tougher than me," Corby said with a faint smile.

"But you're sick," Marcus told her, "or something close enough to it. I'll feel much better if you ride."

"We'll all feel better," Erick amended.

Elissia sat up, eyebrows bunched. In the glow of the fire, Erick thought he saw hints of verdigris in her dark complexion. *Please say yes*, he thought. *I don't want you to—"*

He wasn't sure how to complete the thought. He didn't know what might happen to her if Saburoc, or whatever was in her, returned. Would it kill her or use her like a *talba*? It had some ability to control her, though she fought it. As she got weaker, her ability to resist would wane. If it possessed her, could he bring himself to kill her? Would he be able to?

Elissia nodded. "If it makes you feel better, I'll do it," Elissia said. Erick let out his breath. Elissia grinned. "But only because you asked nicely."

They all laughed, though the humor was short-lived. They redistributed supplies on the mule to both lighten its load and give Elissia room to sit.

"I need to borrow a knife," Marcus told his sister. "At least until we find those bastards and I get mine back."

"I'd rather we not find them," Corby said as he extinguished the fire.

"It's not your favorite dagger they took."

Elissia gave one of the daggers from her boot to Marcus and then, with his help, got on to the mule. They began the trek down the road. Erick didn't know how well he could ride a horse, but he was ready to find out. It had to be better than walking.

They had only been twenty minutes on the road when Marcus said, "That doesn't look promising."

Something glowed on the horizon, no bigger than a firefly, in line with where their road led them.

"Maybe they found their horses missing and organized a search party," Erick said.

"You don't believe that any more than I do," Elissia said, sitting on the mule.

He didn't. As they drew closer and the glow grew brighter, there was no doubt of the cause.

The village was on fire.

As the group drew closer, like moths to a flame, they discovered it wasn't the entire village. Only one building burned.

"It's almost like someone had a specific target in mind," Marcus said.

Erick didn't need to ask where the horses had been. The large building at the far end of the town blazed. Separate from the rest of the structures, it burned alone. Rather than attempt to put it out, a futile effort, villagers stood with wet cloths and watched for errant sparks. Others had ladders, ready to throw against any building should an ember land on a roof. No breeze blew in the still night; only the violence of the fire stirred the firebugs.

Erick estimated thirty people stood in the road, either watching in horror or assisting in prevention. No one paid Erick's party much attention as they drew closer.

"Is anyone injured?" Gabrielle yelled. "Anyone injured?"

A few heads turned their way. Most turned back to watch the blaze, their farmer's faces full of worry. An older woman, one eye permanently shut and gray hair tangled, walked toward them with a limp.

"Who are you?" she asked. Her good eye took them all in.

"Travelers seeking a place to rest," Corby said.

"Then you have to seek elsewhere," the woman said, her voice raspy. "We don't take strangers into our home. And we have other problems." Her eye returned to Erick. "We need no more right now."

Erick turned from the unnerving gaze and saw a stocky, weathered man approaching. He stopped behind the crone and placed a large hand on her shoulder. "Who's this, ma?"

"Travelers seeking rest."

"At Melteth's hour?" Both the man and woman touched their three middle fingers to their forehead, a gesture against speaking the insane god's name. "From where do you come? Why do you travel at night?"

Erick wished they had avoided the village, especially as it seemed there were no injuries. "We come from Prospector's Camp and are going to Dorfork," he told the man. "We travel late because our companion," he pointed to Elissia, "is sensitive to daylight." He winced at how his excuse sounded. Lies didn't come easily to him.

"Then you best keep traveling," the man said.

Others had begun to move their way. A few had farming implements that could quickly turn into weapons.

The man's dark eyes roamed to the burning barn. "We already have one mystery. We'll not welcome more."

"Then we'll be on our way," Erick said. "We want no trouble."

"Are you sure no one is hurt?" Gabrielle asked.

"I'm a healer and can tend our own," the old woman said. Reflections of the fire made her good eye glitter in her lined face. "If I wanted help, I would find someone who travels in better company." Her gaze fell on Erick.

Erick nodded as fear tightened his chest. True healers, those who received their abilities through the worship of Caros, Krinnik, and Talan, could often recognize the tainted power of *elonsha* surrounding Necromancers. These healers had no love for what they saw as a corruption of their domain. Why she didn't immediately expose him to her fellow villagers, Erick didn't know. Nor did he want to stay to find out.

"We'll leave you be," he told her. "Thank you for your understanding."

She nodded, her wrinkled lips pressed tight. Her fire-lit face offered neither love nor outright animosity.

"Come on," Erick said to the others. They walked through the village, the heat almost more than Erick could bear as they passed the roaring barn. He remembered another barn that burned. The animals of his manor had screamed as the flames consumed them within their wooden home as his house also blazed.

When they had gone several hundred feet from the village, Erick stopped and gathered them close. Blink landed and joined them.

"Nobody followed us," the familiar told him.

"Good," Marcus said. "I'm tired of being attacked every time we go into or walk out of a town."

"What now?" Gabrielle asked.

Everyone looked at Erick. His stomach knotted. Leading his band of friends and having them rely on his decisions had not grown easier. Anything he did could end up with someone dead.

The onus fell on him, nonetheless. Stopping Eligos was his task. Much as he had tried to dissuade them, they insisted on aiding him. It pleased and infuriated him. It seemed now he had to offer his desperate plan. The burning barn and the dead horses left only one option he could see. "Corby, do you know how far it is to Dorfork?"

Corby turned his head up to study Talan's Tears, the stars hanging in the clear sky. He pressed his lips together and ran a hand through his shapeless hair. "Roughly fifty miles," he told them.

"How long will it take to get there if we keep walking?"

"Through the night? With no stopping?"

Erick nodded.

"Thirteen to seventeen hours," Corby said. "Depending on how quick we walk and how accurate my calculations are."

"Then that's what we do," Erick said. "We walk. Elissia rides the mule, and we walk and don't stop until we get there."

The going was easy at first. Erick told everyone to keep a wary eye out for Keven and the other man. Nobody may have followed them from the unnamed village, but the two men might be lying in wait ahead of them.

Wide-open farmland gave them excellent visibility, helped by the clear night and thin moonlight. Erick occasionally sent Blink ahead to scout. The familiar reported nothing but open road ahead.

Erick set a quick pace, taking advantage of the level ground. He held the mule's reins and walked beside it. He wished he had put them on this path earlier. They could have been hours down the road already and not had the scare of Corby and Marcus's capture. He needed to think things through better.

Don't beat yourself up too much, Blink thought. *You didn't know Elissia was so sick. Saving her brother might have been the only reason you discovered Saburoc. And this isn't going to be an easy march.*

I know, but it's the best thing I can think of.

Nobody spoke, conserving their energy. Though Erick would have liked Corby to offer a story or song to pass the time, the scholar needed his wind as much as any of them.

Erick tried not to brood and worked to not consider the impossible task before him. In the perverse way the mind works, the more he wanted to not think about it, the quicker it leapt to the front of his thoughts.

We've done impossible before, Blink reminded him. *No reason we can't do it again.*

Erick smiled. *Ever the optimist.*

Someone has to be. You're as grim as a bird staring at a snake.

The familiar's bright disposition never failed to cheer Erick. They *had* done the impossible. Why couldn't they do it again? This task might be easier than getting to Broken Mountain. They had faced several attacks on the journey to the mountain, ambushes planned by the Fist of the *Inconnu*. Erick had been easy to find then, since his enemies knew his destination. Now no one knew where he traveled. He only had the barest idea himself.

Erick glanced at Marcus. He walked ahead, Corby at his side, Gabrielle trailing behind. The *morazol* marking the thief concerned Erick, as evidenced by the recent abduction. Still, Eligos could organize only so many resources. He was a powerful being, but he was only *one* being. As long as they kept moving and stayed alert, they should be as safe as anyone could be while being hunted by an evil entity bent on taking over the world.

That's the attitude, Blink thought.

Erick offered a fleeting smile. One thing he learned from the recent encounter was he would no longer let his band of friends separate. If they did something potentially dangerous, they did it together.

"We need more guards."

Erick started at Elissia's voice coming over his head. When he had glanced at her ten minutes ago, her eyes had been closed. He thought she had fallen asleep riding. "What do you mean?"

"Like Geran," she said. "We need undead to protect us in case someone attacks. If Marcus has this beacon on him, then the more we have the better."

Erick nodded. Why didn't he think of that in Prospector's Camp? He could have reanimated some of the warriors he had released after the fight. Yet another mistake. "That's a good idea. Once we get you cured, I'll see if I can't make a squadron for us."

Elissia gave a light laugh that put goosebumps on Erick's arms. "That might be a bit obvious. Two or maybe three would be best."

"I could do that." Any herbs he didn't have, they would hopefully find in Dorfork. The trick would be coming up with bodies he could reanimate. He wanted to kick himself for missing the opportunity at Prospector's Camp.

You had other things on your mind, Blink reminded him.

I can't keep using that as an excuse. He put his hand on Elissia's, which rested on the mule's back. It relieved him that her hand felt normal, not the brand of fire nor block of ice from earlier. Maybe whatever lurked inside her, the spirit of Saburoc or something else, expended itself during its struggle with Elissia. He had no illusions that the entity left. Hopefully, the fight for control, and Elissia's use of the power to injure Keven and the Sterran, weakened it enough to give them the time to free her.

"What if you can't cure me?" Elissia asked as if she had read his mind.

"I can't think that way," Erick told her. "We have to cure you. I need you to help me with this."

"Really?" She teased. "And here I thought you wanted me to stay away."

"I did. I do. I want you to be safe. But since you're not going to do that, then I'm going to insist you help. You may regret you didn't stay back in Kalador."

"I haven't regretted it yet." She squeezed his hand, and warmth spread from his hand to his heart. The thought of losing her almost made him stumble. He held himself together, put on a brave face, and walked, his hand in hers.

12

To anyone who says to me that my brother and cousin didn't deserve happiness, or that they got what was coming to them, I've got a six-inch steel blade I'd be happy to introduce them to.

   -Elissia of Kalador, as told to Aralin, Kaladorian Archivist

As the sky lightened, Erick thought he had never felt so tired in his life. Whatever energy Denech gave him had been short-lived, and his fatigue redoubled. The chain shirt dragged on his shoulders like a boat anchor. His legs groaned at each step. The endless walking made the journey through Broken Mountain carrying Elissia seem like a spring day jaunt.

Had this been the start of their journey, like the day they left Draymed two months ago, he might not feel so punished. They had gone so many days with so little sleep, endured weeks crossing the Ruins, hours moving through the sloping halls of Broken Mountain, and more hours coming back out. The scant respite they got in the mountain had done little to refresh any of them. Their brief rest in camp before Elissia's terrifying struggle did even less.

"Please tell me we're almost there," Marcus said.

Corby shook his head. The motion made him stumble, but Marcus kept him from falling. "We're maybe halfway."

"I'm going to sleep for a week," Marcus said.

Erick thought he might too.

Only Elissia and the mule seemed to have any energy. The slowly brightening orange light made her skin glow with health. It heartened Erick to see no trace of the strange green coloring.

"You need to take a break," she said. "You're not going to be any good if you get there and can't think straight because you're so tired."

"No," Erick said. "You're sick."

"I feel fine. Better than I have in days. Fifteen minutes isn't going to make a difference one way or the other. Right now, I look better than any of you. Stop and rest before you fall and hurt yourself."

Erick didn't want to stop. They needed to get to Dorfork, but Elissia had a point. Gabrielle had to be able to focus on what she needed. If she was all but sleepwalking, she might make a mistake in the cure, and that wouldn't do any good either.

He had to trust that Elissia was truthful with him. They could all use a break. "Stop," he said.

The others did and gathered around him.

"We'll rest for twenty minutes. Eat, drink, and anything else necessary. Then we start again."

Erick pulled the mule to the side of the road and helped Elissia slide off. Corby opened one of the packs and passed out slices of meat and bread they had taken from the tavern.

"I'd give my teeth and a foot for a wagon to come along now and take us the rest of the way."

"I'd give your other foot for a soft bed," Elissia said with a smile.

"Thanks, sis. Glad to see you have the energy for a sense of humor."

"Who said I was joking?" A small giggle escaped her, and Erick's heart soared at the sound.

They sat by the side of the road and ate. Erick's feet throbbed. He looked at the scuffed, beaten shoes he wore—veterans of a long campaign. The left one had a hole at the top. The coloring on the toes of both had worn away, revealing the brown leather beneath. He felt as battered as they looked.

After he finished the sparse meal, he closed his eyes. He would rest for a few minutes, and they would leave again.

~

E lissia watched as her companions dozed, Gabrielle asleep before she finished eating.

They all needed sleep, and she wasn't going to begrudge them rest. She had it easy, riding on the mule. She felt surprisingly energetic considering everything that had happened. Even if she had been deathly tired, she wouldn't close her eyes for fear of what might happen if she did. The bubbling voice might speak again, might tell her to kill herself so it could be free.

She shivered. Then she considered what had occurred hours ago when Keven and the other man had shown up. The memory fuzzed at the edges like a dream but remained clear enough that she knew it had been real. And she had come close to losing herself.

Incensed at the treatment Marcus and Corby had been subjected to, she discovered within her some strange power. The same bubbling voice that demanded she die had shown her what to do. It had been easy. Some words, a gesture, and violence burst from her. It felt *good* to hurt them. They had kidnapped her brother and cousin to use in a ploy to take the man she loved. She didn't have punishment enough for them. She would watch them fester and melt beneath her wrath. The entity made it all too pleasurable. This was a weapon she could enjoy wielding.

Then, it all changed. Whatever was in her sensed something in Keven and the other man. Suddenly, the thing rose in her mind. "Stop," it burbled at her. Then it used its force against Erick.

She would be damned if that would happen. Agony split her mind as she fought the invader, as she had fought to keep the knife from her chest. This time there would be no Blink to knock her unconscious. This time she protected someone whose life she cared for more than her own.

She demanded the creature cede the power. It struggled. Within her mind and body, they waged battle as physically as if they swung swords. She had never been in a fight so dire or difficult, had never known her mental abilities could be so strained without destroying her.

In the end, it almost *had* destroyed her. She refused to fail, to see those she loved die. She railed against the beast with all the fury and strength she could muster. Her love for Erick, Marcus, and Corby turned to anger. She demanded the creature leave her be. She pounded upon it as if she could shatter bones and crush rocks.

To her amazement, it retreated.

Its sudden withdrawal left her hollow, empty as a thieves' warren at night. It hadn't fled her body. She still felt the pulsing sickness of it deep within. But she had beat it, and it cowered. Exhausted beyond all measure, she had fainted.

Now, as she watched the five others who traveled with her, she wondered how long she could protect them from the thing within her. She had won the struggle with her unwelcome guest by a breath, and it cost her. If it recovered from its quiescence and tried to regain control, she didn't know if she would have the will to resist. Whatever cure Gabrielle sought in Dorfork for the poison, it had to work on this corruption within her, too.

For now, the thing slumbered. The battle had taxed it also. It would not recover for a while, and so, Erick and the others could sleep. They had time.

They didn't have forever, though. If Dorfork didn't have the antidote, or the antidote didn't work, Elissia feared what would happen next.

E rick started awake and had to slam his eyes shut to keep the sun from blinding him. He turned away from the glare and opened them again. Elissia sat beside him, tearing blades of grass into lengthwise strips.

"You're awake," she said.

"I shouldn't have been asleep," he accused himself as he sat up. His head thrummed, and he wanted nothing more than to lay back down. The others still slept in various spots on the ground. "How long?"

"Maybe three hours," Elissia told him. "I've been keeping watch."

"Why didn't you wake us?"

"Three large caravans and one cadre of Queen's Roadmen went by, and none of you stirred. You needed sleep. I'm feeling better, and I think the time was well spent. You could probably sleep some more if you wanted."

"No, we need to go." Some deep inner sense told Erick their time was short. Not necessarily because of Elissia's condition. Keven's escape with the bandit had him on edge. Any delay gave his enemies time to set up an ambush or make some plan to stop him. Their wounds had looked severe, and they might be dead, but Erick didn't believe that was the case. He wanted to meet them again to correct his mistakes by killing them both.

"That's pretty dark thinking," Blink said as he opened his eyes and stretched his wings.

"I'm in a dark mood," Erick said. Compassion had brought him only grief. It was time to try a different tactic.

"Wake up," he shouted as he clapped his hands.

So fast it made Erick step back, Marcus stood, Elissia's knife in hand, and scanned the area. "Where are they?"

"There's nobody," Elissia said. "Nice to see your reactions are sharp."

As Corby yawned and rubbed his eyes, Marcus said, "Then why the hell did you bellow?"

"We shouldn't have been sleeping," Erick said. "We need to get moving again."

"That's all fine." Marcus returned the knife to its sheath. "But a gentle shake and a 'get up' would have worked."

They took a few minutes for everyone to drink some water. Erick considered removing his chain shirt to make his life more comfortable, then recalled ambushes and sharp swords. Gabrielle made another mixture. Elissia downed it with a grimace and hauled herself back on the mule.

As they walked at a quick pace, the day grew warm but not uncomfortable. It was the kind of day Erick would have enjoyed if not for the fear their three-hour delay engendered in him. He kept throwing covert glances toward Elissia. He didn't know what he expected to happen.

"I'm not about to turn into an ogre," she snapped after at least his tenth fearful gaze. "I feel almost normal. Gabrielle's medicine must be working, at least for now."

"Sorry," Erick said, again grasping her hand.

The sun had almost hit its highest point before they reached Dorfork. The short nap after the lack of sleep had Erick's head buzzing. His joints ached. He could only imagine how bad everyone else felt.

They spotted the city as a dark smudge when they crested a rise in the road. A few hundred feet away, a caravan of wagons rolled toward them. They took to the roadside to allow the carts to pass. As the procession drew closer, two guards on horseback, dressed in gray tabards with a gold diagonal slash, spurred their horses toward Erick and his companions. They wore long swords, high riding boots, and leather caps.

"Merchant's Guild guards," Corby told them.

The guards reined in their mounts ten feet from the group. Both typical Zakerin, with brown hair and somber faces, they studied the travelers. Blink had thrown his cloak on and put the hood over his head to conceal his face.

"Where are your guardians?" the guard on the right asked.

That wasn't the question Erick expected, and he sputtered, trying to think of something to say.

Marcus stepped up and nodded to the guards. He indicated himself and Elissia. "Our parents are with the wagon a mile back. It has a cracked wheel, and they've sent us ahead to purchase a new one and return with it."

The guards eyed them. Marcus and Elissia, with their half Straphan blood, bore the unmistakable resemblance of siblings, while Erick and the others, pure Zakerin, looked nothing like them.

Marcus must have discerned the guards were thinking something similar. He continued. "Cousins on our father's side. All of us going to Dorfork on our way to Kalasan to start our trade."

"They sent all of you?"

"Wagon wheels are large. They wanted us to take turns rolling it." Marcus offered a disarming smile.

Erick wanted to tell the men to mind their own business. They were merchant guards, not Royal Guardians. Though he suspected they had no right to be interrogating them, he wasn't sure enough to challenge them. And doing so might make them more suspicious.

The guard considered them all a moment longer, then shrugged. "Any news from the road?"

"The road is clear, other than our aunt and uncle's wagon," Corby said, carrying on Marcus's lie. "However, much of Prospectors' Camp is burned. They'll need provisions and supplies to rebuild."

"What happened?" the guard asked as both men's eyes went wide with shock.

Erick hoped Corby wouldn't tell the true tale.

"Something about an attack from the Ruins. We were passing through and didn't stay to hear much."

"The Ruins? Haven't heard tell of anyone living in them. Certainly not enough to attack a town like Prospector's. We'll sell them what we can, but most likely a special supply run will have to be made. Someone needs to let the *Wecleit* know what's happened so that they can send a patrol."

"Our parents will report what we saw to the Arms Master," Corby assured the guard. "Hopefully those who fled have returned and there are no further attacks until the Queen can send reinforcements. One of them mentioned sending a message to Kalador."

The guard nodded. "A good idea." He glanced back and saw the caravan had drawn almost even with them. "Dorfork is another mile. Safe travels."

The guards took up their positions at the head of the caravan. Erick watched as ten massive wagons passed, all stacked high with goods. A pair of guards rode beside each cart.

Once the caravan cleared, Erick and his companions took to the road and continued walking. It took effort for Erick to start moving again. He wanted to lie in the sun and sleep.

Walking backward, Marcus watched the retreating caravan. "That's something we're going to have to deal with soon."

"What?" Erick asked.

"None of us has our majority. We've been lucky that we haven't encountered any Royal Guardians who've asked to see travel documents. We need to do something about that. It would be a stupid thing to lose the world because you were sitting in the Queen's dungeon or they shipped you back to your burned down home."

"I reach my majority soon," Erick offered.

"How soon?" Marcus turned around and walked forward again.

Erick considered it and realized he didn't know the date. He knew it was early fall, likely the month of Krinnik. Other than that, he had no idea. He lost count of the days during the interminable travel through The Ruins. "I'm not sure. Less than a month, I think."

"When is your birthday?" Corby asked.

"Denech seventeen."

"Born in Denech." Corby smiled. "That makes sense. Your birthday is forty-four days away. Today is Krinnik thirteen."

"How do you know that?" Erick asked.

Corby pointed at his head. "I have keystone events each day. By remembering them backward, I can tell how many days have passed."

As it always did, Corby's intelligence amazed Erick. *He should have been the Necromancer,* he thought wryly. *This would all be over by now.*

"Not soon enough," Marcus said. "We're walking across the monarchy on one of the main roads. We're going to encounter patrols. We need to come up with forged documents for at least you, Erick. Elissia might be able to pass, but not the rest of us."

"I'm the same age as you," Elissia protested.

"Yeah, but you were lucky enough to grow. I keep waiting to jump up five inches and sprout face hair."

"It's not as fun as you might think." Erick rubbed the itchy patches of stubble on his face. As much as anything, he wanted a bath and a chance to use a razor.

They drew closer to the city. Much like when he arrived by sea at

Kalador, his first large city, the smells overwhelmed Erick. He found all of them unpleasant. The first thing he caught was a mixture of burning wood and urine.

"They have a tannery," Marcus said.

"Yes, they do," Elissia agreed. "So glad it's not summer."

"Where would we find the apothecary?" Gabrielle asked.

"If they have a market district," Corby said, "it will most likely be there."

"We could ask someone where it is," Elissia said.

"I should stay behind again, shouldn't I?" Blink said.

Erick sighed. "Probably." He didn't like it, but Blink's appearance caused them too much trouble in the past to take a chance.

They eventually reached a fork in the road and a sign with an arrow pointing west and another north. The western arrow read, "Kalawen," and the northern proclaimed "Kalasan."

Where the road forked, the city began. A ramshackle building of packed clay with a thatched roof came right up to the road. More such buildings, most in poor repair, lined the streets on the inner areas of the fork. On the outer edges, there was no construction, only grassland. It was as if the roads were dams that kept the city from overflowing its banks.

"What the hell?" Marcus asked. "Who builds a city on only one side of a road?"

"It's political," Corby said. "These roads form the border for the three bercs. Dorfork belongs to Dorberc, hence the name. The other two bercs value the land too much to let the city build on it."

Marcus stared around at the empty land on either side of the roads that made up the fork. "Value it? They're not doing a damn thing with it. Why not sell it to Dorberc and make use of that money? Or lease the land and collect taxes?"

Corby shrugged. "I just know the reasons; I don't make them up."

Marcus shook his head. "For such a practical people, Zakerins can be stupid sometimes."

"You're half Zakerin," Corby reminded him.

"And I've been known to do stupid things occasionally."

They followed the road into the city. Noise and people assailed them as they entered the lower-class section of the town. Children dressed in rags came up to them begging for money.

"Do we look like we have any money?" Marcus snarled, indicating his dirty, travel-worn clothing. The children ran away after one offered an obscene gesture.

They passed more downtrodden houses. A few women gave them desultory gazes. As they rode by pits full of offal, Erick wondered how anyone could live in a city with such smells for any length of time. Already light-headed from fatigue, the odors dizzied him.

"Do we have a chapter here?" Elissia asked her brother.

"We do," Marcus answered. "And I imagine word about us has reached here, so we need to be wary. Undead and Eligos aren't the only things that can hurt us."

Great, Erick thought, *because I don't already have enough to worry me.*

They passed the tannery, a large open-air building where men dipped hides into foul-smelling vats, while apprentices plucked feathers and scraped fine down from bloody ostrich skins. Not a soul working there looked happy.

Next to that, men poured large barrels of water into troughs. Others worked the tanned leather, using the water and dyes to color the skins.

They passed other industries. A charcoalier had a vast space where he and his apprentices turned wood to coal. A blacksmith hammered metal while men Erick's age and younger stoked amazingly hot fires to melt ingots. None of them wore shirts. To a man, they were thin and muscular.

"Maybe we should talk to some of them and see if they want to join us, as long as they keep their shirts off." Marcus hit Corby in the shoulder and pointed. "What do you think?"

Corby blushed and refused to look. "I think we're fine with the people we have."

"I agree," Gabrielle said, a frown on her tan face.

A slaughter yard full of ostriches, cattle, and sheep reminded Erick of Kalador, where he had reanimated the carcasses of pigs to save Marcus from hanging. The racket of dying animals sounded from the building at the back of the yard. Though his manor had been a working farm tended by undead servants, Erick had never considered how much went into keeping a city running.

Not soon enough for Erick, they left behind the more odoriferous part of the city. The buildings changed from clay to wood. People's clothing, though still modest and mostly bland colors, showed better care. Two large structures caught Erick's attention. They were the tallest buildings he had ever seen, one at least thirty feet tall and the other not much shorter. The lower portion of the first building was open to the air, supported by wooden columns. Wagons of various sizes and shapes sat on display. A sign attached to the wall declared it "Kylesun Wagoners."

"That would be the way to travel," Elissia said. "Certainly better than riding this mule."

"At least you're not walking," Marcus said with a grin.

The other building was closed on all sides except for a set of large open double doors. The pleasant scent of hay and horses came from the open doorway, the first enjoyable smells Erick had found in the city. The sign above it read "Carette Ostlers," obviously created by the same maker of the wagoner's sign.

"That's a perfect symbiosis," Corby observed.

"A what?" Erick asked.

"Symbiosis. It's when one organism helps another to their mutual benefit. Wagons need horses, and people buying horses might also want a wagon. Smart business."

Elissia rolled her eyes. "Excuse me," she said to a dark-haired woman wearing simple homespun and carrying a wooden bucket of water in each hand. "Where is the apothecary?"

"North," the woman said without stopping. "End of town."

"At least we're going the right way," Marcus said.

"Then let's go there," Erick said. He wanted to get Elissia healed. Then he wanted to sleep a day and a night before they did anything else.

After another five minutes, they spotted a merchant pushing a cart with meat pies. Erick's mouth watered but food would have to wait. "Can you tell us how to get to the apothecary?"

"It's at the end of Merchant's Way, next to the barber," the grizzled man said. His ragged brown hair gave the impression he knew the barber only in passing. "Merchant's Way is three streets down and turn left. Go to the end, and you'll see them."

"Thank you," Erick said.

They continued moving through the street, which had grown crowded in the midday hour.

Corby pointed. "There's the barber pole."

Erick saw it through the crowd, a tall, thin wooden pole with a thick ribbon of brown hair hanging from the top. Beside it, he saw a juniper bush in a large clay pot. "Is that a symbol for an apothecary?"

"It is," Gabrielle said.

Erick almost cried. They had reached what they needed. Elissia would get cured, they would sleep, and then he could consider the next part of the journey.

As they drew close to the apothecary, five men walked out the door. Erick's senses went into alert. He had learned to recognize thugs, and these leather-clad, short sword-wielding men fit the description.

They spread out in front of the door, hands on swords. Erick had the brief hope they were guards for a merchant or noble patronizing the store.

The appearance of Keven and the Sterran warrior walking out behind the other men dashed such dreams.

"You didn't want to come in here, did you?" Keven asked, a malicious grin on his scarred face.

13

We boarded the ship, thinking it was abandoned and easy pickings. Then the undead poured out of the hold. There was nothing we could do. It took at least five of us hacking with all our might to stop even one of them. Most of the crew was dead before some of us were able to escape. We were thankful they didn't try to board us, seeming content that they repelled us from their craft.

-Privateer Belindin Reacj, quoted in *Stories from the Second Inconnu War*

Both Keven and the other man looked the worse for last night's encounter. Craters of tattered flesh pocked their faces and arms. A few off-white blisters stood out on Keven's neck. His eyes appeared puffy and bloodshot, and his jagged facial scar gleamed an angry red.

Erick's shock at finding them here disappeared when he remembered they had ridden horses. More important was, how had they known Erick's destination? Marcus's *morazol* would lead them to the thief's current location. It didn't give the foresight to know where Marcus would travel. What brought them here?

Eligos, Blink thought to him. *They told him what happened, and he correctly guessed what we would do.*

Erick then saw the new mark on Keven's cheek. The symbol of Eligos. Did the Master already have a new *talba*? Had killing him been nothing but a minor inconvenience? Erick wanted to scream. His head throbbed. "Let us pass."

"I don't think so," Keven said, his voice ragged. Erick remembered the blood pouring from the other man's nose and mouth. Had his throat been damaged? "They're closed for business today."

Erick's companions had taken up positions behind him, ready to defend themselves. The market crowd, perhaps sensing the tension as the two groups glared at each other, found better things to do on the other side of the street. "And if we decide to come in anyway?"

"Then, these men will kill your friends, and we'll take you to our master." He grinned, his scarred face hideous. "Of course, you can come with us, and we'll all go peacefully. Like you could have last night."

"Or I can finish you off like I could have last night," Elissia said.

Keven's eyes narrowed in wariness, and he didn't look as sure of himself.

The pale-skinned bandit wasn't as impressed. "If you could have, you would have. Give us the Necromancer and the pet, and you are free to go."

There's that word again, Blink thought as he fluttered his wings in agitation. He hated being called a pet.

"First, you wanted Erick, and now you want them both?" Elissia smiled as she pulled her dagger. "I don't think so."

Erick's skin tightened, and his head cleared as violence became inevitable. He couldn't give himself up, not even to save his friends. Last night's indecision disappeared. He would fight and die rather than surrender. He had been ready to sacrifice himself in the ritual to destroy Eligos; now, he would die to thwart him if necessary.

Gabrielle, a healer, wouldn't fight, so it was seven to five. Knowing how his companions performed in combat gave Erick some confidence in the odds, although he didn't know how well Keven's cohorts fought. That they looked ragged didn't mean they weren't proficient with their weapons. The thought of losing even one of his group made his chest hurt; the thought of failing in his mission pained him even more.

Marcus rubbed his hands together in nervous agitation. "You're not going to give yourself up, are you?" he asked Erick.

"I'm not."

The thief glanced up and down the now almost deserted street, his eyes narrowed. "Never thought I'd wish to see the city guard."

Keven grinned. "The city guard has been persuaded to stay away for an hour or so."

All of Marcus's nervousness vanished, and he offered his lopsided smile. "Have they? Glad to hear that." He let out a low five-note whistle.

Like ants boiling out of a disturbed hill, people emerged from the alleys between the buildings, each brandishing a knife. Some wore tattered clothing, like beggars, and others wore the workaday garb of laborers or merchants. With a range from Erick's age to several years younger, they all shared the grace and fluidity Erick had come to associate with members of the Procurer's Guild.

The warriors backed up in surprise. Their hands dropped to their blades.

"I wouldn't do that," one of the Procurers said. Tall and long-limbed, with hair the color of beach sand, he flipped a jeweled dagger from hand to hand. Erick recognized him as Callon, one of the thieves that helped them escape Elissia's father. "I can put this through your eye, and half of my companions can do the same."

Callon had at least twenty "companions." They all stared at Keven and his henchmen with deadly grim faces.

"Good to see you again, Marcus," Callon said without turning his attention from the fighters in front of the apothecary. "You too, Elissia."

"Yeah," Elissia said. Erick could tell this turn astounded her as much as it did him. Her gaze went to Marcus. "Can't wait to hear how this happened."

"Later," Marcus told her. "Right now, why don't we get inside? Gabrielle can find your antidote, and we can chat with our new friends."

~

K even stared at the unfriendly faces glaring at him. It felt as if
every weapon pointed toward his heart. How had this all
turned so quickly?

The pain from last night's attack had been almost unbearable. He
had wanted to crawl into a hole and die. NalTalva wouldn't allow it,
forcing them to ride until they returned to the unnamed town. Only
there did he stop and take time to examine the extent of their damage.
Painful as the injuries were, they had not been as bad as Keven feared.
Water washed away the pus and blood but left behind deep scars of
red flesh. His throat felt raw as a scraped knee, and it hurt to gargle
away the blood. The air pressed like teeth against his injured face. He
might want to die, but it seemed he wouldn't. Not yet.

When they had tended their injuries as best they could, NalTalva
put his finger against one of the broken spots on his arm. When he
pulled it away, a smudge of blood covered his fingertip. He placed this
against the mark on his cheek. *"Enay, solpeth ol."*

Keven found that, unlike before, he understood the warrior's
words. *Master, hear me.*

And in his mind, faint as a whispered dream, came the master's
response.

Speak, for soon I will not hear. The distance is great.

NalTalva told their master how they failed in the Necromancer's
capture. Rather than anger, a faint sense of pleasure came across
Keven's mind. *Then my brother is returned.*

Eligos told them what to do and where to go. They need not hunt
for Erick and his companions. The Necromancer would foolishly
walk right into a trap.

Yet somehow, he and NalTalva had been the ones ensnared. How
was that possible? Eligos was supposed to protect them. He was
supposed to be better than the god Keven abandoned.

Keven touched a sore on his face, wincing at the pain. He placed
the blood against the mark on his cheek. *"Enay, solpeth ol."*

He got no response. Either the master was too far away, or Keven
didn't have the same gifts as NalTalva.

Erick pointed a finger at Keven. "Don't speak another word in that language, or I'll have them kill you where you stand."

The chill in Erick's voice unnerved Keven. He stepped back, cowed again by the Necromancer. Keven told himself it wasn't Erick; it was the score of thieves at his back. Anyone could be brave when they outnumbered someone.

Keven saw no way out of this trap. Though he could fight, he had little training as a swordsman. NalTalva could be the second coming of Myrmidon Agatar himself and still not best so many opponents, even with the help of five hired thugs.

"You heard the man," the tall, blond one named Callon said, his arms thrown wide as if hugging his opponents. "Get inside the apothecary. But first, leave your weapons out here. *All* your weapons."

Keven placed his sword on the ground. He had no other weapon. NalTalva put a sword and knife down, and the other men also relinquished their swords. Two also surrendered hidden daggers.

"Very good. In we go."

Keven didn't want to return inside. The small building stank of plants and potions. They had been destroying the apothecary's inventory when the others arrived. Shattered glass, ripped cloth packets, and shredded greens littered the floor. The owner of the shop had protested the destruction until NalTalva silenced her with a knife across her throat.

"Against those shelves, all of you." Callon pointed with his dagger. Keven pressed against the shelves, NalTalva beside him. The bottles they hadn't destroyed rattled.

"What are we—" Keven started to whisper.

"None of that," one of their captors said, stepping up to him. She couldn't have been more than twelve. Keven would have laughed if she didn't have a knife pressed against his stomach.

Erick, Elissia, and the others walked through the doorway, followed by ten more of the thieves. Before the door closed, Keven saw the others collecting the discarded weapons.

The rest spread out in the shop between the cramped shelves. Close to panic, Keven hoped they didn't explore too deeply. That they didn't find the small storage space. He glanced at NalTalva. The pale warrior remained stoic. Keven wished he could be as calm as the man appeared.

Erick's companion, a plain-faced girl with brown hair that Keven didn't know, studied the destruction, her eyes glistening and mouth quivering. "I don't know if the antidote will be here. Even if they had it, it might have been destroyed."

Another of the thieves said, "Magary labels everything except the special things she makes us. What are we looking for?"

"It's called Calea's Comfort. It's dark green and smells of orange and rose."

Five of the thieves searched among the shelves and floor. *As long as they don't go behind the long wooden counter and open the door back there,* Keven thought, *we might get out of this.*

Callon turned to Marcus. "What do you want to do with them?"

Marcus hiked a thumb at Erick. "That's his decision."

Erick walked over and stood in front of Keven and NalTalva. Nothing but hate shone from the Necromancer's blue eyes, set deep in his dirty, haggard face. Those deadly eyes turned to NalTalva. "What's your name?"

The warrior didn't answer.

"What's your name?" Erick repeated.

The Sterran remained silent.

Erick shrugged. "I don't guess it matters. Kill them."

A collective gasp rose behind Erick. He didn't care. His compassion had reached an end. Concern about the lives of anyone other than his friends had brought him nothing but misery. The nameless man killed a town of two hundred people. Keven helped him. Another town had been destroyed by Eligos, residing in the body of a man Erick let live. The concept of mercy to his enemies no longer appealed to Erick.

"That seems harsh for this," Callon waved a hand to indicate the store. "We're not in the habit of killing people if we don't have to."

"They've done far worse than this," Erick said. He didn't take his eyes off the two men. Keven's eyes widened, and his body trembled at Erick's pronouncement. That pleased him.

"Yes, they have," Elissia said. "But they're killers. We aren't."

Erick turned toward Elissia, incredulous. "What do you mean? You've killed." His gaze took in his other companions. "All of you have, except Gabrielle."

Corby blanched at Erick's words, while Marcus returned his stare without expression.

Elissia, however, glared at him. Her eyes filled with angry fire. This was no otherworldly entity's wrath. This was all her and all aimed at him. "Yes, we have. We've killed to protect ourselves. To protect *you*. We've killed because you can't. And any of us would do it again. But we don't kill people who aren't trying to kill us."

"They killed Draymed. Killed your aunt and uncle. Corby's parents. This is the man from my vision."

Elissia started, and the pinched grimace on Corby's round face made Erick think his friend might vomit.

Elissia regained her composure. She swallowed and, voice strained, said, "And they should hang for that. But that's for the Queen's *Jurleit* or his subordinates to decide, not us."

Her attitude baffled Erick. Out of anyone who would argue leniency, he would never have expected it from Elissia.

The anger in her face disappeared like a snuffed candle flame. Her eyes went soft; her teeth bit her lower lip. She took Erick's hands and led him away from the others. Marcus stepped into his place, dagger ready.

His hands in hers, she looked up at him and spoke so no one else could hear them. "Why can't you kill?"

"You know why."

"Tell me again. And think about it as you explain it."

He sighed. "The Covenant forbids it because it will open me to *elonsha* and make it easier for it to corrupt me when I use it."

"Ordering people killed is no different."

"Yes, it is. If I don't do the killing, I'm not in danger."

She shook her head. "You're wrong. It may not corrupt your soul, but it will eat at your mind. None of us want to kill. It haunts Corby's nights, though he would never tell you. Sometimes in my dreams, those I've killed talk to me. Keven and this other man have done horrible things. They—"

"If I had told Blink to kill that man, Draymed would still exist. Your aunt and uncle would still be alive. If I killed that other man, Mar—"

"But you didn't," Elissia said, her voice fierce. "Because you have compassion. You care. I wouldn't change that about you."

"Compassion is useless."

"It's not," Elissia said, some of her anger returning. "You're trying to save this world. If there were no compassion in it, it wouldn't be worth saving." She pointed at Keven and the other. "I don't want you to become them."

"I would never become them."

"Are you sure? Once it becomes easy to order two people killed, how much harder is it to order ten? A hundred? If you don't have to do it yourself, it's just words."

Erick dropped his head. Ordering the two killed without a chance to repent might condemn them to the Festering Hells. Although they deserved such a fate for what they had done, it wasn't Erick's place to send them. "You're right."

"I found it," a chipper young voice said. One of the boys held up a dark blue bottle sealed with a cork, one side covered with a small white label.

Gabrielle walked over and took the bottle. She examined it a moment and then nodded.

"Thank Caros," Erick said.

Gabrielle almost ran over to them, bottle clutched to her chest. Her usually calm face flushed with excitement. She handed the bottle to Elissia. "Drink this and it will destroy the poison."

E lissia took the bottle and stared at the blue glass. "Are you sure this will work?"

"Positive," Gabrielle said.

It will kill you, the voice inside her said.

She frowned.

It was the same voice that made her try to stab herself. The dripping, thick sound in her mind made her want to claw out her brain.

She read the label—*Calea's Comfort*, written in small, precise letters of black ink. A thin band of white wax held the cork in place.

"What's wrong?" Erick asked.

"Nothing." She broke the seal and pulled the cork. As Gabrielle had told them, Elissia caught a strong scent of oranges with an undercurrent of rose petals. The combination made her stomach gurgle, and she winced.

It will kill you, the voice repeated.

Her skin crawled. The voice brought to mind every time she had been ill. Every fever and bout of flux rode on the words.

That's what you want, isn't it? she thought; the idea of conversing with the thing inside her made her want to retch.

Yes. Kill yourself and free me.

Something wasn't right.

Many things weren't right, starting with the visions of maggots that tried to cloud her thinking. Something was off about the voice. Elissia had spent her life dealing with duplicitous people driven by selfish motivation, her father foremost among them. If the vile creature inside her wanted her dead so it could break free, why warn her? If the potion would kill her, all it had to do was wait until she drank it.

Which meant it was lying. Or trying to make her think it was lying.

"Drink it," Erick said, hands clasped together. Concern radiated from every line in his body.

"I'm—" she paused. The thing inside her shared her mind and had tried to control her. She had managed it for a time. Had made it do her will and fought it when it wanted to bend her to its purpose. She was its equal. Perhaps she could read its mind. *Are you lying?*

No.

It was. Before it could hide the truth, she saw it. Drinking the potion would not kill her. It would destroy the creature within her.

She downed the elixir.

No sooner had it hit her stomach than incredible pain struck her as if someone slammed a mallet into her torso. She doubled over and collapsed.

Voices spoke around her. She had no time for them. Heat radiated through her limbs, and fire boiled her blood. Her teeth clenched. She wanted to scream but her mouth wouldn't open.

Noooo, the voice slurred, thick and dark as tar.

Another sensation followed. It started in her stomach and spread from there like cold water on a burn. Relief encompassed her, as if a fever that plagued her had broken and been cured within seconds, all sickness purged from her system.

It left her exhausted yet deliriously happy. She hadn't realized how ill she had been until she became well. And she felt no presence of the putrescent being within her.

"Elissia?" Erick asked.

"I'm all right," she croaked, laying on the floor. It was the truth. She gave Erick a genuine smile of joy. "I'm cured."

Erick's face split in a wide grin. Marcus, hovering behind him, also smiled.

Elissia sat up. The energy flowing through her made her feel like a new woman.

As Erick helped Elissia stand, he wanted to dance with joy. The deep olive color had returned to her skin, no longer tainted by the sickly pallor. Her blue eyes were bright, alert. She was cured.

Things suddenly seemed more possible to Erick. He would ask the Procurers to detain Keven and the other man or see them in prison for their crimes. Then he and his companions could be on their way without fear of another ambush. Erick still had plenty to concern him, but he could take one of his worries off the list.

"Dirty bastards," a strangled voice shouted from some unseen place. Erick saw Keven flinch.

A young man, close to Corby's age, emerged from a spot hidden by a wall next to a waist-high counter. He glared at the two men against the shelves. "They killed Magary."

Every Procurer in the room regarded the captives; their expressions ranged from unfriendly to murderous.

Callon's angular face was in the latter camp. "That changes things. Magary was under our protection. Looks like you're going to get your wish, Erick." He pressed his dagger against Keven's throat, who released a terrified squeal.

"Wait," Erick said. An idea struck him like a bolt of divine inspiration. For all he knew, it *had* come from the Gods. It made perfect sense. "Do you have any poison?"

"Poison?" Elissia asked. "Why do you want poison?"

A noise at the door drew everyone's attention. A female Procurer with curly auburn hair stepped inside. "City Guard."

"Help!" Keven shouted.

Erick jumped at the unexpected noise.

Callon's reaction was more practical. He lashed out with a fist and hit Keven in the jaw. His scarred face rocked back and slammed against the shelf. He slid to the floor, dazed.

Callon shook his hand and looked toward the door. "How many and do we know them?"

"Four," the Procurer answered. "The leader is Gwennon."

Callon winced. "He's expensive. Tell him to give us five minutes. And let him know the body wasn't us."

With a nod, she left the building.

Callon offered the unnamed Sterran a bright grin. "You're not the only one who can persuade the City Guard. Procurers, let's hit the warren."

14

And so as mankind came to the power of fire, Caros asked who among his children would take dominion over this new discovery. Vidali offered to be its steward, much as Caros tried to dissuade him to not take these natural enemies on to himself. Vidali would not be gainsaid, and soon learned the price of ever warring with himself.

    -Excerpt from "On The Insane God" in *Tales of Ten Gods; a History of Religion in Krinnik*

Two hours later, Erick and his companions had bathed and received new clothing, most of it as close to black as it could be without violating the law. Erick had managed a shave with actual cream, scented with lilac and honey. It was the best thing he had smelled since arriving in Dorfork. Relieved of wearing his chain mail for the moment, he felt light enough to float.

He almost couldn't recognize his friends, cleaned of all the grime. Elissia's gleaming black hair hung down to the middle of her waist, and her face shone. Corby's hair had been returned to its scholar's cut, shaved on the sides with a top fringe like a thatch of brown weeds. He had not managed to find any sandalwood oil for it. His apprentice's ruby, which had been dulled by dirt, gleamed red against his left earlobe.

Now Erick sat with all his traveling companions and Callon in a small room in the Procurer's warren. Like the burrow in Kalador, this one was hidden inside a sewer and accessed through a secret door. Though not as luxuriously appointed as the one in the larger city, it was comfortable enough. Far cozier than any structure underground had a right to be. They rested on soft cushions while two of the younger Procurers, a boy and a girl, placed bowls of beef and barley soup in front of them. The warm, salty smell made Erick's mouth water.

Once the two servers had placed bread and glasses of ale, they departed. Erick picked up the ale and downed a healthy gulp.

"Are you sure this is what you want to do?" Elissia asked.

Erick sat down the mug and took a spoonful of soup before he answered. He had explained to them all why he wanted the poison before Elissia and Gabrielle left for their bathing chamber, and spoken more with the others while they bathed in a separate room.

"It makes the most sense," Erick said. "We can't leave them alive. I don't know how powerful their mental communication with Eligos is. They might be able to speak to him and arrange a rescue wherever we put them. For all I know, they've already done it. You said we need extra guards with us for traveling. This takes care of both problems. And it serves as punishment for what they did. Especially to you two." This last, he offered to Elissia and Corby.

"It does fix a lot," Elissia said, though her hesitancy told Erick she wasn't convinced. "It's just..."

"It's the perfect solution," Corby said. He ran a hand through his hair, a habit he stopped while it had been dirty and shapeless. "Killing them outright serves no purpose and wastes resources."

"Resources?" Gabrielle sat up with her hands clenched. She hadn't touched her soup. "They're human beings."

"Barely, based on the things they've done," Marcus said. "It puts them to good use for once."

Gabrielle turned to Erick. "I thought you couldn't kill anyone."

"I wouldn't kill them." His eyes went to Callon.

"Happy to," the blond thief said as he tore his bread in two. "They killed Magary. She was a good source for things we need." At Gabrielle's horrified stare, he added, "Herbs for our healer, and soporifics to knock people out. She was also a kind person and didn't deserve that fate."

"And you can get poisons," Erick said, confirming what Callon said in the bath.

"We can. We don't use them ourselves, but we know people who do."

Erick nodded, then took Elissia's hand. "I want us all to agree to this. If there's something else you want to do, say so."

Elissia bit her bottom lip as she stared at those around her. Finally, her blue eyes settled on Erick. "You're not the same person who complained when I took the money from those bodies on the road."

"No, I'm not," Erick agreed. "The world is a much darker and more vicious place than I ever imagined."

~

E lissia flinched at the despair in Erick's words. She didn't want the world's savagery to rub off on him. His naivete had once driven her crazy. Now she wished he still had some.

The damnable part of it was that they were all right. Keven and the Sterran, whose name they didn't know, deserved to die. They deserved to die hideously, but she hated the thought of Erick as executioner, even by proxy. Some instinct warned that if he did this in cold blood, something in him would change irrevocably. Some part of his soul would be forever blackened. "And you're sure giving the order to kill isn't the same as killing them yourself? It won't violate your Covenant?"

Erick frowned. "The Gods seem to think the Covenant is flexible, so I'm willing to take the chance. They can't be allowed to live."

"Why are you so against this, 'Lissi?" Marcus asked.

"Because she's a decent person," Gabrielle said.

Marcus rounded on her. "So am I. Decent doesn't mean stupid. I'm not even sure why this is a debate."

"It's the lives of two people." Gabrielle's face reddened, and she looked close to crying.

"Two murderers."

"I can easily settle this for you," Callon said in a calm voice.

They all turned to regard him.

"Those two killed one of the people under the Procurers' protection. That makes their lives forfeit under our laws. You know this, Elissia. All we're deciding now is how they die."

"Then why in the hells didn't you say so?" Marcus asked.

"It seemed important to Elissia to get out her objections. She always had more conscience than was good for her." Callon turned to her and shrugged. "You did."

Heat suffused Elissia's cheeks, and she hated that she was blushing. With irritation, not embarrassment. "Sorry I didn't want to be a plaything for lecherous old men. Or open my legs for any of you."

Callon waved a dismissive, long-fingered hand. "I'm not talking about that. They shouldn't have forced you into the teachings of Amare. Nor should you be forced to bed with anyone you didn't want."

"Thank you," she said stiffly.

"What you shouldn't have done," Callon continued, "was betray the Procurers. You shouldn't have told the priests of Amare everything you knew. No matter how much you hated Torin, you should have thought about what your actions would do to the rest of us."

Elissia bowed her head. After her father banished her, she thought only of her pain. She never considered how what she did affected anyone else—affected her brother. In many ways, she was as selfish as the father she hated.

"I'm sorry," she said.

Callon shrugged. "Three years heals a lot. Most of us forgave you for Marcus's sake. Many understood why you did it, even if they didn't agree. It's past. Now, we move on."

Elissia nodded. She didn't know if she deserved such easy forgiveness. She could only accept it and vow to do better.

Marcus picked up a piece of bread and broke it in half. "Speaking of moving, how did you end up here?"

"And how did you know where we were going to be?" Elissia added.

"Second question is easier. Marcus saw one of ours and signaled for us to follow."

That surprised Elissia. Marcus had seen a Procurer, and she hadn't? She gave him a questioning look, and he replied with the hand signal for "later."

"As for coming here, the skirmish in the warehouse botched things for several days. Those of us who helped scattered to the boltholes. Unfortunately, several spots were compromised by whips loyal to Torin. Darius waged a holy war against us. You would have thought we killed his mother and skinned his cat."

"Father never had trouble inspiring loyalty," Elissia said. "It's love that caused him problems."

"Love is overrated," Callon said. "Anyway, after a week, they captured or killed seven of us. That's the ones I know for certain. I gathered those I could find and fled for a friendlier home, which we found here. After we convinced Mundar we weren't here to absorb them into Kalador, they accepted us readily enough. I want to think we've shown him he didn't make a mistake."

"How many escaped with you?" Elissia asked.

"Eight."

"Did Calligan make it?" Marcus asked.

The pain in Callon's face told Elissia everything, but he answered anyway. "I wasn't there to see it, but I heard they killed him in the common. The man with the priest cut his throat."

"Son of a bitch," Marcus said.

Moisture gathered in Elissia's eyes. "Another mark on father's ledger."

"I'm sorry I brought all this down on you," Erick said. Elissia noticed he touched little of his meal. "Death follows me everywhere."

And you're about to make more. She gasped in horror that she would have such a thought. Erick was right about the need to rid themselves of Keven and the other man. They were all right. So why couldn't she accept it?

Erick stared at her. "Are you okay?"

She nodded, afraid to speak.

~

E rick watched Elissia, her eyes wet, a hand to her mouth. *She still thinks it's wrong,* he thought.

Perhaps, Blink thought. *But it's the best option.*

It is. Then why did it feel like he was doing the wrong thing?

They finished their meal with Callon and Marcus talking about how the Procurers assimilated with their new warren. Erick ate, though the meal went down grudgingly. His stomach knotted at the thought of what he must do. Should he leave them alive and—

Stop second-guessing yourself, Blink told him. *Do it and accept the consequences.*

After he finished eating, Erick reached out and took Elissia's hand. She gripped his. Though she smiled, Erick saw the haunted gleam in her eyes. He wished he had a mental connection with her, so he could make her see things from his viewpoint.

She leaned over and rested her head against his shoulder. Lilac perfumed her hair. A thrill drifted through Erick.

She put her lips against his ear. "I understand," she whispered. "I just wish there was some other way."

He turned to whisper "thank you" when their lips met. Erick forgot everything. The sensation dizzied him. It again hit him how much he loved her and would do anything to keep her from harm. It pained him how much he kept failing.

A loud throat-clearing from Callon interrupted their kiss. Everyone stared at them, a smug grin on Callon's face. For a moment, Erick hated the blond-haired thief.

"It seems everyone has finished eating," Callon said. "You ready to take care of this?"

15

One of the many misconceptions about Necromancers, no doubt perpetuated by certain factions with animus toward them, is that they drain the blood of innocents to use in their Rituals. This is patently false. They use either their blood or the blood of those in their immediate family.

-Corberin of Draymed, *On the Necromancer's Art*

They stood and followed Callon from the small chamber. A few turns through lantern-lit hallways brought them to another doorway. Callon opened it and escorted them inside.

Once they stepped in, he said, "I'll be right back." He closed the door, leaving the group alone.

The room stood twenty feet to a side, carved from the soil and supported by thick roof timbers and columns eight feet apart and along the walls. Lanterns on the columns illuminated the room in pools of light. Unlike the other chambers Erick had seen, this one was unfinished, the ragged earthen walls lacking brick and mortar. A damp, loamy smell permeated the room.

The closeness of the ceiling pressed on Erick. The whole space had the feel of a cold grave. Considering what was about to happen, it seemed fitting.

As they stepped into the center of the room, Erick saw Keven and the Sterran against the far wall. They sat in wooden chairs, their hands and legs tied with thick rope, mouths bound with strips of burlap. Keven's eyes darted from person to person, sweat gathered on his brow. He tried to speak but only produced muffled sounds. The Sterran's dark eyes had locked on, of all people, Blink. He tracked the homunculus as if Blink were a worm and he was a bird.

"Cheery in here, isn't it?" Marcus said.

"Hardly," Corby muttered.

"It shouldn't be," Gabrielle said. "There has to be—"

Erick cut her off. "There isn't. They don't deserve any better for their crimes. The Procurers were going to execute them anyway. This way, at least they'll serve some purpose."

Gabrielle didn't respond. Her eyes went dark, and she frowned.

Elissia squeezed his hand and gave him a soft smile.

Conversation lagged, and the group stood uncomfortably, waiting. Keven continued to make muted sounds that grew louder and more insistent.

"Shut up," Erick finally shouted at him.

Keven's head jerked back and his eyes widened.

The door opened, and Callon stepped into the room. "Everything okay?"

"Upright as a coin on edge," Marcus said.

Another man trailed behind Callon. Tall and slender, he had a nose thin as an ax head and ears that protruded from under his short black hair. He wore a snug gray shirt with short sleeves and tight blue pants. They walked to the center of the room where the others stood.

"Mundar," Callon said, "this is Erick, the man I told you about. Erick, this is Mundar, the leader of the Dorfork Procurers."

Mundar offered a thin, long-fingered hand on which he wore a thick gold band set with a gleaming emerald. "Kiss the ring," he said.

Erick hesitated. Was this a joke? Did this man think of himself as royalty? Erick glanced at Callon, who gave no indication. "No offense," Erick said, "but I'd rather not."

Mundar dropped his hand. "Well, that's disappointing." He eyed Callon. "It never really does work, does it?"

"Hasn't so far."

"You'd think a self-proclaimed King of the Thieves would get more respect from his subjects." He gave a dramatic sigh. "I'm destined to be under-appreciated in my own time." He glared at Erick. "Why are you here?"

The sudden question startled Erick. "I'm...we..."

A smile broke so wide on the man's narrow face that it looked in danger of swallowing his nose. "Relax, I'm jingling your bells. Life is way too serious to take at all seriously. Welcome, all of you, to our warren. Sorry the circumstances are what they are, but that can't be helped. We make the best of what we get."

Erick found himself already liking the tall man. Though he held the same status as Torin, Mundar was as different from Elissia's father as a dog from a ghoul.

The two Procurers who had served them their meal entered the room, the boy carrying a tray laden with squat wooden mugs, the girl wielding a clay pitcher.

"Ah, here are Lila and Alon with refreshments. I trust the meal was adequate?"

"More than adequate," Erick answered. "We greatly appreciate that and the baths."

"I'm glad you are pleased with our hospitality. We should have a drink of ale, shouldn't we?"

Erick was about to wholeheartedly agree when Gabrielle stepped forward, hands clasped before her. "What are you doing?" she asked, her usually timid voice harsh and demanding. "You want to celebrate two men dying?"

Mundar's smile faltered but didn't entirely disappear. "That's not what we're celebrating. We'll get to them in due time. We're celebrating a meeting of new friends, and welcome to our house. Friends of Callon's are friends of ours. Is that not worth a toast?"

"I don't feel it's appropriate to do in front of them. Mockery of death offends the Gods."

Mundar's smile disappeared. "It's only inappropriate if you care what dead men think. They lost the privilege of having opinions when they killed Magary. And I mock nothing. Their death will receive the seriousness it deserves. I won't force you to join our toast, and you are still welcome. But I won't let the hurt feelings of dead men interfere." His smile returned. "Now, who will join me?"

All except Gabrielle stepped forward, their mood subdued.

"Excellent," Mundar said as he took the pitcher from the girl, deliberately turning his back to the two bound men. He poured the ale into the short cups. The nutty, yeasty smell filled Erick's nose. Mundar handed each filled cup out until all who wanted a vessel had one. He filled the last and held it toward Gabrielle, his smile returned.

"Procurers' warren, Procurers' ways," Marcus said, standing beside her.

Gabrielle's mouth formed a flat, grim line. "I'm not a Procurer anymore."

Mundar nodded and set the spare cup back on the tray. "As you say." He lifted his cup and held it at chest height. "Welcome, friends, to my warren. Consider it your home for as long as you need it. Our food is your food; our drink is your drink; our hearth is your hearth. Or would be, if we had any hearths." He winked at Erick, who found himself grinning at the man's friendliness, even as Gabrielle's discontent weighed on him.

"I drink to your good fortune," Mundar continued. "May the pockets you pick be deep and full."

He drank, and the others followed. As he always did, Erick enjoyed the earthy liquid. This was cold and smooth. He hated there was so little when he finished in three gulps.

The young thieves who served them gathered the mugs and left.

Mundar wiped his mouth with his gray sleeve. "Now we can get serious, as the healer wishes." He offered a nod to Gabrielle. She did not respond. "Callon, since we've finished with the drinks, you can go get what we need."

As Callon left, Mundar told Erick, "Didn't want there to be any mistakes."

Erick didn't quite understand what the man meant and decided it was probably better.

Mundar walked over to the two prisoners seated against the wall. The Sterran's eyes finally left Blink to focus on the Procurer leader. All smiles and any trace of friendliness left Mundar's face. The wiry muscles in his arms corded as tension played over his body.

"I'm going to remove your gags," he told the men. "Don't do anything annoying, like screaming or shouting. It won't do any good. No one who cares will hear you. All it will earn you is a sore mouth and maybe a few lost teeth when I punch you. So, I take off the gag, and you stay quiet. If you agree to the terms outlined, signify by a double nod of your head."

They both nodded, though the warrior hesitated slightly longer than Keven.

"Good." Mundar removed Keven's gag.

"Elissia, ple—"

The slap sounded dull in the chamber, any echo absorbed by the dirt walls. Keven's head rocked at the hit.

"And already we're in breach of agreement," Mundar said. "Quiet is defined as a lack of sound, which includes not talking."

Keven glared at the Procurer but said nothing more. He worked his jaw back and forth.

Mundar removed the Sterran's gag. The pale man licked his thin lips but made no noise.

"So, we see who the master is here," Mundar said. "I suspect you're the one who killed our dear friend, the apothecary. You have the muscled build and deadly gaze of a trained warrior." He turned to Keven. "You just look like a bully who would piss his pants at the first sign of any true resistance."

"That's pretty much him," Erick said, remembering their confrontation on the temple steps in Draymed.

"Yes, Callon mentioned some history between the two of you. Care to elaborate?"

"Keven hates me because I'm a Necromancer. The priest he followed preached against my family, so he learned to hate me before he knew me. He tried to push me around, but I wouldn't let him. So that made him hate me more."

"I hate you because you stole Elissia from me," Keven blurted, his face red.

Fast as a spider leaping upon an insect, Mundar wheeled around and slammed his fist against Keven's mouth. Keven's head thudded against the wall. Blood trickled from his split lip.

"Not the brightest candle, are you?" Mundar said.

Elissia walked over and looked at Keven. Erick didn't understand the pity on her face; it wrenched his heart, nonetheless.

"I was never yours for anyone to steal," she told Keven. "Why could you never see that?"

Keven opened his mouth, stopped, closed it, glared at Mundar.

Mundar shrugged. "Go ahead. But only as long as she's asking questions."

"Why wouldn't you be mine?" Keven asked. The anguish in his voice almost moved Erick to feel sorry for him. Almost. It wasn't enough to erase the death of over two hundred people. "I had everything. A good family, land, money. What more could you want?"

"The one thing you didn't have," Elissia said. "Personal qualities I could care about."

She pointed at Corby. "You and your friends constantly berated Corby, because you knew he wouldn't fight back. He could have, and he would have flattened your ass."

Keven cast a glare at the scholar, who flinched and pressed against Marcus.

"See? Even now, you can't look past your arrogance, your desire to place yourself over those you perceive as weaker. I already had that in a father. I wasn't going to accept it in a companion. Did you ever try to understand Corby? Or anyone who wasn't up to your presumed level?"

"What's there to understand?" Keven asked. "Corby is an affront to Caros, like his little friend Quinn, until he roasted in Draymed."

Corby gasped and pressed his head against Marcus's shoulder. He shook. Marcus hugged him.

Keven continued. "The things they did sickened us. When I heard his father telling Quinn's father what he had witnessed, I wanted to vomit. We're not the ones who deserve to die. He is."

"Excuse me," Marcus said in a soft voice. "I'll be right back."

He kissed Corby's tear-streaked cheek, then walked over to Keven, who stared at the small thief with undisguised disdain.

"You're talking about someone I care about very much," Marcus said. "You don't deserve to speak his name, much less belittle him." Marcus clenched his fists together tight and swung his arms like a club. The fists smashed into Keven's nose with a sharp crack. Keven grunted as blood squirted from his broken nose. Marcus stepped back and shook his hands.

"You must be the one who takes it like a girl," Keven grinned through the blood. "You hit like one."

"But I don't," Mundar said. His fist lashed out again, catching Keven across the jaw. He rocked sideways and almost fell over before the heavy wooden chair righted itself. "And I don't care if Marcus is a girl to every boy in the warren. He's a Procurer. We take care of our own. And we protect those they love."

Erick marveled at Mundar's words. Like the sudden under-standing of an elaborate Ritual, it came clear to him. The love between Corby and Marcus was no different than his love for Elissia. Emotionally, it all meant the same thing. It went beyond the physical and into the soul.

He saw in Marcus's defiance and the pride in Corby's wet eyes. No matter what people professed the Gods wanted, Erick had been wrong to question their love.

"Go back to Corby," Elissia told Marcus. "He needs you."

While her brother walked away, Elissia turned to stare at Keven. The pity returned to her eyes as her mouth pinched in the way Erick had come to associate with her anger. "I tried to say you shouldn't die; that it wasn't our place to do it. Now I see I was wrong. There's nothing left in you worth saving. And I suspect the same is true for your friend. It hasn't been nice knowing you. I can only hope you serve us better dead than you did alive."

"What are you talking about? What—" Keven stopped as Mundar brought his blood-speckled fist back up.

Elissia took Erick's hands. "Do what you have to do. I can't watch, though."

Erick nodded. She gave him a soft kiss and left the room.

As she walked out, Callon returned carrying a copper serving tray in one hand and a wooden stool in the other. "She looked upset," he remarked.

"Everyone is out of sorts," Mundar said. "It's been an emotional time."

Erick reflected with wry bitterness that Mundar didn't know the half of it.

Callon presented the tray to Erick. On it sat two blue vials with corks in their tops. Beside them, laid on a sheet of parchment, were the various herbs Erick would need for the two Rituals. "Is this everything?"

Erick surveyed the herbs. "That's them."

The thief set the stool down and placed the tray on top of it.

"Who do you want to start with?" Mundar asked.

"The warrior," Marcus said, his voice so pitiless Erick flinched. He again released Corby and returned to the men in the chairs. He pushed his finger against the scar on Keven's cheek. "I want this bastard to watch and see what waits for him."

"I like your style," Mundar said. "You should stay and work with us."

Marcus shook his head. "I've got places to go with Erick. Then we have our warren to steal from my father."

Mundar let out a boisterous laugh, a deep sound from a slim body. "Good for you. Glad I've never made you mad. Okay, we start with the Sterran."

He turned his attention to Gabrielle. "You may wish to leave, too."

"I will witness in the name of Calea."

Mundar shrugged, picked up one of the vials, and removed the stopper. A bitter lemony smell caught Erick and he winced. The thief stood in front of the fighter. "You wish to do this honorably or do we have to make a spectacle of it?"

"I cannot die honorably," the man said. "That creature dishonored me when he felled me from behind. Coward." He spat on the floor.

"What would satisfy your honor?"

"For the creature to wound himself and spread his blood upon my face so that I may go to Sangara with my enemy's blood on me."

"You Sterrans are a strange lot," Mundar said. He glanced at Erick. "Will you allow that?"

"I will not," Erick answered. "He lost all honor when he killed two hundred innocent people in my town. Besides, he won't be seeing Sangara for a long time."

"Wha—" the warrior started. With astounding speed, Mundar upended the vial and dumped the contents into the man's opening mouth. The warrior clamped his mouth shut, shattering the vial between his teeth.

The Sterran tried to spit and only succeeded in getting the barest amount of saliva from his mouth. Blood dripped from his lips where the glass cut him.

"Any last words?" Mundar said.

"May Eligos curse you all."

Marcus strode forward and pointed at his forehead. "He has."

The Sterran smiled. "Then you are already doomed." He coughed.

They all watched as the poison worked its evil. The warrior coughed two more times. Then his muscles locked. His jaw clenched, and Erick thought the teeth might crack. The warrior shook. The chair made vibrato *tock* sounds against the floor. A spume of foam and blood poured from his lips. His bowels loosened.

Gabrielle fled, choking sobs following her. Mundar noted her departure with a wry smile. Marcus and Corby looked away, arms over each other's shoulders.

Erick forced himself to watch. This man was dying at his demand, just as Keven would shortly. Erick owed them nothing, but he owed it to himself to witness the consequences of his actions.

Less than a minute later, the Sterran exhaled one last breath redolent of lemon and slumped forward, dead.

Keven screamed. He struggled against his bonds, twisting his torso to break the ropes. "Please," he said. "I'm sorry. I'm sorry." Tears poured. "I'll do whatever you want. I'm sorry."

The anguish in Keven's voice nearly changed Erick's mind. They only needed one undead to follow them. He didn't need Keven to die.

Then, he recalled Draymed.

The bloody, fiery demise of an entire village. Destruction perpetrated by two people. One of the criminals had already received punishment—it was time for the other.

"Shut up," Erick said. The command in his voice brought Keven to silence. The man stared at Erick, face dripping with tears and snot.

"I'm doing you a favor," Erick told him. "Only Alakaneth judges, but with the deaths of two hundred on your soul, his only judgment would be the Festering Hells. Serve me long and honorably enough, and maybe that judgment will change."

Hope lit Keven's brown eyes. "Yes. I'll serve you. I'll do whatever you say."

"Yes, you will." Erick motioned to Mundar, who moved toward the tray.

"I'll obey your orders and perform well."

"Yes."

"Free me, and I'll show you how loyal I can be."

"I'll free you, but only after I've returned you."

Keven's hope changed to puzzlement. The scar on his jaw twisted as he frowned. "Returned? To Draymed?"

"No," Erick said. "You once called me corpse boy and said I wasn't so tough without a bunch of undead around me. In some ways, you were right. They protect me. So, I'm going to make sure I have two new bodyguards." Erick offered what he hoped was a twisted smile as his stomach roiled with what he was doing.

Keven's eyes widened, and his mouth gaped. "No."

Mundar moved, but not quick enough. Keven saw him and slammed his mouth shut. The Procurer barely avoided wasting the vial's contents and pulled the glass back before he poured it onto Keven's closed mouth.

In the end, it took Callon and Marcus prying Keven's mouth open. Keven thrashed and screamed, making sounds Erick had never heard from a person. Sounds he hoped never to hear again.

Though it took longer than Erick ever expected, they eventually accomplished the task. Everyone backed away, and all the fight left Keven. He slumped in the chair as if already dead. After a moment, his eyes found Erick. "You're an abomination, just like Corby. You may command me, but I will fight you with anything I have." He glared, then his face crumpled, and he cried like a child who has lost his family. "I don't want to die."

His wish had no bearing on his fate, and Erick again watched until the inevitable end. It surprised him to find tears on his face once Keven had gone.

"This was the right thing, right?" Marcus asked, voice shaking.

"It was," Corby said, although his voice wasn't much stronger.

"I need to be alone," Erick told them. "It's going to take some time to bring them back."

No one argued. They departed, leaving Erick with Blink and the two corpses.

16

The phrase "Sangarans can't lie, their God won't let them" is one of the biggest lies out there.
    -Mundar, Head of the Dorfork Procurer's Guild

E rick looked at the herbs on the tray: two slivers of willow bark, four dried geranium petals, two sprigs of cowslip, and two each of lavender, cat's claw, and milk thistle. The cowslip wasn't as fresh as he hoped—the yellow flowers faded, the stems and leaves beginning to wilt. The condition of the others showed they had been scooped from the floor of Magary's shop. A few slivers of glass lay among some of the leaves.

It would all suffice. The geranium petals, the crucial ingredients in this Ritual, were intact and sound. They would suppress the recently dead men's remembered emotions, making them easier to control and open to Erick's suggestions.

With Blink's help, Erick untied the bodies from their death chairs and laid them on the floor. He pulled off their shirts and tossed them aside.

As Erick requested, a small cup, similar to the ones from which they drank the ale, sat on the tray. A small, slender knife with a hooked blade sat beside it. He recognized it from Elissia's description as a purse cutting knife. One of the first tools a Procurer learned to use. He picked up the blade, held his thumb over the cup, and sliced his pad. The sharp edge had blood flowing into the cup before the sting of the slice hit Erick.

He gritted his teeth and squeezed his thumb to keep the blood flowing until the cup was half-full. He put his thumb in his mouth to stem the flow of the coppery blood, then wrapped it with a thin strip of linen he hadn't requested, but someone had thought to provide.

As he broke the willow bark and dropped it into his blood, he went over the Ritual in his mind. It was a variation of the one he used to bring back Geran, the Royal Guardian who had tried to return them to Draymed. He died in an ambush of bandits attempting to capture Erick for Eligos, but Erick resurrected him as a protector.

This time, the Ritual would be more difficult and more dangerous. He had kept that information to himself since he didn't want Elissia objecting more strongly than she already had. Despite his good intentions, guilt plagued him over the deception. He assuaged it by telling himself it was nothing she needed to know, like she hadn't needed to know his part in the Ritual to fight Eligos.

He wished she still didn't know that.

Now, he placed himself in jeopardy by summoning two souls with enmity toward him, and returning them from an unknown place, since their ascendance to the Heaven of Caros wasn't likely. He had never tried anything like this. The geranium would stifle their enmity. As for the other variables, he could only trust the power of the Covenant. A power that had recently shown itself as more dependent on whim than he would have imagined.

He crushed the geranium petals into the mixture and stirred it with the knife. Lavender, cat's claw, and milk thistle joined the gory soup.

He took one of the cowslip sprigs, dipped it in the liquid, and stepped in front of Keven. He didn't know the man well, but better than he knew the Sterran. It would make the binding of Keven's soul easier. It would also be easier to dispel and send him back if something went wrong.

At least, he hoped it would be easier.

Erick painted the blood and herb mixture onto Keven: an X on the forehead, a dab on both eyes, a line on the throat, dots on both wrists, and a circle surrounding the heart. He connected all of them with thin lines he painted with his finger.

"*Mucalz col cnila phamah allar soygha. Alakaneth, amde sibsu, dluga mucalz deteloc pham allar soygha. Krinnik, amde sibsu, dluga mucalz decalz ar anoan allar soygha. Denech, amde sibsu, drix aldor mucalz od cnila de allar soygha.*"

As *elonsha* swirled through the air, bringing its rotted onion smell, Erick steeled himself to hear Eligos whisper to him. The *elonsha* tugged at him as it always did, its force taunting him to use more, to revel in its dark power. With Blink's steadying presence, Erick always resisted. The return of Eligos had made it harder, the malevolence of his voice weakening Erick's will.

This time no voice came to him. No whisper or presence of Master of Shadows. Had the battle at Broken Mountain severely hurt Eligos, limiting his power? It was a comforting thought even if Erick didn't believe it.

A string of silver appeared in the air. Keven's *nanta*. Traces of black tangled through the glimmering string, the stain of Keven's deeds. The line of *nanta* drifted toward the symbol painted on Keven's forehead, its doorway back into his body, and entered. Smaller strands arced from this conduit and touched the other painted areas.

Seconds later, the last of the shimmering soul disappeared, and Keven opened his eyes. They appeared clear brown to Erick, but he knew others would see the barest hint of lifelessness in them. If anybody studied him, they would surmise the scarred man either suffered from illness or recently recovered from a prolonged infirmity.

"I am your master," Erick said in *lonsh*, the language of *elonsha*. The language the dead spoke.

The brown eyes regarded Erick. "You are my master. Why am I here?"

Returning from death didn't destroy the memories embedded in Keven's soul. He was newly dead enough to remember he and Erick had been enemies and that Erick had poisoned him. The energy of the geranium used in the ritual made such knowledge unimportant, so Keven had no desire to resist or try to attack Erick. Though undead Keven hated Erick, he could not resist commands as long as Erick asserted power over him.

"You are here to help me," Erick answered. "You will use your skills to protect my companions and me. For now, stand and wait."

"As you command."

Erick turned his attention to the Sterran. He considered leaving him dead since he had caused much of Erick's woes. Certainly, he would go to the Festering Hells and deserved it. It could be argued Keven saw no choice and was led astray. This man was the leader and firmly a creature of Eligos.

The more protection, the better, Blink thought. Erick nodded. He didn't know if more ambushes waited for him and his friends. And he had no idea what to expect on the road, especially when they reached the Sterran swamps. Having someone familiar with the land would be useful. Corby might have knowledge from books, but this warrior had experience.

Again, Erick dipped the flower into his bloody mixture. He painted the symbols, the liquid shockingly red against the warrior's pale skin. Erick recited the Ritual. The *elonsha* gathered, passing through him with the vague nausea it always brought. Once more, no voice came. Erick fully expected Eligos to attack him this time. After all, the Master's servant was being put in thrall by his last remaining enemy. The absence worried Erick almost as much as it pleased him.

The *nanta* shimmered into being, seemingly created from nothing. It hovered around the body, as much black as silver. Erick hesitated and frowned. Did he want a soul that evil under his command? He had no experience controlling multiple Revenants. He didn't know if, suppressed emotions or not, they could turn on him. Another thing his aborted education left unknown to him. He had to decide before the Ritual released the *nanta*.

Blink?

You can always dissolve the Ritual.

Could he? He knew he could release the souls of *quana*, the simple undead used as servants. But Revenants were much higher functioning beings. What if Erick released the soul, and it didn't want to leave? So much uncertainty.

He had to take the risk. The benefits of a native guide to Starrasen were too much to let go.

He recited the Ritual a second time.

The *nanta* slid into the forehead symbol. The Sterran's eyes opened. So much hatred showed in them that Erick took a step back. "I am your master," Erick said, exerting his will upon the creature.

Several long seconds passed before the Sterran responded. "You are my master."

If Erick didn't know better, he would have sworn he heard sarcasm in the voice. "What was your name in life?"

"NalTalva."

Erick shook his head. "Nal is an honorific from the Master of Shadows. You are Talva. You no longer belong to Eligos."

The warrior did not answer.

Erick sensed struggle within the dead man. He pressed his will against the resistance. "You no longer belong to Eligos."

"I am not yours," NalTalva shouted. His anger and defiance staggered Erick. He fell back at the power of the warrior's rage as NalTalva leapt toward him.

"Protect me," Erick shouted.

The Sterran's fist came up and slammed into Erick's face. The last thing he saw as blackness took him was Keven rushing toward him, arms outstretched.

～

Elissia and Gabrielle sat in one of the warren's smaller rooms on opposite sides of a square wooden table. A lantern provided dim illumination. That suited Elissia. It matched her mood. For the first time since she threw her lot in with Erick, she questioned the wisdom of her choice. Through all the fights, the fires, the sickness and death, she had never wavered. She held steady because she believed in Erick's inherent goodness despite the malice of the ability he wielded. She had chastised him several times for being too gentle.

Now she wondered if she, or his power, had pushed him too far in the other direction.

"I'm scared," Gabrielle said, her round face a charcoal sketch of misery in the dim light. "I don't think I can keep traveling with you. Erick scares me. I ignored what he did before because it was necessary. I can't ignore what's happening now. I can't keep violating my oath."

"It's your choice," she told the girl. "I'm going. And that means Corby and Marcus are going. I imagine this warren could offer you a place if they need another healer. If not, it looks like the position of apothecary has come open."

Gabrielle nodded. "I've considered that."

"But," Elissia continued, "we're going to need you before this is over. It's a long way, and we may get hurt. We may not ever make it. We can't stop trying, though."

Elissia thought the Healer's Oath not to aid Necromancers was ludicrous in the extreme, but she completely understood the fear. She stopped short of confessing it. If she told anyone, it would be Marcus, not this girl she only sort of knew, despite the last month of travel together. She would continue the journey and do everything possible to make sure Erick didn't disappear into the abyss. Her love outweighed her fear of what he might become. She had to cling to the hope that with her and Blink at his side, he would maintain his humanity.

And if she was truthful with herself, she couldn't be certain Erick was wrong. Maybe the best fate for Keven and his companion was helping those they had tried to hunt down. They deserved death for their actions against Draymed. That was justice. She didn't know if being turned into undead slaves against their will was. Most believed that only Alakaneth judged. She cared little for how the Gods worked, though Erick had knowledge beyond any of them. Perhaps he received instructions the rest of them wouldn't understand, and he hadn't told them. His decision not to mention his part in destroying Eligos, including his ritualistic death, told her he wasn't beyond withholding information. He might well be resurrecting Keven and the other on instructions from Caros.

Unaccustomed self-doubt made her want to scream. Dwelling on it would only have her ready to hit somebody, and Gabrielle was the only one close.

I'll deal with it later, Elissia thought. *I'll talk to him and make him understand my concerns. And he'll put my mind at ease that he's not going to become a heartless monster.*

That's what she hoped.

"There you are."

She recognized Marcus's voice. He and Corby walked into the room, both pale and with queasy expressions. "Erick sent us out so he could finish…whatever it is he has to finish."

They sat in the remaining two chairs. No one spoke for several seconds, then Marcus said, "That was a lot tougher than I expected. It's much easier to kill someone when they're trying to kill you back."

"Then it almost becomes too easy," Corby said. Elissia knew he must be remembering how he had lost control in the first ambush they faced. He had beaten a man with his staff until the warrior's head had been unrecognizable as such. The bloodlust hadn't hit him since, though everyone knew it was there. Lurking.

"Gabrielle wants to leave us," she told the others.

"Why?" Corby asked.

"Scared," Gabrielle said. "Confused. Unhappy. You can find another healer."

"We don't want another healer." Marcus leaned his elbows on the table. "We want you."

"No, you don't." Gabrielle's lower lip quivered. "Not the way I want. I'm a distraction for you." She pointed a shaky finger at Corby. "And you're a reminder of what I can't have."

Marcus glanced at Elissia. She had been brought into something private. She should leave but didn't know the warren well enough to know where to go.

Gabrielle continued. "I thought I could accept that it would get easier. It hasn't." Her eyes, red and wet, fixed on Corby. "It would be so much better if I could hate you. I can't. You've been nothing but kind to me. Kind to all of us. You and Marcus are happy together. That makes me happy for you. And miserable for me."

Elissia didn't move. Barely dared to breathe. This was the most Gabrielle had spoken. Elissia feared if she did anything to distract her, the healer would retreat into her shell. Painful as it was, the girl needed to confess.

The others must have thought the same. They waited as Gabrielle took a shuddering breath and let it out. She clamped her hands together and regarded Elissia. "You have Erick. Corby and Marcus have each other. Who do I have?"

"You have all of us," Corby said softly.

"As friends." A bitter smile quirked her lips. "I had friends in Kalador. I had to deal with Valarie, but I didn't have to deal with the constant fear of being attacked. I didn't have to contend with the hardship of travel. I didn't have to face people dying and returning from the dead."

"We can—" Marcus began.

"Let me finish." Her brown eyes blazed with anger that surprised Elissia as it fell on her. "Erick is a gentle soul. Were he not a Necromancer, I think you two would find long-lasting happiness." Her hands fell to her lap, and she focused on the table.

Elissia braced herself. Whatever Gabrielle had to say, it scared her to do it while looking at Elissia.

"His power is an affront to Calea and Talan. A perversion of everything I hold sacred. It pained me every time I healed him. In the end, it will consume him and turn him as evil as the one he fights. Today, you witnessed some of what it will make him." Her head came back up. Her eyes had gone flat, anger replaced with the sadness of a lost child. "It will only get worse. Everywhere he goes, there will be death."

Elissia sucked in a breath. The healer's words sounded like a distant echo of the warning Elissia's aunt had given her when Erick first came into her life. The dire pronouncement had angered her then. It infuriated her now. "If you felt that way this whole time, why didn't you say something? Why did you stay with us and act so damn happy and accommodating?"

Gabrielle's eyes flicked to Marcus before they returned to Elissia.

Of course, Elissia thought.

"Because I had to try," she said, again staring at the table. "I had to see for myself if I could overcome my prejudice. If all the things I had learned about Necromancers were a lie." She shook her head, expression forlorn. "I can't and they weren't."

A sudden noise in the hall stopped the angry retort on Elissia's lips. A crashing door followed by fearful shouts and a snarling growl that almost froze her with dread. Her stomach dropped. It was the sound of—

"A prisoner has escaped," someone yelled. A meaty thud followed.

Elissia's heart lurched. Unless they had other prisoners, one of Erick's undead had gotten away.

"Come on," Elissia yelled as she ran from the room. She knew how she had gotten here, so she headed toward the chamber where she left Erick. Something she shouldn't have done.

Two turns down rough-hewn corridors found her back in the hallway to the prisoners' chamber. Corby and Marcus flanked her. She stopped short as four Procurers in the hall, daggers in hand, faced the room. One of theirs lay on the ground, unconscious or dead.

The undead Sterran warrior stood in the doorway with a grimace on his pale face. He charged the quartet.

Two of the Procurers moved in with dagger thrusts—one aimed for under the left armpit and the other for the right side. The blades did their work, but the warrior did not indicate that anything had happened. He grabbed the two thieves by their heads and brought them together with a crunch that made Elissia's stomach writhe. They collapsed, their daggers protruding from the warrior.

"Fall back," Corby shouted from behind her. "You can't kill him."

The two remaining Procurers fled down a side passage, shouting warnings as they ran.

The Sterran stared at Elissia, and her blood went cold. A flash of the vile thing that had possessed her passed over her mind. She drew her dagger even as she knew it was useless.

The warrior grinned and charged.

She plunged the knife toward his throat. It pierced right through the side of the neck, and then some force pushed her hand back, leaving the blade embedded, making no more impact than a kiss. The contact left her nauseous.

He pushed past her as if she didn't exist.

Marcus let out an incoherent cry of dismay as the undead fighter slammed into him. Hands wrapped around Marcus's throat, and they both fell to the ground.

Corby grabbed at the warrior's arms and tried to tug them free, to no avail. "Let go of him, you bastard."

The nausea left Elissia, and she could move again. She ran toward her brother with no idea what she was going to do.

Corby pulled his foot back and kicked the Sterran in the face. His head rocked back, and his grip loosened. Corby launched himself into the warrior's side. The momentum carried them off Marcus and into the wall.

"Rope," Marcus croaked from the floor. "Get the rope."

Elissia ran for the room where the undead had escaped. As she rounded the corner, the first thing she saw was Keven standing over Erick, who lay on the floor, blood running from a gash in his forehead.

17

I have read reports from a millennium ago, and what the commanders faced on the battlefield. All I can say is we would be lucky to have it as easy as they did.

    -Report from Archlegate Prine, Commander of the Markern Army

E rick had a vision. He had experienced enough of them; he could tell when one was happening. He also knew he wasn't sleeping. The Sterran warrior had knocked him unconscious.

He stood on a hillside overlooking a shallow valley. White clouds drifted through the sky, moving fast though he felt no wind. A girl whose face he couldn't quite see stared at him from a great distance on another hill. They had once been closer. She had created the gap.

He called to her, but she didn't answer. He tried to remember a name. Nothing.

She doesn't want you to remember.

A man, older than him but not by many years, stood beside him. Black haired and fair-skinned, he wore a tunic decorated with a symbol of eight interlocking circles pierced by an arrow. He had spoken in Erick's mind.

Why? Erick asked.

She thought she could be your friend. Instead, she will become your enemy.

Even in his vision, Erick despaired. Didn't he already have enough enemies? *Why?* he asked again.

The young man shrugged. *Sometimes the ways of humans are mysterious. Another will influence her.*

Am I dead? Erick asked the man, who he now realized was Denech. The Gods had never appeared in his visions. Would he soon be sent to Alakaneth to be judged?

Of course not, Denech answered with a chuckle. *What would be the use of telling you about a future enemy if you were dead?*

Can you stop her? Erick asked Denech.

No. That is beyond what the Covenant allows.

It seems many things are beyond the Covenant.

It was a complex agreement. We Gods are complex beings. Or spoiled brats, depending on your perspective. Your soulmate isn't wrong in her disdain.

Erick now had to wonder if this was a hallucination brought on by the knock to his head. A God was admitting fallibility.

We're all quite fallible, Denech told him. *With maybe the exception of Father. He is wise beyond my ability to grasp. The Covenant was the best he could wrangle with the forces involved. Forces that—*

A boom rumbled across the landscape, and Erick almost fell from the hillside.

The enigmatic girl appeared to take no notice.

Erick looked at Denech and couldn't accept the terror he saw in the god's eyes.

Or had there been any?

Denech's young face now appeared serene, as if the world hadn't just shaken. *I've already pushed the boundaries of the agreement with what I've done for you previously and been reprimanded for it.* He shrugged, and his dark gray eyes twinkled. *If I can't tempt fate, who can?*

The sky changed. Clouds turned black and heavy and a bruised color overtook the blue air. The atmosphere grew oppressive. Erick's breath came in gasps. Lightning, red as blood, flashed, though no thunder followed. Three bolts stuck near the girl.

Again, she took no notice.

Dark times ahead, Denech told him. *I will help as I can, or I won't. It's becoming harder to reach you. There are—*

Another rumble shook the ground, softer this time. A warning.

Denech smiled. *There are things I'm not allowed to do. Boundaries I won't try to cross. Don't rely on Gods. Rely on yourself and your friends. Rely on the one who loves you.*

In an eye blink, Denech was no longer there. Instead, thunder cracked, and lightning split the sky. There was so much he wanted to ask the God of Fate. So many questions. Some deep dread inside him told him he would never get the chance.

Don't rely on Gods.

He would heed Denech's final suggestion. He would rely on himself. And his friends. And the one who loved him.

He stared across the gulf at the mystery girl. A deep red glow surrounded her and obscured her face.

In a flash of black, she disappeared.

Erick's head hurt. Soft lantern light seeped through his closed eyelids. The sharp scent of herbal astringent stung his nose. Something hovered over his face, shadowing the light. A bare hint of *elonsha* tugged on his mind. He touched it to find the presence of the newly raised Keven.

He sucked in a breath and sat up, startling everyone else in the room. Their presence, in turn, made him jump.

"Amare's testicles," a young woman, with her brown hair in a ponytail, swore. "That's a great way to end up with a needle jammed through your skull."

Erick didn't recognize her. She wore the tight, dark clothing Procurers favored. Slim, like most procurers, her arms appeared long enough to hang past her knees.

Something floated in front of his left eye, and he jerked back. The black image followed him. He raised a hand to swat at it.

"Stop it." She grabbed his hand and pushed it back. "You'll jab your hand or tear out your stitches."

Stitches, Erick thought. The mysterious object before him resolved into black thread, from which hung a thin iron needle. Beyond the string, he spotted Keven, standing immobile, eyes on his master.

"You have to quit making a habit of scaring us to death," Elissia said from behind the other woman.

Corby, Marcus, and Blink stood behind Elissia, at the edge of the lantern light. "I'm too young to die from anxiety," Elissia continued. Though her voice was bright, Erick noted apprehension in her eyes.

"What happened?"

"In a moment," the newcomer said. "If you're through dancing, I'd like to finish stitching you up."

"Of course," Erick told her. "Why isn't Gabrielle doing it?"

The others walked closer as the woman grabbed the needle. "She's not here. I'm filling in. Name's Mallow. Close your left eye."

Erick did so. Pain flared in his head as she jabbed the needle into his scalp. Blood ran down his face until Mallow wiped it away with a rough cloth.

Elissia took Erick's hand. The warmth of her touch made the pain almost disappear. "What do you remember?" she asked.

"I returned Keven with no problems," he said. "Then, when I tried with the other one, something went wrong. Either Eligos claimed him, and I couldn't fight it, or I'm not powerful enough to control two Revenants." He saw their puzzled looks. "It's a type of undead."

"How many types are there?" Corby asked. His brown eyes sparkled with curiosity.

"Later," Elissia said. "When we're traveling again."

"Anyway," Erick continued, "either I can't control more than one, or the Sterran's will was strong enough to defy me. Maybe a combination, I don't know."

"Doesn't matter right now," Elissia told him.

It did matter. Erick needed to know his limits and how much control Eligos had. "The warrior attacked me and knocked me down.

I thought Keven was attacking me too and then the warrior punched me in the face, and I went out." A shudder racked Erick as he realized how close to failure he had come yet again, how he brought potential death to his friends. Despite wanting to scream, he held his calm as he asked, "What happened?"

"Keven protected you, as you instructed," Blink said. "He charged the Sterran and drove him away. He stood over you, ready to defend you until I instructed him to let the others help you."

Corby picked up the story. "The warrior fled into the warren and attacked Marcus and some others. We held him back while Elissia grabbed a rope and we managed to tie him up. He fought like Vidali's fury. I'm glad he didn't have a weapon."

"I'm glad you told us living people can't kill undead easily," Corby said. "That saved us wasted effort and unnecessary casualties."

At least there was some good news. Erick dreaded the thought of the havoc the Sterran could have caused as a loose undead. Only then did he notice Corby's black eye and the dark ring around Marcus's neck. Yet another mistake causing harm to his friends.

Corby's mention of casualties made Erick fear the answer to his next question. "Was anybody killed?"

"No," Mallow answered. "We had a few banged up, one pretty bad, but they'll all recover."

Erick allowed himself to breathe again. Things could have gone so much worse. "Where is he now?"

"We shoved him in one of the sewer outlets with bags of sand tied to his feet. He's not going anywhere."

"Then I can de-animate him." *I hope*, Erick thought.

"Good." Mallow did something with her hands Erick couldn't quite see, then leaned in with her mouth near his scalp. He heard a click as her teeth came together. She leaned back, needle in hand, frayed string hanging from it. "There. Ten stitches. You're going to have another nice scar to go with your old neck wound. Gives you a rugged look. I like that in a man."

Erick's cheeks grew warm.

Elissia squeezed his hand. "That's enough of that, Mallow," she said, eyes narrowed.

Mallow laughed. "Loosen your purse strings, cutling. I've no interest in your territory."

"I'm no cutling."

Erick appraised the other woman as she and Elissia stared at each other. Erick thought they appeared of an age, although something in Mallow's brown eyes spoke of witnessing things better left unseen. Erick could empathize.

She was taller and thinner than Elissia, her breasts less developed. She had the brown hair and fair skin of most Zakerins who didn't spend their life farming, less attractive than Elissia's olive complexion and ebon hair.

"I'll wager I'm as trained and experienced as you," Elissia added.

Mallow's large eyes, the same color as the small bronze hoop piercing her left nostril, flashed. Not with anger, but challenge. "I'll wager not. I've cut the purses from nobles and their kin, all the way up to the Queen herself. Broken into homes protected by no less than twenty guards, carried out sacks of valuables, and taken the house cat with me. I've—"

"Telling tall tales again, Mallow?"

Erick turned to the doorway. Mundar stood there in his dark clothing, a tray and cup in his hand. Though he hadn't caught it before, Erick immediately saw the resemblance between the thief leader and Mallow in the ax-thin nose and large ears. "She's your daughter?"

"She is," Mundar confirmed, "and how I raised such an outrageous liar and provoker, I'll never know."

Mallow gave a mocking bow. "I learned from the best."

Mundar walked into the room with graceful strides and presented the cup to Erick. "Drink this. It will help the pain."

Which pain? Erick thought. His heart ached as much as his head. He had unleashed terror on unsuspecting people. If they had not been able to grapple it, there was no telling how much damage the undead warrior could have managed. What had gone wrong? Why had his binding failed?

He went after Marcus when he couldn't get you, Blink thought. Is it possible *the* morazol *was stronger than your command?*

Why him and not Keven?

Blink shook his head.

Erick drank from the mug. It was ale with a bitter under taste, a medicinal herb. He winced but swallowed. The thought of herbs brought him back to an earlier question. "Where's Gabrielle?"

His companions shifted uneasily, casting glances at each other. No one seemed willing to answer, and Erick feared the worst. Had the resurrected warrior killed her? No, they already told him no one died.

"Gabrielle will be staying here with us," Mundar said. "I'm happy to offer you Mallow in her place."

"I'm a better healer anyway," Mallow said with a smile.

"Another outrageous lie," Mundar said with no rebuke in his voice. "You are a competent healer, and you have skill with a blade. You also have your majority so that's one less set of forged documents we need to pay for."

So, Mallow is older than Elissa, Erick thought.

"I promised we'd pay you back," Marcus said.

Mundar waved his hand dismissively. Erick had missed whole conversations while he was unconscious. He took another gulp of the bitter liquid. Though his head had grown less painful, he couldn't say the same for his other ache. "Why isn't she going with us? Is she ill?"

Again, his companions seemed discomfited. It was not at all like them, especially the acerbic Marcus.

"Someone tell me something," Erick demanded.

"They're your friends, so they don't know how to tell you," Mundar said. "I haven't known you long, so I have no care about your feelings. I had a nice chat with her while you were taking a nap and letting dead things knock around my people."

Erick opened his mouth to offer an apology when Mundar held up a hand and waved his long fingers in a dismissive gesture. "It's okay. I know that wasn't your intention. You were doing what you thought best. And the healer said you are always doing what you consider best. She also said that you're an abomination, and she can't travel with you anymore."

Erick's face went numb with shock. His brain had no idea how to react. He knew healers could have that reaction to Necromancers since that's what their calling taught them. He had hoped—no, assumed—Gabrielle had overcome such revulsion. Hadn't her time with them shown her anything of his true nature?

Which true nature? He thought. *The one where you can't kill anyone and care for your friends, or the one where you have two men murdered for convenience?*

You're being too harsh on yourself, Blink thought. *You did what was necessary.*

Perhaps, he thought. But he was changing. The Erick from a month ago wouldn't have done such a thing.

The Erick from a month ago was naive.

"You sure know how to break something gently, don't you?" Elissia said.

"He's an adult," Mundar told her. "He can handle blunt words." He regarded Erick, and his face took on a kindly expression. "She took no pleasure in anything she said, and it's tearing her apart. But she has to be true to herself, as we all must." His eyes went to Corby and Marcus. "I suspect she has other reasons."

"Fine," Marcus said, throwing up his hands. "Good riddance." He looked at Mallow. "Welcome to the jester troupe." He stormed out of the room.

Corby's mouth flattened, and eyes narrowed. He appeared to Erick as if someone had hit his dog. "Marcus," he shouted as he chased after him.

"You people are going to be a cask of chuckles to travel with," Mallow said. "I should go pack." She also left the room.

Draining fatigue hit Erick as if he had been dragged behind horses and was then forced to run uphill. He could no longer remember a time when he hadn't felt tired. His whole body ached, despite the numbing drink. Another desire to return home struck him. Except he had no home.

"You're welcome to stay the night and rest, and then we'll help you with provisions and send you on your way. The healer didn't say as much, but I gather you have a long journey ahead of you."

"Can I speak to Gabrielle?" Erick asked in a flat voice. It was becoming harder to talk and to concentrate. It must have been some-thing in the herbs they gave him.

Mundar shook his head. "She doesn't want to see any of you right now. She's afraid you'll try and talk her into continuing with you."

"I wouldn't do that," Erick said. "I just wanted to say goodbye. But I'll honor her wishes. We'll leave first thing in the morning."

Lethargy overcame him. He wanted to care that Gabrielle was leaving. At the moment, he couldn't. He also needed to do something about the undead but didn't have the energy. "Is there somewhere we can sleep?"

"I'll have pallets brought here. We're a small warren with only one guest room." He shrugged. "I already offered it to Gabrielle."

Erick nodded. None of it mattered right now. What had been in that drink? "That will be fine."

Mundar left the room. As Erick lay there, Elissia holding his hand and stroking his hair, words from his talk with Denech came back to him and broke through the numbness.

She thought she could be your friend. Instead, she will become your enemy.

He shivered.

~

Corby spotted Marcus rounding a corner of the hallway, his pace brisk. He gave chase. Taller than his friend, he soon caught up. "Wait," he said.

Marcus offered no response, only kept walking, his head turning left and right as if he sought something. Corby reached out and grabbed Marcus's hand. Marcus didn't pull away, but he didn't stop walking. With no choice, Corby followed. They had to stop sometime, and he could wait.

After turning down a few passages and passing people who got out of their way and offered quizzical looks, Marcus must have found what he sought. He stared at what Corby saw as nothing more than more a dark earth wall, barely illuminated by dim lanterns at long intervals.

Marcus eased his hand from Corby's grasp. With both hands, he felt the wall. Corby watched, fascinated, as Marcus pushed five spots on the wall. Divots, Corby realized when he looked after the fact. On the fifth push, something clicked, and the wall swung in. Marcus stepped inside, paying no attention to Corby. Corby followed anyway.

The door shut, putting Corby in complete darkness. "What is this?"

"Bolthole." Marcus's voice came from close by in the darkness.

Corby didn't dare move, afraid he would trip over something.

"She betrayed us," Marcus said.

"She didn't betray us." Corby put his hands at the wall behind him, needing something to anchor him. The darkness made him feel as if he might fall in a pit, even standing still. "She's looking after herself, as she should. She could have left anytime, but she waited until we landed someplace safe. You can't fault her for that."

"I damn well *can* fault her," Marcus said. Noise indicated he was moving around the room, searching through items. Corby wished he had Marcus's ability to quickly see in darkness. "If she didn't want to come, she should have stayed behind. If she didn't like Erick, she shouldn't have come. If she had a problem with us, she—"

There was a sharp *wicking* sound as something metal flew across the room, slammed into the wall, and hit the floor.

"Marcus?" Corby asked in alarm.

"I stood by her," Marcus said. "When Valarie berated her, I defended her. When my father said she was useless and ugly, I came to her side. She was my sister when Elissia wasn't there. Why couldn't she accept me as I am? Accept us. Accept Erick."

"I don't know," Corby said. The emotions were almost too much for him. He didn't know what to say, how to make things better. He could have named any number of logical reasons for Gabrielle's behavior. None would answer Marcus's questions.

Feet shuffled across the floor and Corby found both his hands in Marcus's. "Please tell me you'll never betray me."

"Gabrielle didn't—"

"I don't care about her right now. I care about you. Tell me you won't betray me."

"I have no plans to betray you," Corby said. It wasn't quite the same, but it was the best he could offer. Who knew what the future held?

It must have been enough for Marcus. He released Corby's hands, wrapped his arms around him, and pulled him close. The heat from Marcus's body dizzied Corby.

"Decide right now. Do you want me or not?"

"I do," Corby said, his voice husky with roiling emotions that threatened all sense of logic.

"Do you care what the Gods think?"

"I—" He didn't know how to answer. He cared, though all of a sudden, it didn't seem to matter. "I don't know."

"Yes or no," Marcus whispered in his ear, and Corby shuddered at the sensation. "Do you care what the Gods think?"

"I do," Corby said, barely able to speak. "But I think Elissia is right. They don't care. Not about this."

Marcus didn't move for a moment.

Corby held his breath, teetering on the precipice of disappointment.

"Good enough," Marcus said. His hands slid down the front of Corby's pants. For a long time after, Corby gave no thought to the Gods' feelings.

18

Be kind to all you meet and do good while you can; you never know when Alakaneth will call.

　-Amelan Proverb

The next morning, Erick awoke with an arm around Elissia, his body pressed against hers. They lay on a thin cushion, curled under wool blankets. He had no memory of being moved to put the sleeping items under him.

He shifted, and arrows of pleasure shot up his back.

"I feel that," Elissia said drowsily as she put her hand on his arm. "Too late now. We should have done something last night."

"Could we have?" Erick asked, the idea thrilling.

She rolled over to face him. Her passionate kiss mollified his disappointment at the loss of contact. "Probably not. The herbs Mallow gave you to help with the healing had you asleep on your feet."

"I remember," he said.

She gave him another kiss. "We'll be together soon. I think I'm finally ready."

Her words set his every nerve tingling.

"I am too," he said. He kept his tone sober in spite of the giddiness. He feared if he acted too excited, as he had back on the hill when his manor burned, he would scare her into reconsidering. They kissed once more.

As he pulled back, she stretched. He watched her chest, pressed against her tunic, and smiled. Soon he would see it without clothing in the way.

Stop it, Blink thought. *You're making me ill.*

Then get out of my mind, he thought back, kindly. He was in too good a mood to be upset. Whatever had been in the ale had done wonders for him. The cut on his head didn't hurt. He sat up, pulling his eyes away from the enticing view, and stretched.

His mood dropped a notch when he spotted Keven standing where they left him last night, his eyes focused on Erick. Even being used to undead, the sight unnerved him. "I am your master," Erick said, sending his will toward the Revenant.

"You are my master," Keven echoed, no trace of anything beyond repeating the statement.

Erick relaxed.

He found Corby and Marcus asleep on the other side of the small room. Corby lay on his back and Marcus on his stomach. Marcus's hand rested on Corby's chest. Erick had been concerned when the two of them hadn't returned to the room before they decided to go to sleep. Elissia assured him he had no reason to worry. Marcus had cause to be angry and needed time either alone or with someone he cared about. Elissia suspected the latter, considering Corby hadn't shown up, either.

The happiness Erick felt seeing them beside each other surprised him. Now that he decided not to let who they were bother him, he realized how silly it had been to allow it to affect him in the first place.

Elissia sat up, her shoulder against his.

"It's really okay, isn't it?" Erick said, nodding his head toward the two sleepers.

"It is. And I'm glad you see that. It's bad enough we lost one over feelings she couldn't overcome. Glad to see it won't happen to you, too."

"She's partly responsible," he told Elissia. "What she thinks of me is wrong, so it stands to reason what I thought about them was probably wrong, too."

Elissia nodded. "Life would be better if people tended more to their own warrens and left others alone. Of course, it wouldn't be nearly as exciting." She smiled. "Hey, wake up!" she shouted across the room.

Marcus sat up, eyes bright and alert, a dagger in hand before the small echo died away. Corby sat up more slowly, his eyes half-open as he ran a hand over his head.

Elissia giggled. "Never gets old."

"That's damn rude, sis," Marcus told her. "We had a late night."

Her grin threatened to reach her ears. "I'm sure you did. And now, you have an early morning. We need to get on the road."

"Back to sleeping on the ground outside," Marcus grumbled.

"Not if I can help it," Mallow said, standing in the doorway. She had changed into traveling clothes: tan, dull, and rugged. No dark colors to attract unwanted attention. Her hair still wound in a ponytail, the wooden holder she previously wore replaced with a leather tie. Her thick leather gauntlets and leather breastplate surprised Erick.

"Procurers wear armor?" Erick asked.

"Smart ones do," Mallow answered.

"You mean those too slow to get out of the way," Elissia said.

Mallow cocked her head and gave a smile that seemed half amused, half exasperated. "You and I are either going to become the best of friends or kill each other. Get up. There's breakfast in the common, and we've supplies and horses waiting for us at Carette's."

"Horses?" Erick asked with dread.

"Horses?" Marcus echoed. Erick heard the same reservations in his friend's voice.

"Did I walk into a chamber of parrots?" Mallow asked. "Yes, horses. You may love the idea of walking a thousand miles, but all it does for me is make my feet hurt. Let's go."

Breakfast was porridge, ostrich bacon, and a wedge of cheese washed down with a glass of goat's milk. They were the only ones in the small common area because the bulk of the Procurers had gone to rest after their night's work.

As they neared the end of the meal, Callon came in with four pieces of parchment and handed one to each of them. "Travel papers," he explained. "Erick, yours has your birthday, except the clerk miswrote the year, so you have your majority. Elissia, yours has a forged birthday, which gives you your majority, since you are close enough to make it believable."

Elissia looked at the document. "It says I'm from Masca. Where is that?"

Callon shook his head. "Your mother is Straph, and you know nothing about her homeland?"

"Our mother isn't the most forthcoming person we know," Elissia said.

"Masca is a city in central Straphan. Bigger than here, smaller than Kalador. Both you and Marcus are from there."

"Makes sense," Marcus said, "with us being twins and everything. What doesn't make sense is her having her majority and not me."

Elissia laughed. "Well, you are the younger one."

"No offense," Callon said with a shrug, "but you're not physically big enough to look like you have majority."

"I could show you something that would beg to differ."

Corby's cheeks turned bright pink.

"I don't think so," Callon said. "I've been to the baths with you."

Elissia let out an unfeminine snort. "He's got you there, Mar."

"You said yourself you've been lucky," Callon reminded him. "If you're taking the Routh Awen, you're going to run into checkpoints. The goal is to make those encounters smooth and raise no questions. Easier to convince someone you're under majority, and Elissia is your travel guardian."

"I guess," Marcus said. "But I don't like it."

"Corby, Erick is your travel guardian."

Corby nodded, his cheeks still flushed.

"That covers it," Callon told them. "Everyone ready to go?"

"Not yet," Erick said. "I have one more thing to do."

Erick stood in front of a deep hole in the sewer, staring into the depths. Blink stood beside him with a torch so Erick could see without using their connection. Rank smelling water ran from a channel in the tunnel and fell twenty feet into the chamber below, where it washed out to a specially constructed pit south of town. Callon told them, with a smile, to be thankful the wind hadn't blown from that direction during their visit.

The light played against the well walls. Erick stared down at the man that had called himself NalTalva. Bags of sand tied to his feet kept him immobile. Rope bound his arms tight to his body.

Even at this distance in the flickering light, Erick could see hatred gleaming in the undead's eyes.

As complicated as Rituals were to create, they were surprisingly simple to undo. Erick held his right hand, palm out toward the undead. *"Amde lonsa Caros od sibsu, ol tiab nonci. Undl oala quin yolca."*

For a moment, nothing happened. Erick feared the release wouldn't work. Then, he would have to take time to dismember and bury the warrior in separate graves; the only way to be sure it couldn't break free and cause problems.

The body shuddered. Its *nanta*, black with few hints of silver, broke through the chest. As it dissipated, the body collapsed. It fell forward until the head struck the wall with a deep crack.

It was now just another corpse. Something it should have been a month ago when Erick first met the warrior.

All taken care of?" Callon asked as Erick rejoined his companions in the warren's gathering hall.

Erick nodded.

"Great," Callon said. "We'll make sure he gets washed out to the pit with all the other shit."

"That won't cause any problems with the local watch?" Corby asked.

Callon smiled. "I would think you'd know by now that we have ways to make sure it doesn't. Let's go."

He took them through the warren to the same spot they'd entered. Mundar waited with Mallow, who had a large bright red backpack slung over her shoulder.

"Goodbye to all of you," Callon said with a wave. "Luck of Denech and Blessings of Caros."

"Yeah, that and a *teres* will get us an ale," Elissia murmured.

"Thanks for taking us in," Marcus said. "Someday, we'll go back home, and you'll be right there with us."

"I count on it." Callon departed.

Mundar offered Erick his hand. "Mallow is going to take you from here. Remember, believe only sixty percent of what she says. Thirty if she's talking about her skills. Best of luck in your journeys."

"Thank you," Erick said, taking his hand, bemused by his comments. "And thank you for sending Mallow to help us."

A grin cracked Mundar's face. "You jest. I'm getting a far better healer. I should thank you."

Erick glanced at Mallow. Her face was impassive, as if her father's comments did not affect her. He released Mundar's hand. "Tell Gabrielle goodbye for us. Tell her we have no ill feelings."

"Tell her they have no ill feelings," Marcus said. "Tell her I said she can rot."

"Marcus!" Elissia said.

"I will tell her you all send regards," Mundar said smoothly. "You'd best go now." He turned to Mallow and kissed her on the cheek. "All my best, love. Try to be honest at least once a day."

She smiled. "No promises."

Following Mallow, they exited the warren through a sewer cover and into a narrow alleyway filled with stacks of wooden crates. The sun hung low enough that much of the alley remained in shadow.

"I'll meet you a mile outside town," Blink said. Before Erick could say anything, the homunculus took to the air and disappeared over the roofs.

Erick sighed.

"Fall is here," Corby said. "Soon, it won't be unusual for him to wear a hooded cloak, so he can stay with us."

"One good reason to look forward to it," Erick said. One of the few: fall was a time of rain and chill. It was not as cold as winter, but much wetter, at least in Zakerin. He had no idea if things were different in Starrasen, their destination, but they would all be wearing hooded cloaks within the next fortnight. He didn't look forward to the unpleasantness of that travel.

Maneuvering through the crates brought them to a street where few people roamed, all heading one way. Erick caught a whiff of roasting meat and toasted bread.

"This way," Mallow said and led them in the opposite direction.

Despite only passing through once, Erick recognized the road as the one they traveled yesterday, heading back out of the city. "I thought we were getting horses."

"We are," Mallow said. "You came in from the east, right?

"Yes," Erick said. "Down this same road."

"Remember the large building you passed that smelled of horse manure? Bet you can guess what they sell there."

Erick nodded. He decided it might be best if he stayed quiet for a while.

"Don't remember horse manure," Elissia said, her voice tight. "Couldn't smell it over the piss reek of the tannery."

"I'm sure your little town has industries that stink as much," Mallow said. "No need to be snide."

"Funny, I was thinking the same thing," Elissia plastered on a fake smile.

Erick wanted to groan. He knew Elissia was only defending him, but he didn't want her alienating their new healer. He hated losing Gabrielle; he certainly didn't want to see Mallow chased away, too.

As they moved down the streets, more people stepped outside of shops, opening doors and setting out wares as the city prepared for the day. No one paid much attention to Erick's group, just another group of citizens. The day promised to be warm and pleasant, a fine time to be on the road. Erick would take it while he could.

They soon left the market district and drew close to the large wooden building that housed the horses and wagons.

"Wait out here," Erick told Keven as they reached the double doors leading into the building. "Look stern and unapproachable."

The Revenant set a menacing grimace on his face. With his long scar and fierce demeanor, he managed Erick's request as well as any living person.

"Hand on sword and scan people," Erick added. "Look like a bodyguard."

"What are you doing?" Mallow asked.

"If he speaks, no one will understand him but me. I want to keep people from being interested in talking to him." Erick already noticed people shying away if they drew too close to Keven, repelled by a vague sense of unease. That didn't mean some enterprising merchant wouldn't overcome his anxiousness and try to sell Keven something.

Mallow shook her head. "People don't talk in this city unless they want something. Bring him in with us if you're worried."

"He'll spook the horses if he's too close. When we travel, I'll have him ahead of us until the animals get used to him."

"I'll stay with him," Marcus offered. "I don't need to see the horses, and I can divert anyone who tries to get friendly."

Erick nodded.

The small thief affected a stern posture. With his slight build and a dagger as his only weapon, he made a far less menacing figure than Keven.

Erick and the rest went through the large open doors. The smells of horse, horse manure, and hay dominated the building. It was the largest stables Erick had ever seen, at least sixty feet deep and again as wide. Panels on the roof twenty feet above were open to allow in the early morning light. Four rows of stalls ran down the length, divided by wide walkways. A contingent of young men worked the stables, some with wheelbarrows and shovels cleaning up after the animals, others with buckets of feed or water that they loaded into each stall's troughs.

The horses ran the gamut of breeds. On Keystone Island, horses were a luxury used for travel only if necessary. Erick had seen drawings in his mother's books but never encountered one until Kalador. Here, in one place, were at least three times as many horses as he had seen in his life.

At the front of the building, before the stalls began, hung any number of items Erick didn't comprehend. The saddles on the ground, he understood; he had no idea what the other gear might be.

A man walked toward them. He was bulky, tall, and his long face was made longer by a protruding black beard, which hid his mouth. He wore a leather apron over a gray shirt and carried a mallet in one large hand. "Expected you twenty minutes ago," he told Mallow in a deep, rumbling voice. "Got better things to do than wait on you."

"Our guests don't believe in dawn," she told him as she pointed at Erick and the rest.

His dark eyes fell on them, full of irritation. He addressed the group. "I'm running a business. Can't be waiting for lazy people."

"Sorry," Erick mumbled, taken aback by the man's rudeness and Mallow's willingness to sling blame.

Elissia stepped up and put a hand on his arm. "Did you get paid on time?" she asked the man.

"I did," he acknowledged.

"Then you can damn well wait, however long it takes."

The man's eyes narrowed, and his hands twitched. Erick wondered if the merchant wanted to throw the hammer at Elissia.

"Jorome," Mallow said in a conciliatory tone even as she flashed a warning at Elissia, "why don't you show us where it is, and we'll get out of your beard."

His eyes not leaving Elissia, Jorome pointed with the hammer at a doorway behind him. "Through there. Ascan will help you."

"Thank you," Mallow said. "Let's go," she told the others.

Erick remained tense as they walked past the muscular man. Elissia seemed unconcerned, her stride casual, her movements loose. The horseman watched as they walked to the doorway. Erick confirmed it with a glance over his shoulder.

The doorway put them back outside, where they found two horses

PAUL BARRETT

hitched to an open wagon loaded with crates that rose five feet over the retaining board. A man, a few years older than Erick, stood with his hands on something running between the two horses' heads.

"What is this?" Erick asked.

Mallow wheeled on Elissia. "You really should learn when to keep your mouth shut. We're helping you out, and you repay us by being rude to one of the people we do business with? Is that how family behaves in Kalador?"

"If you mean 'do we repay rudeness in kind,' then yes."

Mallow's eyebrow arched. "You thought that was rude? Rude is calling you a sniveling little brat with thin skin and no sense of propriety. Jorome was acting like a businessman."

Elissia stepped forward, fists clenched.

"Please," Erick said, reaching to grab Elissia's arm before remembering she hated that. "We have enough enemies without making them among ourselves." He almost apologized on Elissia's behalf, and thought better of that, too. "Let's consider it a misunderstanding and get going. Okay?"

Several tense seconds passed as the women glared at each other. Then, Mallow shrugged. "Good as a gold coin to me."

Though it took Elissia far longer, she eventually unclenched her fists. "We're going to have to come to an understanding at some point, though."

Marrow offered a feral smile. "That we are."

Erick wanted to pound his head against the wall. Could he not have a group of companions who all liked each other? "Like I said earlier, what is this?"

"It's a horse and wagon," Mallow said. "Isn't that obvious?"

"It is," Erick said, keeping his voice even. "What is it for?"

"An actual explanation, please," Corby said. "Not the sarcastic one you were about to offer."

Mallow frowned for a moment, then smiled. "You're no fun. Fine. I know none of you can ride horses. While I'm one of the best riding instructors that ever lived, I don't want to waste my time and talent training you, so we have a wagon. Everyone can ride in comfort. If patrols stop us, we're part of a merchant consortium taking goods to market in Kaladan. The wagon will let us move faster than walking, and we won't be as beaten up as if we rode horses all day." She smirked at Corby. "Is that a satisfactory explanation?"

Corby nodded.

Marcus cocked his head. "And what are we taking to Kaladan?"

"Just the supplies we need to make the journey."

Marcus shook his head. "I was born on Skyday, but it wasn't last Skyday. The leader of a Procurer branch doesn't send his daughter with four strangers out of thiefly camaraderie. You're transporting something, and we're the protection. That we all happen to be going the same way is a happy chance."

"You are a clever one," Mallow said. "Yes, we are taking some goods that may be less than acceptable in law-abiding circles."

"We're smuggling?" Erick asked.

"Say it a bit louder," Mallow snarled as her head darted around the yard. "I don't think they heard you in the Awenholt."

"I don't know that I'm comfortable with that," Erick said.

"I don't expect you to be." Mallow shrugged. "You can always walk and find your own supplies. Of course, we'll have to charge you for the healing I did and your lodging last night." She grinned.

For a moment, Erick shared Elissia's irritation. He found himself wanting to punch Mallow's smug face.

Then she said, "Look, maybe we should have told you sooner, but it wouldn't have changed anything. If you want, you can consider this as repayment for saving your ass in the market square." She pointed a finger at Marcus. "Pretend the smart one didn't figure it out. If we get caught, and we won't, I'll happily say you knew nothing about it. Either way, we should get going before Jorome chases us out of here or reports us himself. We're on thin ice now." She turned her gray eyes on Elissia. "It's why he was irritated we weren't here on time."

Elissia nodded. "If you had been up front with us, I would have acted differently."

"Probably." Her gaze returned to Erick. "This is your grand adventure, so it's your decision."

Yet again, Erick found himself in the position of having to make a choice that affected other people. He didn't know if he would ever be content with the idea of being a leader. "I don't have much choice."

"Not really," Mallow agreed.

"Then let's get on the road," Erick said, hoping he wasn't making a huge mistake.

19

There are those who say perhaps war could have been avoided. That we could have negotiated peace. You don't negotiate with invaders. You can't talk peace with a sword at your throat.

-Excerpt from lecture by Corberin of Draymed, given at the University of Straph

W hen Fathen stepped into The Firstlast Inn for the second time, he was a changed man in many ways.

For one, he wasn't a man anymore. Even more than his first meal of the miner's son in Prospector's Camp, the various people he consumed on his travels down the Routh Krinnik proved it. Three yesterday and two today.

Though not needing to sleep allowed him to travel without stopping or fearing an attack, walking made him so hungry. The food and water he once subsisted on did nothing but sicken him. Only the taking of blood and flesh from a creature with a soul sated his appetite. The meat was so sweet, like the finest beef: the blood, a wine of exquisite vintage.

At first, some deep part of the priest he had once been cried at the desecration, screamed that it would be better to be dead and damned than to commit such vile acts. That part of him became less convincing with each mangled body left behind. By the time he returned to the hamlet of Firstlast, it had all but disappeared.

He stared at those gathered in the tavern and smiled. A few glanced his way and then returned to their business. He was just another patron, nothing special.

How wrong they were.

Late in the first day of his journey south, he discovered by accident what his new status allowed. In the town of Devin's Rest, he lured an unsuspecting chambermaid into his room on the pretense of needing fresh linens, and then snapped her neck as easily as wringing a chicken and gorged on her flesh.

The door opened, and another young girl, no more than sixteen, walked in with sheets in hand. Lich and maid stared at each other for a shocked instant. Fathen could only imagine what the girl saw: a supposed harmless customer with blood and gristle on his chin as he chewed on the leg of her companion. With a cry of terror, she turned to run.

"Stop," Fathen said with all the force he once used to cowl the followers of his former god. To his wonder, she did. Her face went slack as she turned back to him and stared as if waiting for further commands.

Is it that easy? he wondered. "Drop your burden."

With only the briefest hesitation, she opened her arms, and the linens fell to the floor.

"You are mine to command," Fathen said.

"I am yours to command," the girl agreed.

Fathen smiled.

Before he left Devin's Rest, he experimented on people in various ways to discover his capabilities and limits. Some people were harder to control than others, and some he couldn't touch at all. Nonetheless, he had no doubt he could perform the tasks Eligos had set before him. He wondered why his master had not told him about the powers he possessed.

Unease bubbled up from within as he considered this omission. Had Eligos said nothing because he used this same mental domination to snare Fathen back in Draymed? On that night over a month ago, Fathen choked the life from a prisoner so Eligos could possess the dead man's body. Eligos had said kill, and Fathen willingly obliged. Had it been his will or the Master's? Had Eligos forced Fathen as Fathen forced the young chambermaid? Who had made the decision that ultimately led to where Fathen stood now?

As much as it might ease him to think he did what he did because his will was not his own, he couldn't. The choice had been his. His hatred of Erick's family had driven him as much as his hatred of Draymed. He was miserable, and Eligos offered a path away from that misery. In his deepest heart, he might question what that decision cost him, but he would never say it hadn't been his.

Eligos said nothing of his new abilities because it must be a test. If Fathen couldn't discover his power, he wasn't worthy of serving the Master.

Fathen departed Devin's Rest, in a set of freely given travel clothes of brown leather and a fur-lined cloak of blue, confident in his new-found capabilities. He would use his mental prowess, his force of personality, and his undead stature to deal with the Prelate and win Kalador for his master.

But before he did, he had matters to settle at The Firstlast Inn.

Gert, the portly, crimson-haired proprietor of the establishment, spotted him and said, "Have a seat where you will, good sir, and we'll see to you momentarily." She gave no recognition of him, though he had been here little more than three tendays past. She doubtless saw many patrons. An exceptionally tall, black-haired man probably didn't stand out in her mind any more than another, even if that black-haired man had traveled with a Necromancer and his homunculus and had been unceremoniously booted from the inn while the other patrons laughed.

Fathen had no issue with Gert. She had been kind to them, and only fear of lost customers made her reluctantly turn them out. He didn't blame her. One could seldom work against the will of the mob.

As he walked through the small room, he spotted those he did blame. The brown-haired Wilser sat with three other rough-looking, bearded men. They wore leather coats pocked with squares of metal over the heart and kidneys. Rough linen shirts and pants in dirt-coated shades of brown made up the rest of their attire. Wilser also wore thick leather chausses. Swords in battered scabbards hung at their sides.

Fathen grinned and walked toward the men. Neither arms nor armor would do them any good.

He stopped in front of the rugged would-be warriors. Mugs of ale and the remains of a meal littered the table. It took a moment before they noticed Fathen. When they did, Wilser offered a companionable smile. "Can I help you, friend?"

Fathen offered his own grin. "I want to sit at this table."

"Then you'll have to wait until we leave."

"And when will that be?"

"When we damn well please," Wilser said. The other men laughed. One slapped Wilser on the back as if he made the best jest ever told. A strong scent of ale drifted up from the quartet.

"But I want the table now," Fathen didn't compel them, though he could have. Their table wasn't what interested him.

Wilser's smile disappeared. "You'd best move along before we send you on your way."

"You mean like you did near thirty days ago when you sent my companions and me into the night because you decided we consorted with demons?"

The room had grown quiet as people sensed the brewing tension.

Gert drew near, a pitcher in her hand. "Look, good sir, I don't want—"

Without casting an eye toward her, Father held out a hand. "Say nothing more." He put his power behind it. "These men will pay for the insult they laid upon us."

Wilser studied Fathen. "Oh, I remember now. Yes, the boy and his demon, and you, a priest of Caros." He laughed. "You'd best move on. There are four of us who are well-trained and will not hesitate to kill a priest."

"And yet here you sit at the same table as the last time I was here. Why aren't you on campaign, raiding villages, or scaring children? So well-trained that no one will hire you? Mercenaries with no work? I'm terrified."

The man on Fathen's left stood, hand on sword. "You'd best leave n—"

Fathen reached out his long arm, his hand crooked in the shape of a claw. His fingernails extended as the hand latched on to the man's throat. He clenched down and tugged. The man's larynx came loose as easily as loam. He gurgled as blood gushed from the wound. Fathen took the chunk of flesh and threw it at Wilser.

Chairs thudded and mugs shattered as people screamed and rose to flee. Gert's pitcher clattered to the ground as she fainted. Wilser paled as his companion's ruined throat landed in his lap.

The other two men, after a moment of shocked hesitation, rose to draw their swords. Claws extended, Fathen lashed at the second man's face. Long nails raked across the mercenary's eyes, tearing into the tender orbs. He fell back as his hands reached toward the destroyed tissue.

The third fighter thrust his sword into Fathen's side. The blade sunk deep. Fathen noticed it only as pressure no worse than a child running into him, annoying but nothing more. He reached out and grabbed the man's head. The warrior struggled to no avail. Fathen pulled him in, tilted the head to the side, and plunged his teeth into the man's neck. His teeth met the man's skin, and he wrenched back. Blood splashed as the large artery tore open. Fathen chewed and swallowed even as he released the man. The mercenary dropped to the floor as his life gushed from the wound.

The inn had cleared in short order, the door left open as the last patron fled into the night. Wilser had not moved, frozen by the bloody chunk of meat that still lay in his lap.

Fathen pulled the sword from his side as he regarded Wilser. Though longing for revenge still burned, this man might have a better use. Fathen was more potent than he had ever been as a priest of Caros, but he was only one person. Eligos had set two important tasks upon him. Wilser could help with a third task Fathen had considered. If the Fist of the *Inconnu* were to grow strong again, it would need many converts. Like his master, Fathen could create undead using the flow of *elonsha*, a draining process that necessitated renewal by consumption of flesh.

Unlike his master, Fathen could destroy himself if he overextended his powers. Releasing *elonsha* was akin to bleeding himself, and if he bled too much, he would cease to exist. His limited abilities made it more efficient to bring the living to their side as members of the Fist. With them as an army, and undead to bolster them, they could destroy those who might stand against them.

Fathen knew the Fist still existed and would as long as humans had reasons for serving Eligos. They would be ready to see their master's return to power. Once Wilser found them, they could recruit among the downtrodden who might find a better life under Eligos. While Fathen worked on those in power, the Fist would be gathering from those who had none.

Eligos never said Fathen couldn't obtain assistance with his tasks.

His eyes locked with Wilser's frightened orbs. "I'm not going to kill you. I have a task."

Eight hours of travel brought Fathen and Wilser to the Great Temple of Caros in the city of Kalador as the early morning sun gleamed across the stone. Since his first days as an acolyte, Fathen dreamed of serving in the Temple. As he trained in his home of Kalaser, several days west, he always saw himself coming to the capital and taking his place in this holy building. In those wistful days, he dared aspire to the exalted position of Prelate, head of the Temple. He was naive enough to believe it within his grasp.

As he stared at the awe-inspiring building, he realized his dream was still within his grasp, although in a completely different way than he ever expected.

"That's the most beautiful thing I've ever seen." Wilser stood beside him, his eyes rimmed with exhaustion yet filled with enchantment and entirely in Fathen's thrall. Turning him had been simpler than Fathen expected, so uncomplicated was the mercenary's mind.

"Yes, it is," Fathen agreed. And it was the truth. Even now, he appreciated the structure's beauty. Built of washed yellow granite, the domed roof rose thirty feet above and was topped with gold. On the steps leading to the temple, sunstones gleamed, set into the stone in seemingly random lines. Fathen knew the stones formed the eight-rayed symbol of Caros when seen from above. It had been created so the god could witness his worshipers' devotion. For those who came to worship, the same icon crowned the top of the golden dome, giving the temple another twenty feet of height.

Larger than any of the buildings near it, the temple projected strength and confidence.

If only the god it represented had been as strong, he might still hold Fathen's heart.

"You understand your instructions?" Fathen asked Wilser.

"I do," Wilser said. "Find someone from the Procurers, tell them to inform Torin you would speak with him, and to send word to *The Bell Sonnet.* Then I'm to show this paper around the docks and see who recognizes it."

Wilser held up the cheap pulpreed parchment upon which Fathen had drawn a sword with an arrowhead as the tip of the blade. A wavy pattern ran the length of the sword, thick in the middle and tapering at each end. Under the sword, he had drawn three circles, the center bigger than the two on either side. Fathen was no artist or calligrapher, and though crudely drawn, the pictogram represented well enough what it was: the symbol used by the Fist of the *Inconnu.* Few would recognize it. Those who did would be the people Wilser wanted to speak with, to organize and spread the word that Eligos survived the battle at Broken Mountain. The Fist would rise again. It was time to cause trouble.

An enemy of Eligos might recognize the symbol and kill Wilser. The Temple of Caros had agents who kept watch for such people, although they spent most of their time rooting out those who worshipped Melteth or Vidali, the Insane Gods. It was a risk Fathen could accept. If someone killed his thrall, Fathen would find out who, kill them, and then locate another ruffian to do the work. There were always ruffians.

"Go about it," Fathen said. "I have my own tasks to perform."

Wilser nodded and headed east toward the docks.

Fathen walked up the temple steps. Others nodded as they passed: priests, supplicants, a pair of guards. He did not deign to nod back. The life around him proved distracting. It was growing time to feed again. Once he took care of this matter, he would find a suitable meal.

He reached the top of the steps and walked across the landing. In gleaming yellow plate armor with the sunburst pattern of Caros etched in the breastplate, guards stood on either side of the large, open doors. They held halberds and wore short swords in yellow leather scabbards. They wore no helmets, both clean-shaved, their brown hair long and braided, in imitation of the sun god's ever-reaching rays of light. Fathen's black hair still hung almost to his waist, though he had not braided it since taking up service with Eligos.

As Fathen drew closer to the doors, his steps slowed. Uneasiness filled him. His vision grew hazy. The closer he got, the harder it became to move. Dim yellow light filled the doorway, making it difficult to see the chamber beyond.

He stopped. He physically couldn't move anymore. Nausea welled up in him. Pain racked his body, physical discomfort he hadn't felt since his master returned him. The sanctity of this building hurt his mind. He had to force himself not to turn and flee.

"Are you well, sir?" one of the guards, little older than a child, asked.

"I'm fine," Fathen said through gritted teeth. "A mild spell of dizziness, but it is passing."

He knew what stopped him.

The power of Caros.

Or the power of the belief of those inside. The building itself, hundreds of years old and enshrined to the worship of the sun god, stood wrapped in divinity. It rejected what Fathen had become. It worked to thwart his entrance.

He would not let it.

Fathen had left Caros because the god no longer had the strength he should. Eligos was the stronger being now. He imbued Fathen with a measure of his ability and had handed Fathen a task to prove he was worthy of his elevated position.

He would not be balked.

As he worked to take another step forward, he imagined knocking down a cliff would be easier. With great effort, his foot moved. One step. And another. His vision clouded more. The radiance in the door brightened and grew solid, obscuring what lay beyond. His head thrummed.

You will not stop me, he told his old god, although he had no idea if his old god still listened.

Another step forward.

It felt like walking through rock. He had gone completely blind. His ears rang. He almost fell back but refused to do so.

You will not stop me, he repeated. *My master is stronger than you.*

Yes, I am, a voice whispered in his head, so faint he thought he imagined it. *You are not up to this task yet, but you did not falter. That is worthy of praise and assistance.*

Power filled Fathen's mind and body. A surge of energy infused him as if he just consumed ten lives.

The pressure fell away.

The blindness left his eyes.

He almost stumbled at the absence of resistance and caught himself before he fell through the doorway. If the guards noticed, they gave no indication.

The yellow barrier had disappeared, revealing the large foyer. Priests mingled, speaking to supplicants or acolytes. A giant statue occupied the center of the room. A man in yellow robes, his face obscured by the sunlight that shone on it: the visage of Caros, too bright for any to gaze upon.

The strength of Eligos surprised Fathen. Though he believed his master had great power, with Fathen's reincarnation as proof, this display of puissance over such a distance was more than he expected.

I grow stronger, as you will, Eligos told him. *The twins offer praise and sacrifice to me.*

The twins—the Necromancers who offered their souls and prowess to Eligos—were the last Necromancers other than Erick.

I will hold back the faith shine of your bastard god, Eligos whispered. *But you must prove your worth. You will have to best his representative yourself. If his supplicants destroy you for blasphemy, you will go to whatever fate awaits you.*

Fathen couldn't shiver anymore, but the memory of that sensation played through his mind as he considered again facing the judgment of Alakaneth. Fathen knew too well his fate if that came to pass. It steeled his determination to bend the Prelate to his will.

He crossed the foyer toward a clump of priests in yellow robes with gold chains on their necks and wrists. Not long ago, he had been one of them. Now he despised them and would happily see them burn.

"Your pardon," he said, doing his best to don a mask of politeness and not seize one of them by the throat. "I seek an audience with Perius Oerus."

The priests regarded him with skepticism, no doubt disdaining his attire. Though well-crafted, his outfit was that of a merchant or road-man, not a priest.

One of them, a foot shorter than Fathen with scant hair and a sizable paunch, said, "He does not give audience to just anyone. Do you have an appointment?"

Fathen offered a smile. "No. I suggest you take me to him anyway." He exerted his will on this unctuous man.

The priest took a step back, and his eyes went out of focus for a moment. Then they returned and stared at him. "If you wish." He turned to his four fellows. "We will continue our discussion when I return."

The other three gave their companion puzzled looks, as if uncertain why he acquiesced to this unknown man. They made no move to stop him, however.

"He won't see you," one of the others said as they walked away.

"Yes, he will," Fathen said.

They strolled across the foyer and into a wide hallway covered with granite and sunburst symbols created from gold. The hall gleamed in the lantern light. It hurt Fathen's eyes. The ostentatiousness angered him.

A wooden door sat at the end of the hall, a sizable sunburst symbol upon it. The priest opened the door and stepped into a small room with another door on the opposite wall—an antechamber.

A brown-haired acolyte, perhaps sixteen, sat at a desk crammed into the room. He looked up as they entered.

Fathen spoke before the boy could. "You are dismissed."

The child offered no struggle. He stood and left the room, his overly large yellow robe dragging the floor.

"You may go, too," Fathen told the priest. The older man departed with as little fuss as the acolyte.

Fathen smiled. He could grow to enjoy such command of people.

He walked to the door and paused. He sucked in a breath he didn't need as he prepared to confront the man who had sentenced him to twenty years on a backwater island amid people he despised—the man who ultimately chased him away from the light of Caros.

Fathen opened the door.

Like his acolyte, Prelate Perius Oerus sat at a desk, though it had far more style and ornamentation than the clerk's simple desk. Large and mahogany, it gleamed from the oil that polished it.

The man who sat behind it also shone, but with the vigor of good health. Despite knowing the Prelate was at least twenty years his senior, he appeared to Fathen as if they might be of the same age. The Prelate's long white hair hung in eight braids, each wrapped with thin, gold wire. Wrinkles lined his high forehead. The eyes in that round, caring face glimmered in the lamplight, bright with vitality. His hand moved across the parchment with surety and no sign of weakness or palsy.

That coruscating life made Fathen growl with hunger. He wanted nothing more than to drain the Prelate's vigor and take it into himself. Such a soul would sate him for days. He regretted his task would not allow him such an indulgence.

That life also frightened him. Such a strong soul might be able to escape before he could subvert it to the will of Eligos. He pushed aside the fear. Fear would make him doubt, which would make him falter. Health and faith were not the same. Fathen would gladly match his faith in a strong master against the Prelate's loyalty to a weak god.

213

"I'm busy, Landin," the Prelate said without looking up. His voice had a deep, commanding quality. Fathen imagined the rare sermons given by the man swayed followers in significant ways. "Whatever it is, it can wait."

Fathen shut the door. "Writing more letters condemning priests to solitude and desolation?"

That got the man's attention. He stopped writing as his face jerked up, and his eyes settled on Fathen. "Who in the name of Caros are you?"

"I am no one in the name of Caros," Fathen said. Speaking the name filled him with rage. "I am here in the name of a greater being, and you and I are going to reach an agreement."

"Who are you? You are not allow—"

"Shut up," Fathen said. He didn't try to exert his will. He would save that for the important matters coming soon. Fathen also had an imposing voice, and his command brought shocked silence. He advanced toward the Prelate as he spoke.

"I am Fathen Malnun of Kalaser, one of your former priests. Twenty years ago, you condemned me to an island because I spoke truth no one wanted to hear. Then when I requested to chase away a family of Necromancers, you denied my request. So, I stayed, and I waited. Now the staying and waiting are over. I have found a better path than Caros. You are about to join me on that path."

Perius stood, no recognition in his green eyes. "If I sent you away, I'm certain there was a good reason. The Necromancers are sacro—"

"Yes, sacrosanct. I know," Fathen's voice overrode the older man. "So you said in your letter. Sacrosanct they may be, but most of them are now dead, and two have returned to their former master. The time is upon us for Eligos to claim this world, as he did long ago, and you are going to help."

Alarm aged the man's lined face. Fathen saw the Prelate was an old man, strong or not. He had lived well past when he should have.

"Landin, summon the—"

Fathen's long arm reached across the desk and latched on to the Prelate's throat, stopping his useless shout. With strength he never possessed while alive, Fathen dragged Perius across the desk. Paper scattered, kicked by flailing legs. Black ink spattered the Prelate's yellow robe. Sheathes of parchment followed the living and the dead as the men dropped to the floor, Fathen's weight on the Prelate's throat. "Time for you to join us."

Perius's eyes bulged, green and bright in his rapidly reddening face. His hands gripped Fathen's arms and worked to pull them away. Strong as the man was, he could not match Fathen, who had both leverage and the anger of twenty years behind him.

In time, the struggles grew weaker. Fathen watched as the life slowly left the Prelate. It took all his willpower not to sink his teeth into the flesh before him. When this was over, maybe he would feast upon young Landin.

The Prelate of Caros died.

The light disappeared from the aged man's eyes as his *nanta* prepared to go before Alakaneth. Now Fathen would need all his will.

The silvery *nanta* slipped from the Prelate's body. As if born with the instinct, Fathen reached out mentally and grabbed the soul.

Images filled him. Fragments of the Prelate's life: a man devoted to his temple and loving his god. All Perius Oerus did, he did with the best interest of the Temple. The images ended with the man's death. They showed Fathen a man not afraid of the end. Perius died a happy man; now he would be with the god he served faithfully all his life.

The Prelate's arrogance enraged Fathen. No man should be so certain of a thing. He would show the smug bastard how wrong he was to have such faith.

The *nanta* spoke to him, not in words, but in abstract images that translated to concepts Fathen's corrupted soul could understand.

Are you Alakaneth?

Fathen sent forth a string of images. *No. I am the one you will serve.*

You are not Caros.

You no longer serve Caros. You will serve that which serves the Master of Shadows.

The *nanta* rebelled. Tried to break free. Fathen held tight. *Submit.*

Never.

Submit. Fathen forced his will on the soul. Poured his rage toward the sins of the living man into his desire to subvert the dead one.

Promises of power and position could sway some men. Fathen had accepted this lure, and gladly. Perius Oerus was not such a man. He would not be won over or seduced, only cowed.

Fathen pounded on the man's *nanta*. Pressed upon him the hope-lessness of life. Showed him the pain he would endure if he did not submit. Lashed at him with psychic tooth and claw and tore at his defenses.

Perius resisted. Once, he almost escaped the hooks Fathen had set. Fathen's fear of the consequences of failure drove him harder. He pummeled the soul. Bore onto it with all his energy, slammed it with his conviction.

In the end, Fathen's belief in Eligos and fear of damnation wore down the Prelate and overtook his faith. With mental anguish that rocked Fathen's mind, the *nanta* of Perius Oerus shifted from silver to black speckled with shades of deep red. *I submit*, the soul told him.

Then live again, Fathen told him as *elonsha* poured from him and into the body of the dead Prelate.

Fathen slowly became aware again of his body. He didn't know how much time had passed, though it felt like hours. Hunger bore on him as physical pain, as if he had starved for days. His head spun, a living feeling he thought gone.

Beside him, Perius Oerus, former Prelate of Caros, stirred. He sat up a changed man. His hair had transformed from ghostly white to the black of coal. Lines still wrapped his face, but they had dimin-ished, so he now appeared no older than forty. He looked at Fathen, wonder in his green eyes at what he had become mixed with hatred for the one who had done it.

Fathen didn't care. His servant could hate him, so long as he also obeyed. And Fathen knew Perius would obey. He lost any choice when he submitted. Fathen smiled. "Are you hungry?"

"Yes," the Prelate answered, his voice soft with fear.

"Then summon young Landin. We will feast. And tomorrow, we will seek an audience with the Queen."

20

The front-line soldiers died in such quantities that the living corpses used the dead corpses to cross the river as easily as they would use a foot bridge.
  -Calin Srend, Commander of the 7th Archery unit of Rostin

Eligos, now in the body of Min the miner, sat at the crossroads that formed the truncating border of Dorfork. He paid little attention to the smells from the nearby tannery. Such scents did not bother him, serving as nothing more than sensory information. The aroma of roasting meat or baking bread told him only that they would provide sustenance for the *talba*, which needed such things to function. Eligos took no pleasure or dislike of the food his adopted body consumed. He would eat a sumptuous cut of beef or raw fish with equal apathy.

The one thing he did not eat was human flesh. Such creatures served as retainers or slaves, either living or dead. They were not food. His *nequa*, the higher-functioning servants he created from *elon-sha*, like the priest, required such provender to survive. Eligos had no idea why this was so and didn't care enough to figure it out. Once he ruled this world and his people settled it, then he might take leisure time to study the phenomena. Until that long-sought day, he had more pressing matters to attend.

He cast his *elonsha* outward, seeking the mark on the child that killed his last *tabla*. He found it, a day's walk west, doubtless following the Necromancer.

Eligos tried to reach NalTalva and Keven. He found nothing. Unlike Fathen, who Eligos could contact at any distance because the priest had died and returned under the power of *elonsha*, his communication with the warrior and acolyte had limits. If they pursued Erick, they might be out of reach. They had not yet sacrificed the Necromancer. That, Eligos would feel.

Min's face frowned as Eligos considered whether he should take the time to hunt the Necromancer himself and end him. It would not be the same as having another sacrifice the boy in his name, but it would take care of the unexpected nuisance Erick had become.

Anxiousness outweighed his desire for vengeance. He wanted to reach the twins and learn what their studies garnered. That would serve a much higher purpose than killing the Necromancer. There was nothing more Erick could do on his own with no other Necromancers to aid him.

Though he didn't like to admit it, he had to accept that he wasn't strong enough to be sure he could destroy Erick and his companions. The defeat at Broken Mountain and acquiring a new *talba* had cost him a great deal of energy. He had further drained himself returning Fathen to his service, an act that, so far, was not proving to be the mistake he feared. His power would take time to rebuild. In this weakened state, he wasn't sure he could tell when the Necromancer used *elonsha*, as he had when the boy's father first returned him to this world. He had detected no stirrings since the battle at the Mountain. Erick might not have found a reason to create more undead. After all, if he thought his enemy dead, what need would he have of protection?

Still, Eligos didn't believe it. There should have been some whispers of *elonsha* from the Necromancer. And Eligos should have felt them.

He wouldn't confront Erick, not now. They couldn't kill him, but to lose another *talba* so soon would set him back and delay his arrival at the twins' home. He was counting a great deal on using what they had learned.

Eligos walked down the road and into Dorfork. Though he wouldn't hunt down the Necromancer, he wanted the child captured and used as a sacrifice. The power he could provide would strengthen Eligos and accelerate his plans. With no Necromancers left but those under his sway, the world would fall.

He had underestimated Erick and his companions enough. He wouldn't do it again. It was time to lay better traps.

As he rode through the poorer section of town, he kept his eyes open for signs of a Procurer, though this town might be too small to support a guild. The roads were mostly quiet, with people about their work. He passed a small temple to Caros and smirked.

He didn't find a likely candidate until he reached the town's market, a labyrinth of stalls and buildings that wound down a wide street and branched on to several side roads. On one of these offshoots, a child sat against a building. A patch of linen and cotton batting covered his left eye. Burns scarred his right hand. Grease matted his black hair to his scalp and stained the linen wrapped around his head.

"*Tera* for an orphan," he said, asking for copper pieces with his burned hand out. Most of the market customers ignored him, though at least one tossed a coin at him. Eligos doubted the boy earned enough to survive from day to day. He also suspected that wasn't the child's primary purpose for being here.

He strolled over to the child and tossed one of the gold *aesta* he pilfered from the ruins of Prospector's Camp. It landed in the child's hand. The uncovered eye regarded him with suspicion.

Eligos knelt close to the boy. "Where is a nearby tavern?"

"*The Shielded Swan*. Gold Coin Lane." The boy nodded his head to his left. "That way two streets and turn left."

He moved to put the coin in his pocket. Eligos grabbed the small hand with Min's large, calloused one. The boy darted his free hand toward his pants, where he no doubt had a knife hidden. As Eligos placed another gold coin in the trapped hand, the child paused and stared expectantly with one brown eye.

"Tell your master I would meet with him and ask a favor. I will wait in *The Shielded Swan* for his reply."

Before the boy could answer, Eligos stood and walked away.

~

Hopeful he had been correct in assuming the boy's connection with the Procurers, Eligos waited in the *Shielded Swan* to see if anyone would show up.

The tavern was like many others he had seen, with the same smells of old drink and unwashed clothing. The faces might vary, the menu might have different foods, but they all blended in his mind. Little had changed since he first came to this world a millennium ago. There had been some technical advances, but the people were as slow-witted and easy to manipulate now as they had been then.

He ordered a drink for appearance and sat studying the useless humanity that occupied the tavern at this time of day—those without employment, or those seeking less than legal endeavors. Eligos would happily see them all enslaved to his peoples' will or washed away in blood and fire. This world begged to be remade, and he was the being to do it.

Ten minutes later, a woman in dark brown clothing and light brown hair stepped into the dimly lit building. Her eyes fell on him, and she walked his way.

"The beggar says you want to speak to the king," she said in a low voice.

"If the king is what you call your master, then yes, I do."

"Will you submit to bound blinding?"

Eligos nodded. He mused on how much such a thing bothered the priest when they met the Procurers in Kalador.

"Follow me."

"What about my horse?"

She gave him a crooked smirk. "It will be safe. The only people who would steal it belong to us, and we don't steal horses."

They left the tavern, ignored by the other patrons. Three quick turns through the market took them into an empty alleyway.

"Turn around," the girl said.

Eligos did so. Others might have feared treachery at this point, but Eligos didn't. If she tried to stab or subdue him, she would only succeed in losing her life.

She did neither, only putting a thick black piece of cloth around his eyes. She spun him five times, and he dizzied, still ruled by many of the *talba's* human frailties.

He heard a door shift and was led down a set of stairs. They passed through a series of tunnels, and Eligos didn't try to figure the turns. The location of this secret place did not interest him.

They soon stopped, and the young woman removed his blindfold. He stood in an open chamber lit by three lanterns. The scent of honeysuckle filled the room. A man, thin as Torin had been fat, sat in front of him with one leg folded over the other on a large wooden chair. He held a cup, and a pitcher sat on a small table beside him next to a silver handbell.

The beggar child stood at the man's right side, the patch missing from his good eye. His hand still showed the burn scars. Eligos assumed he had not taken time to clean off the makeup since he would be back on the streets soon.

"Oh, that's completely real," the man in the chair said in a light voice.

"What?"

"I saw you looking at Spar's hand, wondering if it was fake because his eye patch was. It's not. He had an accident when he was younger."

Eligos nodded. "You are perceptive."

"You don't become the leader of a group like this by being unobservant. For instance, I see someone who looks like a miner, and I wonder where he comes up with the means to casually fling gold at my man."

Eligos smirked. The "man" puffed up his chest at the mention.

"Don't misunderstand," the seated one continued. "Mining is an honorable profession, but *aestes* aren't the sort of coin they see regularly, which means either you stole them or you're something more than you appear. If you stole them, congratulations, but you are well above apprentice age, so we don't have a place for you. If you are more than you appear, consider me intrigued."

"I found them," Eligos said in Min's husky voice, "and the former owners no longer needed them. I have many more that I can pay for a task."

"Now, I'm more intrigued. I'm Mundar. Your name?"

"Min."

"Min, the miner. That has a nice ring to it. Is this the same man, lad?"

Spar nodded. "That's him."

Mundar clapped the boy on the back. "Good job. Back to your spot. Sila is a good lass but hasn't gotten the knack for spying. Best you take over and hope the quarry hasn't slipped away."

Spar nodded again and ran from the room, eye patch in hand.

"Now then, what is this task? It doesn't involve killing, does it? We're not assassins."

"I only need you to deliver a message to Kalawen. It needs to be there within three days."

"I think you've mistaken us for the Royal Post."

Mundar's disarming smile allowed Eligos to ignore the rebuke in the man's words. A good thing, since he did not take reproach lightly. "It must go to a member of the guild there. Does the Royal Post have your address?"

"It does not." Mundar's grin changed to contemplation. He tapped a slender finger against his equally slight nose. "That will take horses and the loss of a man for at least a tenday. He'll need stimulants to keep him alert on the road and time to recover from—"

"I'll pay you five *aesta*."

"Five? You paid two simply for a meeting. I was thinking more along the lines of ten."

Eligos gritted his teeth. He checked the impulse to kill this man for his insolence. Such an action would ensure no cooperation from the Procurers, and they would kill this *talba* in revenge. He could not handle a whole warren, not in his weakened condition. Even if he survived their retaliatory onslaught, it would be a waste of potential resources. The limitations of the bodies he had to use chafed him. He longed to regain his strength, when he could kill a man with one swipe of a blade and return him to fight seconds later. "I will give you eight. With the two you already have, that will be ten."

The finger again thumped his nose for a few seconds. "Done. When will you have the message ready?"

"Within the next half hour, if you provide writing supplies and sealing wax."

"We can do that." Mundar offered his charming grin once more. "We won't even charge you extra." He picked up the handbell and rang it. It gave off a surprisingly piercing metallic sound.

A short time later, a large, plain-looking girl walked into the room dressed in a shapeless white robe. "What do you require?"

"Writing supplies, sealing wax, and a candle," Mundar said. "If you don't know where they are, and I suspect you don't, Ralim can show you."

She nodded and left the room.

With great difficulty, Eligos kept the surprise from showing on Min's face. "Who is that girl?"

"A servant. Nobody special."

Mundar wasn't as good a liar as he thought. Or maybe Eligos heard the falseness because he knew the girl. She might not be special herself, but she had recently traveled with some special people. "I'm traveling north and could use a servant to help. How much to buy her?"

"Yet again, you seem to mistake us for something we're not." There was no smile this time. "I don't sell people. She is free to come and go as she wishes."

"Is she not a Procurer, subject to your commands?"

"For as long as she wishes to be."

"Then how much for you to command her to travel with me until I no longer need her, when I will send her back to you?"

"You couldn't afford her."

"A simple servant? I think I could. Three months at what, five *tera* a week? Less than two *aesta* total. I'll give you three."

"No."

Eligos lost his patience. He took the pouch from his side and threw it at the indolent thief. "You may have all that is in there."

The pouch landed in Mundar's lap. He stared at it like one might study mud on a boot.

Eligos stepped forward and brought his fury and power to bear on the man. *Elonsha* danced over his skin and coursed in his eyes. He grabbed the man's collar and pulled him close. "Plus, I won't destroy you and your pathetic little den of cutpurses. When I come to rule, you will have a place of standing such as you've never had. Or you will be killed and fed to dogs. Your choice, but choose quickly."

Mundar tried to shrink away from Eligos's grasp. Fear covered his thin face, which had paled. His nose wrinkled at the smell of *elonsha* radiating from Eligos.

"Choose before the girl returns, or it will go poorly for both of you."

"Take her," Mundar said. "Take her and leave this place."

The anger slid away from Eligos as quickly as it came. He stepped back and released the thief, who fell against his chair, the pouch at his feet. The *elonsha* faded, and Eligos again became Min the miner. "I'm glad we could reach an agreement. Open the pouch. You will see I have not cheated you."

Mundar tipped the pouch. In addition to a few more gold and silver coins, several quality gemstones fell into the thief's lap. The wealth now in his possession could finance two healers for a year. His eyes widened in surprise, and he gave a shaky laugh. "If you had offered a fair price in the beginning, we wouldn't have had such a nasty disagreement."

His resilience impressed Eligos. Perhaps he *would* give the man a place in the world to come. "I offered a fair price for a servant. Not a healer."

His eyes left the fortune in his lap and rested on Eligos. "You knew she was a healer?"

"I have seen her before with some friends. You must learn that there are times when a lie is not the best action."

He shrugged. "It serves me well most of the time." He scooped the coins and gemstones into the pouch.

"Did you meet her friends?" Though Eligos asked the question casually, Mundar tensed, and his eyes grew wary. "Don't lie again, or—"

"Yes, I know. It will go poorly for me. You're quite persuasive, and I'm convinced you're much more than a simple miner. Who you are and why you have such questions doesn't concern me. They came here for shelter because two of their number were Procurers. They stayed one evening and left."

Eligos had a deep suspicion there was more to the story. Mundar was the kind of man who gave nothing away unnecessarily. He prepared to probe further when the girl returned, bearing a small writing table upon which sat all the materials necessary to pen a message.

"They're for him," Mundar said.

Eligos smiled. He could find out everything he wanted to know. She had remained behind for a reason. That might work to his advantage.

She sat the desk down in front of Eligos and offered a deferential tilt of her head. "Will there be anything else?"

"Min, meet Gabrielle. Gabrielle, meet Min. You are his new traveling companion."

21

There are many who believe that the Necromancers, because of the Covenant, should be considered holy and blessed by the Gods. Should you know a person who has such views, it is within your discretion to refuse to heal them, and the Guild will not hold you at fault and you will not be punished.

-Excerpt from the *Healer's Guild Book of Laws and Strictures*

For the second time in as many days, Fathen stood before an ostentatious building. This time it was the royal palace, home of Queen Alekita, the sovereign leader of Zakerin. In both the Grand Temple and the palace, typical Zakerin practicality gave way to beauty.

Prelate Perius Oerus stood beside Fathen, stance firm, and skin flush with the healthy glow of one who has feasted well on fine cuisine. They had both partaken this morning of the rest of the Prelate's young acolyte. Tomorrow, they would report him missing to the Temple Guard, who would begin a fruitless search.

Last night, the Prelate had resisted the desire to consume flesh for several hours. Some deep part of Fathen had felt shame at how quickly he had given in to his first meal. The newer part of him rejected the thought as foolishness. One couldn't outlast the hunger, so why torture yourself with the effort?

Eventually, the sobbing Prelate had torn into the soft skin and eaten. Tears flowed as he slurped the blood and gnawed the meat. This morning, there had been no hesitation and no tears, although the haunted gaze had not left the cleric's soft brown eyes. Fathen almost believed his own words as he assured Perius the guilt would subside.

Four of the Temple Guard flanked them, escorting them across the three wide avenues that separated the Grand Temple from the palace. Fathen stopped because Eligos whispered into his mind, instructing him. The Master had received no word from Keven and NalTalva concerning the capture of the Gods-blessed Necromancer. He knew the marked one lived because the *morazol* revealed his location. It was all too possible Erick and his companions had killed the other men. Eligos had conceived the first part of a new plan and needed Fathen to implement the second part, using his access to the Queen to assist him.

I understand, Fathen thought. After Eligos left his mind, the question Fathen dared not consider finally came. Would Erick avoid these traps as skillfully as he had all the others?

Unlike the Grand Temple, the palace sat level with the street. "Accessible to the common people," the crown liked to proclaim. Fathen suspected the two soldiers standing before the large, jewel-encrusted door turned away more commoners than they allowed in.

Fathen and Perius walked toward the two-story structure, passing through the lush gardens and well-manicured lawn surrounding the building. It took up an entire block of the city, flanked by houses almost as large—the residences of nobles or relatives of the Queen.

As they followed the white stone path, Fathen observed the servants who worked the gardens, some planting fall flowers while others pruned bushes. The hopeless, bored looks on their faces made Fathen think he was more alive than they were.

When they reached the door, the two guards crossed their halberds to block the entrance. Sunlight winked on the many jewels attached to the door, casting a rainbow of colors.

"What is your business here?" The guard on the left asked. He had brown hair and a nose that seemed to cover half his face.

"Do you not recognize me? I am Perius Oerus, the Prelate of Caros. This is my supplicant, Fathen of Draymed. We demand an audience with the Queen."

Fathen didn't appreciate being called the man's supplicant. He had to let it pass for now and deliver a rebuke later.

The guards stared at them for several seconds, puzzled and skeptical. Then, the one who challenged them gasped. "Your forgiveness, Grand Holy Master. I did not recognize you. You look...different."

He looks two decades younger, Fathen thought.

"The strength and vigor of Caros fill me," he said, "and I am blessed. Now let us pass."

Fathen wondered how the Prelate could use the name of Caros without flinching in discomfort. Maybe he was better at hiding it.

The guards uncrossed their weapons. "At once. Please enter."

Fathen pushed open the door, and the two men stepped into the palace foyer. The grand room extended fifty feet deep and half as wide. The fresco-covered ceiling reached the height of five men. The artwork celebrated all the Queens that had ruled Zakerin, from Aralena, who reigned over three thousand years ago, up to Alekita, the present monarch. Each queen wore a crown with oversized jewels sparkling from the points. Those gems represented the best examples of the wealth from Broken Mountain, displayed for all visitors to see. If he still cared about such things, Fathen would have found it a criminal waste of resources.

A grim-faced man noticed them and walked over. He wore the royal livery, a blue waistcoat with a silver rose embroidered on the lapel. What little hair remained on his head was gray and slicked with oil that gave off the scent of ambergris, an expensive pomade this far inland.

"May I assist you...Grand Holy Master?" The man's bushy white eyebrows rose, showing the same skepticism as the guards.

Perius nodded. "Sheridan, isn't it?"

A blush came to the man's face. "I'm honored you remember, Most Holy. It has been many years."

"Nonsense. I always remember those who treat me well and those who don't." He threw a sideways glance at Fathen. "My supplicant and I would speak to Alekita."

Now Fathen knew the man was calling him that to irritate him. He could have his little game. He would learn soon enough who the true supplicant was.

Sheridan frowned. "Protocol requires an appointment to petition the Queen."

"I realize that, but this is an unusual circumstance. This man is Fathen, a priest of Caros from the town of Draymed, on Keystone Island. He has come with dire news concerning the holding in Prospector's Camp, and it should not be delayed."

Sheridan's frown turned to concern. His brows bunched as his eyes narrowed. "Dire, you say?"

"Most dire," Fathen confirmed.

The man nodded, and another wave of ambergris washed over Fathen. "Follow me. I will request that she attend you posthaste."

Sheridan led them up the grand flight of stairs and down a well-decorated hallway. The royal colors of blue and silver dominated the corridor, broken by red roses in crystal vases on tables spread at regular intervals. The hall ended in another door, this one with the silver rose emblem created by diamonds embedded in the wood; the wealth brought by the mining of Broken Mountain was on gaudy display.

"Wait here," Sheridan told them. He gave three soft knocks and entered the room, closing the door behind him.

They didn't have to wait long. The door opened, and Sheridan motioned them in with a well-lined hand. "Her Royal will see you now."

They walked in as another man in expensive clothing of green and gold bowed before leaving the room. He gave them a hard glare as he passed. Fathen paid it no mind.

Alekita was a young queen, no more than twenty-five. Sitting on an oak chair studded with rubies and emeralds, she appeared even younger. Her brown hair curled down to almost cover her pale face and hung to just below her shoulders. In every way, she reminded

Fathen of a child's doll: small, delicate, and coddled. Three servants stood near to hand as another poured wine from a pitcher into her gold chalice. Her pale blue eyes regarded them as they walked toward her, treading on a blue runner with silver edging. Her mouth looked no bigger than a bottle opening, the lips painted cerulean. Silver makeup dusted her cheeks and eyelids, distracting despite the lightness of its application.

When they had approached within ten feet, Sheridan held up his arm to stop them. "Your Royal," he announced, "I present to you the Prelate of Caros, Perius Oerus, and his confederate, Fathen of Draymed."

"I remember you," Alekita said as she gestured toward Perius, her voice surprisingly throaty and deep. "You are looking well. Being Prelate agrees with you."

"The strength of Caros sustains me, your Royal. You are as dazzling as I remember, though when I last saw you, you were still a child. Now you are truly a woman of power and poise."

"I should hire you as my chief flatterer," she said with a breathy giggle. "But enough pleasantries and foolishness." Her icy eyes regarded Fathen. "Sheridan has told me you have news concerning Prospector's Camp. Speak without delay."

The command in her voice surprised Fathen as much as its depth. Perhaps her doll-like appearance hid a true ruler. "Yes, your Royal," he said with a slight inclination of his head. "I fear the town has burned, and many of the inhabitants have been killed or fled. The mining has shut down."

"It's a town of stone buildings. How could it burn?"

"Even stone buildings have wooden structures within. There was enough flammable material that the conflagration was immense. But I have not told you the worst of it, your Royal. Flames did not kill the majority of the people. Creatures raised by Necromancy killed them."

All the servants went pale. Two appeared as if they might faint. The color drained from Sheridan's face.

Alekita leaned forward in her chair, sloshing red wine from the cup she held. "You're talking nonsense. Necromancy hasn't existed for a thousandyear."

"Pardon my insolence," Fathen said, "but you are incorrect. It is true the *Inconnu* were banished long ago. However, the six who survived the battle of Broken Mountain raised descendants, the evil power passed to them by the Covenant struck between the Gods and the Necromancers. They remained quiet, and perhaps most have forgotten they exist, but they and their hideous magic never truly went away."

"I can attest to the truth of this," Perius said. "Fathen here was my man on Keystone Island, tasked with watching the Necromancers to make sure they remained contained. Though the Gods would not allow us to harm them, we could make sure they did not cause havoc."

Fathen wondered if that was how the Prelate saw the matter or if he only went along with the story Fathen started. Either way, it was twenty years in a place Fathen grew to hate.

"I fear I failed in that task, your Royal." It took all of Fathen's willpower to say the words without choking. It helped that the only thing he hated more than Keystone Island was Erick. If his words saw to the child's capture, he would say anything necessary. "The Necromancer there killed his parents, burned our village, and fled to the mainland. I followed to try and stop him, but I must confess he was too wily for me." The admission pained him. "He summoned an army of abominations and used them to kill and destroy Prospector's Camp."

"Whatever for?" Alekita asked, distress in her voice.

"He seeks to weaken the kingdom. Much of Zakerin's wealth comes from the mountain. If the merchants find out, they will have their excuse to depose you."

Fathen learned of the monarchy's trouble with the merchants from the Procurers. He had no idea if the merchants would try to topple the Queen, but he counted on the paranoia of those in power. "Without the wealth flowing from the mountain, you won't be able to pay your soldiers."

The queen sipped wine and then waved dismissively. "Nonsense. We have more than enough reserves to last for two months without trouble, and I imagine we can have Prospector's Camp up and running by then. I'll speak to my advisers."

Fathen frowned. The Queen's appearance and youth made him underestimate her. He couldn't start a coup and bring the kingdom to Eligos without an unstable government. He had hoped she would panic and do something foolish that he could use to incite others into overthrowing her. He would have to rethink his tactics.

"However," the Queen continued, "we cannot let someone wantonly destroy a Zakerin town and get away with it. What more do you know of this Necromancer? We will have him captured and executed for this crime."

Fathen grinned. At least the second part of his plan could go smoothly—time to lay the trap. "I can give you a detailed description of him and his companions. He was last seen heading west from Prospector's Camp. I would recommend great haste, so he does not elude your justice."

She nodded. "Sheridan, bring the Royal Artist. We will create posters to give the citizens and our patrols. We will use our sounder eagles to deliver them to Kalawen and the Five Walled Cities."

She turned her gaze on Perius. "I will need your illuminators in those cities to make at least a hundred copies of the artist's rendering. We'll want it done quickly and have the Royal Post disseminate it to the towns as rapidly as possible. We can't let him escape to Starrasen, or Falan-Dar if he ends up turning north. Neither of those savages would let us enter their lands to capture him."

"Send word with your dispatch, your Royal," Perius said. "They are at your disposal."

Fathen waited for the man to continue. They had discussed what he would say if all went well, and the Queen agreed to hunt for Erick. Perius only stood there, a slight smile on his face.

"Then we will—"

"Your Royal," Fathen interrupted.

Alekita's eyes narrowed, and her lips pressed tight at his presumption.

Pushing down his pride, he continued. "Again, I apologize for my rudeness, but it is the will of the Temple that you hand over the Necromancer to us for punishment."

"And why is that?"

Perius finally spoke up. "The Gods protect the Necromancers, and we would not want Zakerin to feel their wrath should they kill the Necromancer without the correct rites. Turning him over to us will make sure he leaves this world with proper obeisance made. His other companions you may do with as you will, but the Necromancer *must* come to us."

Fathen waited to see her bristle. Instead, she took another drink of wine and then put her hand on her chin and her elbow on the throne, considering his words.

"I see your reasoning," she said after several seconds. "It would be most unfortunate if the Gods turned against us, although for the life of me, I don't understand why they would protect such a horrible person in the first place."

Perius shrugged. "We are only servants. They are the masters."

Alekita nodded. "As you say. Very well. Capture the Necromancer and return him here. Place the others in prison for aiding in the destruction of Royal property. Sheridan, get the artist. Mala, get our guests some food and drink."

22

I would sooner fling myself over the falls that lead into the swamp than venture in there again. We never saw the creatures that followed us, but we heard them and felt their presence. I expected any day to die at their hands.
-Explorer Talleen Barmack, concerning the Starrasen swamps

Erick had experienced many emotions in his travels, from happiness to panic. The one feeling he never expected to encounter was boredom. For the past tenday and a half, their routine had taken on a monotonous sameness. They awoke near dawn, ate what they could afford at the inn where they lodged the night before, then boarded the wagon and left.

The well-tended road never varied. It drove straight on across the flat grassland, broken up by farms now surrounded by harvested fields and pens of cattle or ostriches. Erick had thought the birds stupid-looking when he first saw them. Having seen more of them than he ever knew existed, his opinion hadn't changed.

Every day they stopped and ate a cold lunch when the sun reached its peak. They then rode another six hours across more of the same landscape. Caravans and other travelers offered a brief break to the dullness, but these encounters were usually little more than waved greetings as they passed, or perhaps a brief update on the road ahead. These reports were always the same: no trouble, nothing exciting. Marcus was able to keep his agoraphobia in check as long as he stayed close to Corby or wore a hood and kept his eyes forward.

The two times royal patrols stopped them amounted to nothing. The men perfunctorily checked the forged travel documents and sent them on their way. Erick didn't want a fight, but any excitement would have been nice. Even the uncertainty of them asking about the boxes in their wagon would have been something. They hadn't bothered to look.

Haven't you had enough excitement for one lifetime? Blink asked.

Yes, but... He had no real way to explain the discontent he felt, the need to be doing more than walking or riding down a road. The worst that had happened was an occasional chilly rain.

Enjoy it while you can, Blink had suggested. *It won't last.*

Near the end of each day, they would come upon a town sizable enough to have lodging, either an inn or small boarding house. Despite there always being at least another hour or two of daylight, nobody seemed inclined to press on. They would eat a meal in the common room and retire to two separate chambers, Elissia and Mallow in one; Erick, Corby, and Marcus in the other. Blink joined them if they could open the window. If not, he slept on the roof. Though the rooms were cramped and sometimes not entirely clean, no one complained. They had all spent enough time sleeping in bedrolls, and the weather tended toward uncomfortably cold in the evenings.

Remembering Elissia's promised affection, Erick tried to wrangle his way into a room with her.

"That would mean a third room," Mallow said, "since I'm not sleeping with those randy clowns. No telling what they get up to at night, and I don't want to hear it. We can't afford a third room."

Erick started to tell her that they didn't get up to anything until he remembered waking a couple of times to low giggles and other sounds. He gritted his teeth and resigned himself to waiting a little longer, thankful he could sneak away to the privies occasionally to relieve his frustration.

The meals were boring, too. Mallow controlled the funds the Procurers provided, and she was as miserly with dining as she was with lodging. They always got the cheapest fare the inn could provide, inevitably boiled vegetables with scraps of ostrich meat for dinner, or oatmeal with bits of whatever the local fruit might be for breakfast. All of it was edible, none of it satisfying.

On the fifth day, they caught their first sight of the Awenholt, and Corby told them it was the largest forest in Zakerin. This provided a temporary diversion while Corby relayed what he knew about the wood, which he finished with a surprisingly beautiful song about the love between a lumberjack and a wood nymph. On the sixth day, with the trees a mile away on their right, they approached the city of Kalawen, which straddled the Zakador, one of the realm's three main rivers. As they drew close to the walled city and spotted the river docks, Erick took the funds they scrounged in Prospector's Camp and counted.

"What are you doing?" Mallow asked.

"This is the only city we'll see before we get to Kaladan, isn't it?"

"Yes."

"I thought I'd buy us all a real dinner."

"Put that away," Mallow said in her sharp voice. "We have a long way to go and no telling what trouble we might run into before we get there."

"We *are* thieves," Elissia told her. "We can always steal more."

"And if you get caught, then what?" Mallow asked. "The Procurers can't save you every time you get trapped."

Though she grumbled, Elissia had no real answer to the question.

And so, they traveled the relentless days as the wind blew colder. It no longer looked unusual to be wearing hooded cloaks, so Blink rode in the wagon without fear of being noticed as anything other than a cold child.

Corby did his best to keep them entertained, but despite his extensive repertoire of stories and facts, he had to rest his voice. And if

Erick were honest, sometimes everyone got tired of hearing the scholar talk.

"I never thought I'd miss the days of getting attacked by the Fist every few miles," Erick joked once. No one laughed. Then he caught a glimpse of the *morazol* on Marcus's forehead, and guilt kept him quiet most of the day.

Erick often occupied his time watching Elissia for unusual signs. Though he admitted it to no one other than Blink, he wasn't entirely convinced the illness had left her. The poison was gone. That much was evident in the healthy copper tone of her skin and the easy way she smiled after a long day's journey. Still, now and then, he caught a look on her face that reminded him too much of the evil that once possessed her. As the days passed, he grew less concerned, though he did his best to remain vigilant.

Keven was another anxiety that nagged at him. Erick had begun to regret both the acolyte's death and subsequent revival. Keven returned with enough intellect to retain his memories of the life taken from him. He knew how he died and who had been responsible. Impotent anger seethed in Keven's undead brain; a desire to destroy Erick and the others who harmed him was barely kept in check by the herbs that returned him.

Venomous thoughts from the Revenant pounded on Erick throughout the days, easing only in the midday hours when Erick put the creature to "sleep" so the *elonsha* could refresh, keeping the link between them secure. When he "woke" Keven, he would reinforce that link with the mantra, "I am your master."

So far, Keven responded with, "you are my master," and Erick maintained control.

The effort taxed Erick's strength. It required Blink's constant vigilance to ensure the *elonsha* didn't slip into Erick's soul, weakening him and allowing Keven the freedom to attack. Having the former acolyte around made Erick feel like he had a loaded crossbow aimed at his head with a finger on the trigger. One slip could cause irreparable damage. Until they could come up with better protection, or Erick could find more compliant undead, it was the best he could manage. As long as he and Blink remained on guard, they would be okay.

Even vigilance had taken on an aura of rote necessity. And he knew the danger of complacency.

The morning of the fifteenth day dawned like all the others, sunny and chilly. Erick arose to find Corby and Marcus curled next to each other on the small second bed. Jealousy tugged at him. He wanted to snuggle like that beside Elissia.

He walked over to the window and pushed open the thin curtains that did little to block out the early morning light. At least the view was different, with a forest of oak and ash a hundred feet outside the town instead of plain grassland. Their leaves barely showed the first turns of color. They had spotted the wood yesterday afternoon; Corby had no stories about it other than naming the trees. Mallow entertained them for a time with a bawdy tale about a forest sprite and a deer hunter that had Erick's face heated and Corby blushing.

Erick slipped on his clothes. He had taken to sleeping in his small clothes despite the discomfort. He wasn't used to anyone but Blink seeing him naked. His face always flushed when he remembered that both Elissia and Corby had seen him without clothes when they cared for him after his battle with the vampire that had been his father.

"Wake up," he said, kicking the other bed.

They woke, Marcus stretching and yawning while Corby sat up and rubbed at his eyes. Marcus leaned over, kissed Corby on the cheek, and then wrinkled his nose. "We may need to tell the harpy to let us spring for some baths, or we won't be able to stand each other much longer."

They had taken to calling Mallow "the harpy" behind her back. They still liked her, and Erick had to grudgingly admit that things seemed less tense than they had with Gabrielle.

However, Mallow tended to impose her will and make the decisions without consulting anyone. It didn't bother Erick. He relished not being in charge for the moment. It annoyed the rest, though—Elissia most of all. She and Mallow had almost come to blows at least three times. Gabrielle had held things in, whereas Mallow happily screamed and yelled and browbeat, and then promptly forgot about it. Even on the few matters she lost, she didn't hold a grudge. The group had never seen the depth of Gabrielle's frustration and hostility because she never told them. Mallow had no such compunctions.

"From what she told me, we'll reach Kaladan today," Erick said. "I'm going to get us rooms at a decent inn and order baths for all us, no matter how much she gripes."

"That's the Erick we know and love," Marcus said. He stood and put on his clothes. Erick turned to stare back out the window. Marcus did not share Erick's modesty. "Take back your role as the leader."

"Don't get excited," he said. "I'm not going to go crazy. She is right. We need to save money and not steal unless we end up with no choice." He turned back to them. "It will be a communal bath, not a private one."

"That's fine with us." Marcus wagged his thick black eyebrows while Corby turned crimson with embarrassment.

"Yeah," Erick muttered. "I figured it would be."

Breakfast was oatmeal with chunks of strawberry and a cup of watered-down milk. Erick didn't like strawberries, but he ate anyway. He wished he could get a glass of ale. He had tried to get one early in their journey at the other inns despite Mallow's disapproving frown. He had no luck. In Zakerin fashion, the innkeepers stuck to the rules. His forged travel documents had changed the year, not the day. He had his majority, so he was old enough to travel, but he needed majority plus one to drink, a stupid law if there ever was one. He looked forward to his birthday next month. He wondered where he would be then.

"We'll reach Kaladan today?" he asked Mallow to confirm what she had said two days ago.

"We'll have to travel a little longer than normal, but yes, we'll get there."

"We should have traveled a little longer every day and we could have been there yesterday," Elissia said.

"Assuming we lived," Mallow countered. "We would have been

camping outside at night, which is when bandits like to ambush people."

"We survived well—"

"Please," Erick said, holding up a hand to each woman. This was an old argument they would never settle. How Elissia and Mallow managed to sleep in the same room without killing each other was a mystery. "We'll be there tonight, and that's all that matters. We could have traveled faster, but none of us complained about sleeping on beds while we were doing it."

"Figures you'd take her side," Elissia murmured. Erick would have felt hurt if he hadn't caught the smile Elissia tried to hide.

"Yes, she and I are secretly in love," Erick said with his own grin.

"That we are," Mallow said. "Once we get to Kaladan were going to lift the bar in the House of Caros and then move to a country manor in Makern."

"You'd lift the bar with someone who would force you to live in the deep north?" Elissia asked. "Then you two can have each other. Way too cold for me."

Everyone chuckled, and they finished their breakfast in good spirits. Getting to Kaladan didn't mark the end of their travels, but it marked a substantial milestone. Erick contented himself with that.

They hitched the horses to the wagon, a task Corby had taken to effortlessly, and prepared to leave. Keven assumed his place at the rear as Erick instructed. The Revenant served as a guardian over the contraband they carried, leaving them all free to sleep, although Erick not as well as the others. Despite sleeping, a part of him stayed alert to maintain mental control over the undead.

Had anyone disturbed the cargo, Keven would have fought and alerted Erick and his companions. They all agreed it was time Keven did something useful, although Elissia seemed ill at ease around him.

"I knew him all my life," she explained to Erick when he asked. "Yes, he was a jackass and probably dangerous. Still, I knew him."

Corby had a much more practical reaction. "He made the wrong decisions, and he paid for it. Now, he's serving his atonement."

They loaded up, and Mallow took the reins. "Here we go."

"One more day of boring roads," Erick said.

Mallow laughed and handed Erick a piece of folded parchment she pulled from inside her brown traveling shirt. "Have you looked at this?"

Erick recognized it as the map the Procurers provided as part of their supplies. Corby had been amazed at being trusted with such a treasure. Erick didn't understand the reaction. All he saw were a bunch of squiggly lines that more or less represented landmarks. He knew he needed to head west until he reached the swamp in Starrasen. After that, he had to rely on help from the natives who, according to Mallow, might be less than cooperative. He regretted the loss of NalTalva, both because he wanted the man to pay for his crimes by serving them, and also because he would have been the perfect guide.

"I've looked at it," Erick said. "It doesn't have Alais's location on here, so it's useless."

Mallow chuckled. "Open it up."

He frowned and opened it: lines, a sketch of forests, circles with dots in the center that indicated cities, the names written beside them. It showed none of the smaller villages, where they had spent most of their nights.

"See the numbers at the bottom?" Mallow asked, pointing to a line on the left-hand side that stretched across roughly a quarter of the parchment and had numbers spaced at even intervals.

"Yes," Erick said.

"That's a mile scale. It tells you how many miles each tick represents, so you can use a string or your fingers to measure and get a sense of how far something is. I drew this map. I'm pretty much the best cartographer the Procurers have ever seen."

"Was that before or after you became their best bullshit artist?" Elissia asked from the wagon's back seat.

"It all goes hand in hand," Mallow tossed over her shoulder. "You don't have to bother measuring," she told Erick. "I wouldn't want all the math to hurt your brain." She removed her right hand from the reins and pointed at one of the circles with a dot. "Know what this is?"

"Kaladan," Erick said, reading the name under the circle. "That's where we're heading."

"Smart boy," she said. She pointed at a dotted line that traced a haphazard pattern across the map until it hit the bottom. "This is the border between Zakerin and Starrasen, which we'll cross tomorrow shortly after we leave Kaladan." She moved her hand way to the left of the line and pointed at a drawing that looked like a bunch of lines pouring over another line, "This is the Surris, and everything between that is the grasslands of Starrasen. As you can see, we're barely at the halfway point. We have at least another five hundred miles to reach the falls. And who knows how long we'll spend in the Swamps?"

Erick stared in disbelief at the map. At least another fifteen days on the wagon? He wanted to cry.

"Best enjoy the roads while you can," Mallow continued, her words an unconscious echo of Blink's. "I've never been to Starrasen, but my understanding is roads there are little more than a suggestion, towns with inns a foreign concept, and warmth to strangers all but non-existent. Boredom can be a good thing."

On that cheery note, she snapped the reins, and they continued their travel down the flat avenue.

Dusk was still an hour away when they approached the bridge over the Zakador. A hundred feet beyond the bridge, they saw the twenty-foot-high walls of Kaladan. The road led through the open gates and a few wagons rolled in to disappear beyond the gray stone.

Well-maintained shacks stood on either side of the bridge, both painted in blue and with the rose engraved on the front and painted silver. A wooden pole, striped in blue and silver, spanned the bridge, which was also wooden and wide enough for two wagons to cross easily. Four guards in chainmail and wielding pikes stood in front of the barrier.

"That seems like a lot of guards to collect a toll," Mallow said. She slowed the wagon but didn't stop.

"It's a border city," Corby said, "so perhaps a greater military presence is to be expected."

"On the border side, maybe," Mallow said. "It's certainly more than I remember seeing the last time I was here."

Beside her, Marcus said, "Could someone have ratsnaked about the goodies?"

"Possible, although I have no idea who or why." She turned and looked at the others behind her except for Blink, who flew over the nearby woods. "Let me handle this. A lot of times they're looking for an extra toll. At the worst, we get arrested, and the local Procurers will pay our fine. Won't look good with the boss that we got caught, but not the end of the world."

"*We'll* get arrested?" Elissia asked. "I thought the rest of us didn't know anything about this."

Mallow gave a wide grin, which seemed to Erick almost malicious. "Haven't you been a Procurer long enough to know they won't believe that?"

Elissia's hands curled into fists.

Erick gently put his hand on her arm, careful not to make it seem like a grab. He had learned his lesson. "Let's wait and see what happens."

Mallow brought the wagon to a stop ten feet from the guards. "Hello, good—"

"Get off the wagon," the man on their far left said. His silver epaulets marked him as a sergeant.

"You're very rude," Mallow huffed. Nonetheless, she jumped down, and the others did the same. At a mental command from Erick, Keven joined them and stood beside him.

The sergeant had a piece of parchment in his hand. Erick couldn't see what was on it. As the sergeant consulted the document and studied first Corby and then Marcus, Erick suspected he knew the paper's contents.

What do you want me to do? Blink asked.

Nothing yet.

Mallow held out her long-fingered hands in a placating gesture. "Come, gentlemen. We are in a hurry and have been on the road a long time. What can we do to be on our way? Perhaps a contribution to the Royal Watch Apothecary Fund."

The sergeant's face, already stern beneath his metal helm, went rigid. "You attempt to offer us a bribe? I had no interest in you, but now I wonder who you are and why you feel the need to bribe us. Guard to stance."

The other three men lowered their pikes so that they pointed at the nervous horses. At the same time, more guards, armed with swords and shields, emerged from the sheds beside the bridge. As Erick watched, ten more men surrounded the wagon, shields raised, swords drawn.

The sergeant stared at Erick. "Sir, on the personal orders of her Royal, Queen Alekita, you are under arrest for the destruction of Royal property and murder by Necromancy in the attack on Prospector's Camp."

Confusion and anger roiled through Erick at the sergeant's pronouncement. The destruction and murder had not been him. Once again, others blamed him for things over which he had no control. How had the Queen found out and sent word so far so quickly? He thought they had left the few citizens they met in Prospector's Camp on friendly terms. Had they reconsidered?

The sergeant turned his attention to Mallow. "Now, let's see what you have in your wagon."

"Why do I always get the do-gooders?" Mallow muttered.

So, Blink thought, *here's some of that excitement you wanted.*

23

We weren't heroes; we just did what we had to.
   -Elissia of Kalador

F athen felt as though he were reliving parts of his life, only now with the chance to do things the way they should have been done the first time.

Once again, he sat in front of the rotund Torin in the sewer home of the Procurer's Guild. After being in the palace and Grand Temple, the counterfeit splendor of this thieves' abode was even more apparent. They surrounded themselves with stolen niceties to disguise the fact they lived surrounded by shit—a layer of filth overlaid everything. The carpets, once finely woven, were threadbare and covered with stains. The paintings on the wall hung in tarnished frames. At one time, a place such as this would have disgusted Fathen. Death removed all such squeamishness.

The heavy-jowled leader of the Procurers tapped his sausage fingers on the arm of his chair as he drank wine and stared at Fathen. A cup sat beside the former priest's arm, untouched.

Another man sat beside Torin, as withered and parchment skinned as Torin was florid and robust. Slate gray eyes stared at Fathen with guarded consideration, as if Fathen were a snake that may or may not be poisonous. The aged man's long nose and pointed chin gave him the appearance of one accustomed to looking down on others. Considering the things Fathen had learned about this man, such an attitude made little sense to Fathen.

The two men also dressed in a dissimilar manner. Torin wore everyday, dark clothing that did little to hide his ample size. The other man wore the gaudy attire befitting his station as a Count. Silk dominated his clothing, colored green and gold, his pantaloons blossomed and frilly. Around his neck on a gold chain hung a gold amulet in the likeness of a Zakerin *aesta*. He wore a gold ring on each hand. One had a carving of a rose, the other a coin. These were the trappings of his office as a *Geleit*, the finance minister of Serberc, the southern land of the monarchy. Though he was Zakerin, his fashion was anything but. Fathen neither knew nor cared where the man's pompous wardrobe came from. Alekita, for all the garishness of the palace, at least wore sensible attire.

Fathen had requested Torin invite this man since he would need the help of someone in such a powerful position. He wondered how much compromising material the guild master had on the noble to get him to enter these dank surroundings—most likely a great deal.

After he drained his wine, Torin stared at Fathen, dark eyes set deep within his pitted face. "I allowed this meeting because you and your master helped me root out a serious infestation within my nest," he rumbled. "It was for the best, despite all the heartache it caused. But tell me why I should help you with this plan."

Because if you don't, I will destroy you and everyone within this pit you call home, Fathen thought. The old Fathen might have said something very like that. Now, he would show discretion at least until they gave him a reason not to keep his restraint. "I expect you would profit greatly from an unstable government. I seem to recall you were having problems with the Royal Guardians. Has that improved in the last month?"

"It has not," Torin conceded.

"So, if the Queen were busy dealing with a merchant uprising and demands, you would be left alone to do what you do. A lucrative endeavor."

Torin tapped a sizable finger against his grizzled chin. "It has merit."

The older man gave a disdainful snort. "Why did I agree to this meeting?"

"Because you didn't want me to ruin your life," Torin said.

Fathen smiled. As he suspected from his previous visit to this warren with Eligos, the Procurers had blackmail on the old man.

"What you propose is nothing short of treason," the man blustered. "I'll have no part of it."

Fathen glared at the man. He had little use for Torin, thief that he was. He had no use for this wretch and his unnatural fascination with children. Were it not an express command from Eligos to utilize the finance minister, Fathen would happily remove the man's heart and eat it while those dead gray eyes watched. Fathen leaned forward in his chair. "You will do everything and anything I tell you to do, dear Count D'Arascant. If you don't, I will inform both the Prelate of Caros and the Paramour of Amare who you are and what you do."

The man's eyes blazed, the first sign of any emotion. "I will not sit here and listen to this nonsense." He put his palsied hands on the rails and began to stand.

"Sit down," Fathen said, putting power into his voice. The Count collapsed into his chair as if a hammer had slammed into his head. "I would just as soon kill you and leave you for the rats, defiler of children."

"Who are you to throw such baseless accusations at me?"

"Baseless?" Torin rumbled. "I have it from the mouth of my son the things you do to youngsters."

"That was your little gutter rat who stole my ring?"

"It was. And you'd best watch your tongue if you want to leave here with it."

"My seneschal is aware of where I've gone. Harm me, and this warren will cease to exist by nightfall."

"Enough," Fathen said. He wanted to get out of here and return to dealing with the Queen and the Prelate. He enjoyed tormenting his former superior far more than dealing with these two. "Count, you will report to the Queen the dire financial situation the monarchy finds itself in. I don't care how, and I don't want to know, but convince her you have less than a week's reserves to pay the Royal Guardians. And do it where her guards and as many servants as possible can hear. I want the rumor to have wings. If you don't, I will spread your shameful secret to any who will listen. Many of the nobles may not care since they are as disgusting as you. The common people, however? And most certainly the Sect of Amare. After all, if you aren't using sanctioned concubines, they aren't getting paid. And the only thing they love more than lust is their money."

"Torin, your people will spread the rumors among the Guardians and the merchants. Let word slip that Zakerin is on unsteady footing. It's possible pay will not be forthcoming soon. Go on a crime spree, too. Stir things up. I want this city ready to riot within a tenday."

"That's a tall order," Torin said. "The monarchy is stable, and there is little discontent. What are you going to do to help bring this disorder about?"

Fathen offered a grim smile. "Soon, people will learn why their ancestors feared Necromancy."

Two days later, Fathen stood in one of the side rooms of the Grand Temple with twenty-three members of the Fist of Eligos. Wilser stood beside him. Though the number of people was smaller than Fathen wanted, they would do for a beginning. Considering the difficulty of ferreting out members of an outlawed faction, the ability of his new lackey to find this many so quickly impressed Fathen.

A rough-looking group, they dressed in the patched and soiled garb of menial workers. As Fathen and Wilser escorted them through the decorated halls of the temple to this chamber, they received more than a few stares. None of the gaping acolytes or priests said anything, however. They had been told in no uncertain terms by the Prelate to leave the new arrival alone and allow him and any guests to come and go as he pleased.

This was a good start. Fathen already pictured himself ruling Zakerin in Eligos' name, bringing his old home into his new master's fold.

"Gentlefolk," Fathen said, "you are blessed, for you are here at the dawning of a new age. The day many of you thought in your hearts would never come is now upon you. Your perseverance through times of doubt will be rewarded. The age of the *Inconnu* has arrived. Stifled a millennium ago by traitors, this time has been too long coming. And yet, we should be grateful to those seditious Necromancers."

Grumbles of discontent greeted this statement. Fathen raised his voice over the mutterings. "We are grateful because we are alive to see the beginning of this glorious new reign. We are the spark that will light the fire. In years to come, they will say, 'Here in Kalador, it began. Here started the rise of the Master of Shadows' new reign. Fathen and his Fist were the ones. Their power and skill were the avalanche that buried Kalador and put the world on the path to its true destiny.'"

Boisterous shouting and cheers followed.

Fathen smiled. "Are you ready to sow the destruction that will help bring this city under our control?"

Cries of "yes" and "praise Eligos" filled the room.

Fathen was thankful for the thick doors and solid walls of the temple. Prelate's edict or not, such utterances might bring reprisals if the faithful of Caros heard them. At one time, Fathen might have feared the wrath of Caros himself, vengeance for uttering such blasphemies in his grandest house. Now, he knew better. The Gods either no longer cared or were powerless.

Fathen rolled up his sleeve, revealing the thick black symbol that marked him as his Master's man. "Show your allegiance."

Each member revealed the symbol of the Fist on their arm: two black lines stuck straight out of a circle with three dots in a triangle pattern inside it. Fathen nodded proudly at this show of solidarity.

Now came the crucial moment.

Fathen pointed at a table on which sat a collection of pewter goblets half-filled with wine. "We shall drink in celebration of this auspicious beginning. Take forth a cup and raise it above your heads."

Dropping their sleeves, the men and women shuffled over in a disorderly fashion, each grabbing one of the vessels. When they all had a goblet and more or less returned to formation, Fathen also grabbed a cup. He did not offer one to Wilser, who had remained standing where Fathen told him before this ceremony began. Fathen raised his goblet. "To the greatness that is Eligos. Do you pledge to offer yourselves for his greater power?"

"We do," the voices said in a ragged chorus.

"Will you give all to ensure his dominance in all things?"

"We will."

"Are you now and forever loyal to the glory of the *Inconnu*?"

"Yes."

"To the beginning of a new world." Fathen put the cup to his lips and drank.

The others followed suit, slurping down the wine. Fathen made sure to provide a fine vintage so his recruits would want every drop. He also acquired a strong-flavored varietal to hide the taste of poison.

After everyone drained their cup, Fathen said, "To the glory of Eligos, I offer you as sacrifice."

He saw it as they began to realize what had happened. The wide eyes of surprise and the astonished gasps as the venom roiled through their blood. Fathen had acquired the deadly liquid from Torin. The Procurers weren't assassins, but they had access to an assassin's tools.

The convulsions started. People fell to their knees. A few of them glared at Fathen and walked toward him, hands outstretched as if they intended to strangle him. They got no further than three or four steps before they collapsed.

"What's happening?" Wilser asked, fear in his deep voice.

"What must," Fathen said.

A minute after they drank the wine, all of the Fist members lay dead on the floor, some curled in on themselves, others sprawled as if stretched out to sleep.

While Wilser stared goggle-eyed at the death, Fathen stepped behind him. "Thank you for your help," he whispered into the mercenary's ear. "I offer your blood to Eligos. Let it bring forth your brethren."

"Wh—" Fathen drew a knife across Wilser's throat, and the man's question dissolved into gurgling. Wilser pushed his hand against the wound, trying to stop the gush of blood.

"To your glory, Eligos," Fathen said. He put his hands under Wilser's throat and let the man's life coat him. *Elonsha* roiled around him, dancing through the blood and coursing over his body. It was the closest he had felt to his living self since he returned. He resisted the urge to lick his hands. There would be time to feast later.

He went to the first dead body, a young woman, and touched a finger to her lips. *"Gholar a cnila de Eligos mirc nonca,"* He intoned. *Rise with the blood of Eligos upon you.*

The girl sucked in a breath, and the blood disappeared into her mouth. Her eyes opened.

Fathen grinned, giddy with the power at his hands. Twenty years as a priest of Caros had never given him this.

After returning ten of his supplicants, he needed more blood. He returned to Wilser, dead in a pool of gore. Fathen dipped his hands into the cooling liquid and gave in to the temptation. He licked his index finger and savored the coppery taste. *Elonsha* continued to rage across his nerves. Now, he not only felt alive; he felt more so than he ever had when he had lived.

He finished his work and soon had twenty-three *vohquana* standing before him, ready to kill at his command. He stared at Wilser's body. The man had served his function, and Fathen had no desire to bring him back. He saw no need to reward one who insulted him.

Yes, a voice said in his head. *And what if I had thought that way? You would not be standing there.*

You are right, Fathen thought. *But his throat is slit.*

That matters not to the dead.

Fathen relented. He had hoped to feast on Wilser's body with the Prelate as a final indignity to the man. Eligos was right, however. The mercenary had proven himself resourceful. He should have the opportunity to continue to do so.

Using the man's blood, he touched his finger to Wilser's lips. *"Gholar a cnila de Eligos mirc nonca."*

Wilser's eyes flew open. He sat up as if a spring pushed against his back. "What have you done?" he asked. His words had a slight mushiness and whistling undertone.

"I've made you immortal," Fathen told him. "Or as immortal as one can ever be. You will want to wear a scarf in public."

Wilser touched his neck, feeling the gash across his throat. His mouth fell open as he brought his fingers up and saw the blood. Then, to Fathen's surprise, the man smiled. "Well, ain't that something. Amazing. What do you need me to do?"

"There will be plenty tomorrow. For now, all of you wait here. I'll have instructions soon."

He left the room, closed the thick wooden door behind him, and headed for the Prelate's chamber, which they now shared. Perius knew the city, knew who had power and influence and in what measure. It was time to figure out who needed to die to cause the most confusion and terror.

24

Undead we were used to. We had seen plenty of them. But when the portals
opened and these new creatures spilled forth, any hope of survival died.
  -Anonymous commander of the garrison at Esteri

E rick and Blink sat in darkness so dense even Blink's night
vision revealed little. There wasn't much to see in any case:
nothing in the carriage but a splintered wooden floor with a
chamber pot secured in one corner. They had been stuck in a stuffy,
windowless carriage for two days, heading back to Kalador to stand
trial before the Queen. Keven sat in another corner, his hands and legs
chained. The guards had quickly realized Keven's true nature and
brought him along as proof of Erick's "unholy powers."

As the carriage jostled down the road, Erick wondered if they
should have fought at the bridge. His initial instinct had been to do
just that. The grim faces of the soldiers surrounding them had
dissuaded him. The Royal Guardians weren't wayward bandits or
untrained ruffians. They were seasoned warriors well-versed in the
use of their weapons. Erick's friends would have shown well, but the
numbers were against them. Keven would have killed many of the

guards until they overwhelmed and bound him, as the Procurers had done with NalTalva.

Erick briefly hoped Blink would remain free, unknown by the guards. That hope was dashed when the sergeant demanded Blink join them upon threat of death to his master.

He could ill afford this delay. He had two options: one was to persuade the Queen of both his innocence and the importance of his mission. Given the reactions of most people to his abilities and the Queen's efforts to have him found, that prospect held little promise.

His other option was to escape and continue on his own. His chest hitched as he considered leaving his friends imprisoned in the Kaladan jail, charged with aiding in the destruction of Prospector's Camp, and the transportation of illegal goods. If he escaped, could he somehow rescue them?

One thing at a time, Blink told him.

You're right, Erick thought back. He focused on his situation. Their escort consisted of four guards and a driver. Now and then, through the squeak and clatter of the carriage, he could hear their muffled voices and the occasional burst of raucous laughter. They had manacled his hands with thick-chained cuffs, a situation that proved decidedly inconvenient when he tried to use the chamber pot.

Blink's hands and feet were chained. His wings and tail remained unfettered since the soldiers had no easy way, short of hogtying him, to accomplish it. Still, the chains on his squat legs were so short that they threw off his balance anytime he tried to walk. At best, he might be able to sting one with his tail and fly away. That would leave four remaining, Erick captured, the guards alert, and Blink no better off since he had no one to remove his chains—nothing useful there.

Erick considered Keven. He was their best bet if he could somehow get free. The first day the guards had stopped at noon and in the evening to empty Erick's pot and give him a flavorless mush with a few bits of ostrich meat and a cup of water.

When they stopped for the night, they allowed Erick to sit for an hour in the fresh air before sealing him back in the carriage. His attempt to converse had been met with threats of being returned to confinement immediately.

When they let him out tonight, he needed Keven ready to attack. The assault would create momentary confusion and might allow Blink a chance to subdue one or more of the guards. With luck, Erick could get his chains around the neck of one of the men and render him unconscious.

That was a lot of favor to ask from a god who recently told him not to rely on Gods. And it still left two men free to stop them.

It would be a lot easier if I could free Keven's hands, he thought.

Why can't you?

How? Erick asked Blink. *I don't have any lock picks and couldn't use them if I did. And I don't think they'll give me a blade.*

He doesn't feel pain. Break his hands.

Erick winced at the idea. Then, he realized Blink was correct. The thing that had been Keven experienced no physical pain. He could break the Revenant's hands and have him slip out of the manacles at the right time. The extra surprise would give them an advantage. Being able to use his arms fully would make Keven much more effective at attacking. The clamps on his legs would be a hindrance, but he could do nothing about that. Even if Erick broke Keven's feet, the shackles were too tight to slip through without amputation.

He won't be able to hold a sword, Erick thought.

One thing at a time, Blink reminded him. *He won't be able to help at all if we're in prison and they put him in a hole.*

Erick had no way of judging time. He only knew it was past midday because they had already stopped for their noon meal. His stomach's protests told him it must be close to evening. That could mean another thirty minutes or two hours. It didn't matter. Keven would sit until Erick told him to move.

On his hands and knees, Erick shuffled to the corner where the Revenant sat quietly.

I want to kill you.

It sounded in Erick's brain like a whisper. He shivered as he first thought Eligos had found him. The Master had doubtless found a new *talba* and was rebuilding his strength. It was only a matter of time before that sinuous voice returned to haunt Erick anytime he used *elonsha*.

But he had not been reaching out for *elonsha*. This was Keven's anger.

I know you do, Erick thought. *You can't.* He stated it as a fact, not a boast.

Someday.

Chills ran up his back again at the fury in the voice. Fear transformed into anger. Keven had brought this fate on himself with his heinous actions. "Put your hands against the floor."

The chain clinked as Keven obeyed.

In the darkness, Erick had to use his hands to find where Keven had placed them. This was going to be difficult. *Blink, look at Keven.*

Erick connected with his familiar as Blink watched the undead. His vision gave Erick at least a vague outline of his servant. Keven's hands lay spread, the chain taut between the shackles on his wrists. Erick grabbed Keven's left hand and turned it edgewise, so the thumb sat on top. Putting the manacles together, Erick took a few practice passes to make sure he aimed correctly using Blink's vision, offset from his own.

On the fourth time, he struck. His stomach lurched as the bones cracked, as clear as breaking sticks over the clatter of the carriage. The hand crumpled and lay limp like a dead spider.

Then Erick realized that though Keven didn't feel pain, he did. His hands throbbed from the impact. As he pulled back, a trickle ran down his right forearm from where the manacle had cut him. "Melteth's tits," he swore under his breath.

As the pain receded, Erick looked at Keven, who had not moved. "Pull your hand out."

Keven tried. The manacle slid with him until Erick held it, then the hand slipped out easily.

"Put it back."

He obeyed, and the hand went back in as smoothly as it had come out.

Erick smiled. They might stand a chance. A regular person couldn't have done that to Keven. *Elonsha* protected the undead from most injuries, failing only under a major blow or an overwhelming assault. As Keven's creator, Erick could cripple him as easily as he created him.

Picking a better angle, he broke Keven's right hand.

Shaking his hands from the pain of the second strike, Erick said, "Sit by the door."

Keven repositioned himself.

"When the door opens, pull your hands free. After I leave the carriage, subdue whoever is near me. After you take him down, go after anyone else who is free."

I will subdue them, Keven acknowledged in Erick's mind. *I still want to* kill *you.*

Erick frowned. This was his first time dealing with such a high functioning undead. Were they all this strong-willed, or did Keven's hated of Erick lend him power? Yet another piece of his vast lack of knowledge about his calling. He might have to release Keven soon before ill will somehow turned into deadly action.

He turned to Blink. "After Keven attacks, I'll attack whoever is closest. You go after whoever you see."

"Okay," Blink said. "You sure this is going to work?"

"Not at all, but I can't go back to Kalador. This is the best option we have." *Or at least the best one I can think of.*

Erick sat against the rough carriage wall, staring at the door he couldn't really see. All they had to do now was wait.

He had no idea how long he waited as the wagon trundled over the road. The steady motion made him sleepy. He started out of a half-doze when the movement stopped. His heart pounded, and his throat clenched. He tried with little success to calm himself. He didn't want nervousness to betray him. As his hands shook, he wondered if he might convince them of a sour stomach if they asked why sweat dotted his forehead.

Muffled sounds reached him. The carriage rocked as the men dismounted. They spoke a moment, and then Erick heard the metallic rasp of the key inserted in the lock. He wiped his forehead and again tried to stop his hands from shaking.

Calm down, Blink said. *They aren't going to kill you, and they can't kill Keven. The worst that happens is you fail.*

They could kill you. And they could hurt me a lot without killing me.

Blink gave a grim nod. *Then let's do our damnedest to win.*

The door opened. Erick blinked at the evening light, almost unbearably bright after his confinement. He brought his hand up to shield his eyes, which also hid his sweaty forehead.

"Come on out and stretch," the guard said. "Bring the pot with you."

Erick knew none of their names. With their every-day Zakerin features, Royal Guardian livery, and heads covered with half helms, little distinguished one from the other. It was just as well. Not knowing them made it easier to attack. He didn't want Keven to kill them, but accidents could happen.

I didn't use it, Erick almost said, then realized it could be a weapon. He walked over to the pot, which he *had* used earlier, and unfastened the bolt that held it against the wall. He picked up the container and walked toward the door, careful not to slosh. Having it in his hands gave him something to concentrate on and kept him steady.

As he reached the door, from the corner of his eye, he saw Keven letting the manacles slide from his broken hands. The wagon had no steps, so he had to make an awkward jump to the ground. He deliberately stumbled into the guard as he landed.

"Careful what you're doing," the guard barked as he jostled Erick into a stable stance. "You almost—"

The soldier fell forward with a whoosh of breath as Keven slammed him from behind, broken hands smashing into the guard's head. Keven followed up by dropping his body down and burying his knees into the man's spine.

Erick didn't wait to see if the assault was successful. He spotted another soldier ten feet away, surprise just beginning to register on the man's pocked face. Erick ran forward with the chamber pot above his head. After a few feet, he flung it. It hit the man square in the nose.

Yellow liquid spumed from it and coated the soldier. His helm fell backward.

Even as the guard sputtered in disgust, Erick plowed into him with his full body weight, slight as that was. They collided with the ground. The guard grunted and wiped at his closed eyes while Erick swung his chained hands with all his might. The metal cuffs connected, slamming the man's right wrist into his nose. There were two crunches as wrist and nose broke. The man wailed. Blood burst from his nostrils and stained his neck.

I got one, Blink told him. *The driver is running.*

Find the other guard. Erick pushed up using the downed soldier's chest for support. The wounded man moaned as he clamped his nose with his left hand. His right wrist had already started darkening. He wouldn't be gripping a sword anytime soon.

Erick backed away and prepared to turn when someone wrapped strong arms around his chest from behind. Panic seized him. Had Keven turned on him?

"Stop struggling, or I'll crush the life out of you," a gruff voice said in his ear. His breath smelled of meat.

Erick quit moving.

Blink flew toward them, the movement jerky and awkward because of his bound hands and legs. Keven also lurched in their direction.

"Tell your pets to stop, or I'll kill you."

"Then they'll kill you," Erick told him.

"Perhaps they will. That won't do you much good, though, will it?" The soldier's concerned tone surprised Erick. He was used to aggression or disdain, not compassion.

Even without Erick's command, Blink stopped several yards away. He hovered, wings flapping to keep him aloft, gray face grim. Keven had also stopped since Erick instructed him to attack only those who weren't engaged.

"I don't want to kill you," the man said. "My job is to take you to Kalador. I have nothing against you, but I have to do what the Queen commands."

"I can't go to Kalador," Erick said. "Any delay only helps Eligos and the *Inconnu*. I have to go—" he stopped. If he did escape, unlikely as that seemed now, he didn't want this man knowing his plans. "I have to stop him, or it will be the *Inconnu* War all over, only much worse. I'm the only one who can stop him."

"You have a very high opinion of yourself."

Erick wanted to scream in frustration. "I'm not bragging. I'm a Necromancer."

"And I'm a guard. My job is to get you to Kalador. So back in the wagon with you, while I get my mates re—"

With a thud of leather against flesh, the man's mouth smacked into the back of Erick's head, rocking Erick forward and making him grunt in pain. The guard collapsed, still clinging to Erick. Erick pulled himself ahead, disengaging from the man's grip. He spun around, prepared to defend himself.

A man, older than Erick but still young, stood there. Skin the color of burnished bronze peeked through the loose clothing the man wore. The garment, mottled in patterns of light and dark gray, covered all but his hands and face. Even his feet were hidden where the cloth dragged the ground, dusted with dirt and bits of grass. The fabric appeared to be one piece, like a bedsheet. A dull white cord cinched it at the waist.

He stood in a slight crouch. In his hand, he held what looked to Erick like a small, black cucumber. A leather strap kept it secured around his wrist. He stared at Erick, coal-black eyes gleaming in the dying light.

"Who are you?" Erick asked.

"Your savior. You should probably say thank you."

Erick had never heard his accent before, clipped and sharp. The tone hadn't been humorous. Instead, a certain arrogance lay upon the words. This man honestly considered himself Erick's savior. In a way, he was right, although he only saved him from inconvenience. The soldier wouldn't kill him.

It was going to be a severe inconvenience, Blink thought as he flew beside Erick and landed under the newcomer's watchful gaze. *And for all we know, it might have ended with you hanging. Say thank you.*

260

"Thank you," Erick told the man. "I'm—"

"Erick the Necromancer, I know." The man stood from his crouch and slid the strange black object into a fold of his clothing. Though he was taller than Erick, the flowing cloth hid his size. "I am Sangay, of the Bozba tribe of Falan-Dar."

A Sakenin. That explained his skin color and, presumably, his strange clothing. It didn't explain much else.

"How do you know who I am?" A sudden fear that this man was a member of the Fist trembled through Erick. Had he traded one captor for a worse one?

"I am with the Procurers from Kaladan. We have seen the posters. Word of your plight reached us from the prison, and I came to track you."

The Procurers again. Erick gave a wry smile. They were going to start charging him.

The man continued. "I was planning a time when I could approach the men and negotiate your release without violence. Your ill-conceived escape attempt complicated matters."

Erick's smile disappeared. "Ill-conceived? It was my best opportunity."

"Then your opportunities lacked woefully."

Erick already found himself irritated at Sangay's smugness. The Sakenin had a way of making every sentence sound as if it were irrefutable truth, provable or not.

"I'm sorry," Erick said, making sure his tone indicated he was anything but. "I didn't know I had a savior to magically talk my captors into abandoning their duty and freeing me."

The man tilted his head. A string of black hair had worked its way from under the cloth on his head and hung between his eyebrows. "I would have. Your disbelief does not make it any less likely."

Erick blew out an exasperated breath. *I think I was better off with the Guardians.*

They were undoubtedly less obnoxious.

Erick knelt beside the guard, taking his eyes off Sangay. Blink was watching and would protect him. He rolled the man over with a grunt and unbuckled his sword belt. Though he wasn't much good with swords, it was better than bare fists. Erick considered Sangay's words. "How exactly has my escape attempt complicated matters?"

"I have saved your life. Now I must travel with you until you save mine."

25

Blood will flow in the name of Eligos, and the newly dead will rise.
　-Ritualistic assassination chant of the *Eligoi*

E rick stared at Sangay. "Don't you have that backward?"

The young man frowned. "Have what backward?"

"The custom is that if someone saves your life, you owe them a debt."

"Perhaps in the uncivilized world beyond the desert. The Sakenin code says I am now your protector until you save my life and absolve me of my duty."

Erick disliked the idea of yet another companion. The ones he had worked well despite the occasional personality clash. He didn't want to add any new factors.

Then he remembered his friends were prisoners.

"You don't owe me anything. That man wasn't going to kill me. He was going to put me back in the wagon and take me to Kalador to stand trial."

"Yes, I know all that. The Procurers overheard while the raven-haired girl, the scholar, and two others were taken to the east gate jail."

"You saw them?"

Sangay gave an impatient shake of his head. "No, it was another. We should leave. These men will wake soon."

Erick couldn't argue with that. He could sort out the rest later. "Should we take their carriage?"

"Yes." Sangay moved toward the front of the vehicle, where the horses stood placidly. "Do you know how to drive one?"

"Not really," Erick said.

"Then you are lucky that I do."

Sit behind us, Erick told Blink. *If he does anything he shouldn't, stop him.* Erick had learned the harsh way not to trust anything at face value. Sangay might say he was from the Procurers, but that didn't mean he was telling the truth.

Get back in the carriage, he told Keven.

After the Revenant entered the carriage, Erick closed the door, then lifted himself on to the hard wooden bench. Blink settled on the roof, wrapping his talons around a small luggage rail.

"There is plenty of room on the bench," Sangay said as he took up the reins.

"I prefer him up there," Erick said, "in case he needs to leave in a hurry. He doesn't always get the friendliest reception."

Sangay shrugged, the motion barely perceptible under his loose clothing. "As you say." He shook the reins and made a sound from the back of his throat. The horses began walking. Sangay turned the wagon around, and they started the journey back to Kaladan.

None of them spoke as the carriage rolled down the road and the sun settled on the horizon. It surprised Erick to find it a rougher ride sitting outside. After a few minutes, Blink had taken a seat on the bench.

I can watch him from here, he thought to Erick. *If I keep trying to hold on up there, my legs might snap off.*

His job done, Sangay didn't seem inclined to talk. Erick was too busy racking his brain, trying to decide what to do. He needed to get to the jungle. From what Mallow had shown him on the map confiscated by the Royal Guardians, it would take at least fifteen days by cart to get to the lower part of Starrasen, where the Surris turned the Upper Serpent River into the Lower Serpent. That assumed no further delays, an unlikely prospect at best. And if Starrasen had no roads, they might end up walking instead of using the wagon.

Once they reached the jungle, he had no idea how long it would take to track down the *wicaesir*. Then, they had to convince her to help, something he had no concept of how to accomplish.

He realized he was thinking in terms of all of them, when right now, "all of them" consisted of himself, Blink, and Keven. He didn't know this new man well enough to consider having him follow them for such a long distance, perceived debt or not.

He needed the others. Without any Necromancers to help him, his friends had become his cohorts. He relied on them and didn't think he could do it without them. Not only that, he missed them, even Mallow, who he had come to like in a surprisingly short time despite her dust-ups with Elissia. He couldn't leave them behind any more than they would abandon him.

That meant he needed to free them.

"You say you owe me until I save your life?" he asked Sangay.

"I have said that."

"Then, I need your help. We have to break everyone out of prison."

Sangay frowned and didn't speak for several moments. "It will be easier if we break just your friends out."

It was Erick's turn to frown. Was Sangay joking, or had he taken Erick's phrase literally? At one time, Corby had been literal-minded about things, though Marcus's sarcastic nature had diminished that quirk. Was this Sakenin the same way? "I meant my friends. I don't want to free criminals."

"There are those who say your friends *are* criminals."

"There are those who say I'm a criminal. I'm not. And neither are they."

One of Sangay's thin eyebrows arched.

"Okay, I guess technically Elissia, Marcus, and Mallow are criminals, but I don't care. Are you going to help me or not?"

The older man sighed. "I suspected you would ask this. I will help how I can. The Procurers will not. They do not wish to deal with the problems if we are caught. We will be doing this with no help."

Erick grunted, his mouth flat. "I've got some experience with that."

~

They paused before they could see the bridge leading over the Zakador. They had plodded through the chilly night and slightly warmer day with few breaks to drink from streams and eat the dried meat and hard bread Sangay shared. They had not slept. Now, evening drew near again. Though tired, Erick was anxious to free his friends. It had been four days since their arrest.

A sudden thought tore at him. *What if they aren't there? What if they've gone to trial and been hung?*

Don't think that way, Blink told him.

He couldn't help it. He also wasn't going to let it stop him from trying.

"We will leave the animals and wagon here," Sangay said. "They will be recognized."

"So will I," Erick said. "We have to get in some way other than the bridge."

Sangay shook his head. "They have captured you. They will not be looking for you anymore."

Erick wasn't sure he agreed with that logic. "Are you certain?"

"Guardians follow orders and little more. Pull your shirt up to hide the scars on your neck, and in the dim light, you will look like any other male Zakerin child."

Though Erick bridled at being called a child, he let it go. It wouldn't do to start an argument. He agreed with the rest of Sangay's assessment. There was nothing special about his appearance, especially now that his brown hair regained some length and curl.

Sangay took the time to free the horses from their tethers to the wagon, then he and Erick walked toward town, leaving the animals to nibble at the grass. Having been given no other orders, Keven followed.

"I'll find a place to hide nearby," Blink said. "Shout if you need me." He took to the air.

As they drew closer to the bridge, Erick's pulse raced, and muscles tensed. Sweat broke out on his forehead, despite the cool air.

"You must relax, or they will grow suspicious," Sangay told him.

Erick did his best to will himself to calmness. It didn't work. Despite Sangay's assurances, he knew the soldiers would recognize him. The uniform dress gave him no idea if any of the guards were the same that accosted them earlier. What if they asked for his majority papers, which had been taken?

Calm down, Blink told him. *Don't borrow trouble.*

Erick took a deep breath. The best course would be to keep his eyes forward and not acknowledge the guards. If they didn't see him, they wouldn't have cause to recognize him. They wouldn't spot the guilt in his eyes. He knew it was there, even as he knew he had nothing to feel guilty about.

They stepped onto the bridge.

The guards regarded Sangay with curious eyes. Erick held his breath and focused on the far side, not trusting himself to do anything else. They paid him no attention and gave only a cursory glance at Keven, who walked with arms limp at his side. Sangay nodded to the guards. They nodded back.

That was it. Forty feet later, they were in the city of Kaladan.

"You must learn to trust me," Sangay said. "I will not tell you wrong."

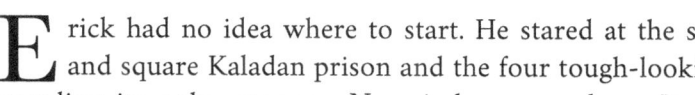

Erick had no idea where to start. He stared at the solid brown and square Kaladan prison and the four tough-looking soldiers guarding its only entrance. No windows anywhere. It was one of several in the city, according to Sangay. This one happened to be the one that held his friends.

The bleak structure made Erick's stomach knot as he thought about Elissia stuck in there.

He and Sangay stood in an alley between the tax collector's office and the land records building, both structures as boring and practical as their functions required. The city was beginning to come to life in the early morning as citizens went to work. Few people glanced their way. A vendor selling skewers of meat started toward them with a bright smile that turned into a scowl as Sangay waved the man away.

The longer Erick stared at the building, the more hopelessness plagued him. It had to be impossible to break into. "Do you know anything about the inside?" he asked Sangay.

"Not from personal experience, since I have never been caught," Sangay said with deep pride. "The Procurers have extensive information from others not so skilled. I have read the reports."

"How do we get in?"

He nodded toward the door. "That is the only way. In addition to the guards outside, another four stand inside before an inner door. The outer door is locked from the inside. One of the guards inside must open it. He only does so after hearing a coded knock that changes every day.

"If you can get past those eight men without them raising the alarm at the City Guard station, the inside is easy." He pointed at another squat, ugly building across the street from the jail. A sign hung above the door, a painting of two crossed swords overlaid with a silver rose. "Thirty cells. Easy locks. Someone brings food in the morning and evening. Leaving the cells is easy. Getting out of the prison is difficult."

"Are the prisoners allowed to have visitors?"

"Only if they've hired a...what is Zakerin for one who speaks law?"

"Judiciary," Erick offered.

"Yes, judiciary. And the judiciary must have signed papers allowing entrance and is searched upon entering and leaving."

Erick frowned. He had no experience with this sort of thing. He needed Marcus or Elissia. Without at least fifteen men and knowledge of the door code, he wasn't getting in through the front door. Or any door.

A squeak caught his attention. He turned toward the sound. Behind Keven, a rat stood near the wall, chewing on a desiccated carrot. After a few seconds, it stopped and stared at Erick, mouth hovering over the half-eaten vegetable. Then, as if Erick chased it, it dropped the carrot and ran toward the shadows in the alley, passing a metal grate embedded in the ground.

"What about sewers?" Erick asked.

Sangay regarded him, head cocked. "Yes, tunnels run under the building, but there is no entrance large enough for a person to fit through."

"I'm not thinking about a person," Erick said. "Is it possible to get me some herbs and other supplies?"

Elissia sat in her cell and stared at the food on the thin tin plate. In the dim, sputtering torchlight, it was hard to tell what the meal was, other than brown and lumpy. She didn't think more light would help. The smell reminded her of something similar to meat. All the meals she had eaten the past four days had been much the same. Bland and full of undercooked vegetables with chunks of some indeterminate animal. It hadn't made her sick, so at least it was thoroughly cooked. As she scooped it up with a piece of unsalted bread, she tried not to think about what she might be consuming.

"I'd give my left testicle for something with the barest hint of flavor," Marcus said from his cell, two doors down from hers. They had all been put in separate cages, able to see each other in the flickering torchlight and close enough to talk as long as they didn't mind shouting.

There were five other prisoners here at the moment, though none of them seemed inclined to be social. That suited Elissia. She wasn't in a convivial mood herself. Four days with no word on when they would go to trial had her ready to chew through the bars. She knew the trial would be as much of a sham as the charges. Well, the transportation of contraband charge was real enough, but that usually meant a fine and confiscation of the goods. The local Procurers should have already had a judiciary down here taking care of that, as well as the ridiculous, trumped-up accusation of aiding an enemy of the realm.

She ate the flavorless food to keep her strength. Whatever time she didn't spend pondering what might happen to her and the others, she worried about Erick.

She stopped eating.

"He's okay," Corby said, sitting in the cell next to her.

"What?" Elissia said.

"Erick. He's okay. I seriously doubt they'll hurt him. They need him to stand trial. If he appears overly abused, the Queen's advisers will look favorably upon him, which could reduce whatever over-reactive sentence she might impose."

Elissia didn't want to consider the punishment for a town's destruction. "How did you know I was thinking about him?"

"When are you not thinking about him?" Corby said as his gaze drifted toward Marcus.

Elissia smiled, pleased her cousins had found love. It had bothered her at first that they were also related. But they couldn't have children, so what did it matter? She was also glad Erick had come to understand and support them.

Now, she hoped they all survived long enough for their feelings to thrive.

A wave of sadness washed over her, an unusual emotion. She wanted to yell and cry at the same time. Four days with no light but torches and no air but the fetid reek of people in cells was enough to drive her mad. How long before she went crazy?

A soft squeak caught her attention. She looked toward the gate at the front of the corridor, thinking the guard had opened the door. It remained closed, as did the cell doors.

The squeak sounded again. Movement across the floor drew her eye.

A large brown rat scuttled toward her, its thick tail trailing behind it. Something about the rodent's movement seemed off, as if it didn't quite understand how to operate its body. It stopped and stood frozen for several seconds, not even its whiskers twitching. Then its arrow-shaped head moved from side to side. One beady eye fixed on Elissia.

She shivered. She had no great love for the dirty creatures, but, having seen more than she could count while living in the warren before her exile, she had never been repulsed by them. This one made her skin crawl. Its unnatural movements made her think of the jerky way Erick's servants moved when she first saw them at the manor.

The thought gave her a jolt.

No, she told herself. *That's not possible.*

As the rat drew closer, skittering straight toward her, she saw it wasn't the rat's tail behind the beast. It was a brown leather bag tied to the creature's waist with a dirty gray cord.

"Corby," Elissia said, unable to keep the excitement out of her voice. "Look."

Corby pressed his face against the bars between their cells and stared where Elissia pointed. "Is that a rat with a coin pouch tied around it?"

"You're so observant you must be a scholar," Elissia said, giddy with happiness. The rat stopped at her feet. Its beady eyes, flat and lifeless, stared up at her. It squeaked. The animal had to have been sent by Erick, which meant not only was he free, he was also close.

"Is that you, Erick?" she asked, feeling only a touch foolish as she crouched down.

The rat stood on its hind legs, squeaked, and spun a circle.

"What's going on over there?" Marrow asked from her cell across the hallway and two doors down.

"Talking to an old friend," Elissia answered. Anger fought with joy. Erick shouldn't be risking himself to free them, though she couldn't help but be glad he was.

Perched on its hind legs, the rat exposed the knot tied around its stomach. It also revealed the hole in its throat, and blood-stained fur.

Elissia reached down, hoping all the fleas had already abandoned the rodent's carcass and untied the knot. She picked up the leather pouch that was as big as her hand. Something clinked inside it. She upended the bag. A set of lock picks, and a scrap of parchment tumbled onto the stone floor.

A thrill as if she had just gotten her first kiss ran through Elissia. She scolded herself for an idiot as she picked up the parchment and unfolded it. Though she had never before seen Erick's haphazard handwriting, she immediately knew he wrote the note.

I know you're going to be mad at me, it began, *but I couldn't leave all of you in there. I'm being selfish. I can't do what I have to without you. Use the lock picks. I don't know how you can get past the guards, but I trust all of you can come up with a way. Sangay and I will be waiting with mounts in the alley two buildings past the guard station. Luck of Denech be with you. I want to see your beautiful face again.*

Elissia grinned, her heart swelling, and handed the note to Corby. Though she had no idea who Sangay was, she knew Erick didn't make a habit of carrying lock picks, so he must have found a Procurer. Or one found him. She should have kept faith that the local chapter would know what was happening in their domain and deal with it. After all, their contraband had been confiscated. Even if the Gods didn't keep tabs, the Procurers did.

She snatched up the picks and walked to the door. This would be easy as punching through parchment.

She hesitated, considering the other prisoners. Were they all prisoners, or did the guards have a spy in here watching for someone trying to break out? She wished she knew more about how these things worked. She wished Marcus was closer. He might know.

"What are you waiting for?" Corby asked.

"Shh," she said.

Across the hall, Mallow watched, face bunched in curiosity. A squeak behind her made Elissia turn. The rat stared at her, its head tilted as if also perplexed.

Elissia returned her attention to Mallow. Would she know? Only one way to find out. Using the hand signals known among the Procurers, she asked, *Do guards spy for escape?*

Seems waste given secure, Mallow answered. *One way to know.*

Elissia smirked at the unconscious echo of her thought. She put picks to lock, and, within seconds, the door opened. She stepped out.

"Hey," the man in the cell across from Mallow said. "How did you do that?"

Elissia didn't answer. As quick as she could, she released her three companions. Fear rattled her every moment. She grew certain tonight would be the night the guards broke routine and returned for the food trays early.

Soon, they all stood in the center of the room. The other captives stared at them with envy.

"Let us out," the man who had spoken before said. "There's four of you and eight of them, and they have weapons. You'll need our help."

"What are you in for?" Mallow asked.

"Debts."

"And you want to add escape and assaulting Royal Guardians to that?" Marcus asked. "That's not a great idea."

All the prisoners stared at Elissia. She did a slow spin, and with hand signals, asked if any of them were Procurers. Two of them answered her with signs.

The rat squeaked at her. When she looked at it, it ran several lengths toward the door and then turned to her again.

"In a minute," she told it, hoping Erick could hear her and that she wasn't just foolishly talking to a rat. She went to the cell of the first Procurer. "In or out?"

"Out," he said, his voice nasal to match his pinched nose and thin face. "How did you train a rat to do that?"

"It's a long story. I'll tell you someday if we're ever back this way." She worked on the lock and popped it open. The others gathered near the exit, ready in case one of the guards unexpectedly came in. She pointed at the man who professed to debts. "Can the chapter cover his debts?" she asked the Procurer.

His stare told her the Procurer wondered after her sanity.

"No one should be here because they can't pay. Will you make sure he's helped?"

He hesitated, then nodded. "I'll do what I can. Name's Kandin."

She returned the nod. "You'll be out soon," she told the debtor. "You have Kandin's word." She had no idea if the Procurer would follow through, but she couldn't worry about it now.

"Thank you," the man said.

She went to the other thief, tall and slender with frizzy hair and one eye puffed shut. "In or out?"

"Out," he told her. "Those bastards roughed me up more than they needed. Me and some of the boys might get a little payback."

Elissia didn't like the anger in his voice. No time to be choosy, though. "What's your name?"

"Doesn't matter," he said.

"Fair enough," she said. Some Procurers didn't like to give their names to strangers, even strangers who professed to be Procurers. She respected that. She opened the door.

"Appreciate it," he said as he cracked his knuckles.

"What about you two?" she asked the other men. "What are you in here for?"

"Being drunk," a man with a blotchy red face said. "I'll be out tomorrow."

"I'm in here by mistake," the other said, his hand wrapped around the bars. "I'm innocent. Let me out."

Elissia noted the scrapes and bruises on his knuckles and a cut on his chin. He had been in a fight of some sort. He might be handy in this situation, but she didn't know him, and he wasn't a Procurer. "Sorry," she said.

"Hey," he shouted. "Come on, let me out."

Elissia ran to join the others. She worried the man would keep shouting and attract the guards before she and the others had a plan. After his initial outburst, though, he said nothing more.

"How do we do this?" she asked her huddled companions.

"Jump them when they come in," Mallow said. She pounded her fist on the wooden door. "Somebody help me," she shouted.

"What the hell?" Elissia said.

"Get ready." Mallow pounded her fist again. "I need help!" she yelled.

A key slid into the lock.

Mallow stepped away from the door and put herself in the center of the hall so she would be the first thing the guards saw. Elissia was ready to use the momentary distraction. Her stomach clenched, and her senses cleared as the energy of an imminent fight raced through her. Marcus stood on her left, the frizzy-haired thief with no name on her right. Corby and Kandin stood nervously across from them. They would be behind the door when it opened. Corby could fight if he had a staff. She had no idea how he would do bare knuckles against armed men, so she was glad he wouldn't be in the initial attack.

She was about to say something encouraging when the door opened. A guard stepped through. He had not drawn his sword. When he saw Mallow, he said, "What are you— "

That was all he got out before Elissia and Marcus charged. She struck low while he went high. Shoulder down, she slammed into his knee. The hit jarred her, but the man stumbled backward with a shout and fell. Elissia pushed the advantage and kept moving, heading for the foyer. She would leave Marcus to finish the man.

The other three guards weren't as unprepared. They had drawn their weapons. Elissia hesitated as Nameless threw himself at the nearest man, hands clawing for the guard's face.

"Duck," a voice screamed behind Elissia. On instinct, she did. Mallow flew over her and slammed into the guard in the center. He smashed against the wall as she brought her clenched fists down on his face. He fell toward the floor, sword dropping from his hand. The guard on the left pivoted to swing at Mallow's exposed back. Elissia leaned forward and charged. She rammed him with her shoulder, bounced back from the solid mass of the large man, and landed on her ass. Dazed, she saw him aim for Mallow again.

With cries of fury, Corby and the thin-nosed Kandin ran past Elissia. Kandin grabbed the guard's sword arm while Corby reached for the knife on the man's belt. The soldier turned his hip, trying to keep the weapon from the scholar's grasp. This gave Kandin the advantage. He wrenched on the guard's arm and slammed it against the wall, trying to knock the sword loose. The guard held on and head-butted Kandin. He fell back.

Elissia pulled herself off the floor, forcing her brain to work. The guard, his sword hand free, aimed the pommel for Corby's head. He caught the scholar's shoulder instead. Corby fell back with a cry.

Elissia moved in, her eyes fixed on the dagger on the guard's belt. He saw her and swung his sword. She halted, and the blade whooshed past her. Before he could recover, she rushed in and grabbed the knife. Something struck her back, and stinging pain seared her. She ignored it and sank the knife into the soldier's midsection. He grunted. She yanked the blade free and struck again. Blood welled over her hand.

Something moved to her left.

Kandin had returned. A thin rill of blood ran from his forehead. He grabbed the soldier's arm and once more tried to wrench the sword away. This time, it worked.

Elissia stepped back, dagger in hand.

The ferret-faced Procurer slammed the pommel of the stolen sword against the soldier's head, much as the soldier had tried to hit Corby. Kandin's aim was truer. The pommel smashed into the wounded man's temple. He collapsed, blood running from his perforated midsection.

The other two were down. Marrow stood up from her unconscious man, shaking her scraped hands.

Marcus came into the room, three deep scratches along his cheek. He had a dagger in hand. "'Lissi, you're hurt."

Before she could inquire about his injury, a knock sounded on the other locked door. "What's going on?" a voice asked.

The wild-haired Nameless grabbed the sword from one of the unconscious guards. "Help us in here," he rumbled in a deep voice. "They've gone crazy."

As the guard fumbled for his keys, Nameless put his newly acquired sword to his downed foe's throat.

"No," Elissia said. "We're thieves, not assassins."

The man frowned but had no time for a rejoinder. The key turned in the lock, and the door opened, hindered by the unconscious guard leaning against it.

"Help us," Nameless shouted.

"We're trying," a voice said.

With hand motions, Mallow had Marcus assist her. They grabbed the downed man and yanked his body away from the door.

With the weight gone, the door flew open, and the guard stumbled inside. Fresh night air rushed into the room. Nameless swung the sword at the guard's back. He cried out in pain and fell to the floor, though Elissia saw no blood. His armor had protected him.

"Run," Marcus shouted.

Elissia pushed past the other three guards, dodging a wild sword swing. The night air brushed her body as she ran, only noting the others as fleeing shadows near her.

"Alarm!" one of the guards shouted. Footsteps followed. "Alarm!" he shouted again. Behind Elissia, a door opened, and loud voices spoke.

"You better really be there, Erick," she said.

It seemed to take forever to run past the two buildings to reach the alleyway. She expected an arrow in her back any moment. She wondered if you felt the one that killed you.

The wound in her back stung like a hundred bees had struck her. Warmness ran over her lower back. Blood, she realized.

Corby ran beside her, Marcus and Mallow ran ahead. She didn't see the other two and guessed they had gone a different direction. Fine with her.

The second building finally came to an end, and they turned into an alleyway. Elissia almost ran into Marcus, who stopped short.

Erick stood in the alleyway with Keven and a man in a flowing beige garb. Between them, motionless and patiently waiting, stood seven ostriches.

2 6

There are many people who envy my eidetic memory. Often, I envy those who don't have one. I would give almost anything to be able to forget much of what happened.

-Corberin of Draymed, introduction to *The Cadre*

As best he could through the rat's vision, Erick observed Elissia and the others fighting. His nerves jangled, wanting to leap out of his skin at every hit and thud. All he could discern in the dim light were blobs of muted color. He wished he had the rat's keen sense of smell.

He recognized Elissia by her long hair. Mallow was the tallest. He had trouble discerning Marcus and Corby from the other two prisoners they had freed.

He had to stifle a shout of joy when they broke through the first barrier of guards. As the second wave entered the room, Erick abandoned the rat, blinking as sharp angles and color returned in the dim light of the alley, his vision better than the rat's less keen sight. He needed to be ready when they came around the corner.

The ostriches waited with the patience of newly risen *priquana*, recently bled for butchering and processing. It had been a nasty business getting them down from their hooks with Erick fearing capture. But Sangay had been efficient and quick. Erick performed the ritual on each animal. His thumb throbbed from the cut he made to get blood.

"You're sure we can ride these?" He asked Sangay for probably the fourth time. "They seem fragile."

Sangay prepared to answer when a cry of "alarm" sounded from down the street. Erick nearly screamed at the unexpected noise. He heard running footsteps, shouts, and another roar of "alarm."

The footsteps drew nearer. Sangay put his hand on his sword. Erick clasped his weapon, his throat dry. Blink brought his tail up and flared his wings. Keven waited for instructions.

Marcus and Mallow rounded the corner with Elissia and Corby on their heels. They skidded to a stop.

"Ostriches?" Elissia said.

"Yes," Erick said. "Get on; we have to leave."

"How do we ride them?" Marcus asked.

To Erick's surprise, Corby answered. "Grip them under the wings where they attach to the body. Steer by pulling a wing. And hang on."

Erick nodded. "Let's go."

Every one of his companions looked dubious. Erick couldn't blame them. It was their only choice. They had no horses and wouldn't outrun mounted guards on foot.

"Move," Sangay said. Something in his voice broke through their paralysis. They ran for the ostriches.

"We'll follow Sangay and head for the border," Erick said as he ran to his feathered mount.

"What is it with you and undead animals?" Elissia asked.

Erick smiled as he slipped his arms under the creature's wings, took a firm grip, and pulled himself on to the animal's round, plump back. It smelled of dirt and hay, as well as an indefinable scent of wildness. Coppery blood underscored it all.

His smile disappeared as he heard the clop of hooves. The guards had taken to their horses, just as Sangay had warned.

Once everybody had awkwardly mounted and appeared ready, Erick shouted to Sangay. "Go!"

Blink took to the air.

With a shout and a kick to the bird's legs, Sangay launched toward the alley's far exit. Erick did the same and almost fell off as the bird ran.

Keven, follow me, he thought.

As the ostrich trundled down the road, Erick had no time to wonder how the others fared. It was all he could do to hang on.

Sangay exited the alley and turned left. Erick prepared to pull on the ostrich's left wing. He ran into the street.

"There," a voice shouted from his right. Even as he tugged hard, Erick's head wrenched back to see three men on horseback less than twenty feet away. He spun back, disoriented for a second, and then saw Sangay ahead, bird dashing down the cobbled street in a gait that would have been comical any other time.

He kicked the bird again, and it increased its speed, eerily silent in its run. Erick chanced a glance back. On his bird, Marcus dodged, doing his best to avoid the wildly swinging sword of a guard behind him. Shadows and forms told Erick the others were also being menaced.

Blink, can you help them?

I'll try.

Erick leaned forward in time to see Sangay turn right down a side street. Erick yanked on the wing, and the bird reacted, the agility of the movement again almost dismounting Erick. A man and woman on a walk watched with mouths agape at the spectacle.

Shouts reached him, cut off as he rounded the corner of a building. Every instinct told him to stop and help his friends.

That ended when he cleared the building and almost ran into a horse.

The mounted guard pulled short, avoiding a collision as Erick veered left to pass him. With the skill of an expert rider, the soldier wheeled his mount and pursued Erick, only feet behind.

Blink! Erick let out a panicked shout in his mind.

I'm busy, Blink shouted back.

Erick feared to reach for his sword, terrified he would fall from the ostrich. The guard drew closer, weapon ready. He would be within striking distance in seconds.

In desperation, Erick yanked back on the ostrich's wings. The creature lurched to an almost stop. As the guard barreled past, his sword whistled through the air. Erick ducked. The weapon passed close enough to ruffle his shirt. There was a *thunk* of something hit, followed by a louder thud. Erick sat up to find the guard wheeling his horse back around. The ostrich's throat had taken the sword strike. Its head and a foot of neck lay on the ground.

Erick met the guard's eyes.

The man smiled, no doubt expecting his opponent's mount to collapse.

Erick kicked the bird's legs, and it launched into its bone-jarring run.

The guard's shock was a memory Erick knew he would hold a long time, assuming he lived a long time.

The soldier recovered quickly, and soon hooves pounded behind Erick. He didn't dare glance back.

What's happening?

I got one of the guards. Elissia got another and shoved him off his horse. There are three more following us. I'm doing what I can, but they like swinging swords at me.

Erick didn't see Sangay. He panicked for a moment until he came to a broad street and glanced right. He spotted the robed man, who had slowed and looked back. When he saw Erick, he again kicked his ostrich into a run. Erick wrenched on the right wing. The bird turned, feet skidding on the cobbles. The movement tilted Erick to the left, and he gripped with all his might to stay mounted. His left hand slipped, and, for a moment, he knew he was going to slam into the cobbled street. He desperately gripped feathers and tugged himself into an upright position. A few plumes pulled away and floated past him.

A snort of air blew across his back, the puffing of a horse as it pulled up beside him.

"Halt," the guard raised his sword and shouted, his voice thin in the whipping wind. "I don't want to hurt you."

Erick might have believed him if the soldier hadn't already swung at him. Knowing he would most likely fall and break his neck, Erick released the bird's wing and drew his stolen sword. In desperation, he raised the loosely gripped weapon against the soldier's oncoming strike. The swords clashed. Erick's hand spasmed as the weapon wrenched from his grip. The blade barely missed his leg as it clattered to the road. Pain burned on his palm. The hilt had sliced the skin as it tore from his grasp.

The guard brought his sword back and swung again. Erick ducked backward, his legs gripping the ostrich's torso so hard they cramped. The sword whistled past him and slashed into the bird, sending more feathers flying. Before the soldier could withdraw, Erick latched on to the man's wrist. Pulling forth *elonsha*, he tugged on the man's soul, a clean and lively spirit. Delicious, ethereal *nanta* flowed into Erick, the closest to the Heaven of Caros a living person could ever attain. He drew it to him, reveling in the bliss and pleasure coursing through him. The pain in his legs disappeared. Light and wonder poured over him, soothing him.

Stop, Blink told him. The command had little force.

The stricken guard wrenched back and fell from his horse. Reluctant to break contact, Erick almost tumbled with him. Gravity forcefully yanked the man's wrist from Erick's grasp, and the guard rolled across the cobbles. The riderless horse dropped from its gallop to a trot and then a walk.

Erick gasped; his heart hammered with energy. His nerves ran hot with the power flowing through him as he pulled himself upright on the ostrich. He had wanted to absorb the man's entire soul, which would have killed him and irrevocably damned Erick, tainting his power and ensuring he would become all but powerless against Eligos.

A shudder ran through him at how close it had been. He couldn't think about it now. Sangay was ahead of him, and the city wall just beyond. They were almost out of the city.

We're coming in behind you, Blink said.

Erick turned his head and saw the others drawing close, pursued by at least five guards on horseback. Would the men stop at the city gates?

He stared over the stump of the ostrich's neck as the wall drew closer. Indecipherable shouts floated in the rushing wind. Four guards ran from the gatehouse and put themselves in Sangay's path. Sangay's hand moved in a blur from his side. Something white and powdery drifted in the air. Three guards reeled back, clutching at their faces. Sangay's mount trotted past the other, who drew his sword.

Then Erick was on the soldier. He threw a sloppy kick at the man's head. The guard jumped back with a shout as Erick passed through the gate into open ground. He ducked as arrows whistled down from the walls and struck the ground around him.

Once he thought he was out of bow range, Erick shouted, "Sangay, slow down," though he didn't believe the other man would hear him.

Sangay's ostrich changed gait, and soon, Erick caught up and rode side by side. The Sakenin did a double take when he saw the condition of Erick's ostrich. A glint of fear showed in his eyes.

"Three miles to the border," Sangay shouted. "Will these beasts make it?

"They'll make it to the World's Circle Ocean if I let them," Erick yelled back.

Sangay shook his head and muttered something Erick didn't catch.

We're right behind you, Blink told him.

Erick glanced back to see his group almost upon them and the five mounted soldiers on their heels. That answered Erick's question about whether the guards would stop at the city. He hoped they'd stop at the Zakerin border. The ostriches could run to the ocean, but he and his companions couldn't.

The three-mile ride was the longest Erick had ever endured. Blink flew above the group, doing his best to harass their pursuers, with little success. Their longswords, even awkwardly handled, kept the homunculus at bay. Erick expected any minute to hear the cry or scream of one of his companions as they fell from their mount, struck down. He felt alive and vibrant, thanks to the *nanta* he had absorbed, but that only served to make his fear more acute, his nerves more on edge.

Dust and grass seed swirled around him, kicked up by the birds' churning legs, and dried his throat. Dander from the feathers clung to him. The occasional glance back showed him all was the same. He kept hoping to find the horses dropping back, but they remained in close pursuit.

"Over that ridge," Sangay shouted and kicked his bird. It poured on a burst of speed. Erick followed and hoped the others did the same.

He crested the short rise and saw a river gleaming black in the starlight. He couldn't tell how broad it was, but he could see the opposite bank. They could make it across. Or could they? He had no idea if ostriches could swim.

In less than fifteen seconds, he found out. Cold water splashed Erick as the bird ran into the river. He gasped, sucking in dander that choked him and made him cough. He held onto the ostrich. It soon lost footing as the water deepened. The ostrich kicked to propel itself, and a bony knee knocked Erick's shin. Wincing at the thudding pain, Erick folded his legs up to keep them out of the way. Splashes behind him told him the others had plunged into the water. He tried to count how many, but they were too close together. He clung tight to the wings and glanced back.

The Zakerin soldiers had stopped at the river's edge.

His companions held to their birds as the undead animals swam across the slow-running river.

One of the guards on shore shouted a command. The others sheathed their swords, wheeled their mounts away, and headed back for Kaladan.

"We did it," Erick shouted with joy.

Marcus waved. The others didn't react.

After Erick didn't know how long, but certainly less than a minute, the ostrich's feet found the bottom, and they left the river and waddled up the slight embankment. Everyone gathered fifty feet from the river. Erick turned the bird to face his friends. "We did it," he said again. "We're in Starrasen."

"I'm glad," Corby said, his voice weak. "I think I need to rest." He slumped and slid off the ostrich. An arrow protruded from his back.

"Me too," Elissia said. She jumped off her mount, then fell face forward. Through her water drenched shirt, a long sword gash ran with blood.

In the end, it was decided we shouldn't burn our stores of herbs. While it would have deprived the Necromancer of ingredients, it would also have prevented us from performing our work.
 -Excerpt from *On the Evil Ones*, by Master Herbalist Howrena.

I n the past tenday of travel, Gabrielle had grown fond of her new master. When Mundar sent her out with the stout man, she feared he would want her for more than healing services. So far, he had shown no such inclination, treating her as he might a daughter. True, he made her fetch water for the horses and care for them when they stopped at midday. It was she who prepared their noon meal, who gathered ale or food from the trestle in taverns that didn't employ servants. He required her to do much of the menial work necessary for traveling. She didn't mind. Valarie had taught her the meaning of hard work, and Min was far more gracious than that old woman would ever be.

He also seemed genuinely interested in her as a person, which was more than she could say for her last traveling companions. Marcus knew enough about her that she wouldn't expect him to ask anything, but the others never thought to question her about her likes or dislikes. They didn't care what she hoped to accomplish or if she had dreams beyond her present existence. To them, she was nothing more than "the healer" to be called upon when they needed tending, then set aside until required again.

At first, she had put it aside to her manner. Though she was not one to speak out, that didn't mean she had nothing to say. She chose to wait until they asked. The problem was, they never did.

From the beginning, she had difficulty reconciling healing Erick with what she had learned. To heal a Necromancer was an affront to the three Gods she served. She did it because Marcus wanted her to. And because Erick seemed a genuinely good person, despite what he did. She had asked forgiveness every time she did it and hoped the Gods listened.

"Why so quiet?" Min asked. They rode on a small wagon, heading north toward Kalasan. Their journey would take them across the Inner Trade Ocean and up the Nallicus to Masca, the capital of Straphan. A visit to old friends, Min told her. Woodswomen living in the Lisphin, the forest many days east of Masca.

"Thinking how glad I am to be away from the others." Glad wasn't the exact word, but she had no easy way to explain the conflicting emotions that plagued her.

"As you should be," Min told her. "They didn't appreciate you. No one in your life has ever appreciated you."

And that was the crux of it. Min knew how she felt without her having to say it. He knew her better in a tenday than Marcus did after ten years. He appreciated her more than Marcus. He cared more about her talents, cared more about *her*. "It's the truth," she said.

"Even the Gods don't appreciate you."

Gabrielle frowned. She had more trouble accepting this idea. Such comments occasionally slipped from Min's lips. Much as she didn't want to believe it, she thought he might be one of those rare people who didn't believe in the Gods. Or at least, didn't revere them as was proper. Maybe what he said was true, that the Gods didn't appreciate her. Considering who she had aligned herself with, and who she had healed, she didn't deserve love from any of them. "It is not the Gods' duty to appreciate us," she said. "It is our duty to worship them."

"Why?"

"They give me my power. Because of them, I am a healer."

"You are a healer because you worked and studied. The power to heal comes from within you, not from the Gods."

She squirmed on the wagon, as she always did when the talk turned toward blasphemy. She could contend with Min's doubt. Who didn't doubt, from time to time? She found it harder to accept when he was outright irreligious.

"The Gods made me who I am," she said with as much force as she could muster. She wanted the conversation to end and return to more comfortable topics, like their mutual interest in flora. "It is through their grace that I can do what I do, and the ability to work and study, as you say."

"So, they gave the Necromancer his abilities?"

Almost from the beginning, Gabrielle made her displeasure with Erick well-known to Min. Although she couldn't help but like Erick as a person, and like the irrepressible Blink even more, the longer she witnessed what Erick did, the more she despised what he was. The killing and resurrection of the two men in Dorfork had been the rock upon her spine that snapped it. Even Blink was an abomination. He had been born of no creatures on Krinnik but created in some unnatural way. "The Necromancer's power comes from beings known as the *Inconnu*. Evil entities from somewhere outside Krinnik."

"Why don't the Gods take his powers away from him?"

"Because of the Covenant between the Gods and the Necromancers," Gabrielle said. "Do you not know this?"

She assumed everyone knew the story of the *Inconnu* War and the Covenant. Then, she was a learned person, and not everyone, especially miners, had the benefit of an education.

Min shrugged his broad shoulders. "I had little time for learning."

"Would you like to learn?"

He shrugged again. "We have a long road. It will pass the time."

Gabrielle smiled. Though she wasn't as eloquent as Corby—another reason to dislike him—she enjoyed sharing knowledge with others. It was part of the Healer's Creed to strengthen minds as well as bodies. So, Gabrielle explained the story of the *Inconnu* War and the

Covenant as she knew it. She told him how the three *Inconnu* had brought power from someplace outside Krinnik, a place of darkness where no living thing could survive, and gave the power to those they corrupted to their foul purpose.

"And what purpose was that?" Min asked with a faint smile.

"To overrun the world with their creatures and destroy it."

Min nodded. "To what end?"

"I don't understand."

"Why destroy a world? What does that gain the *Inconnu?*"

Gabrielle frowned. "I can't speak for the *Inconnu*. I wouldn't want to."

"Continue your story."

She went on, explaining how the Necromancers, at last, saw the damage they caused and turned to the Gods to aid them in stopping the *Inconnu*. The Gods agreed that if the Necromancers fought against what they created, they could keep their evil powers in case such a crisis again struck Krinnik.

"So, the Gods needed the Necromancers to fight the creatures brought about by the power of the *Inconnu*," Min said. "The Gods couldn't do it themselves?"

Gabrielle frowned. "I don't know that they couldn't do it. Perhaps they didn't want to."

"Why?"

"I can't speak for the Gods either. They are wiser and more powerful than I can imagine."

"Are they? Maybe they aren't as powerful as they want you to believe."

Gabrielle squirmed as her skin prickled, and her face burned. She didn't want to hear this kind of talk, especially from Min, whom she had come to admire. His questions sounded more like something the blasphemous Elissia might say or logic Corby might use. "Can we talk about something else?"

"Of course. I didn't mean to upset you. These are philosophical questions I ponder over ale with my friends."

That admission perplexed Gabrielle. She didn't know miners could have such intangible ideas. She had never met any laborers who expressed deep thoughts. She had to admit, though, she lived a sheltered life in the warren after her parents died, and she didn't mingle with many outside the Procurers. "You don't speak like I expected a miner would."

He offered another smile. He did have a pleasant face if you looked past the hard edges. "Just because we mostly use our muscles doesn't mean we don't know how to use our brains."

She offered a tentative smile in return. "I look forward to more stimulating conversations with you. But maybe not about religion. At least, not for a while."

~

A s you say," Eligos offered in Min's voice, keeping the smile back this time. He thought too much of that expression might make the young woman more uncomfortable. He had started to gain the trust of the healer who once traveled with Erick, and today, probed to see how much work he had to do to turn her against not only her traveling companions but her beloved Gods.

She had false notions deeply ingrained and would be resistant to his efforts. Eligos welcomed the challenge. They had at least another half-month of travel before they reached the twins in their wooded cabin. That was plenty of time to slowly subvert the child's will and poison her mind.

Eligos wished his brother Bolfri were still with him. A flutter of rage at what had befallen them in the battle with the Necromancers made Eligos want to kill something, to release violence. He resisted hitting the girl. Such an outburst would not help win her soul. Instead, he gave the wagon reins a sharp crack. The horses let out startled whinnies and picked up the pace.

"Is something wrong?" Gabrielle asked. The girl had a healer's empathy. He would have to take great care to hide his emotions.

"I want to reach Kalasan by evening, so we must move faster." It pleased Eligos that he could speak the truth. He did want to reach the city, and the sun already hung low. Lying did not come easily to him. The perceptive Gabrielle might sense his falseness.

Bolfri was the one with the gift of speech. He spun lies like a weaver spun cloth. He would have Gabrielle believing herself a god who could perform miracles by the time they crossed the Inner Trade Ocean. Bolfri had brought the Necromancers into service to the *Inconnu*. Believing the lies spoken by Bolfri, the Necromancers abandoned their souls.

But Bolfri was dead. And unlike Saburoc, the Master of Disease, Bolfri could not replicate himself. There would be no return of the Master of Lies, no poison-coated blade that would let him fester within a living being and work his will.

A shame, Eligos thought, and rage again tightened his muscles. To take his mind from such destructive thoughts, he turned to Gabrielle.

The quiet girl had opened up to him, pleased to have someone interested in her. Though he knew more about her than he cared or wanted, he had also learned much about Erick and his companions. He could use this information to turn the healer against her former friends. Though it would be easier to kill her and bring her back as a thrall, it would not be near as sweet as having her willingly turn against them.

He also needed to conserve his strength. If the twins had found a way to do what he bid them, he would require every measure of power he could muster to ensure success.

It would take time to turn the healer, but they had plenty of it. There was time to do nothing but travel and talk, time to work his magic, to let his power of persuasion leak slowly into her and push against her will.

And if she ultimately would not come to his way of thinking, the twins had ways to subvert her. Healers weren't the only ones who understood the effects of herbs and how to use them.

28

I don't know which is more appalling: that the Gods were bullied into accepting the Covenant, or that the people didn't immediately reject the Gods for their capitulation.

-Tarn Reaker, former priest of Caros

A knock at the door interrupted Fathen's discussion with the Prelate.

"Enter," the Prelate said.

The door opened, and a sandy-haired acolyte stepped in, a parchment in his hand. "A message from the Royal," the young man said.

"Bring it," Fathen said with an impatient wave of his hand. It was a significant breach of protocol for Fathen to speak for the Prelate in his chamber. Fathen didn't care. If the acolyte noticed, he gave no indication. The man strolled across the room and handed the parchment to Fathen.

"Dismissed," Fathen said. He waited for the acolyte to depart before he broke the seal on the parchment

"We could have feasted on him," the Prelate said.

"No." Fathen glared. The Prelate's green eyes were glassy with hunger. The dead man had taken to the consumption of flesh with a vigor Fathen found disturbing. Fathen thought of their meals as nothing more than something they needed to survive. He likened it to eating mush or beans. You did it because you must eat. That didn't mean you liked it.

The Prelate, however, relished the terror in their victims' eyes, the shouts as they died with teeth in throat. He took to the desecration of flesh with the same zeal he brought to service of the god neither would speak of.

"The acolytes are too well-known among each other," Fathen explained to Perius's disappointed frown. "There will be another delivery tonight."

He had made arrangements with the Count D'Arascant to have a young man or woman delivered every day. In the six days that followed, the meal had brought itself to them, unaware of its fate. The Count also was not aware of what happened to them and hadn't asked. Had he known, he might have refused, the threat of exposure or not.

So far, only one of those that came to their chamber had been a female. Given the Count's lusts, that didn't surprise Fathen.

"I'm hungry now."

"And you shall remain hungry until evening," Fathen told him. "You will learn to control yourself, or you can go before Alakaneth and suffer your judgment."

"No," Perius whined, flinching from Fathen's stern gaze.

Fathen had assured the man that succumbing to the will of Eligos had damned him. When Perius's unlife ended, the punishment of the Festering Hells waited for him. Fathen would see the same fate when his end arrived. Another reason to kill and eat the meals that came to them. Those unfortunates must be assured a place in the Heaven of Caros. And he had no desire to go to his doom any time soon, if ever.

"I'm sorry," the Prelate continued. "I will control myself as you wish."

Fathen grinned. How wonderful to control another's life, especially the life of the man who had controlled him for so long. He returned to the message.

The Necromancer has fled across the Starrasen border, and my soldiers could not follow. He is lost to us.

His smile disappeared.

The Queen had signed the message.

Fathen crumpled the parchment and flung it across the room. "Could not or would not, the spineless cowards?" he shouted. Erick had the luck of the Gods on his side.

Perius turned his head as if looking to see who Fathen addressed. "What's the news?"

"Erick escaped. I wanted to bury a knife in his heart and offer his soul to our master, then feast on his corpse." That particular meal he *would* enjoy.

"What do we do now?" Perius asked.

Fathen reached out to his master to give him the news.

That is disappointing, but not disastrous. The thought came back to him in a faint whisper, as if from a long way away. *I suspect they have killed your acolyte and the warrior, or perhaps turned them to their service.*

Unless he was dead and returned, Keven would never serve Erick. The thought of his protégé under the bastard Necromancer's control infuriated Fathen. Nothing to be done about it now.

Where are you? he asked Eligos.

Traveling north. What of the other tasks I set for you?

Fathen's grin returned. *That goes much better.*

He relayed to Eligos how the campaign of disinformation spread by the Procurers had the city grumbling. Reports came daily of disgruntled soldiers and Royal Guardians, nervous merchants, citizens complaining of robberies and violence. The Queen herself had confided her fears to Fathen and the Prelate. She asked the Prelate to call for calm in the name of Caros in his sermons. Fathen allowed it, knowing it would do little good. The Prelate's words were no longer as convincing as they had been now that it pained him to speak the name of his former God. Much of his fiery energy had ebbed.

For someone reluctant to cooperate, Count D'Arascant had done his job well, stoking the Queen's fears about the lack of money in the treasury. Though mature for her age, she had not been Queen long enough to learn guile, and she believed her advisers when they told her lies.

D'Arascant insisted they needed to get Prospector's Camp working again. The treasury was low, and while their exports of fish and timber might keep them afloat for a time, they weren't enough to sustain the realm. It would be at least a month, perhaps longer, before wealth could flow again from the mountain. By then, it might be too late. Much of Zakerin's military would abandon them if not paid promptly.

Fathen already considered ways to disrupt trade further so it would take longer to get Broken Mountain running again, should such a tactic become necessary. Perhaps the Court could issue unfavorable conditions with Amelan and Straphan, the nation's two biggest trading partners.

When the Queen asked how the treasury had come to such a dire state, the Count blamed it on the merchant guilds, who refused to extend large amounts of credit to the crown and demanded almost immediate payment. Such a lie played right into the Queen's not unfounded fears that the guilds sought a way to limit her power, if not outright oust her.

You have done well, Eligos told him. Fathen beamed in the praise. *Continue with the plan. Do not reach out to me anymore, for I will soon be otherwise occupied. I trust you to do all in my name. I will contact you when I am ready.*

As you say, Fathen answered, pleased he had once again earned his master's trust.

The presence of Eligos left his mind. He suddenly found himself hungry, longing for the taste of blood and flesh. Still, as he commanded the Prelate, he would control himself and wait the long hours before a new sacrifice arrived.

E nergy flooded through Fathen, as it always did when they finished feasting. The Prelate's green eyes gleamed with false life. Fathen knew his eyes must be doing the same, although he had never looked to see. He avoided mirrors. They reminded him of the man he once was. He longed to be that man again, even as he wanted nothing to do with him.

"Clean," he told the servants who stood in the corner of the candlelit chamber. They had been the Prelate's valets, older men who tended to the things required by a man of the Prelate's station. They now served Eligos and Fathen and would no longer grow older.

The men moved to gather the offal, bones, and meat that remained of their meal. Even two of them could not consume an entire person. The servants would take the remains through an escape tunnel, eat what they wished, and dispose of the rest in the ocean.

A bucket of warm water and a bar of honeysuckle-scented soap allowed Fathen and Perius to scrub the blood from their faces and hands.

"I must prepare my weekly lesson for the acolytes and priests," Perius said. He paused. His once lined face, now youthful and filled with color, bunched in confusion. "I don't know what I will say to them. The words no longer come to me, just as I no longer know what to say to the masses. Why is that?"

"You know why." Fathen's eyes went to the gnawed limbs being placed in a burlap sack. Perius followed his gaze and frowned.

"Don't let it trouble you," Fathen said. "You made the right choice. Postpone this week's lesson. Tell them the troubles in the city and consultation with the Queen have occupied your time. You will speak to them next week. Then, we will plan. When it is necessary, I will speak to them."

Once they finished cleaning themselves, Fathen and the Prelate left the room, a "meditation chamber" below the main floor of the temple. Only the Prelate and those he invited were allowed entrance. They strolled down the dark hallway, a flickering torch at the far end their only guide. They reached it and headed up the steps. The doorway at the top brought them into the back entrance of the Prelate's chamber. As soon as they entered the room, the sound of running feet caught their attention. While Fathen closed one door, a fist pounded on the other.

"Enter," the Prelate said, a sense of unease in his voice.

One look at the panic-stricken face of the young man told Fathen he was about to be pleased by what he heard.

"Your Most Holy," the boy gasped. "The docks are on fire."

2 9

The toll of death is unimaginable. It will take months before we have a full accounting.

    -Report to King Relham of Amelan

Erick leapt off his mount and ran toward Elissia. Worry overrode his concentration, and he lost mental control of the ostriches. They collapsed, dead again, accompanied by a muffled "oof" as Marcus spilled to the ground. He rolled out of the fall and ran toward Corby.

Erick reached Elissia at the same time as Mallow and dropped to his knees.

"Pull the shirt away from the wound," Mallow said as she also knelt.

Erick did so as carefully as possible, tearing the fabric at the top and bottom of the garment. He winced as he exposed the extent of the long slice through her pale flesh.

"It's not deep," Mallow told him as if she could read his thoughts. "How's the thinker?" she shouted.

"He's got an arrow in his back," Marcus yelled back, his voice high with stress. "How the hell do you think he is?"

"Is he still breathing?" Mallow asked.

"Yes," Marcus answered, "but it's shallow."

Mallow pointed at the ground. "Scoop up some of that mud and place it on her back," she told Erick. "It will stop the bleeding. I have no idea how I'm going to stitch it up."

Erick nodded to Sangay, who stepped forward. He pulled a pack from his shoulder and lowered it to Mallow.

"What is this?" she asked.

"I would think it obvious," Sangay said. "It is materials for practicing your profession."

She took the pack and opened it. A smile crept onto her face. "You thought to get me a healer's pack?"

Erick shrugged. "I have a bad habit of letting my friends get hurt."

"Think you could quit gawking and make use of it?" Marcus demanded.

"Forget using that," Mallow said as Erick grabbed handfuls of the sticky mud. She pulled a tightly wound bundle of linen from the pack. She unrolled it and folded it into a long, narrow strip. "Use this instead. Cleaner and better. I need to attend Corby."

Erick wiped as much of the mud as he could from his hands and took the strip of linen. He pressed the cloth against Elissia's back. She didn't move or make any noise. Despite Mallow's assurance, Erick feared the worst. He said a quiet prayer to Caros and Denech to keep both his friends alive and well.

His concern shifted to Corby as he watched Mallow work on his friend. She examined the arrow, which protruded from halfway down Corby's back. From his vantage, he couldn't tell if the arrow had hit the spine. He wished Gabrielle were here. He knew her proficiency, as she had recovered them from a number of injuries. He had no idea of Mallow's capabilities.

Marcus's face was a mask of tortured concern as he waited for the diagnosis.

Mallow pushed at the inflamed area where the shaft penetrated. Bright blood welled.

Erick winced, and Marcus gasped.

"Standard Royal Guardian arrow," Mallow said. "That's good news."

"Why?" Marcus asked. The eager hope in the question broke Erick's heart.

In answer, she pulled the shaft from Corby's back. It slid out smoothly, and more blood leaked from the puncture.

"Not barbed," Mallow said, dropping the arrow. "We're not barbarians, like some." She removed a vial of light green powder from the kit, sprinkled it on the wound, and held her hands over it. "Krinnik, by your power are we given our means. Talan, by your power do our means thrive. Caros, by your power do our means grow. By the Triad am I granted power to mend what is broken. I am your servant."

Dull white light suffused her hands. Erick remembered the pain of that holy power. A pain only he felt because of the evil nature of the *elonsha* that made his abilities possible.

A grunt drew his attention. Keven snarled as he watched. Erick had forgotten about the Revenant in his concern for his friends. "Keven, *undel.*"

Keven stared at him. The snarl stopped, but his eyes did not close.

Undel, Erick pointed the thought at Keven. After several seconds, Keven's eyes closed, and his posture relaxed into the meditative state Erick had used on his manor workers at night. It allowed their spirits to return to the Heaven of Caros to be with loved ones and the *elonsha* to renew. As a Revenant, Keven had been trapped before being judged and thus could not leave his body. He still required the renewal of *elonsha* so Erick could maintain control.

He's starting to resist me openly, Erick thought to Blink. Another worrying development stacked on top of Keven's ingrained hatred of him. *I may have to release him soon. Something's not right.*

Can't you release him and turn him into a priquana?

Erick considered it. He suspected Keven would not ascend to the Heaven of Caros, considering his role in the destruction of Draymed and the death of the herb shop owner. No ascension to Caros, no return to his body.

No, he told Blink.

How about if you talk to him? Blink asked. *Not as his master, but as a person. Well, as much as you can consider him a person. Tell him if he serves you, he may redeem himself enough to find his way into Caros's favor.*

Would that work? Could an undead obtain redemption like a living person?

Erick put the questions aside as the glow died away from Mallow's hands. Sweat dotted her forehead. "You might as well plan to rest here," she told him. "He'll need at least a day to recover."

Erick kept his disappointment to himself. Mallow's skill was impressive. A wound like Corby's would take weeks to heal if tended by normal means. But Gabrielle would have had him mobile in hours. Erick missed her and wished he had done more to learn about her unhappiness.

"Come," Sangay told Marcus. "We will forage the means of a fire." He spoke as if it were a foregone conclusion Marcus would obey him. To Erick's surprise, the thief, after a worried glance at Corby and Elissia, followed him into the grassland. Erick had no idea how they would find anything to burn.

Mellow knelt next to him. "Let's take this off."

When she removed the blood-soaked linen from Elissia's back, Erick was happy to see the flow had stopped.

"She'll be fine," Mallow assured him.

"How come she passed out?"

"Exertion and blood loss," Mallow said. "Not enough to be dangerous, just enough to weaken her. They didn't exactly feed us a banquet in the cells."

"I'm sorry," Erick said.

"For what?"

"That we got caught. That it took me so long to get you out. That I have no supplies, and I don't know how we're going to survive getting to the swamp."

She stared at him, amusement sparkling in her brown eyes. "You have been told you're only one person, right?"

"What does that mean?"

"You don't have to do it all yourself, and you shouldn't blame yourself for things you can't control. You thought far enough ahead to get this kit." She smiled. "Give yourself a pat on the back."

Erick thought about this as Mallow searched through the healer's kit. She pulled out a spool of black thread and a long, curved needle.

"What's that for?" Erick asked.

"I'm going to stitch up the wound."

"Can't you just heal her with your powers like you did Corby?"

Her amusement disappeared. She settled back and stared at him, her mouth set in a flat line. "I don't know what this Gabrielle was like, other than she didn't have the will to stick with you, but I don't squander what the Gods gave me. If I can mend someone almost as well with mundane means, I will. This thread and a few herbs will have her recovering near as quick as my gifts, and it won't offend the Gods."

Erick nodded, although he didn't see how the Gods could be upset at Mallow using the power they gave her in the manner they intended. Still, he had never been a healer; perhaps the rules were different.

"She may wake up when I start stitching. I'll need you to hold her down and explain what's happening."

"Blink," Erick said. Knowing Elissia's strength and litheness, he had little confidence he could hold her alone. The homunculus waddled over and grabbed Elissia's legs above the ankles.

Erick gripped her arms and then placed his face next to hers. "You're going to be okay."

Mallow threaded her needle, pressed the separated flaps of skin together, and pushed the point into the tattered edges. Elissia flinched but didn't wake. Mallow drew the edges together.

When Mallow pushed the needle in the second time, Elissia's hands clenched, and she drew in a hiss of breath.

"Melteth's tits, that hurts," she said.

"You're going to be okay," Erick repeated.

"Nice to know," Elissia said through gritted teeth. "It still hurts like hell. Don't you have anything for the pain?"

Erick looked at Mallow.

The young woman shook her head. "Don't believe in it."

"Of course you don't," Elissia growled.

Though Elissia did her best not to struggle, Erick and Blink had to keep her from trying to curl in on herself. She made no further complaint as tears poured from her eyes. Erick tried to offer soothing words of comfort until she snarled, "Stop it. You're making it worse."

Several minutes later, Mallow finished the last stitch and tied off the thread. "Help her sit up."

Erick helped Elissia roll to her side, then pulled her into a sitting position. Though he tried to be as gentle as possible, she winced.

"Sorry," he said.

"Don't be. I'll survive."

He didn't bother to tell her he was sorry for everything that happened. Anytime he had tried before, it did nothing but make her angry. Besides, Mallow's words had given him something to think about. Maybe he was too hard on himself.

Mallow reached back into her pack and pulled out several jars. "Now I can give you something for the pain."

"Now? Why couldn't you do it earlier?"

"All the mixtures I can make with this kit thin the blood. I didn't want you to start bleeding again."

"You could have told me that to start."

"I know," Mallow said. "But if you invoke the name of one of the Insane Gods around me, I'm going to take it ill."

"I wasn't invoking it; I used it as a curse."

"Doesn't matter. They still hear it and mark it. You need to try and sleep on your stomach tonight and stay off the wound, if possible. I don't have enough linen to wrap it."

Realizing Elissia's shirt was now useless, Erick removed his and handed it to Mallow. "Here, she can wear this."

"You can't do that," Elissia said.

"You need it more than I do," he said. "You have to keep your wound clean in case you roll over. And you can't go around with...well...with..."

"With her teats hanging out?" Mallow offered.

Erick's face burned. "Yeah, that."

"You're cute when you're embarrassed. Why don't you look over there while she changes? If you get that red just talking about them, you might melt if you see them."

Erick wandered over to where Blink sat. They both stared across the field, although there wasn't much to see at night.

"Want to look at her through my eyes?" Blink asked with a wicked grin.

"Shut up," Erick muttered.

～

T he next day, they walked across the trackless land of Starrasen, heading in a roughly western direction. With Corby and Elissia wounded, it was slow going, though they were healing well according to Mallow's morning examination. She suggested they take a relaxed pace to not reopen their wounds.

"We'll be able to move quicker tomorrow," she promised Erick.

Erick relayed the story of his escape from the guards, with small input from Sangay. When questioned, the Sakenin said little, only that word of Erick's need had reached the warren in Kaladan. They weren't inclined to aid the Necromancer, so Sangay set out on his own to do so.

"Why?" Elissia asked.

"Many nights in the *boda* did we hear the stories of the *Inconnu* and the Necromancers, and how their war split tribe against tribe in Falan-Dar. I would not see that happen again. So, I aid you before war comes again."

As the day wore on, unseasonably sunny and mild, other matters concerned Erick. They lost their pack animals when they were captured. As he had confessed to Mallow, his desperation to rescue his friends pushed aside considerations of resupplying them.

If he were honest, he thought getting provisions would be easy once they were together again. It never occurred to him they would find themselves in such a desolate land so quickly, with both food and water in short supply. They had found one thin stream and drunk their fill several hours ago and had seen nothing since. Small, burrowing rodents that none of them had seen and Corby knew nothing about ran over the scrub, but the party had no bows, and the little beasts were too alert and quick for Blink to catch.

Erick briefly considered backtracking to Zakerin and trying to sneak back into Kaladan or going to the next village to the north. He decided against it because he had no idea how widespread the net was to catch him or his companions. If they got captured again, their captors would undoubtedly make it nigh unto impossible to escape.

"We're going to need to find a settlement soon," Erick informed everyone, although he suspected they all knew it.

"And hopefully one where their warriors don't kill us on sight," Mallow offered. "Sterrans aren't known for their friendliness to outsiders."

"That's why I like you," Marcus said. "You're always full of cheery news and information."

Mallow offered a broad smile. "I could always not tell you and let it be a surprise."

"According to the map, we should come across one in another day or so," Corby told them. Despite their slow pace, sweat dotted his forehead. "The scaling was off, so I don't know how large it will be."

Erick wished he had been able to control NalTalva, as the bandit would be most useful now

"What map?" Mallow asked.

"The one the Procurers gave you."

"It got taken with everything else."

Corby tapped his forehead. "I've got it here."

"Really?" Mallow's voice bristled with amused disbelief.

"Yes, really," Marcus snapped. "He's the smartest person you'll ever meet."

"I'm the smartest person I'll ever met," Mallow corrected. "But I'll take your word for it that he's the second smartest. If you say he's got the map in his head, he does. The biggest problem will be finding the town. Unless you also have an unerring sense of direction, all it takes is getting a bit off in our walking, and we'll go right past it."

"No, we won't," Erick said. "We'll travel another half-day tomorrow, and I'll send Blink to scout for us."

As they trekked across the grassland, Erick studied Keven, who walked beside them, arms limp, hands broken. He considered what

Blink had said yesterday. Could he appeal to Keven's better nature? Or at least a sense of selfish fear?

He opened his thought to Keven. *Do you want to go to the Festering Hells?*

He didn't respond immediately, only continued to walk as he stared ahead. His expression didn't change.

Do you? Erick asked again.

I don't, Keven thought, more fear and sadness in the simple statement than Erick would have imagined.

I could release you now, and that's where you would go.

Only Alakaneth judges.

Yes. And how do you think he will judge you?

Again, Keven didn't respond for a long moment. Then, the creature's shoulders slumped. *I didn't want to die.* Anguish poured through the thought.

Erick couldn't help himself. He pitied Keven, who wasn't evil, only arrogant and easily manipulated. Having Fathen as a mentor had been the worst thing that could have happened. *Serve me. Treat me well, treat my friends well. Protect me. Atone for what you've done. Before I release you, I will find a priest of Caros and tell him you proved your remorse and did your penance. I will have him bless you. Only Alakaneth judges, but I will help him judge you more favorably.*

Keven's head raised, and his brown eyes locked with Erick's. Erick, who saw such undead as if they lived, couldn't miss the hope in Keven's expression.

I will try, Keven thought, *but I still hate you.*

Erick shrugged. *Maybe we can change that too, someday. I never wanted to be your enemy.*

Keven returned his gaze to the land ahead and continued walking.

They spent that night on the ground in the open air, bellies grumbling and mouths dry. Thankfully, the early fall evening was comfortable. Although, at this point, Erick wouldn't have minded rain. At least they would have been able to drink some of it.

He and Elissia lay a short distance from the others. Mallow, who had first watch, patrolled a wide perimeter around the group.

Erick stared up at the sky with Elissia curled against him. She lay on her side to stay off her wound. Her warmth tingled through his body. He took her hand and kissed it, relishing it against his lips. "I should have planned this whole thing better. We need supplies. It would stink to have gone through all this only to die because I forgot a water skin and a backpack of food."

"We're not going to die from that," Elissia said. "We'll find something tomorrow, and we'll be fine. It's not like we're roaming the desert."

"Close enough," Erick said. "It's certainly not like Zakerin."

"It isn't," she agreed. "You need to not take so much on yourself. You're not the only one here."

She lightly ran her hand over his arm, and he couldn't think for a few seconds. When his brain cleared, he said, "Mallow said the same thing."

"So at least that's one thing we agree on."

Elissia's mention of the desert made Erick think about Sangay. He wondered if the man from the arid land of Falan-Dar might have some special knowledge for finding water. He had not offered such wisdom; Erick suspected he wouldn't unless explicitly asked. He was as tight-lipped as Gabrielle.

Something else came to mind. "Are there a lot of Sakenin Procurers?"

She considered it a moment. "I can't speak for every chapter, but there were certainly none in Kalador. I suspect there are thieves of every stripe, though. Except Amels, maybe. Way too puritanical for their own good."

Erick nodded. "I'm glad you're safe. I was worried about what might be happening to you."

"No more than I was worried about you," Elissia said. She snuggled closer. Her breasts pressed against his bare chest and warmed him in numerous ways.

He leaned in to kiss her. She joined him. Their mouths opened, and sparks lit his brain as their tongues touched. He put his arm around her. She winced and drew back.

"Sorry," Erick said as he withdrew his arm.

"It's okay," she said. "You stay still." She leaned in and kissed him again. Their mouths interlocked; her hand rubbed over his arm. Goosebumps raised. She took his hand and placed it on her hip. Then her hand touched his hip. His mind danced with pleasure and thrilled at the thought of what might be next. Were they going to do what he hoped, right here in the open sky? As she pressed against him and almost sent him over the edge, he thought they were.

Footsteps intruded into the sensations bounding over him. They grew louder. He reluctantly drew back from their passionate kiss. "What's that?"

Elissia didn't have to answer. Seconds later, Mallow came into view, running and panting. She stopped next to them and announced to the camp. "Everyone up. We have visitors."

～

Erick jumped up as Elissia slowly stood, and the others joined them. "Who is it?" Erick asked.

"Considering where we are," Mallow said, "I assume they're Sterrans."

They didn't have to wait long to find out. Twenty men on foot ran into view, their short spears gleaming under the moonlight. They wore leather breastplates and vambraces. Their boots, also thick leather, ran up to their knees. Their dark gray shirts blended with the night and couldn't hide the muscles beneath.

Erick and his companions unconsciously drew into a circle.

"Don't make any sudden moves," Mallow said. "Erick, don't draw your sword. That's a sure way to end up dead. If we stay passive, we may be able to get out of this."

Pulling a weapon against a score of warriors had been the furthest thing from Erick's mind.

They waited as the men approached and broke into two lines that surrounded the small party. Every man stood at least six feet tall, and Erick felt dwarfed, both in numbers and size. Their skin shone pale in contrast to their dark hair. Their faces appeared neither hostile nor friendly.

Once the Sterrans had the group surrounded, they dropped their spears to aim the points at the small party. One stepped forward from the circle. More muscular than the rest, he also stood much taller than the now-dead Fathen, which made him almost a giant to Erick. His black, short-clipped hair settled at the top of his ears. A close-trimmed beard dominated much of his face. He wore no insignia Erick could see to mark him as the leader and held no weapon. He scanned the whole group as he spoke.

"Sipad landa da mangopo andalo mencero antanah okamo?"

Other than being able to tell it was a question, Erick had no idea what the gigantic man had said. Considering the situation, he had a good guess, but no way to answer. He hoped Corby's studies included languages.

To his surprise, Mallow stepped forward, crossed her hands over her chest, then lowered them. *"Okama telaa malirikano dir dar kezlimin tanaha taimura din belindun. Okama mendti dangen nit tiaka skitom dangrn mencar haan parsahobaton ando plint. Ando akin membunta okamo?"*

The man considered her words, and Erick stood on edge, wishing he could follow the conversation. "What—"

"Shh," Mallow said from the side of her mouth.

Erick had no choice but to defer to her and hope she knew as much about these people as she seemed to. He looked at the others and saw his confusion and concern echoed on every face.

One of the men behind the leader pointed at something in the group's midst. *"Lihan, mahlak separ-manasian yan kati dabarituhu."*

Erick realized his companions had gathered Blink in their center in an attempt to hide him. The ruse had not worked. Erick tensed, wondering if these people would react the same as anyone else who had seen the homunculus. If so, they were in a great deal of trouble.

"Adkah mahlak ini malak ando?" The leader asked Mallow.

"Di adkah tadik ad. Belia adlah aba huaih merayaka dirapudu tentra okamo, gargoyle pergungoa utora."

The leader shook his head. *"Untak barbhung adlah untuk mengdapa kamuraan da Sangara. Dilah kehidotun yonga bisa. Dia adlah maluk kapodo sesrang."* He pointed at Keven. *"Dan arong itud tadik lag berfas dangen."*

The astonishment on Mallow's face ratcheted Erick's concern higher. The few words in Zatrim he recognized suggested they were talking about him. Even so, the man had said something that caught Mallow off guard. Her hesitancy evident in her taut muscles, she pointed at Erick. He began to get an inkling of the questions they asked.

The man and his comrades turned to regard Erick. "*Hali dano jaga ditikan, pemlah kehidipan.*"

Erick shook his head. "I'm sorry, I don't understand."

"My sorrow," the man said slowly in Zatrim as if making sure he used the right words. "You are the one makes the death back to live?"

Hope left Erick.

They knew he was a Necromancer.

Though his friends had proved to be stalwart fighters, there was no way they could win against twenty seasoned soldiers. Their fights had been against castoff renegades, the best the Fist of the *Inconnu* could muster. These men were from a culture that prized battle above all; that lived for the chance to die in combat. Erick and his companions probably wouldn't offer a fight worthy of the name. They couldn't kill Keven, but that didn't matter. All they had to do was kill Erick, and Keven would wander until they trapped him or tossed him into a place he couldn't escape. Eventually, the *elonsha* would wear away and the undead would die. Even a lie wouldn't work. Though it had been phrased as a question, Erick could tell the man already knew the answer.

Tense, ready to draw his weapon and give as well as he could, and hoping the others would do the same, Erick said. "I am a Necromancer."

The man nodded.

Then, all the fighters dropped their spears to the ground.

The leader spoke. "We expect you and happy you survive to here. We take you to our home."

30

Join the Inconnu army and live forever.
　-Graffiti on a wall in Kalador

Bad dreams plagued Gabrielle's sleep. Visions of zombies and skeletons shambled through a burning town. Erick stood on a tall building, flames dancing around his feet. Elissia stood beside him. Next to them, Marcus and Corby sat on a single chair, Corby in Marcus's lap. They all glared at Gabrielle. She stood below them, tears on her face at the destruction around her.

A growl drew her attention. She turned as a zombie lumbered toward her. Before it reached her, a girl crossed its path. No older than eight, terror suffused her face. She stopped before Gabrielle, placing herself between the healer and the monster.

"No!" Gabrielle shouted.

The girl paid no mind. She faced the zombie. The slavering beast grabbed the child by the arms. A squealing scream burst from the girl as the zombie sank its teeth into her throat. The shriek turned to gurgles as the throat tore, bands of skin and muscle pulled like taffy.

Gabrielle sobbed at the lost child. All around her, similar scenes played out, death on a scale she had never witnessed.

Laughter reached her ears.

She pulled her eyes from the devastation and stared at the quartet above her. Their faces gleamed as they chuckled. Erick pointed at her, and their laughter redoubled. Corby and Marcus fell off their chair—so intense was their merriment. The laughter echoed around her, mocking her tears.

"This is your fault," she screamed at them, flinging her arms wide to encompass the whole of the burning town.

"And I'll do it again," Erick said, his voice the whisper of dry leaves over sand. "And again. And again."

Gabrielle screamed.

And woke up.

Her breath came in panting gasps. Sweat dotted her forehead. Disoriented and in the dark, she had no idea where she was.

A gentle swaying brought it back to her.

She was on a trader ship, the *Convex*, that called the port city of Masca home. They headed there now, sailing up the Nallica, the river that ran from the Tortured Mountains to the Inland Sea. They had left the Inland Sea three days ago and would arrive in Masca tomorrow. Another six days overland would bring them to their destination. Gabrielle looked forward to that. She was tired of travel.

She rolled over in the bed and placed her hand against Min's broad back. The curly hair tickled her palm. His earthy scent did the same to her nose.

She had surprised herself many days back when she realized she had fallen in love with the stout miner. And astounded herself more their first day on the Inland Sea, when she had given herself to him. She had offered her body on this very bed as the ship rocked on the water.

And why not? He was the best thing to happen to her in her seventeen years. He gave her the love and attention she once dreamed Marcus would offer. He listened to her, talked to her, let her share her doubts and fears, knew about her. And he did so without the mockery that always seemed behind Marcus's blue eyes. Mockery that only intensified when he met Erick and Corby and when he reunited with his sister.

With Min's gentle questioning and counsel over the past weeks, Gabrielle had come to realize how Erick and his comrades had duped her. She was the outsider they tolerated because she could help them. They had been the couples. They had been the friends. She was the plain-looking girl no one loved. Marcus wanted nothing to do with her so badly that he turned to perversion rather than care for her.

She marveled that she had been so blind for so long.

Min comforted her. His presence warmed her and opened her to reality. He told her people were often too close to a situation to see the truth of it, and only fresh eyes could show them what they overlooked.

"If you stand too close to a building, all you see is a single brick," he said. "Only by stepping back do you see the truth of the structure."

She had stepped away by leagues and tendays and now saw the truth. Erick was an abomination, a blight to Krinnik. She should have turned him in to the Healer's Guild as soon as she saw him. She should have never traveled with him. Worse, she had *healed* him. Had healed them all, even Corby, who had stolen Marcus from her and drawn him from the light of Caros and into the wrongness of loving other men. Before Corby, Marcus had a chance to see the wisdom of being with her. Now he was damned as much, if not more, than Erick.

She drew close to Min and pressed herself to his naked back. Warmth flooded her. Here was a man, a real man, who loved her and cared for her more than any ever had. More than her parents, who gave her over to a cruel mistress before they died. More than Valarie, who harangued and belittled her at every opportunity. Even more than Torin, who had done nothing to find her when she fled the Procurers to travel with Erick, a journey she should never have made.

And yet she couldn't curse her path, for it had brought her to Min. She gave his back a gentle kiss, not wanting to disturb him even as she hoped he would wake. As well as opening her eyes to Erick, Min had shown her so many things she had never known. He could be gruff and taciturn at times, but he was also caring and gregarious. Often, she thought he was two different people, silly as she knew that to be. And though she sometimes felt uneasy around him, as if she sensed some sinister presence behind his brown eyes, she considered that more likely her nervousness and distrust, for he offered nothing but kindness and care. If she wished anything more from him, it would be that he showed faith in the Gods. She had not pressed him on this matter, for he had only expressed disinterest and gentle uncertainty, neither of which were sins. He wasn't like Elissia, who openly blasphemed and called the very motives of the great powers into question. Yet another reason for Gabrielle to be grateful she no longer traveled with them.

Pressed against Min's warmth and confident all had become right with her world, Gabrielle fell back into sleep.

~

Min woke her early the next morning with a kiss, as he had every morning since she gave herself to him. His prickly stubble tickled while his rough lips thrilled her. Warmth radiated from him. Warmth and...something she hadn't been able to define since she first encountered it. It was either her paranoia or his raw intensity; she wasn't sure. It unnerved her as shivers of yearning played across her skin. Power emanated from his dark eyes, as if he had untapped strength.

"Time to rise, my pet," he said in his husky voice. "We should reach the city within the hour."

She yawned and stretched. As the rough woolen cover slid away and revealed her nakedness, Min gave her an appreciative stare.

Heat flushed through her cheeks. No one had ever looked at her with that intensity. No one had ever desired her.

He smiled, the hard edges of his face softening. "You are beautiful."

Beautiful. A word she never expected to hear about herself. He stood before her, his nakedness revealed in the lantern light. His pooch-bellied, heavily muscled body belonged to her. He wasn't the most attractive man she had ever seen, but she didn't care, just as he didn't care that there were many women comelier than her. He thought she was beautiful. She thought he was as handsome as she could ever want or deserve. He cared about what she thought and how she felt. And wasn't that more important than physical appearance?

She sat on the bed and shivered as she watched his body react to her. "We don't have to get up just yet, do we?" she asked.

He didn't speak for several seconds, still smiling. "No, not yet."

He slid back into bed with her.

~

Two small craft pulled the ship into the cove at the riverbank, one of several half-moon shapes carved into the land and built up with docks.

With deft maneuvering, the tow pilots brought the *Convex* into the wooden pier where men with poles held it from smashing into the dock while sailors tossed ropes over. The well-seasoned crew moored the ship and lowered the gangplank.

Min offered his farewells to the captain, a friendly-faced Straph with the olive skin and black hair that marked his people. Gabrielle found herself beginning to dislike the Straphs, if only because they provided constant reminders of what was behind her.

As they walked through the city, with its strange dome-shaped buildings of painted wood, her hatred grew stronger. Everywhere she looked, she saw Marcus's clipped black locks or Elissia's almond-shaped blue eyes. She paid little attention to any beauty the city might have offered because she fixated on the people.

"Are you okay, sweet?" Min asked. "Miss the ship already?"

She offered a small smile. "No. Just trying to remind myself these people aren't the people I left." *The people that left me first.*

"They aren't," Min said.

"I know, but it's difficult." They were going to be in this land for a long time, so she would have to either overcome such prejudice or drive herself crazy. She reminded herself that Marcus was only half Straph. He no doubt inherited his less savory aspects from his Zakerin father.

"Don't fret. A day will come when those you helped will suffer for the wrong they did you. And maybe you can help."

Gabrielle frowned. What did that mean? "I have no wish ever to see them again, but I don't want them to suffer."

"Are you sure?" Min asked. Something in the soft, whispered quality of the question sent goosebumps up her arms. This question came from the other Min, the one she had named the Vengeful Min. Even as it chilled her, the cold strength he exuded made her reconsider. He had brought perspectives into her life she had never thought about. This was another. Did she want them to suffer? If she no longer desired to see them, why should she care what befell them?

Min didn't rush her. He always allowed her time to mull through, in her methodical way, whatever question he posed.

They passed several market shops, painted in garish colors and fronted with signs proclaiming their wares in the calligraphic Straphan writing, before she spoke. "The others can suffer, but I wouldn't want anything to happen to Marcus. I still care about him."

"More than you care about me?"

That brought a deeper frown to her face. She had known Marcus most of her life and Min less than a month. Could he truly expect her to care for him more in such a short time? She might in time, but not yet.

Another chill washed over her and brought a thought with it. *Why not?* Why shouldn't she care for Min more? Marcus betrayed her by giving his love to another. Another woman would have been bad enough, but a man? Such a thing stung worse than anything she had known.

Though as much as she should hate Marcus, she couldn't. They were no longer friends, but she couldn't make him an enemy. And she couldn't drive eight years of love, even unrequited love, from her heart so quickly, much as she might want to.

"I don't know," she answered truthfully—miserably.

"It's okay," Min said. "I understand."

The hurt in his voice told Gabrielle he didn't understand, despite what he said. That made her more wretched.

~

Eligos pulled back the *elonsha* he had directed upon Gabrielle. As was his wont, he had pushed too hard, too fast. Her way of thinking wasn't bending toward his desires as quickly as he wanted. He had little time left. Seven days travel across Straphan would see them in Phinsa, the village closest to the twin Necromancers who had joined his cause. Even days to convince her to willingly help destroy the world she knew and remake it in the image he sought.

It was a mission he had begun to doubt he could complete. Gabrielle wasn't like the priest, who had been easy to bring into the fold since he was so full of biting anger toward Erick. She wasn't even the original Necromancers, who had come willingly for the power he offered them: the control of life and death. Gabrielle's pure soul and firm belief in the Gods made her more resistant to the pull of *elonsha* than he had ever suspected. He had to offer his suggestions subtly, infect her slowly with the thoughts he needed her to possess. She would unconsciously sense too much power forced upon her and resist more, making his task harder.

He considered throwing the full force of *elonsha* at her mind, overwhelming her, and taking control. Two things stopped him. It was better if she came willingly. Less resistance meant more control.

And, he wasn't sure the effect such an influx of *elonsha* would have on someone with her magic. It might kill her.

Worse, he might discover she could resist him, even at his full might.

Full might? He thought bitterly. *If only I had such a thing. No one could resist me.*

He was getting stronger, but until he had more people sacrificing in his name, more *elonsha* flowing into Krinnik, his might was a distant memory. The events in Kalador fed him slowly, evidence the lich priest was succeeding at the task of destabilization. *Elonsha* dribbled to Eligos, feeding him and building his strength. It wasn't nearly enough.

He hoped the twins were as successful as their messages indicated.

"Now who's being quiet?" Gabrielle asked. "I'm sorry if my answer displeased you. I've known Marcus too long to throw him away so casually, though he hurt me deeply."

"I'm not displeased," Min lied. "I just don't understand. But then, I've never had a love like you had."

Her brows bunched in confusion. "But you were married."

"It was an arranged wedding. We never had children." That was another lie, but she had no way of knowing about Min's sacrificed offspring. Eligos again wished for the gifts of his brother, Bolfri. Early on, Gabrielle noticed the garnet pinkie ring on Min's finger and inquired about his wife. Searching his *talba's* memories had shown the woman five years dead, and Eligos had given her the information. Days later, he "lost" the ring to avoid the inconvenience of that question anymore.

She nodded, though she still looked confused. "I care for you a great deal. I dare say I love you. I will come to care for you more. In time."

Min smiled as Eligos snarled. Time. He didn't want it to take time he didn't have. He had no choice. He would work on her the next seven days, perhaps increasing the *elonsha* and hoping she didn't notice. If they arrived at the sisters' house and she had not acquiesced? Well, an unwilling vessel was better than no vessel.

The city of Masca sat at the split of two rivers, the Nallicus and the Nallican, branches of the Nallica, which flowed from the Tortured Mountains. Masca sat on a hill between the two rivers, and Gabrielle found herself winded as they reached the city center, despite her improved stamina from so much travel.

Questioning a local got them directions to a transportation company on the northern side of the city. A quick negotiation secured them a wagon they could use to travel to Phinsa.

"Just give the wagon over to Balorin when you get there," the cheery wagoner told them. "Ask for him. Phinsa's small enough that you can stand in the center and shout his name, and he'll come running."

The man asked for no deposit, simply trusting the two strangers would use the wagon as stated and deliver it unharmed. For the cost of an excellent meal, they could unofficially own a buggy and horse worth twenty times what they paid. Marcus would have laughed at such naivety.

Just like he laughed at yours, she thought.

They descended toward the Nallicus in the wagon, which was a far more comfortable journey. In an attempt to dispel her gloomy thoughts, Gabrielle said, "The founders of this city had a wicked sense of humor."

"What do you mean?"

"Nallica is the Straphan word for a married couple. Nallicus and Nallican mean man and woman. Masca is a baby. So, the city of Masca is the baby produced where the man and woman meet." A few tendays ago, she might have blushed at making this statement. Now that she knew the joy of that meeting, she felt no such embarrassment. Corby's face would have melted from the heat of telling such a risqué story.

She gritted her teeth. Was everything going to remind her of that betrayal?

That was yet another thing Marcus never learned about her. She might not be as smart as the scholar, might not have a freakish talent like an eidetic memory, but she knew a lot more than they thought she did. She had read books, too.

"Would you like to be Nallica someday?" Min asked with the strange whisper in his voice.

The question caught her off guard. "Married? To you?"

"I was not thinking that far ahead, but perhaps."

"I do want to be married someday." But to someone as old as Min? She loved him, but she knew the age difference could cause problems. "I haven't given it much thought." Rather than consider the matter too closely, she asked, "Have you ever been here before?"

It took Eligos a moment to determine how to answer the girl's innocent question. He had been here, a millennium ago, when

Masca had been half its current size and many of the elegant wooden houses had been little more than huts of dried river mud. Then, the largest city and capital had been Rambaras, at the foot of the Tortured Mountains. He had passed through this fledgling town on the way to the capital to meet with the king, a vain and arrogant man whose name Eligos no longer remembered.

Starrasen, to the south, had claimed the triangle of fertile plains between the Upper Serpent River, the Pellicus River, and the Inland Ocean. Straphan burned to take their territory back, so Eligos and Bolfri had preyed on that desire and the monarch's vanity to stoke the kingdom's righteous ire. By the time the Necromancers betrayed the *Inconnu*, Straphan had retaken almost all they had lost and kept it from the technologically inferior Sterrans, either through sound defense or an uneasy peace.

Eligos longed to tell all of this to the young girl, to reveal his true self. He missed being able to speak openly as he did with the priest. He wanted a confidant.

He restrained himself. He would have two of those soon enough, hopefully three if his persuasion of Gabrielle went well. For now, he searched the memories of Min. The man had led the dull life of a miner since he was old enough to swing a pick.

"I have not," Min told Gabrielle. "This will be my first time seeing my sisters since they left home."

A visit to his sisters was the lie he presented when the healer first asked why he traveled. When she questioned why he wanted her to come along, he told her his sisters requested he bring a servant, someone from the homeland that would make them comfortable. They didn't care for the domestics they could find close to hand. Eligos had been proud of that particular lie. He didn't think Bolfri himself would have come up with much better.

"It's an interesting city," she said. They drew close to the bridge that would take them across the Nallicus and onto the road leading to Phinsa. "A lot like Kalador, yet different. They have more gardens and greenery than I would have thought. The buildings are strange, and I'm curious how they create the colors for their paints and keep them from fading after a season."

Eligos cared nothing about any of that. He could have told her that cities all over Krinnik were much the same, at least on this continent. Only the architecture and customs changed. They were all crowded, stinking places that imagined themselves as the height of culture.

When Eligos and his people eventually claimed Krinnik, he would raze such population centers and scatter the people he didn't enslave. A dispersed population was less likely to foment rebellion.

As Min, he said, "Yes, it's strange to see so much wood covered with such strange colors. The buildings are perhaps more elegant, but I wonder how they fare in a fire." As he said this, he pushed *elonsha* toward her—forced her to remember and despair at the destruction wrought by her friends.

~

Another chill passed through Gabrielle at the mention of fire. She shuddered. Images of the conflagration in Prospector's Camp slammed against her. Those buildings had been all stone, yet the furniture inside burned. Flames consumed the street vendor carts. This city burning, its graceful wooden buildings covered in oil paint, would make the Camp look like a candle.

The burning hadn't been the worst of it, though. The undead rampage still gave Gabrielle nightmares. That was the first time she had seen the real evil of Erick's power. She had felt it in her bones. He had used it to save them, but Gabrielle wondered if it would have been better to die than live through the horrors she witnessed. That had been the beginning of the end for her. From that point, the thought of getting away from Erick had grown. And the longer she spent with Min, the better she felt about the decision.

She remained quiet as they crossed the bridge. It was an impressive structure, large enough to allow wagons to go both ways at the same time. It straddled the three-hundred-foot expanse of the Nallicus, ascending in a gentle slope until the midway point and descending after that. Crisscrossed on the sides with thick ropes that led to towers embedded in the river at intervals along the span, it was a more graceful construction than anything Zakerin could dream of.

As they reached the end, a line of people and wagons waited to enter the city. A large pole barred the way on the incoming side. Guards and a tax collector assessed the arriving people and materials and lifted the pole only when the tax was paid, either in coin or goods.

It surprised Gabrielle how long they rode before the line ended. At least a half a mile. "How will they get them all in before sundown?" she asked.

"They are efficient people," Min answered. "Or so my sisters have said in their letters."

As they traveled, Gabrielle marveled at the road. The roads in Zakerin roamed across the realm in mostly straight lines, but they were narrow, not always well-maintained, and made chiefly of packed dirt with cobbles. She expected this road to narrow after they left the city, but it stayed wide enough to allow wagons to pass safely without leaving the path. And rather than cobbles, some smooth black substance, like pitch turned solid, made up the thoroughfare. "What is this?" she asked.

Min shrugged.

Corby would know, she thought. Then she wanted to scream. Why could she not get them out of her mind? She slid closer to Min, put her arm through his, and laid her head on his muscular arm. This was what she needed. A man who cared for her. A man who understood her.

A man who would never disappoint her.

Alekita will burn in the Festering Hells. She betrayed her country and her people, and for that there can be no forgiveness.
   -Marera, Myrmidon of Sangara

F athen sat on the gilded throne in the Temple of Caros and reflected that the last three-quarters of a month had been the best in his long life.

Perius Oerus sat beside and one step below him, as was his proper place. The Prelate had relinquished his office eight days ago when he realized Fathen had a far better grasp of politics.

Fathen also controlled their supply of food. At a word from the priest, young sacrifices would stop arriving, and Perius would whine and plead for Fathen to allow the meat and blood to flow again. Fathen found the old man's mewling disgusting and base. Finally, he agreed to provide an uninterrupted supply if the Prelate gave over his power. Perius did so with a speed and lack of consideration that amused and disturbed Fathen in equal measure.

Fathen became Prelate of Zakerin in a small ceremony entirely unlike the usual pomp and circumstance that heralded a new leader of the Temple. As much as he would have enjoyed a celebration, right now discretion suited his cause better. When Eligos ruled, there would be a fete the likes of which had never occurred.

Now, the two men awaited the hour in which supplicants could appear before his Most Holy and request boons or seek advice. It was the most tedious part of the job, and Fathen did it with little relish. It lasted only an hour, so Fathen tolerated it to stifle the already swirling rumors about his usurpation of the Temple.

Most of the boons he was happy to grant, as they slowly weakened the Queen's base of support. It was mostly merchants seeking recompense for the destruction of their stores and sea captains wanting to know who would cover the cost of goods they could no longer ship because of the burning of the docks.

Fathen offered them money like it was water. Why not? The Temple had funds to spare and credit in surplus. So did the Crown, but Fathen's campaign of whispered lies and outright treachery by the Queen's advisers had worked on the naive monarch far beyond Fathen's wildest dreams. He expected her to show up begging for help from the Temple. Then, the second phase of the plan would begin.

Until that day, though, he still had to deal with the small problems.

A bell tolled somewhere above them, sonorous and droll. It heralded the time of Caros's Grace. Fathen prepared himself for another dull hour of dispensing favors.

The doors swung open. Two of the Temple Guards, dressed in yellow plate mail, stepped inside. A herald followed, wearing a yellow cap with a horn emblazoned upon it. He stepped up to Fathen and the former Prelate. "Your Most Holy, now comes before you the first supplicant seeking succor in the Grace of Caros."

Fathen hid his flinch by bringing his right hand up to rest under his chin as if ready to decide the fate of worlds. Even now, hearing the name of his former God gave him discomfort. He no longer tried to speak the name.

"Bring forth the first petitioner," Fathen announced, "and let him receive the blessing of the Great One." That was the closest he dared.

To Fathen's surprise, three acolytes walked in, their orange robes brushing the floor, their silver chains gleaming in the torchlight. The tallest strode before the other two, who flanked him like goslings following their mother. They walked with great purpose and grim, determined looks on their faces.

Fathen's shock disappeared as they approached. He had expected something like this would happen sooner or later.

When the three young men reached the proper distance and waited at the foot of the throne, three steps down, Fathen motioned to the two guards. "Wait in the hallway and close the doors. I would have no other supplicants hear this request."

The two men nodded and obeyed the order. The doors clunked shut and cut off the hallway, leaving the chamber illuminated only by the lanterns hung on pillars and the wan light coming through the chamber windows.

The three men looked between each other as the guards departed. Doubtless, they had not expected that.

Fathen clapped his hands, and their gazes returned to him. "Speak your name and tell me what boon the Eternal Sun may grant you."

"I am Ian of Kaladan," the one in front said. He had the brown hair and eyes of most Zakerins, although those dirt-colored orbs shone with the gleam of anger. "With me are Cyric of Devin's Rest and Randall of Kalador." Both men wore grim, frightened faces and had brown hair, although the one named Cyric wore his longer than allowed to acolytes.

"I know not what the Eternal Sun is," Ian continued, "as that is not the name or moniker of the god I follow. The boon Caros may grant us is your removal as Prelate. Furthermore, he may also grant us your departure from this hallowed place. You may return to whatever dark cave you crawled from and never trouble this holy ground again."

It took all Fathen's resolve not to leap down the stairs and rip this impetuous cur's head straight off his shoulders and drink his fountaining blood. Although it would make him feel good and would probably please Perius, who would see it as an unexpected meal, it would not accomplish what Fathen sought to do with this rabble.

"Strong words," Fathen said. "And what have I done to warrant such condemnation from a mere acolyte?"

"You know well what you do," Ian said. "I don't know the full manner of your foulness, but your presence is nothing short of unholy. You have made a mockery of this Temple. Men of ill repute and blasphemy roam with impunity and command us like we are dogs."

Ian pointed at Perius. "Furthermore, you have debased our Most Holy and make him follow you as if he were nothing but a manservant. Whether you accomplished this through worship of the Insane Gods or the use of vile potions, I neither know nor care. You will leave tonight and never return."

Fathen admired the man's bravery and spirit. Though no stranger to arrogance, even at his most brazen Fathen would have never dared confront a Prelate. His unwillingness to do so resulted in twenty years of exile on an island, he noted with bitter amusement. "And if I do not depart, as you say, what will you do?"

Ian reached into a fold in his robe and drew out a knife.

Beside Fathen, Perius gasped. "You would shed blood in the House of Caros?" he asked, then put a hand to his head as if someone had slapped him.

"We would," Ian said as the other two drew daggers. One of them menaced the herald, who stepped back with his hands up, showing he was unarmed.

"I see," Fathen said. He dropped his hand to the armrest and drummed his fingers as if considering Ian's proposal. After half a minute, he said, "Very well, kill me."

The shock on the acolytes' faces thrilled Fathen, and he almost laughed out loud. It was a maneuver they hadn't expected.

"What?" Ian asked, his voice faint.

"I choose to stay and remain Prelate. Your mewling god will not grant your boon, so if you wish me gone, you will have to kill me. Hurry up; there are others waiting with requests."

Tense moments passed as the trio and Fathen stared at each other. Ian's hand trembled, the knife catching glints of lantern light as it shook. He glanced left and right. His companions nodded at him.

Fathen smiled. It was easy to nod when you weren't the one having to do the deed.

Ian took a tentative step onto the lowest riser.

Fathen sat back in the throne and opened his arms. "Make it true and quick," he said.

Ian's eyes darted around as he took the second step, no doubt wary of a trick. The third step brought him close enough that Fathen could feel the rush of his rapid breathing and hear the thud of his pattering heart.

"Do it," Fathen said as he leaned forward, "if you have the conviction of your faith."

The acolyte jerked forward, almost as if against his own will, and rammed the knife into Fathen's chest. Fathen felt a dull pressure as if someone had laid a not particularly heavy rock on him.

Before Ian could step back, Fathen thrust his hands out, snagged the collar of the young man's robe, and pulled him forward. Ian let out a squeak of fright and grabbed Fathen's wrist.

"Don't struggle," Fathen said, exerting his will on the youth. After a brief resistance, Ian's hands went limp. "That's it. I didn't think you would do it. You have great bravery."

That bravery had disappeared. Fear replaced the anger in Ian's eyes. Though he no longer struggled, held by Fathen's command, the tautness in his muscles showed that every part of him screamed to flee.

"Had you not had the nerve to try and kill me, I would have destroyed you and feasted upon you. As it is, you will make a serviceable aide." He took the boy's head in his hands. He wrenched Ian's head sideways, snapping the spine and crushing the windpipe. The sharp crack echoed through the chamber.

Ian dropped to the floor like a sack of grain.

The other two acolytes stood frozen in shock for a moment. Then, with cries of terror, they charged Fathen. The herald, already in thrall to the former priest, pulled his knife and stabbed Cyric, the slower one, in the neck. Blood sprayed and drenched the tips of the young man's long hair. He ran three more steps before his knees gave way, and he fell to the floor.

Randall reached the dais and ran up the steps, knife brandished as if he had never held a blade before. Fathen grinned, pulled out the dagger stuck in his chest, and thrust it forward. Too late, Randall tried to stop and couldn't. He ran his eye dead into the extended blade.

Fathen took the jolt to his arm, and Randall stopped, his face puzzled as if he couldn't accept what had happened. Fathen twisted the knife. Randall released a moaning gasp. His hand opened and his dagger fell from it.

"You die as sacrifice in the name of Eligos, the Master of Shadows," Fathen said, twisting the dagger further. *Elonsha* gathered around him and flowed through the acolyte, absorbing the young man's soul.

Fathen yanked the knife from the ruined eye socket. Randall continued to stand and tremble, not realizing he was dead. With one long leg, Fathen shoved the acolyte off the dais. The body flew backward and landed beside his companion. It shook a few more seconds and then went still.

Perius dropped from his chair and knelt over Ian, his mouth moving toward the man's throat.

"Not him," Fathen said, his voice cracking out the command. "I will bring him into our fold. Do what you want with the others."

Fathen addressed the herald. "Inform any other supplicants that the hour of blessing is canceled for today. Tell them we are ill, and they may try again tomorrow. Then, lock the doors and return. We must dispose of what is left."

The herald nodded and walked away. Perius scuttled to the pair of dead acolytes and studied them, head swiveling back and forth. Then, he placed his mouth over Randall's ruined eye socket and made wet sucking sounds.

Fathen knelt beside Ian. The acolyte's brown eyes stared toward the ceiling, glazed with death. Fathen ignored his hunger for the moment. There would be plenty left. Perius was a glutton for the sweet flesh, but he couldn't consume two men in one sitting.

Placing his hands on Ian's neck, he channeled *elonsha* into the cooling body. Receiving his power directly from Eligos, he didn't have to recite stupid chants or crush herbs like Erick. All he needed was a sacrifice, and Randall had unwittingly offered himself.

The energy flowed through Fathen and into Ian. It amazed Fathen to think he had once feared this dark power, had thought it the evilest thing in existence. Now he knew it for an incredible strength, a living force that Necromancers debased and diluted with their presence. Real power lay in being undead, not creating them.

Fathen sensed Ian's *nanta* trying to escape. He poured more *elonsha* toward it, wrapping it in the energy. Like a snuffed candle flame, the *nanta* disappeared and was absorbed by the more powerful force.

Ian jerked. His eyes closed, then reopened. Black filled the orbs and sparks of red flickered through like crimson lightning in a moonless night. Ian sat up, and the darkness cleared from his eyes. He stared at Fathen, his new master. All resistance had disappeared.

"What do you wish me to do?" Ian asked.

Fathen smiled. "Are there others that feel as you did before you joined me? Others who think that I am not fit to be Prelate?"

Ian nodded. "But I was the only one brave enough to confront you." Pride shone in this statement.

Fathen nodded. "And as I said, that is why I have made you special. You see now that you were wrong, don't you? There is nothing to fear from me."

The briefest hesitation, then Ian nodded.

"I want you to convince those who still feel the way you did that they are wrong. Tell them I am taking us in a new direction. Too long have we played second to the Queen and the monarchy. It is time we assume our rightful place as rulers of Zakerin. Soon, the Queen will come to us, begging for our help, and we will spell out our conditions. We want all those who worship the Eternal Sun to be with us. Those you can convince, let go about their business. Those you can't, bring to me, and I will talk with them, as I did with you. And if they don't see reason, then—"

Fathen waved his hand toward the floor. Ian turned. They both watched as Perius, having consumed both of Randall's eyes and most of his nose, now chewed at his throat.

"Go now and do your work," Fathen said. "I'm hungry."

As Ian walked away, Fathen joined Perius. He would let the former Prelate have Randall for himself. He sat beside Cyric and pushed up the sleeve of the acolyte's robe. The tender forearm would be a good start.

32

We may never know why the sects of Vidali and Melteth never joined the Inconnu. Though they are not sizable, they could have done serious damage. One can only surmise that the Inconnu *scared even those insane Gods.*
  -Corberin of Draymed, *The Second Inconnu War*

E rick had been so used to horrible things happening to him and his friends that it took him a moment to realize what the man had said. "You're not going to kill us?"

The man frowned and didn't speak for a moment. "Is that what people think? We kill no reason, like northern barbarians?"

That was precisely what most people thought. Zakerin histories spoke of the barbarous, warlike Sterrans and their desire to conquer lands both north and east. The Straphs to the north were the enlightened people, great inventors and scientists, though lacking in warfare. The thing Zakerins had over their western neighbors was military discipline and better weaponry. Sterran skirmishes with the Straphs had kept both countries at bay during the *Inconnu* War. Zakerin martial superiority dissuaded them thereafter.

Erick didn't think a history lesson or political discussion was the best idea right now, so he went with the truth. "Anybody who learned

I was a Necromancer has either wanted to kill me or imprison me. It's a surprise to find someone who wants to help me."

"More like a Gods-blessed miracle," Marcus said.

"Indeed," Mallow agreed.

Elissia let out a low snort.

The man nodded. "We light fire and speak." He shouted commands to his men. Half of them broke off and ran back the way they had come, while the others efficiently pulled round disks of some dark brown substance from their packs and stacked them on the ground until the mound stood a couple of feet high and a foot round. Then, they stepped back.

Their leader pulled a leather skin from his back, removed the cap, and poured liquid on the stacked disks. A sharp, bitter smell hit Erick's nose as the man struck flint over the pile. As soon as the sparks touched, the entire stack caught flame. In thirty seconds, a beautiful fire burned, throwing off a cheery light and a deep, earthy smell. The warriors set cross-legged on the ground in a half-circle behind their leader.

Erick and his companions said nothing during the preparations. Erick wasn't sure what to say, surprised by this unexpected turn of luck. He was almost afraid to speak, lest he say something wrong and turn the men against him.

With the fire going and everyone seated, the warrior leader spoke. "I, Anaran, *kal* of *plint*." He indicated the men behind him with a toss of his head. "My Zatrim not best."

Better than my Sterran, Erick thought.

The leader pointed at Mallow. "Her Sterran best. We speak, and she tell?"

They wanted to use Mallow as a translator. It would slow things down, but they weren't in much of a hurry. It was still late at night, and if these people were genuinely going to escort them, a multitude of Erick's worries fell aside. Translation would help avoid confusion and misunderstanding.

"Yes, Mallow may speak and tell." Erick smiled as he caught himself mimicking the leader's speech pattern.

So, with Mallow translating, they began to talk. They learned

Anaran was the leader, the *kal,* of the war band, or *plint,* sent to seek them. That lead to the first question.

"How did you know to look for us?" Erick asked, and Mallow translated.

"And where we would be?" Elissia added.

Anaran paused before he spoke as if considering the best way to explain.

"There is a blind girl in our town," Mallow said. "Her name is Venra. She lost her sight while playing in the woods, though she never explained how. When her eyes went dark, she became a—" Mallow stopped, and her brows furrowed. When Anaran continued to speak, she held up a finger to stop him. He paused while Mallow considered. After a few seconds, she said, "My Sterran is the most fluent of the twelve languages I speak—"

"Of course it is," Elissia said.

Mallow ignored her. "But I'm not quite sure what he's saying. The word means 'watcher of skies,' which doesn't make sense."

"He means a shaman or seer," Corby said. "Those who receive visions are known as 'sky watchers' among primitive cultures." Corby's face flushed as he realized what he had said. He gave a fearful look at Anaran. "No offense meant."

Anaran seemed not to have noticed nor understood the slight. He stared patiently at Mallow.

"You're lucky his Zatrim isn't best," Marcus said with a lopsided grin, while Corby's blush deepened.

Mallow conferred with Anaran. It amazed Erick how foreign words flowed out of her as easily and as fast as he spoke Zatrim. The language sounded harsh to Erick, muscular and brutal, as if the people who spoke it lived in constant agitation.

After a brief exchange, Mallow looked at the group. "The scholar is correct. The young girl is a seer." She indicated for Anaran to continue. "Twenty-three days ago, the child came before the evening moot fire. The glaze in her eyes had disappeared, and they gleamed green, as if she could again see. She spoke of a band of travelers who sought the witch woman who dwells in the swamp. This band was bound for Starrasen under great peril and might not survive the journey. If they made it to the greatest land, his words, not mine, they would be bereft and uncertain. They would need aid. Find them and see them safely to the falls. Then the child's eyes returned to white and she collapsed."

"Was she dead?" Corby asked.

"No," Mallow answered after asking Anaran. "Though she had not regained consciousness when Anaran's *plint* left to search for us. They've been patrolling the border in what they considered the most likely place to find us and sent word to other villages to watch for us."

"Twenty-three days ago, we were in the cave under Broken Mountain," Corby said with a sense of wonder in his voice.

"Are you cert—" Mallow began, then stopped. "Yes, I'm sure you are."

"Maybe the Gods were looking out for us after all," Marcus said.

"Would have been nice if they let us know," Erick muttered.

"They don't have to let us know anything," Mallow said. "They are not beholden to us."

Erick thought they were beholden to him, at least to some extent. Didn't they have an interest in seeing their creation remain alive and not spoiled by the *Inconnu*? He didn't feel like getting into an argument, so he kept his mouth shut.

Elissia had no such compunction. "The Gods do need to let us know." She waved her hands to take in most of the group. "Maybe not us, but at least Erick. He's doing a task they assigned him, and so far, he's done most of it on his own, with some help from us and the barest amount from the Gods. So yeah, I think it's time they stepped up and helped slit a few purses."

Erick held up a hand as Mallow prepared to fire off an indignant reply. "Stop, both of you, please. Mallow, you're right, the Gods don't necessarily owe us anything but what they wish to offer. I was speaking out of frustration, and at least some relief. It would have been nice to know help was near. Then, we could have been looking for them. I also wouldn't have worried so much about our situation."

"I can't believe you're taki—"

Erick rounded on Elissia. Something in his face stopped her, although dark spots dotted the olive skin of her cheeks. "You are underestimating how much all of you have helped me. Without you, I wouldn't have made it this far. I probably wouldn't have made it ten miles from Draymed. I remember how much I didn't want you and Corby to come along. I've never regretted you ignoring me." He offered a smile. She didn't return it. "You're also not giving the Gods enough credit. They have helped us, Denech especially. Not always in ways you have seen, but I'm aware of it. If they helped bring this about, I'm grateful. I would be more grateful if both of you would accept it as a boon and not fight."

Elissia considered while Mallow stood nearby with a smirk Erick wished she would lose. Finally, Elissia offered a wan smile. "Sorry, Mallow. Blasphemy is second nature to me. The Gods forgive me, since they haven't struck me dead yet. I hope you will, too."

Now Mallow considered, her eyebrows lowered, though her smirk didn't leave. "As you say, the Gods seem to bless all of you. After all, they gave me to you to make sure you made it here and had a way to communicate. So, we'll call it a slip on both of us due to stress and fatigue."

Erick held the relief inside, happy to deflect another clash between the two hot-tempered women.

You're getting good at this diplomacy thing, Blink thought.

Compared to keeping these two from killing each other, fighting Eligos was cooking soup, Erick thought back.

Anaran and his *plint* said nothing while this exchange took place. Having offered their reasons, they seemed content to wait for whatever came next.

"Mallow, tell them we are most grateful for their help and would gladly travel with them as long as they will have us."

Mallow relayed the message and then gave the group Anaran's reply. "They have food and water. We'll eat and rest this evening, and then tomorrow, we'll begin the trek across the land."

"Bless them," Marcus said. "I'm so hungry, I'm ready to eat grass."

The ten men who had run away returned, hauling two long wagons, which they pulled with large leather straps attached to their broad chests, much like dray horses.

"Did something happen to their horses?" Erick asked.

Mallow answered without conferring with Anaran. "They aren't native to this land, and the Sterrans fear them."

Erick found it difficult to believe these stout warriors would be afraid of such tame animals, but he didn't question it.

In short order, Anaran's men produced skins of water, pieces of dried meat, and dark bread cut into six-inch strips.

"What is this?" Corby asked as he looked at the meal.

Marcus had already placed a piece of jerky in his mouth and chewed with evident pleasure.

"Goat," Mallow answered after asking Anaran. "The bread is made from barley. The skins hold strawberry beer, so don't go sucking it down like it's water."

"Beer?" Erick asked. "Is that anything like ale?"

"Similar," Mallow said, "although I'm not certain how good strawberry beer can be."

Erick ate a piece of the dried goat meat. It was salty and gamy, and the best thing he had tasted in days. His stomach gurgled as the meat landed. He tried the beer, taking a few test sips. Sweet and light, it was much different from ale, though not unpleasant. He took a few more swallows.

"Same warning applies as with the ale," Elissia told him. "Don't drink too much of it."

"You sound like a mother hen," Mallow said, her voice more tease than admonition. "Let the man drink as much as he wants."

"I'd like him traveling without a headache," Elissia said. "He can drink as much as he wants, but when he moans about how horrible he feels tomorrow, you can deal with it."

Mallow considered this as she chewed a piece of the barley bread. "That's a fair point," she said. "You're right."

"Admitting Elissia was right?" Marcus said. "I'm going to die now since I've seen everything."

Their small group chuckled, although Erick had to force his. Marcus's comment reminded him that, help or not, they still had a great deal against them.

Yes, we do, Blink agreed. *But for now, we're safe and fed. Enjoy the moment.*

"I can admit when someone is right," Mallow said. "I'm magnanimous like that. She's right, Erick. Drink only enough to wash down your food. But soon, we're going to have to get you drunk, good and proper. Everyone should experience it at least once."

"We already have," Blink said. "It didn't turn out so great."

Erick had been more than tipsy when Blink discovered Fathen beaten on the road. The priest claimed bandits, though Erick was now certain he'd lied to get in their good graces. "Hopefully, next time will be better."

"Are you not going to eat, Sangay?" Corby asked the robed man.

"I have my own," the man said, removing his pack from his shoulder. "That food is not properly prepared. To eat it would be an offense to my body."

"Have it your way," Marcus said. "I'm going to stuff myself."

Erick had no idea what to make of the Sakenin. He was grateful the desert man had rescued him but wasn't sure why he had done it. Something about him made Erick uneasy. He wanted to tell the man to depart since they no longer needed his help. Especially now that Erick had an escort of twenty natives to guide him across the land. Sangay had made it clear a debt was owed between them, although Erick didn't understand it. Getting the man to leave might not be easy, and Erick didn't want to resort to violence against someone who had aided him.

He's an unknown, Blink thought, *and an unknown can be dangerous.*

It can also be good, Erick thought back. *Why would he rescue me if he meant me harm?*

I don't think he would, but that doesn't mean you need to keep him with us. As you said, we have enough help with people we trust.

You trust the Sterrans?

Blink nodded. *They have less reason to help us than Sangay, unless they were told by someone like this seer they mentioned. And remember, Starrasen didn't join the* Inconnu *during the war. Some of the Falan-Dar tribes did.*

Yes, he alluded to that. I think maybe his didn't.

"What are you two talking about?" Elissia asked, nudging Erick's shoulder.

"How did you—"

"You get this look in your eyes like you're trying to recall your own name."

Erick looked at the others. Anaran's men had settled themselves in a circle, eating and speaking in low, excited murmurs. Mallow was in conversation with Anaran, hopefully learning about what lay ahead. Marcus and Corby sat near, their knees touching as they ate. Sangay sat apart from the group. He had pulled a flat piece of bread and a jar of something dark from his pack. Certain no one paid them any attention, Erick quietly said, "I'm not sure what to think about Sangay."

"What do you mean?"

Erick shrugged. "I don't know who he is or why he rescued me, other than he says he found out about me from the Procurers. He claims to be a friend and to want to not see another *Inconnu* War. But half the tribes in his land joined the *Inconnu*."

"Was his one of them?" Elissia asked.

"I don't know," Erick admitted, "and that might be the first thing to find out. I just...we thought Fathen had become an ally, too." Erick couldn't help but throw a sideways glance at Marcus. "I just don't want to let compassion or gullibility almost destroy us again."

"What about them?" Elissia asked, nodding her head toward Anaran and his men.

Erick shook his head. "Starrasen didn't side with the *Inconnu*. And they could kill us if they wanted us dead."

"Unless they wanted us to walk ourselves to the slaughter, so they didn't have to carry us," Elissia said.

The shocked dread Erick felt at Elissia's pronouncement must have shown in his face. She let out her throaty laugh and leaned against him, her head on his shoulder. "It's okay; I was joking. I'm pretty good at spotting duplicity and Anaran doesn't have it in him. He's a warrior, through and through. Sterrans are loyal to Sangara. That keeps them mostly honest."

"Poor Brannon," Erick said, stabbed by a painful remembrance of the Draymed guard captain, also a worshiper of the warrior goddess.

"Yes," Elissia agreed, her voice solemn. "Poor everyone in Draymed."

Erick squirmed at the reminder of his hometown's fate.

"Stop it," Elissia said. "We've gone over this." She pointed at the motionless Keven. "It's more his fault than yours. He could have stopped the bastard who did it and chose his own miserable life instead."

Eased by her words, he couldn't help the smallest pangs of guilt. To chase it away, he asked, "What about Sangay?"

Elissia shrugged. "I don't know him well enough to say yet. He saved you, which makes him an ally for now. Until I know his motives, I won't call him a friend. I'll watch him."

"Thank you." Erick hoped his thoughts were nothing but paranoia brought about by too much betrayal. He liked the desert warrior, despite his odd arrogance. He didn't want to think of him as another pawn of Eligos, another Fathen, waiting for the right moment to strike.

"What about Keven?" Elissia asked.

"What?" he asked, thrown by the question.

"We have an escort of twenty warriors walking us through their homeland. If we're not safe now, we never will be. We don't need Keven anymore. Release him, so he can go to the Festering Hells where he belongs." The viciousness in her voice would have surprised him at one time. Now he knew how vindictive she could be when wronged, and he didn't blame her.

"That's a good idea." He disengaged from her embrace with regret and stood. "Keven, *fafen.*"

"Where are you going?" Marcus asked, still next to Corby.

"To release Keven."

"Why not just do it here?"

"You want to sleep next to a body?" Corby asked.

Marcus arched an eyebrow. "Good point."

Erick didn't want to tell them that the body would also quickly revert to an advanced state of decay—the condition it would have been in had it never been enchanted.

Blink waddled over on his short legs and followed Erick. Anaran spoke to one of his men, who jumped up with his spear and joined them. Erick almost sent him away and then decided perhaps there were things in the night that required an escort.

Erick judged two hundred feet or so was far enough to keep any predators from bothering the camp should they come to scavenge the corpse. Not that any intelligent predator would assault such a large group.

He faced Keven. "Keven, *nonc zir—*"

The Revenant lunged and struck, using his broken hands like clubs. Erick reeled back from the blows to his head.

You made a promise, a voice shouted in his mind.

Blink, help.

The homunculus moved in, as did the warrior, spear poised to strike.

Keven continued to pummel Erick, who raised his arms in defense. *You promised I could have a chance. I should have known you were false. You're right. I'm sorry.*

Other voices reached Erick. His head throbbed from the hits it had taken. His heartbeat thudded in fear.

Then, the blows stopped. He brought a hand to his temple and winced at the pain.

Keven stood a few feet away, hands raised like a prisoner surrendering. Sangay, Marcus, and two of Anaran's warriors surrounded the Revenant, weapons drawn except for Marcus, who had his hands raised as fists.

Elissia stepped up beside him and put her hand on his shoulder. "Are you okay?"

He nodded as his head pounded in two places.

You promised I could have a chance, Keven repeated.

Erick heard what he hadn't during the attack. Keven hadn't acted out of anger, but desperation and fear.

One of the warriors plunged his spear toward Keven's chest. The tip barely pierced the shirt before the weapon bounced back, pushed away by the force of *elonsha*. The warrior grunted and drew back, ready to make a more powerful stab.

"Stop," Erick said. "Leave him be."

"What?" Elissia asked.

"I made him a promise," he told her. Then he addressed Keven aloud so everyone could hear him. "You are right. I promised you a

339

chance to redeem yourself. To seek the Heaven of Caros with your actions. I was wrong to try to release you now. I will not do it again until you have been before a priest of Caros for his blessing, have shown your remorse, and offered to atone through your actions."

"Are you sure?" Elissia asked. "What happened to too much compassion and gullibility?"

"What happened to not wanting me to become heartless?"

Elissia frowned, her thick eyebrows bunched, then gave a wry smile. "Fair enough, but you sure picked a strange way to understand what I was saying."

Erick shrugged. To Keven, he said, "Do you accept my apology and agree to serve me and protect us?"

"I do," Keven said. Others gasped, no doubt surprised to hear the dead person acknowledge him, although Erick knew they heard only a groan or mutter, not words.

Then stand guard, he thought.

Keven took up a position ten feet from the group and facing away. His hands hung limp. Erick needed to figure out a way to fix the broken bones. Could he modify an existing ritual? That was something to think about when he had time.

He turned to Anaran. "Mallow, translate, please. Now you understand some of what I do. The magic that's around me. You've had it touch you, at least lightly. I'll understand if you no longer want to escort me. All I'd ask is you give us some token that will let us pass unmolested if others find us."

Anaran shook his head before Mallow finished. He spoke, and she followed with his words. "We are bound by our oath and the command of the seer. And the aftereffects of death do not bother us. Let us return to camp. At first light, we will depart as planned."

Erick nodded, pleased. He had almost forgotten that anyone other than his friends could be helpful.

They returned to camp, Keven following, and settled back down. He curled with Elissia, her back pressed against him, her head resting under his chin.

"I hope you know what you're doing," she said as she yawned.

"So do I," he said.

Sleep took a long time to reach him. He stared at Keven, who stood like a statue. Would the Revenant try to make up for the destruction he caused, or was the creature merely another way for Eligos to track and reach him? Erick didn't think the Master of Shadows could touch Keven's mind; then again, he knew so little of the Master's abilities. All Erick could do was hope what he did was right and pray he didn't make any more mistakes.

33

The Fist of the Inconnu *was a threat only because it was difficult to determine its members without a thorough inspection. Though subjugation to Eligos branded the supplicant, the tattoos were easily covered, and any call to inspection might see the Inquisitor dead.*

-Timone Narvis, Scholar of Kalador *On the Inconnu and their Followers*

After a tenday of travel with Anaran and his warriors, Erick hoped the worst of his ordeal was behind him. These Sterrans were a blessing from Caros, or perhaps Sangara, given their skills as warriors. Unlike the stern, humorless men that Brannon and those in the Draymed town watch had been, these fighters liked to laugh, drink, and share friendship. Their rough, crude humor, full of physical pranks and colorful language, often made Corby blush, though none of it was mean-spirited.

Each night, when they set up camp, they would break out casks of beer flavored with blackberries or strawberries, and bottles of *lafark*, a liquor made from barley, goat's milk, and grasses found in the middle of their country. Erick tried it once and choked as the liquid burned its way down his throat. It tasted to him like a cow patty fermented in brackish water. Anaran's men had laughed as he coughed and sputtered. His companions, except for Mallow, also swore it off after one taste.

He found the beer much more to his liking, but he followed Elissia's suggestion and limited himself to two mugs. So far, he had avoided a nasty headache.

Each morning, despite the prodigious amount of alcohol consumed, the men rose early, packed camp, and continued their travel. Ten of the men oversaw the massive wagons that carried the camp supplies, along with plenty of food, water, and beer.

On the first day, Anaran provided them with weapons to replace those lost in their captivity and escape. Though most of the warriors used spears, enough of them had swords that they could equip Erick and Mallow. Daggers were plentiful, so Elissia and Marcus were each given two. Marcus lamented the loss of his favorite jeweled dagger but knew he could do nothing to retrieve it. Corby made do with a sword, since staves were not available and, as Anaran explained, wooden spears were too valuable to give to any but Sterran warriors.

As evening fell on the second day, they came to a village comprising fifteen square dwellings the color of dull wheat with flat roofs. Goats and sheep roamed among the buildings, occasionally nipped at by small, golden-furred dogs if they strayed too far. There seemed no order to the layout of the buildings, just as they had come across no roads in their travels, only well-worn paths.

They spent the night at the edge of the village, and the inhabitants welcomed them with a meal of goat meat, a mashed vegetable that reminded Erick of turnips, and a drink of fermented sheep milk. The drink was sour and almost unpalatable, but Erick forced it down to be hospitable.

On the fourth day, he noticed Corby conversing with one of the warriors. Wondering if the man spoke Zatrim, Erick roamed closer. Corby talked to the man in Sterran.

"Kind of spooky, isn't it?" Marcus asked, walking nearby. "Four days, and he's talking like a native."

"Amazing," Erick agreed. He had picked up a few words, mainly the names for water, warrior, land, and nature break. Beyond that, it sounded like gibberish.

The only stain on their travel was a warrior named Balamin. Almost from the first day, he had made himself known to Elissia. Whenever Erick looked, the tall warrior was close to hand, walking behind them, his dark eyes following her strides. The first tent he always set up was the one Elissia and Mallow somehow shared without killing each other. Every morning, sprigs of sparse purple and yellow grassland flowers lay outside the tent.

"He's absolutely courting me," Elissia said in answer to Erick's question one night before they retired to their segregated tents. Erick and Blink shared a tent with Sangay, while Marcus and Corby took another. Erick thought it unfair they could stay with the person they loved, and he couldn't, but he made no complaint. Having only recently accepted it himself, he had no idea how the warriors would react to the knowledge of his friends' relationship.

"But I'm offering him no indication that it's working," she continued, "and if he tries to take it past flowers and stares, I'll make sure he knows in no uncertain terms that I'm not interested."

"Maybe I should make it clear to him now," Erick said.

Elissia smiled. "You're jealous. That's very sweet, but you have nothing to worry about. I can handle Balamin." She gave him a long, lingering kiss. The sensation of it stayed with him well after he went to his tent to sleep.

Though he said nothing to the warrior, Erick made it clear with every glance or touch that Elissia already had a suitor and had no need for any others.

As they traveled, the barren land surprised Erick. Zakerin had villages within a day's journey if one trekked on any of the larger roads. Here, they would come across camps of a dozen or so tents, with men herding sheep or goats, women cooking over fires, and boys training with spears under the tutelage of an older warrior. But other than the one village, they saw no other large settlements.

"The land doesn't bear large farming," Corby told them on their fifth night. "So, they only have a few towns of any permanence, near prominent water sources. According to Panaka, we'll come to Talvela, one of their larger towns, in another five days. They're going to throw us a celebration."

"As long as it includes a bath," Elissia said, "I'm all for it."

True to the word, the evening of the tenth day brought them to a sizable lake that sprang out of the ground with no sign of a river to feed it. On the shore sat a small town, perhaps half the size of Draymed. The squat buildings were made of the same light-colored clay as the previous hamlet.

"Welcome to Talvela," Anaran said, translated by Mallow.

One of the warriors had run ahead, and cheers greeted Erick and his friends. Women and girls in red wool dresses danced and sang a joyous song, accompanied by drums and a hollow wooden block instrument that made a melodious *tock* when hit with a stick. Three groups of women sang, taking up the song's beginning at different points, so the sound flowed over Erick in pulsing waves.

"It's hard to tell what they're saying because of the overlay," Mallow told him, "but it basically translates to, thanks for coming to save us."

"Save them?" Marcus asked. "From what?"

"The *Inconnu*, I guess," Erick replied.

As Elissia hoped, they were shown to a large clay tub hidden behind a screen of woven grass where they were allowed to bathe, men first, then Elissia and Mallow. Sangay passed on the offer, saying water was too precious to be squandered on such frivolity.

"Precious where you live, maybe," Marcus said. "Here, it springs right out of the ground. You should try a bath. You might like it."

"It is an offense to Talan to waste his tears. You may offend him if you wish. I will not."

Marcus shrugged. "Suit yourself."

Erick, Marcus, and Corby stripped behind the reeds. It no longer bothered Erick to see or be seen naked by Corby and Marcus. After all, it was just body parts they all had. He enjoyed the feel of clean water and the fresh scent of the goat's milk soap. While they bathed, a young boy gathered their clothing and laid out three sets of wool shirts and pants, all dull gray. At Corby's questions, he explained their clothes would be mended and cleaned, as was Anaran's wish.

When they gathered again, Elissia and Mallow also wore the same shirt and pants, the looseness of the garments hiding any hints of their femininity.

"I feel like a farmer's wife who doesn't know how to sew," Mallow lamented. "I should make these fit us better," she told Elissia. "I'm the best tailor in all of Zakerin."

As usual, Elissia said, "Of course you are," but this time, a genuine smile accompanied it.

Anaran greeted them, changed from his travel armor into a green woolen shirt and gray pants. Unlike their attire, his fit well, showing his muscled chest. "The town is pleased you are here," he told them, speaking through Corby this time. "And we will celebrate into the night that you will save us."

"Save you from what?" Marcus asked again, and Corby translated.

Surprise creased Anaran's face. "From the horrors of another *Inconnu* War. From the terror of seeing those you killed return to fight you, their spirits dishonored, and being unable to stop them. From the loss of life and the desecration of Sangara's children. This is our hope."

"Thank you," Erick said, overwhelmed at the responsibility Anaran's words put on him. Before, he fought Eligos because it was why he existed. Only now, after all this time, did he realize what losing that fight would mean. He had known it logically, but the warrior's declaration brought it to him emotionally.

Corby asked Anaran something in his language. The warrior's stern face drooped, his eyes downcast. He spoke a few words, then patted Corby on the shoulder, said something else in a cheerier tone, then left.

"What was that?" Elissia asked.

"I asked him if Venra, the seer, had recovered from her coma. He said she had not, and he was sorry we would not get to meet her and hear from her what our future held. Then he said, 'enjoy the evening, for tomorrow we may all die.'"

"What a pleasant thought," Marcus said.

That night they feasted on lamb, goat cheese, and custard made of goat's milk and berries. Erick ate until he could barely move. Once again, Sangay demurred, taking his food in the building offered to them as a lodging.

After they finished, Mallow said, "Anaran is right. We may all die tomorrow or any day after this. Remember when I said that some night, we need to get you drunk, good and proper?"

Erick nodded.

"I think tonight's the night."

His gaze went to Elissia.

After a few moments, she sighed and shrugged. "Why not? It's as good a night as any. I might even have some."

"I can't wait to see this," Marcus teased, waggling his thick eyebrows.

They went to a long, low bench of clay, where women poured beer from clay urns into clay cups.

"Not big fans of wood here, are they?" Marcus said.

"They live on grasslands," Mallow told him. "Seen any forests since we've been traveling?"

"Fair point." Marcus raised the cup toward his mouth.

"A toast," Corby said, putting his hand on Marcus's arm to stop him. "To the bonds of friendship and a successful end to our quest."

Marcus nodded, smiled at Corby, and added, "To the love of a good person and the bonds of camaraderie."

"You sure you both aren't already drunk?" Elissia asked.

They laughed and drank. The sweet beer flowed down Erick's throat.

As the evening wore on, the villagers taught them Sterran dances. Consisting of a great deal of jumping, mock combat, and falling to the ground, it was energetic, sweaty work. Erick and Elissia continued to drink, as did his friends.

You should stop, Blink warned. *You'll hate yourself in the morning.*

I'm going to live it up, for tomorrow we might all die.

You're drunk. I'm going to bed.

You should let yourself feel it. It's wonderful.

I'm going to bed.

Erick let him go. No sense in trying to bring a spoilsport into the fun.

He lost track of how long they danced and drank. He left to relieve himself at least three times, and each time it grew more difficult to walk than the previous time. He felt as if everything were right with the world, and he wanted to shout his good fortune in reaching this place alive.

Returning from his latest trip to the shadows, Erick spotted Balamin sitting on one of the low clay benches, staring at Elissia. It was the first time he had seen the warrior that night. When he spotted Erick, he turned away, speaking to Otan, another man from Anaran's *plint*.

"I'm right here," Elissia said, grabbing his chin. Her face was flush, and her eyes glistened. "Don't worry about him. Let's find someplace quiet."

"Okay," Erick said, trying to keep his voice calm as a thrill ran through him at her words.

She took his hand, and they walked past many of the baked clay buildings. The air had grown cool and took some of the fuzziness from Erick's head, although he still felt as though he could float across the ground. He chuckled at the thought. Elissia smiled.

Near the edge of the town, they came upon a wooden structure, the first they had seen since coming to Sterran. It was twenty feet to a side, well-built, and with no light shining from inside.

"This will work," Elissia said, and giggled at the slur in her voice. She checked the door and found it unlocked.

"What if someone lives here?" Erick asked, his voice slow and drawn.

She peeked inside. "I think it's a com...comunital..." She shook her head. "*Community*...building." She laughed again.

They walked inside. Elissia closed the door. Erick could see nothing in the dark and had no time before Elissia pressed herself into his arms, smashing her lips against his.

Every nerve in Erick's body burst to life at the contact, firing through his drink-addled brain. He pulled her close, stumbling back at the force of her kiss. He steadied himself and returned it with his own passion.

As he sank toward the ground, Erick's hip hit something hard and solid. He lurched away on instinct and fell hard, Elissia still in his arms.

"Ouch," they both said, and then giggled. She moved in and pressed her lips once more on his.

Every part of him burned with the anticipation of her touch, but some niggling corner of his brain told them wasn't the right time or place. They were drunk. They were—

She pressed herself against his body. All coherent thought left and was replaced by shuddering pleasure. He slid his hands down her back until they gripped her buttocks.

Her tongue slipped into his mouth, and the taste of beer only enhanced his desire. Again, he wondered if this was right, even as his hips thrust against her with a will of their own.

She broke away for a moment and gazed down at him. The ends of her hair tickled his face. In the wan light that seeped in, her beauty shone.

She sat up and reached for the bottom of her shirt.

"Are you sure?" he asked.

"I've been sure for a long time," she told him, no longer uncertain. "We never seem to have the time or privacy. We could die any day, trying to save the world. I don't want that to happen without this happening first." She gripped her loose-fitting shirt and lifted it over her head.

Erick drank in the sight of the beautiful swell of her breasts and the firmness of her stomach. The pressure below increased as lust slammed him. He tentatively reached a hand toward one of her breasts and stopped.

"Go ahead." She leaned toward his waiting hand.

He relished the soft firmness, amazed at the warmth. His heart thudded, and his mouth went dry.

She wrapped her arms around him and sat up again, pulling him with her while his hand caressed her flesh. She moaned as she pulled off his shirt. She kissed him again and pressed her bare chest against his. Delight gamboled through his entire body, chasing away the dulling effect of the drink. Wrapping his arms around her naked back, he pulled her with him to the ground. Dirt scratched his back, but he paid it no mind. He caressed her as their tongues entwined. A shiver ran through him and he felt Elissia do the same.

A brief flash of shame rolled through him as he remembered his actions after his manor had burned to the ground. Grief-stricken and bereft, he had tried to be with Elissia then, pushing her to the ground and throwing himself upon her. She had shoved him away, telling him he wasn't ready. He realized she was right.

Now, things were different. He was ready. They both were.

Rolling her over gently, he again thudded into something hard. Erick realized it was a wooden bench. It registered only a moment before sensation overtook his ability to think about anything other than his need for Elissia.

Her hands traveled down his back and slid under his pants. She pushed against his butt, bringing him closer. He shuddered as pleasure dashed up and down his spine, almost too much for him to handle.

"Wait," he panted, shuddering from the effort.

"Get your pants off," she commanded, her voice husky with need.

He did, and she did. Desire overtook him as he embraced her. Melting into her with a throaty growl, he reached down to capture her lips. Passion took them where pleasure turned into an agony of need. Together, they moved to a rhythm that refuted death and celebrated life. Soon, a cry broke from Elissia. Her body shuddered under him, pulling him willingly into an abyss of desire.

Hours later, they slept in each other's arms when a door slam woke them. Erick opened his eyes and squeezed them shut as torchlight flared, blinding him.

"Wha—" Elissia said, disengaging herself from Erick.

Cold air raised goosebumps on his bare skin. Shielding his eyes with his hand, Erick opened them again and saw four men, spears in hand. Two held torches.

"What's going on?" Erick asked, acutely aware of his and Elissia's nakedness.

No one spoke. When Erick reached for his clothes, one of the men stepped forward, spear raised. Erick stopped. It was Balamin. He gave Erick a knowing smile.

Elissia stood, bare as the day she was born. The warriors stared at her with disgust written across their faces. Erick wanted to punch them. How dare they be dismayed at such beauty. Her black hair gleamed in the torchlight, her body perfect. Even now, Erick felt his lower half stirring at the thought of what they had done. He covered himself with his hands.

Anaran entered, followed by Corby. When the scholar saw them, his eyes locked on Elissia and bulged as if they might leap out of his head. After several seconds, his cheeks flushed, and he jerked back as if struck. His eyes turned toward the ground. Anaran's expression, far from the friendly manner he had shown before, looked grim, his eyes flat and mouth pressed tight. He turned to Corby and spoke for a few seconds.

Corby shook his head.

Anaran spoke more sternly and then shoved the scholar in front of the gathered warriors. The torchlight flickered behind him, casting him in silhouette.

"What's going on?" Elissia asked, standing nude and defiant.

Staring at the ground as if he would bore a hole in it, Corby spoke, his voice breaking as he made the pronouncement. "You are both to be detained and punished for defiling this structure, the holy worship circle of Sangara."

34

To give one's life, to shed blood to save one's people, and to take as many enemies as you can. These are the bonds of Sangara and will see Alakaneth judge you well.

-First tenet of Sangara

A shiver of fear rushed through Erick. What could they have possibly done, having been in this building most of the night? From what he could remember, they left the celebration with little disturbance. Had he missed something in his drunken state?

Corby, still not meeting their gaze, pointed a finger toward Balamin. "You have also violated this man's courtship without observing proper combat rights."

"What is this bullshit?" Elissia asked, taking a few steps forward. Spears turned on her.

"*Berdiki bakah,*" Anaran said. The spearmen fell back, their weapons aimed at Elissia. Anaran pointed at her. "Stop or pain."

She stopped.

"Clothes," Anaran said.

Erick and Elissia quickly dressed. Erick's head thudded with the aftermath Blink promised, making it difficult to think. What had they done wrong, and how could they get out of it?

Once dressed, they stepped outside of the wooden building into the morning sun, which had barely crept over the horizon. Even that dim light made Erick's eyes water and his temples pound.

Blink, please tell me everyone else knows about this.

We do, Blink thought, even as Erick saw, through his squinted eyes, his companions coming toward them in a line, their faces grim. Keven was not among them since Erick had not yet woken the Revenant from hibernation. He saw no reason to do so now. There could be nothing but trouble from such an action.

Other Sterrans followed, people Erick had laughed and danced with last night. None of them smiled now. At least ten warriors clustered around Erick's companions. Not threatening, but ready for trouble. Much of the town had been made aware of what had happened.

Under Anaran's direction, they walked toward a building the same color as the rest, but much more prominent. Erick didn't dare ask questions, afraid speaking might bring further wrath upon him. Corby probably didn't have answers anyway, beyond what he had already told them.

Elissia took his hand, and he could tell from the tremble in it that she was frightened, too.

They filed into the building. The only light available was what little filtered in through thin vertical slits cut into the walls. In the dimness, Erick saw clay benches lining both sides of an aisle. A monstrous wooden chair loomed at the front of the room. Easily as big as two regular seats, it had no ornamentation—a functional, not ceremonial, item.

At Anaran's pointed instructions, Erick and Elissia sat on one of the benches near the front. Corby sat beside them. Erick glanced back to see people filling up the pews behind, although no one sat next to them. Balamin took up a seat on the bench in the opposite row. The two men he had been speaking to last night joined him. Erick couldn't remember their names.

Erick's companions ended up near the back of the room, seated on the last bench.

"I'm sorry," Erick told Corby.

"For what?" the younger man asked, not looking at either of them.

"That you saw us like you did." Erick felt he owed Corby an apology, though he didn't understand why the scholar was so upset. They had seen each other nude plenty of times now. Then Erick realized Corby had probably never seen his cousin undressed. He may have never seen *any* woman naked. Erick certainly hadn't until last night.

Despite the situation, the memory of what he and Elissia shared stirred warmth in Erick. It stirred other things, too.

Stop that, Blink said. *You need to be worried, not randy. This is serious.*

You're right. Blink's sobering thought cooled Erick's passion.

Elissia leaned across him and put her hand on Corby's arm. "You don't have to be embarrassed," she said. "I'm not."

"I'll be okay," Corby muttered. "It's just..." His cheeks went cherry again, and he shook his head.

Elissia frowned and sat back. She put her mouth next to Erick's ear. "And I'm not sorry about what we did last night, though we both had more to drink than we should have. I'm glad I waited. I'm glad it was you."

Erick could die content right then and there. He had no idea if he would ever be happier in his life, however long or short it might be.

Light flooded in from the back of the room as women brought in clay lanterns that burned the earthy fuel the Sterrans used. They placed them in holders arranged along the walls at regular intervals. Anaran stood beside the wooden chair at the front, the butt of his spear resting on the ground.

Tension filled the room.

No one spoke.

Erick glanced over at Balamin and found the man staring, an enigmatic smile playing on his face.

Erick's brain, slowed by the aftermath of his drunkenness, finally began working. Things that should have been obvious as soon as he saw the dark-eyed warrior fell into place. Erick now realized that Balamin must have watched them leave, followed them, and brought their disappearance to Anaran's attention this morning. It had been Erick and Elissia's bad luck that the building they stumbled into was somehow sacred to the Sterrans.

Please help, Denech, Erick thought as he considered his desperate situation.

Erick imagined he felt the briefest flash of warmth on his neck where his mother's necklace rested.

A murmur rose in the room, and people stood. Anaran motioned to Erick with lifted hands. Erick, Elissa, and Corby stood.

From the back of the room came the most massive Sterran Erick had yet seen. He stood a head and a half taller than Fathen, who had been the tallest person Erick knew. Muscles bunched under his red leather shirt and strained the confines of his black woolen pants. His biceps were as big as Erick's head. His black hair stuck out like the bristles on a horse brush, and curly ebony hair formed a thick, short beard. He carried no weapons, yet Erick sensed he was the most dangerous man in the room.

As the giant passed, the Sterrans at the benches held up their right hands, palm facing the sky. The ten warriors scattered around the room held their spears in their left hands, points angled away from the man.

The man strode past without a glance in Erick's direction. He turned and rested his bulk in the chair, which creaked as if it might break under the weight. As he sat, so did everyone else in the room. A moment later, Erick and his two oldest friends did the same.

"Can you translate?" Erick asked out of the side of his mouth, keeping his voice low.

"As long as they don't stop me," Corby said.

The large man's eyes, deep brown, roamed over the room. Finally, they settled on Erick and Elissia. They narrowed, and the beard twitched, as if the man frowned, or tasted something not to his liking.

His attention turned to Balamin. At a nod and a hand wave, Balamin stood and spoke.

"Most puissant priest of Sangara," Corby translated, "I come before you, a warrior-blooded, to level claims of blasphemy upon these heathen Zakerins."

A priest? Erick thought. He had assumed the man one of their leaders. Maybe the town's mayor, or whatever the Sterran equivalent was.

A drone of surprised muttering broke through the room and gnawed at Erick's headache. Surely these people knew the reason he had been brought here before they came in. Or was it just the way of people everywhere to follow the scent of conflict?

The priest held up a hand until the room grew silent. "And by what means do you make these claims?"

"By right of witness," Balamin said. "I watched as these two left the revelry last night. Seeing them drunk and thinking they sought heathen mischief, I followed. When they stepped into the Circle of Sangara, I considered perhaps I was wrong, and they sought to offer praise to the Mighty One for sending rescue. So, I waited to offer them escort back and thank them for their kind worship of our greatest."

Elissia snorted softly. "He lies like I breathe. He followed us hoping he could get us into trouble."

"But they had not come to worship the Father of Battle. Soon I heard the moans and panting made when performing the Rites of Amare." A tremble came to Corby's voice as he translated. "They made worship to the God of Love in the home of combat and death. A blasphemy that must not pass."

Again, voices broke out in low discussion.

A desire to rush at and throttle Balamin consumed Erick. Last night was a time meant for Elissia and him, shared intimacy only they should have known. Yet this jealous warrior intruded on their moment, had listened as they released their nature on each other. Had this craven man also heard the words they shared after, the whispered affections? Had he—

"Three times they performed the Rites," Balamin said, raising his voice to be heard over the chattering. "Three times did this blasphemer profane our faith with lustful spasms and—"

Erick's face burned. "You had no right!" he shouted as he jumped up and advanced on the warrior. "You bastard. You had no right!" Tears of rage welled in Erick's eyes. He shook them away angrily, and his fists balled.

"Alkanta," the priest shouted. His sharp voice broke through Erick's anger. Only then did Erick see Balamin's spear in the warrior's hand aimed at him, less than five feet away.

"Potanti," the priest said.

"He wants you to sit down," Corby told him, tears on his cheeks. Whether in shame for Erick or because of him, Erick couldn't tell.

Erick's stomach knotted as he shook with rage. His fists clenched, wanting to grasp Balamin's neck. Attacking now would get him killed and nothing more. He sat down, his body trembling.

"Is there any other who witnessed this blasphemy?"

The warrior sitting next to Balamin stood. "I am Otan, and I also witnessed this blasphemy."

Corby could barely get the words out.

Erick growled, ready to again leap from the bench. Bad enough that one had intruded on their intimacy. Two were almost more than he could bear.

Elissia took his hand. "He's lying," she said, her voice brittle. "Balamin isn't, but the other one is. He's standing up for his friend."

Erick believed her. She had far more experience with liars than he did. He had to believe her if he was going to keep any sense of wits.

Elissia turned to Corby. "Tell him exactly what I said."

"Are you—" Corby stopped when he saw the fierce glare in his cousin's eyes. He turned and spoke to the priest, who frowned and talked back.

"He says warriors of Sangara do not lie."

"They aren't supposed to lie," Elissia said. "There's a big difference."

"Do you want me to translate that?"

Elissia shook her head. "It won't do any good."

The priest's dark gaze bore down on Erick. "How do you stand against the accusation of Balamin and Otan?"

Erick didn't know what to say. How could he confess before all these people what should have only been for Elissia and him? How could he deny it?

Elissia stood and took a step forward, her head high and eyes blazing, as defiant as the night Erick first saw her. "It is true Erick and I

357

shared our bodies. We did so because we love each other. We are not followers of Amare, so we performed no 'rites.' We shared what men and women have always shared. It was not our intention or desire to blaspheme sacred ground. To that, we can only plead ignorance."

After Corby translated, the priest nodded. His lips puckered and brow furrowed.

Anaran stepped up beside Erick and spoke.

"As right of leader to the witness, I would speak," Corby translated.

The priest nodded.

"This man and his companions are strangers to our lands and customs. It is known by all in our squad that Balamin has desires upon this female. I offer that this may be a plot to remove a rival."

Balamin leapt from the bench and strode toward Anaran. The taller man faced the warrior, whose pale face had darkened with anger.

"Do you wish to combat for right of denial?" Anaran asked.

Balamin stopped as if his leader's question had been a wall of stone. The two men glared at each other. Erick sensed some different tension here, a history he didn't understand.

Eventually, Balamin shook his head and backed away. He resumed his seat next to Otan.

The priest again pursed his thick lips. His eyes fell on Balamin. "What punishment would you seek for this offense?"

"I seek no punishment, Puissant One. I would take the right of warrior and honor Sangara. I would battle the one who committed this blasphemy and so cleanse the temple of its stain."

Elissia stood up. "If he wishes to battle the offenders, then he will fight both of us."

The priest looked at Corby, who had not translated.

"Tell him," Elissia said.

"I'm not sure I—"

"Tell him."

Corby translated. When he finished, laughter rang through the gathering. Even the stoic priest allowed a small smile, barely visible through his thick beard.

"What's so damn funny?" Elissia shouted.

After Corby translated the question, the priest replied.

"Women don't fight," Corby told her.

"I think I could show him differently," she said, her fists balling.

"Don't," Erick said. "Hopefully, he'll take what Anaran said into account and let us go."

"Hope is a horrible strategy," Elissia told him.

"Right now, it's the only one we have."

Murmuring continued in the hall until the priest held up his hands. The room grew quiet.

"As priest of Sangara, my duty is to Sangara. Offenses to him must be answered. If there was ignorance of our ways, that falls upon you, leader Anaran. You should have instructed them during your travels."

Anaran bowed his head.

"What Balamin witnessed was a blasphemy. Love is a weakness in battle, and Sangara wishes no weakness, so no love nor acts of love are allowed in his temple. Therefore, I grant Balamin's right as warrior." He turned his eyes to Erick.

"What is your name?" Corby translated.

"I am Erick Darvaul of Draymed." A shiver ran up his spine. He knew what was coming next.

"Erick Darvaul of Draymed, you will return to the Temple of Sangara. There, you will face combat with Balamin of Anaran's squad. If Sangara wishes reprisal for your blasphemy, he will have it. Where you spilled your seed, you will now spill your blood."

35

And when I looked upon the destruction wrought in the name of the Inconnu, I wept with joy, for I saw then the Gods were nothing compared to my master.
    -Nameless Eligoi member's last words

Erick and Elissia stood in one corner of Sangara's Temple, while Balamin and Otan stood in the other. The wooden worship benches had been dragged against the wall, giving them a thirty-foot space.

In the daylight, Erick saw the details that might have saved him from being in this situation. At the back end of the room sat a rectangular block of red stone. Three weapons lodged in the stone: a two-handed sword, a spear, and a dagger—the weapons favored by those who worshiped Sangara. Burned into the wooden wall behind was Sangara's symbol: a shield broken in half with jagged edges meant to represent sundering by a mighty sword blow. Had he not been drunk, he might have realized the building's wood construction signified its importance.

He only fleetingly noticed these things, as he was almost too terrified to think straight. He knew next to nothing about actual combat, having never learned how to use any weapon until recently when Elissia taught him to fight with daggers. He usually wore a sword to make Elissia happy, not because he was proficient using it. Balamin was a trained warrior out for blood. This wouldn't be a fight; it was going to be a slaughter.

Another flash of heat radiated from his necklace. He jumped, and then it was gone.

"You okay?" Elissia asked.

"Not at all," Erick said. "I'm not going to survive this."

"You have to," Elissia said, her voice trembling. "Somehow, you have to."

How? Erick wondered. As they left the meeting hall to return here, Erick considered telling everyone to run and that he would also flee. No sooner had he thought about it than another ten soldiers joined the crowd and surrounded them. No escape that way.

He considered awakening Keven but again saw no help there. An undead would be useless against so many, especially when they knew the creature's true nature.

He was on his own.

The crowd waited outside, including Erick's other companions. The only ones allowed to witness this combat were those directly involved and the priest. Anaran was also here as Balamin's leader and because he was responsible for him should Balamin fall in battle, which wasn't going to happen.

"I don't care what they say," Elissia said, "if it gets too bad, I'll jump in and help you. A knife in his spine will slow him down."

"You can't do that." Erick watched Balamin pace back and forth in his corner, eyes cold over a mocking smile. "They'll kill you."

"Then we'll die together. Better that than live in a world where Eligos wins."

Erick nodded. He didn't have a rebuttal. It pained him to think he would fail because of something as stupid as this.

Anaran and the priest had been conferring near the weapon-laced altar. Now the warrior walked toward Erick.

Blink, let everyone know that I'm sorry. I tried.

I'm not saying anything. If you fall, then I'll tell them. But don't fall.

If Erick died, Blink died too. Would he have time to give their friends Erick's last words?

Anaran stopped before them with a grim set to his jaw. "You ready?" he asked in accented Zatrim.

"Not at all. Doesn't matter though, does it?"

Anaran frowned, perhaps trying to figure out Erick's words. Then, he nodded. "Go to middle." He pointed a thick finger at Elissia. "You no move. No try weapons."

"No promises."

Anaran glanced back at Balamin, who stopped pacing and now idly spun his spear. Anaran turned back and leaned down until he was close to Erick's face. "Balamin loose..." he paused and considered. "No, he *sloppy* fight. Where eyes go, spear go. Watch and block." He winked, then straightened, again grim-faced. "Go to center."

"Thank you," Erick said, amazed the warrior had shared such information. It ultimately wouldn't help, but at least not everyone here shared Balamin's vindictiveness.

He thought to kiss Elissia and didn't. Their act of love was what brought them to this trouble. Instead, he gave her a weak smile and said, "I'll do my best."

"Do better than that," she said, tears glistening in her blue eyes.

He trudged toward the center of the room. Balamin did the same, his spear held point down. Confidence and swagger blazed with his every step. Erick drew his sword, uncertain if they would start immediately. He tried to run his scattered mind through all the things Elissia taught him about daggers, wondering if such moves would work with the sword and how they'd fare against a spear.

You're better than you think, Blink told him. *You've been in fights and survived. You can survive this one. I'm here if you need me.*

Blink's projected confidence shored Erick's spirit. He had all but resigned himself to dying. He had been in fights and had won fights. He might not win against this trained warrior, but he'd be damned if he'd go down easy.

The priest also approached the middle of the floor, placing himself between Erick and Balamin. He held up his hands, and they both stopped. He spoke to them, looking from one to the other. Erick had no idea what he said, other than the word "Sangara." He could be blessing them both or explaining the rules of the fight. It didn't matter. Erick had no use for rules when someone was trying to kill him.

Finally, the large man stepped back. Balamin raised his spear, and Erick lifted his sword.

"*Aon tapaa sint ka ota nanen*," Balamin said. His face smiled, but his words were hard.

"Caros and Denech protect me," Erick said.

Balamin jumped forward and swiped downward with his spear. Erick leapt back, and the tip of the blade whooshed by, inches from his face. Erick struck. Balamin easily deflected it. Erick again jumped back and brought his sword to the middle, staring at Balamin, the blade between them. Balamin smiled. He seemed in no rush to fight. Erick kept his guard up, watching the other man's eyes, as Anaran suggested. Balamin held the spear in two hands and moved in a lazy, weaving pattern. Erick paid no attention to it.

The warrior's eye darted down and to the right. Erick tensed. The thrust came, heading for his thigh. Erick deflected the shaft, but not before the blade sheared through his pants and sliced his skin. The shallow cut burned immediately. Blood ran down his leg. He pushed away the spear and took a swing at Balamin's stomach. It was the warrior's turn to jump back. His smile disappeared, and his eyes narrowed with deadly malice. He realized his prey would fight back. There would be no more toying.

Erick's nerves lit up with fright.

Balamin's eyes looked left as his spear went into motion. Erick again deflected it with a thud as blade met shaft. Balamin let the spear roll with the hit, spinning it around his back and slicing toward Erick's head.

Erick ducked and swung at the warrior's feet. The blade slammed into the floor, almost knocked from Erick's grasp. Air moved as the spear drove down at him. He dodged too late. The blade sank deep into his left leg. Erick cried out as the agony slammed him like a mallet. Even worse was when the tip withdrew, and the spear raised, slinging blood. Erick felt as if some part of him had been ripped out. He grew dizzy, unable to think or understand what was happening.

His mind shattered as a hot spike of pain rammed into his stomach. He cried out, uncertain where he was and what was happening. The spike withdrew, leaving emptiness and cold. The ground came up to meet his back, and he lay there, his eyes unfocused as his leg and stomach throbbed.

Tears ran down his face. He shivered. A shadow loomed over him. He wondered if it was Alakaneth coming to take and judge him.

The shadow drew closer. Balamin loomed over him; the smile returned to his face. He knelt on Erick's chest. The pressure made it hard to breathe.

Somewhere distant, a female screamed. Erick stared at Balamin. A dagger replaced the warrior's spear. His face gleamed with triumph as he towered over Erick. "*Sangara, sayo menwark kapeda ando kemuli.*"

Numbed and delirious, Erick barely registered the cold blade of the knife against his throat.

Take his soul! Blink shouted in his mind. The force of the command broke through Erick's numbness. It focused him through the pain ravaging his stomach and leg. The knife pressed against his neck.

As quick as a snake, Erick rubbed his hand across his wounded stomach, smearing his palm with blood. He reached up to Balamin's face and slammed his hand against the man's cheek. "Give," he said.

Balamin froze as his *nanta* drew away, infusing Erick. The warrior's soul churned with the petty anger of a man thwarted, a man overlooked, a man scorned. He saw Erick as an easy target.

Erick was about to prove him wrong.

The *nanta* flowed into Erick. The pain withdrew. A scent of clean earth pushed into his mind. His wounds tingled and burned, closing as the man's life energy healed him.

The knife fell away from Erick's throat. Balamin's mouth hung open. His eyes rolled into the back of his head.

Stop, Blink said. *He can't hurt you anymore.*

No, Erick thought. He had been denied the fullness of total absorption once before. This time, Blink wasn't here to stop him. Balamin tried to kill him. Had intruded on his intimacy with Elissia, forever tainting its memory. He would kill Balamin. He would take all the warrior had been, leaving him as nothing, and damn the consequences.

"You *will* stop," a voice shouted. Though it sounded like a child, the command shook Erick. He turned.

A young girl wearing a loose gray gown stood in the center of the room. The others in the chamber stared at her but did not draw closer. Her tied-back black hair revealed a pale, round face with a small mouth and tiny ears. Her eyes glowed a pale, unearthly yellow.

She spoke again, her voice child-like, but not entirely female. Power resonated in her words, and Erick had no choice but to comply. "Erick Darvaul of Draymed, I am Venra, Seer of the eight righteous Gods. You will release that man and all present will attend my words."

36

Stay alive, you bastards! I don't want to have to fight you a second time.
  -Makern battle commander

E rick pushed Balamin off him with great effort. The warrior gave no resistance. His already pale face was close to being translucent; his breath came in harsh gasps. Erick sat up and winced. Absorbing the warrior's *nanta* had healed a surprising portion of his wounds. His leg no longer ached. His stomach still bled, but in a trickle, not the hot gush evidenced by the spread of crimson on his shirt and the floor. Though it ached, Erick knew he was going to survive—something that wouldn't have happened had Blink not reached to him.

I meant for you to heal yourself, not kill him, Blink thought in disapproval.

Sorry.

No, you're not.

He wasn't. He would happily see the man dead, though now that he wasn't in the thick of fighting for his life, he no longer wanted to be the one to do it. Once again, he had almost damned himself and came close to tainting himself so badly he wouldn't be able to stop

Eligos. He wanted to do nothing but sleep, though he had been awake less than an hour.

Otan ran toward Erick. Erick scrambled back and reached for his sword, fearing the warrior would finish what his friend started. But the other man paid no attention to him. Instead, he dropped beside the stricken Balamin and shook him.

The young girl drew Erick's gaze as she walked further into the temple. The priest and Anaran had both dropped to their knees. Anaran held his spear shaft out as if offering it to the child.

Taking advantage of the distraction, Elissia ran over and knelt beside Erick. Tears were drying on her face. "I thought he killed you."

"He had," Erick said. "I-"

"Silence," the girl said, again in a commanding, not quite female voice. "All will attend me." She touched the haft of Anaran's spear. "Place your weapon away. There is no further need to spill blood unless you would kill that one." She pointed at Balamin, his face drawn and mouth slack as he attempted to sit up with Otan's aid. He appeared as if he had aged ten years.

Anaran spoke, and his Zatrim was perfect, his accent non-existent. "You would have me destroy one of your tribe, great Sangara?"

Sangara, Erick mused. *I thought she was a seer. Do the Gods speak through her?*

"I would have you destroy any who fight without honor, or for an unworthy reason. This man was not concerned about blasphemy. He cared only that the woman thief was not his. His fight was for himself, not me. This is a far greater blasphemy than anything the Necromancer did."

Otan spoke, and Erick could understand him. "He denied the combat rites of courtship to a suitor."

The girl advanced as if she might strike him. He did not flinch. "They are neither Sterran nor followers of my tenants. Our rites do not apply to them."

Now the priest spoke, and he also used clear Zatrim. Why had they not spoken this way before? "But great Sangara, your laws..."

She whirled on him. Unlike Otan, the priest shied away from her fiery eyes. "Let us discuss my laws. Would you strike an unarmed opponent with a weapon?"

The question threw the priest. His thick brows bunched in confusion. "No?"

"You are uncertain?"

"I would not," the priest said, his voice firmer. "To do so is cowardly and brings dishonor."

"That is my law. And would you strike an opponent in the back?"

"Absolutely not."

"That is also my law. You profess to know the laws, yet you would let a seasoned warrior fight an untrained youth without benefit of a champion? A youth I deemed protected and escorted, for the good of all? A youth who, as I said earlier, is not beholden to our rites?"

The girl pointed at Erick and Elissia with her small, delicate fingers. "These two committed no crime but ignorance, which could have been fixed beforehand." Her hands spread to encompass the other four men in the room. "Yet the four of you conspired to commit base heresy, and for that, you will be punished."

"Great Sangara," Otan said from his spot on the floor. "We did not mean—"

"Will you also add lying to your sins?" Venra asked. "Be silent."

No one spoke for several seconds. Breathless tension filled the room.

"What punishment must we take to atone?" Anaran asked. He remained calm as the priest shook with fear.

"Panta, priest of Sangara," the girl said.

The old man looked up, eyes wide and cheeks flush above his curly beard.

"You may no longer claim that title. You are exiled from the priesthood and will leave this village with only your weapons. If you have honor, you will find a cause worth defending and devote your life to it. If not, go forth as a beggar and apostate."

The priest's eyes widened and glistened at the proclamation. He brought his hands together, thrust them in front of him, and said, "As you decree, great Sangara, so will I do." His shaking voice robbed his oath of any strength.

The girl's blazing eyes regarded Balamin, who appeared dazed and barely aware of his surroundings. Otan knelt beside him, rubbing his friend's arm as if trying to warm him. "Balamin, soldier of Anaran's squad, you have committed the highest heresy, putting your needs above others and using your weapon in a selfish cause. For that, the only punishment is death."

"Wha—" Balamin began.

"Say nothing," the girl thundered.

Erick felt the compulsion in her command and couldn't have spoken if he wanted to. Elissia's hand slipped into his, trembling.

Venra continued. "You will surrender your weapon to your fellow warriors and command them to end your life. You will do this before the evening descends tonight. Obey me, and Alakaneth will judge you fairly. Defy me, and when you finally do end, you will burn in the Festering Hells.

"Otan, as his accomplice in this matter, your punishment will be to end his life while your fellows watch, and then leave as an exile from this land."

To Erick's amazement, Balamin broke down and sobbed. Tears poured as he fell back to the ground and lay there, wailing at the air. Otan's face paled to the color of bleached linen.

Good, Erick thought.

Is that what you've become? Blink thought to him. *Vengeful and without compassion?*

Compassion almost got us killed twice. It almost killed Elissia. Compassion destroyed Prospector's Camp and nearly allowed Eligos to win. If I'm going to beat him, I must be as ruthless as him.

Blink said nothing, but Erick could feel his familiar's disapproval.

I'm giving Keven a second chance. What more do you want?

Do what you want, Blink said. *I'm only here to ask the question.*

Erick squeezed Elissia's hand and turned to her. "Should he die?" He kept the question as neutral as possible, not wanting to influence her answer.

"His God showed up to give out this punishment. The Gods do so little for us, who are we to stop them when they do?"

"That doesn't answer the question."

"He killed you. Or would have if you had been a normal person. Yes, he deserves to die."

Erick nodded. "That's what I think, too."

While they talked, Venra regarded Anaran. The warrior stood with his head up, watching the girl, neither defiant nor obsequious. The fire in the child's eyes dimmed as if she were uncertain.

Guilt tugged at Erick. Despite Blink's assertion, he was not totally heartless. He had compassion for those who deserved it. Balamin needed to die; Anaran didn't. The commander had been pulled into this by circumstance as much as Erick and Elissia.

"May I speak?" Erick asked.

Venra turned to him. "Yes," she said. "This one is difficult, and I would hear your counsel."

He glanced at Elissia, and she shrugged. "This man has done well by me. He has brought me here safely. He gave me advice on how to defend myself against Balamin. It was not his intention to see me die, but your laws tied his hands. He couldn't defend nor offer aid because of his obedience to you."

Venra, or Sangara, said nothing for several seconds. Then she laughed, the oddly masculine sound chilling Erick. "You are bold to speak so firmly for one you don't know well. Why did you not accept him as your champion?"

Anaran answered. "Panta did not call for a champion. I had no opportunity to offer."

"Would you have done so?"

Anaran regarded first the priest, who stared back at him with defeated eyes and then at Balamin, who wept, oblivious to anything around him. Otan's eyes glared at Erick. "I would have," Anaran said.

"Do you believe him?" the girl asked Erick.

"I do."

"So do I," Elissia said.

"Then what do you propose?"

"That he continues his mission and takes us to the falls. That he receives no punishment since he had no say in what happened. That he be—"

A scream of rage interrupted Erick. Otan stood and charged,

dagger in hand. Before Erick could react, Otan knocked him to the ground, knife raised.

A spear tip rammed into the back of Otan's head and protruded from his mouth. Blood dribbled onto Erick's shirt. The dagger dropped from the warrior's hand and thudded beside Erick's head.

The spear pulled Otan away, and the body collapsed beside Erick. Blood poured from his mouth and spread across the dirt.

Anaran placed his foot on Otan's head and tugged the spear. It came with a grating sound that made Erick's stomach roll.

The stout leader stood, spear in hand, and nodded to Erick. Stunned at the suddenness of the attack, Erick could only stare. Elissia knelt beside him, a dagger in hand she hadn't had time to use.

Anaran turned to Venra.

The girl studied him with an impassive face, the glow in her eyes barely there.

"I have defended him, as I said I would, given the chance."

"So you have," the girl agreed. "Then, I grant Erick's request. You are free to escort him to the falls, with any you choose to accompany you. Depart now and prepare to go."

The glow in Venra's eyes brightened as she regarded Erick. She nodded, then winked. Erick's amulet flashed with warmth, tingling the skin on his chest. Then the fire left, revealing the girl's vibrant green eyes. She stood, dazed and wobbling. After a moment, she said, "*Witä taptu?*"

"Wait outside," Anaran told Erick and Elissia, his accent back, the words more difficult to understand.

Erick nodded. As he and Elissia walked toward the exit, Anaran moved to Venra and spoke to her in low tones.

"What just happened?" Elissia asked.

"I think either Denech talked Sangara into standing up for us, or he impersonated Sangara." Given the luck god's nature, either was possible. "And I think he made it possible that we all understood each other."

Elissia shivered. "Gods," she said. She might say spiders with the same uneasiness. "Sometimes I—" she stopped.

"I know," he said. "They scare me sometimes, too."

They reached the exit and stepped into the fresh air as the first light of dawn touched the sky.

~

H e stabbed you through?" Mallow asked as she stitched Erick's stomach wound. He winced each time the needle pierced his skin, but compared to the pain he recently experienced, this was no worse than a mosquito bite.

They gathered inside the clay house they had been given, the house where everyone but he and Elissia slept last night. They wore their old traveling clothes, which had been cleaned and mended.

With the excitement of the morning past, Erick felt nothing but achy and thirsty. Every part of him hurt. He had no idea if it was from the drinking, the fight, or both. Exhaustion, both physical and emotional, gnawed at him.

"He did," Erick answered. "I would have died if I hadn't taken energy from him. If Blink hadn't suggested it." He kept to himself how close he had come to killing Balamin...how much he wanted to.

Blink stood away from the group, his thoughts closed to Erick. He was mad. Erick would apologize later when they had time alone.

"That's amazing," Mallow said. "I wouldn't believe it if I didn't see it."

"I can't believe they released you," Corby said. He and Marcus sat in chairs made of twisted grass and tanned hides. "The way people spoke while we waited had me convinced they would kill you. I was so frightened."

"We were all scared," Marcus said. "The worst part was we couldn't do a damn thing about it. The soldiers would barely let us breathe, much less get near the temple."

"It worked out," Elissia said. She sat beside Erick, holding his hand. "Thanks to Denech. Or Sangara."

"Offering praise to the Gods?" Mallow asked with an arched eyebrow. "The world may stop spinning."

"Two Gods, not all of them," Elissia corrected. "Still don't know that it makes up for all the shit they don't fix."

Mallow frowned but said nothing else.

Sangay stood to the side, adding nothing to the conversation.

Erick still didn't know what to think of the Sakenin. While traveling, he seemed fine, but in town, he grew reticent and surly, preferring his own company to speaking with others. When Erick first met Marcus, the thief suffered severe agoraphobia. He would panic when they traveled outside a settlement, and only Gabrielle's medication and Corby's steadying influence helped him overcome it. Was it possible a fear of confinement afflicted the desert man?

"I'm sorry you saw what you saw," Elissia told Corby.

Corby's face reddened as he stared at the wall. "It's okay," he said. "It's not like you did it intentionally."

"If I looked like you, I'd be sorry too," Marcus said with a smile. Elissia offered him a rude gesture. "Seriously though, 'Lissi, I'm glad you two finally—"

The curtain at the entrance slid aside and Anaran stepped in. He had changed into traveling clothes of well-worn boots, brown woolen pants, a thin gray shirt, and a cured leather vest.

"Ready?" Anaran asked in Zatrim.

"Just finishing," Mallow answered. She tied off the last stitch and cut the finely spun wool thread. "We'll take these out in a tenday. Try not to reopen it."

"No promises," Erick said. He put on his brown traveling shirt, wincing slightly at the tug on his stomach. Like Mallow, he couldn't believe how close he had come to death, and to damning himself, in such a short time. He stood, every part of him in pain, and had no idea how he'd manage to walk all day.

A young girl entered the home, carrying a tray with five clay mugs upon it. Anaran took a cup in each hand and offered one to Erick and Elissia. "Drink. Feel better."

Erick took the cup and sniffed it. It smelled bitter and tart, a mixture of herbs and sour cheese. He closed his eyes, held his nose, and downed it. It tasted as bad as he expected.

"Amare's testicles," Elissia swore as she handed the cup back to Anaran. "I'm not sure that that's better than dealing with the headache."

Erick agreed with a grimace and licked his lips. Anaran offered the drink to the others, but they all declined.

"I didn't drink that much," Marcus said.

"I didn't drink at all," Corby told them.

"And I can handle what I drink. Hangovers are for the weak," Mallow offered.

"We go," Anaran said.

As they left the house, Erick had to admit he felt better. Though lack of sleep tugged at him, his headache and other pains disappeared.

"That stuff is pretty damn good," Elissia said. "Tell Anaran I said ,'thank you.'"

"Welcome," Anaran said before Corby could translate.

Keven, follow us, Erick thought. The Revenant walked behind them.

They walked to the edge of town, where Anaran's men, minus Balamin and Otan, waited for them with packed wagons. They were a subdued group. Erick suspected all of them knew what had happened. The town was too small for them not to know. More importantly, how many blamed them? He now doubted the wisdom of letting Anaran and his *plint* escort them.

They walked away from town. Erick took Elissia's hand, and she smiled at him. Balamin may have forever tainted what they shared their first time, but the warrior would never do so again. And Erick hoped there would be more such sharing in the future. He tried to find guilt in his heart for wanting Balamin to die. He couldn't. Blink would have to learn to accept it. Erick had no room for kindness to those who would harm him or his friends. The world took no pity on such feelings.

He took a last glance back at Talvela, where one man was dead and another soon to die. Erick wondered how many more bodies there would be between here and the death of Eligos, should they get that far.

And he marveled that he didn't care. All that mattered was that he and his friends survived.

37

Amelans may be great people, but any group that zealously religious makes me want to punch someone.
    -Elissia of Kalador

Min smiled as the wagon trundled across the grassland toward the forest ahead of them, the horse spry despite the long day. They had not turned the cart in at Phinsa, as its owner requested. They had ridden straight through the small town without stopping. Min was intent on reaching his sisters' cabin before nightfall.

It was going to be close. Already the house of the bastard god rested on the horizon, making the small trees dotting the plain cast long shadows. They had three more miles to go, with no road to follow. He had to maneuver the wagon to avoid the stumps and debris left by loggers who harvested the forest. He wondered if it would have been smarter to leave the conveyance behind.

Gabrielle sat beside him, silent and staring at nothing. She had been challenging to sway to his side, her gentle nature fighting him the whole way. Nonetheless, with repeated pressure through words, the mating these beings enjoyed, and the application of *elonsha* against her will, he had succeeded. In the end, he had to use more force than he wanted to subjugate her. Ultimately, it didn't matter. She was utterly in his thrall, and that was the important thing.

"Are you ready to meet my sisters?" Min asked.

"I am," Gabrielle said, her voice dull, eyes lifeless.

"And you want to see the Necromancer and his companions pay?"

"I do."

"And you will do what we ask?"

"I will."

"I love you, my sweet." He leaned across the bench and kissed her cheek.

"I love you, too."

Min smiled, and Eligos rejoiced. He didn't care that she had no emotion left. He preferred it that way. She had become a willing vessel. Soon, they would have an undead demon and a corrupted soul to handle and control the vessel. The defeat at Broken Mountain was nothing but a temporary setback. The world would again know why it feared and revered the *Inconnu*.

❧

Though Gabrielle made no motion when Min kissed her, she cringed in her mind. She wanted to recoil from his touch but had no will to do so. She didn't know who she was anymore. Her mind seemed split, ready to destroy itself. She loved Min, even as she hated him. She hated Marcus yet couldn't quit thinking about him. What had been a dream had become a nightmare.

She wanted Erick and his friends dead. Longed to see them writhe in agony, laid out before her and flayed while they screamed for mercy. She reveled in these thoughts as much as they horrified her.

She could only surmise she had gone insane and had no idea how to fix it. And she wasn't sure she would have the will even if she possessed the knowledge.

It hadn't come all at once, like the madness brought on by consuming the *dyrak* plant. This had been subtle. So subtle that she wasn't sure it was happening. Maybe her desires to see Erick harmed were the natural result of the stories Min told about the *Inconnu* War and the horrors the Necromancers visited upon the world. She had seen Erick commit atrocities with her own eyes. He should suffer for such actions.

She only once questioned how a miner would know such things. Min assured her he knew because he knew. Vengeful Min had said this, and the chill she had come to associate with that aspect of her lover accompanied the words. Of course, he knew. Why wouldn't he know?

Some deep part of her told her that wasn't right. That Min couldn't know such things. She should run. He wasn't who he claimed.

She listened to the voice and reluctantly disregarded it. Min took care of her when no one else had. To be with him, she would deal with the part of him she didn't quite understand—the part that frightened her.

As the days passed, that side of Min revealed itself more often. The voice buried deep inside her, rather than going away, became more insistent. As Min trapped her with his love and care, she grew more frightened of him. It felt as if she, like Min, was becoming two people. She no longer had any idea which person was the right person. Which one had she started as: the loving, caring one who wanted to heal people, or the vile, hateful one who thought Erick and his friends should suffer for defying Min's wishes?

The woman who believed in the power of Talan and the gift of healing seemed weaker, although she thought it was who she should strive to be. Trying to be that person made her head hurt. It was so much easier to let the hatred reign. After all, she had so many good reasons to hate.

She stared at the forest as they drew closer. The sun dropped lower, darkness taking over. Would they stop if it got too dark? Did she care anymore?

As they reached the edge of the forest, she saw a yellow glow within: the warmth of lanterns or candlelight. She shivered. She remembered being warm, but now she always felt cold. Even when she and Min lay together, the chill never left her. She still loved him, but she no longer cared about him. How had she come to such a desperate state in such a short time?

"There's the cabin," Min said.

"Good," she said, no emotion in her voice. Inside, she roiled with agony and seethed with emotions she barely understood. Yet, it seemed too much effort to let any of that seep into her words. It was easier to show nothing. She feared if she let anything escape, it would show her who she was, and that might kill her, or worse, drive her irrevocably mad.

Ten more minutes down a rough path brought them to the door. Night had come full-on, and only the glow from the cabin gave them any guidance.

Min jumped down from the bench and flung the horse's reins away. "Get our bags," he told her.

"Yes," she said, watching as he went to the darkened door. That other person she had been—or was it the one she was becoming?—told her to run. Flee into the woods and never look back.

Near the cabin door, two spots glittered: Min's eyes. He was staring at her.

Another chill racked her body. Running was useless. This was where she was supposed to be, for good or ill. All her decisions brought her here. She would accept that. She had no choice, really.

She jumped from the bench and walked toward the back of the wagon.

M in smiled again as he watched Gabrielle lift their bags from the wagon bed. She was his...or close enough that it didn't matter. She would do what was necessary when the time came.

He turned back to the door and knocked. A handful of seconds passed before it opened. A large *priquana* stood there, dressed in a leather coat and dark pants. Taller and broader than Min, he must have been an imposing man in life. Now, he was nothing more than a servant.

"*Zir kura lapag bogpo*," Eligos said, pushing his *elonsha* at the creature. It stumbled back.

"Master, is that you?" a sonorous voice asked from within the cabin. A figure came up behind the large *priquana*. "*Quana, alang*," she said.

The creature stepped aside to reveal a tall woman, taller than most he had seen in this realm, even a few inches taller than his *talba*. She wore a simple black dress that she somehow made look as regal as if it belonged in the high court. Her face reminded Eligos of statues carved by Straphan artisans: unyielding, haughty, yet beautiful in its sternness.

That severity didn't lessen as she regarded him. "My apologies," she said in a tone lacking any remorse, "I must have misheard. I thought you were someone else. You've come to the wrong house." She moved to close the door.

"*Zir salmanan de noquoda*," he said.

The door stopped. Her eyes, the cold blue of winter mornings, widened. "My apologies," she repeated, this time with great sincerity. She bowed her head. "We are honored to have you in our home. Please enter. And forgive my rudeness. You do not look as I expected."

"And what did you expect?" he asked as he stepped into the room. It was stuffy, warmer than outside, which had grown brisk with the darkness.

A wry smile touched her dark lips and softened her features. "I don't know exactly. Taller and more handsome."

He nodded. "This is a plain vessel, and the only option available when I needed it. But it is sturdy. Vanity does not concern me."

"Of course not. I meant no offense." She pointed to a wooden chair decorated with a green cushion and gestured for him to sit.

He sat. He held the groan he wanted to release after so long on the rough wagon. "To be offended, I would have to care. I do not. I care that you have accomplished what you have said you could."

"We have taken it as far as we were able, and all appears well. The incantations work, and suffering creates the desired effect. We have kept our new friend at the peak of agony until your arrival, so we may complete the ritual as soon as you wish. Did you bring a *quasba perida?*"

As if the question called her, Gabrielle walked into the house, carrying a large canvas bag in each hand. She froze when she saw the undead man standing to her left. "What is this?"

"This is my sister, Almira," Min said, grabbing Gabrielle's shoulder and leading her into the room.

"A pleasure to meet you, child," Almira said, her silky voice smooth. She offered a long-fingered hand.

"Are you a Necromancer?"

"I am."

Eligos tensed within Min's body. Now came the test of his power. Now he would learn if his carefully applied pressure worked as he hoped. Almira had asked if he brought a *quasba perida*, an innocent turned against the Gods, who believed in the ways of Eligos and his brothers. He said yes, though in truth, he didn't know for certain. Gabrielle's reactions would tell them both. He waited, breath held.

~

Gabrielle froze with indecision. She should run screaming from this house, just as she should have fled when she learned about Erick. Yet she stood rooted to the spot, uncertain.

She turned to Min. Despite her attempt to infuse emotion into her words, they came out flat, as if all ability to feel had abandoned her. "All this time, you knew of my dislike of Erick, and yet you hid that your sister housed the same evil. Why?"

"Forgive me, my sweet," he said, bowing his head. "I hoped your love for me would let you overlook things. Truly, was your animosity to Erick that he was a Necromancer, or that he took away the man who was supposed to be yours? After all, you had Marcus until his sister and cousin met him and the scholar that led him into Amare's Curse. Is the evil in the power, or the person?"

Gabrielle's mind churned at the question. She tried to reach back and remember. She had been taught to hate Necromancers. Hadn't she? She wasn't sure anymore. Erick had stolen Marcus from her.

More accurately, Corby had. But they wouldn't have met if not for Erick.

Despite that, Erick wasn't truly evil. He had done horrible things, all in the name of protecting those he loved, but he didn't count her among that group, didn't care what happened to her. If he had, he would have sought her out before she left. But hadn't she demanded not to be seen? Another thing she could no longer remember. There was too much fog in her head, too much unknown.

"Do you love me?" she asked Min. "Truly love me?"

"With all my heart."

Some part of her didn't believe him. Some part knew he lied. It screamed at her to run. He brought her here for some purpose she couldn't fathom.

She ignored it. They shared each other in so many ways. She felt more loved now than she ever had. If it was false love, she didn't want to know. She only wanted to continue to be as happy as she had been the past month. "It is a pleasure to meet you," she said to Almira.

"You don't care that I'm a Necromancer?" the woman asked in her silky voice.

After a moment's hesitation in which the deep voice tried one more time to stop her, she said, "I don't."

"Look at me," Min said.

She turned to him. Red flickers of lightning danced in his eyes, which had become solid black orbs. Those eyes trapped her.

"Welcome," Min whispered. In that soft word, she recognized the voice that spoke in her dreams, that clawed at her brain and weakened her resolve. Too late, she realized that in agreeing with that voice, she lost her soul.

38

A tincture created from celery harvested under a full moon and infused with wheat juice will keep evil spirits at bay.
  -Sakenin folk remedy

Nearly a month after arriving in Kalador, Fathen got the summons he had worked to receive.

Since his arrival, Fathen insinuated himself into control of the Temple. Those he could persuade or force with his will stayed in their positions within the hierarchy. Those who proved too strong, or recalcitrant, found themselves as dinner guests of Fathen and Perius. The priests and acolytes Fathen felt not worth subverting remained in check either through fear or loyalty.

The priest that approached Fathen in the grand chamber was one of the older men, with stringy white hair and stooped shoulders. As he shuffled toward them, a rolled parchment in his hand, Fathen saw the bulky seal holding the scroll shut. Anticipation thrilled through him. It had to be from the Queen.

"What do you bring me?" Fathen asked from the Prelate's throne while Perius stood beside him, now little more than a lapdog. The only thing that stopped Fathen from removing the animation from

Perius was fear that the former Prelate's death would incite the Temple to revolt. The Prelate was still well-liked, and Fathen had no illusions that he had pacified or cowed everyone.

"A missive with the Royal Seal," the priest answered, his voice weak and nasal. Fathen couldn't remember the man's name.

Fathen held out his hand.

The priest handed it over.

"You may go," Fathen said as he stared at the seal on the letter—silver-colored wax embossed with the Queen's rose. Once the priest departed, Fathen broke the seal, unrolled the parchment, and read.

Most Holy Prelate, the light of Caros shine upon you, the letter began. Fathen's eyes watered. Even seeing the name of his old deity affected him. Though he had grown accustomed to the symbols throughout the Temple, this fresh depiction disturbed him.

He continued reading. *I beseech your guidance in these troubled times. These past tendays have seen troubles plague our realm, such as have not been seen since the Dark Times. The Procurers haunt the domiciles of peasant and noble alike. They are like a plague of rats and have violated the tacit agreement that has held peace for so long. The army and Queen's Guard press for remuneration as the merchants reach for autonomy in exchange for loans, all based on rumors of bankruptcy because of the Necromancer's destruction of Prospector's Camp.*

It surprised Fathen that the Queen would put so much privileged information in an uncoded message. Then he remembered she was young and had no doubt written without the aid of her spymaster, wanting to keep the dire nature of the situation secret from him.

Although any spymaster worth the name already knew.

I fear that if word of these troubles reaches our neighbors, those we saw as friends may decide to take advantage of our weakened state. I ask that you seek the wisdom of Caros to guide us in these times of turbulence. Pray for his divine words and advise me on what path I must take to avert disaster. I will attend you at your convenience.

The missive ended with the Queen's flowery signature.

"What does the Queen wish?" Perius asked, his voice scratchy, as Fathen let the scroll wind shut.

"She seeks our counsel on how to handle the problems that plague the kingdom. We should take an audience with her and advise her what to do."

"Yes, we should," Perius said.

Fathen smiled and rang the bell to summon another acolyte. Eligos could be nothing but pleased with him now.

A s the small carriage, pulled by two acolytes, arrived at the palace, Fathen considered how he would persuade the Queen to follow his course of action. He wanted to be compelling without relying on his powers. He had to believe he could be a statesman when required. He had also sensed hidden strength in the young woman and feared she might have a resistance he could not overcome. She might defy him, and that outcome was unacceptable.

The carriage stopped. An acolyte came around and opened the door. Fathen stepped out and was once again awed by the beauty of the palace. Such things in this world made the darkness in his soul bearable. To rule this city from such an elegant structure would please him immensely. When Eligos owned this world, Fathen would ask that this be his reward.

Two guards saw them and approached the carriage. They did not move briskly, as was the usual manner, and they offered no words of greeting or challenge. They indicated with hand gestures that the two men should follow them. Fathen noticed their breastplates lacked the polish of his previous visit. He wondered how long it had been since they had received pay, and how much longer they would remain before seeking work elsewhere as mercenaries.

He smiled.

A great malaise lay on the palace. Fathen witnessed servants with no smiles, their motions lackluster, and manners surly. Much of the palace lacked sparkle, as floors and furniture were left uncleaned. Rumpled rugs and pillows lay askew. In some places, trays of half-eaten food remained sitting out, some of it moldering.

Fathen struggled to keep from chuckling with glee.

They reached the gold and gem-laden doors of the throne room.

One of the guards, almost as tall as Fathen and with a broken nose, pushed the door open.

The throne room was resplendent as always, although instead of ten guards, Fathen saw only four, their manner and appearance the same as his escorts.

The Queen sat on her throne; her shoulders slumped, her face lined with worry. She looked years older than when Fathen had seen her last. Her transformation in so short a time amazed him.

They walked the length of the throne room, the Queen's lifeless eyes watching them. She made no greeting until they stood directly before her. Only then did she straighten in her oak throne and attempt to smooth out the wrinkles in her dress. "Thank you for coming, Holy One."

"We are honored to offer our help, Your Royal," Fathen said.

A frown put more lines in the Queen's haggard face. "Why do you address me when I speak to the Prelate?"

Fathen offered a tight smile. "Of course, Your Royal, you have not been made aware. Perius chose to abdicate his position. I am now Prelate."

A flare of irritation replaced the lifelessness in Alekita's eyes. "What is this? There was no ceremony—no official proclamation. I should have been made aware. The people should be allowed to celebrate."

Perius told the lie Fathen had given him to use. "Our apologies, Your Royal, but despite my hale appearance, I am not a well man, and we did not want the stress of an official ceremony. All the oaths have been spoken, and the documents signed. Perhaps next spring, if I am better, we can offer a ceremony for the people."

The young woman didn't seem mollified, although the anger on her face lessened. "Yes, let's hope we are here in the spring to enjoy such a celebration. The people could use a reason for joy." She regarded Fathen. "Congratulations, Prelate Fathen," she said, though her voice offered little goodwill.

"Thank you, Your Royal," Fathen said.

"You have read the letter I sent?"

"I have," Fathen said. "I am sorry for your troubles."

"They're your troubles, too, since you are now the ruler of the Temple," she said. "I don't need you to be sorry; I need you to help me figure a way out of them."

"Of course, Your Royal." Fathen bristled at the return of her arrogance. He kept his urge to lash out at her in check. "The first thing you must do is send soldiers and a contingent of laborers to Broken Mountain to rebuild Prospector's Camp and restore the wealth they provide."

"I have done this," the Queen said. "I'm not stupid. We should have supply lines and caravans running again so we may pay the soldiers, those who have not betrayed and abandoned their kingdom. But it will be at least a month before pay is consistent, and that's barring unforeseen problems.

"I am more concerned about the merchants and the Procurers. Both are thieves. At least the Procurers are more honest about it. The merchants seek to steal power by raising prices when they know people can ill afford them and then offer loans or credit at usurious rates. I would declare a decree to set prices, but I don't have the men to put down a merchant uprising. They can pay their soldiers better than I. We need some way to keep the city from devolving into open rebellion."

Fathen considered everything the Queen said. "What do you know of the *Inconnu*, your Highness?"

"The *Inconnu*? Very little, only there was some war fought a millennium ago that encompassed the entire continent."

It surprised and delighted Fathen someone with the Queen's supposed education would know so little about her realm's history. It made his job so much easier.

"You are correct, Highness," Fathen said. "There was a mighty war involving the *Inconnu* and many of the realms. The *Inconnu* sought to aid the lands with great magic and much wisdom, but some didn't want their guidance or help, so they rebelled. Zakerin, however, did not. They accepted the *Inconnu* as their mentors."

"Did the *Inconnu* not bring the travesty of Necromancy to the world?" Alekita asked. "The very thing you wanted me to deal with the last time you were here?"

Fathen frowned as he swore to himself. He had to remember the Queen's innocent look hid a sharp mind. "They did, Highness. Necromancy itself is not necessarily evil. It allows loved ones to speak to their ancestors and receive guidance. It can help to solve crimes. The evil came when those Necromancers the *Inconnu* trusted enslaved the souls of people and forced them to fight against their own."

The Queen looked thoughtful, finger tapping her dimpled chin. "It's my understanding the *Inconnu* brought forth armies of the dead first, to use against those who opposed them."

Fathen wanted to scream. Was she toying with him, feigning ignorance when she knew the truth? Only one way to find out. "You are wrong, Highness."

Her eyes narrowed at his blunt statement. "Explain," she demanded.

"The *Inconnu* came as ambassadors from far away, seeking to learn more about Krinnik and how they and we might benefit each other. Because of the hostility that met their overtures from some lands and interests, war came, realm fighting against realm, a battle over ideas. The Necromancers betrayed the *Inconnu* and summoned the dead as warriors. The *Inconnu* had no option but to fight with the same creatures. The *Inconnu* lost, but they have returned to offer their wisdom and strength again. This time they will not lose, for there is only one Necromancer left, a mere lad, and he will soon be crushed. Any who oppose the *Inconnu* will be destroyed."

As Fathen's words grew more ominous, he let some of his energy flow toward the Queen, pressing against her will. She shrank back in her throne. Fathen noticed the four guards become more alert. They watched him with sharp eyes, doubtless sensing his hostility. He had used the stick. Now to offer the honey.

He smiled. "But those who align with the *Inconnu*, as Zakerin did long ago, will find themselves with powerful allies. Their troubles will disappear, and their kingdoms will become radiant with glory and wealth. They will rule over those they conquer. Eligos will lead this world, and he will need one to rule beside him."

Fathen didn't need to push against Alekita with these words. He watched her face as the visions of glory danced behind her eyes. She was strong-willed and smart, but also young and vain. She enjoyed the power she had and wanted more. She also wanted order restored. He read it on her as easily as if she scribbled it on a scroll.

"I find your words intriguing," she said, trying to maintain a neutral tone. "Give me time to speak with my advisers. You may wait in the guest room. Refreshments will be provided."

"As you wish, Your Royal."

Fathen had won her.

They waited less than half an hour before the Queen's chamberlain fetched them from the spacious, well-decorated chamber where the provided snacks and drink remained untouched.

"The Queen wishes your presence," the man said in a voice as long and drawn out as his face.

Fathen and Perius stood and returned to the throne room.

"Honored priests," the Queen said as soon as they reached the foot of her throne, "my advisers and I have conferred. We fear that the unrest in Kalador will grow and spread to the countryside if we do nothing. Already there are rumblings of unrest in our other power centers."

Cities, Fathen thought. *She thinks of them as power centers.* He smiled. She would be easy to continue to manipulate.

Her blue eyes fell on Fathen. "You speak well of the *Inconnu* and offer them as a solution to our problems. Do you do this as sycophant or ambassador?"

"I am no man's sycophant," Fathen said and believed it. Eligos was not a man. "I speak as one entrusted by their master with this task."

"An ambassador then," the Queen said. "Very well, Ambassador, tell the king of the *Inconnu* that Zakerin will align themselves with the *Inconnu* as they did in the past. In return, they must assist us in restoring order and bringing our realm back under my rightful rule. The merchants must come into line, and the Procurers brought to heel or eradicated. Take these words to your liege and return to me with his response."

"I have authority to speak on his behalf," Fathen said. "Your terms are acceptable. The armies of Zakerin should be ready to aid the *Inconnu*, all resources made available, and your fealty pledged to Eligos of the *Inconnu*. All this, and we shall restore your realm."

Alekita frowned.

As she didn't answer, her hand tapping her chin, he wondered if he had pushed too far. She enjoyed her power, but she also had pride. Would swearing fealty push too far against her dignity? It wasn't his fault she hadn't asked the terms beforehand. He prepared to insinuate his will to force her compliance.

She glanced over to a corner of the throne room. Fathen turned his gaze and saw a rotund man standing in a shadowed nook. He nodded.

"Very well," Alekita told Fathen. "Your terms are acceptable."

Fathen nodded. "Thank you, Your Royal. I must return to inform my master. I will join you and your advisers soon, and we will set things right."

"The kingdom thanks you and we look forward to a mutually beneficial alliance," Alekita said

Fathen and the Prelate turned to leave. The unknown man in the nook had disappeared. One of the Queen's advisers, obviously, but who was he and how much power did he have? Fathen would have to look into it. In the meantime, he had another task. One he had wanted to do for over twenty years.

A knock at the door drew Fathen's attention as he swallowed the last bite of the acolyte's heart. Perius, standing near, glanced at the door before returning his gaze to the body. Fathen wiped the blood away from his mouth with a cloth and tossed it to the floor, where it landed beside the corpse. Making sure the dead man was hidden behind his bed, Fathen crossed the chamber and answered the door.

"They have gathered, Holiness," the thin, balding priest said, voice nervous. Fathen nodded.

"Come, Perius," he said to the Prelate.

The older man stared with longing at the bed.

"Come," Fathen barked, putting power into his voice.

The Prelate's head snapped up, hunger in his drawn face. Fathen had refused to let him feast upon their latest meal. He wanted the man weak for what was to come.

"Follow me," Fathen told the former Prelate. They left the room and followed the priest toward the grand worship chamber.

They entered through a side door, which led directly to the dais. Fathen dismissed the priest with a wave of his hand. He scurried back out the side door and closed it. From there, the priest would return to the main doors, enter, and join the rest of the temple's inhabitants waiting in this chamber.

Fathen walked up the two steps and onto the dais. Faces turned toward him as he strolled toward the center, like an actor crossing a stage. Acting is how he felt about his past when he performed as an ineffectual priest to a useless god. This was his real life, where he had power.

Where people feared and respected him.

He stopped and stared at the priests and acolytes, gathered in uncertain clusters near the chairs that sat in neat rows. They spoke in hushed tones, and Fathen saw much-relished fear on many of those who watched him and smiled. If they knew what was coming, fear would turn to outright terror.

The sun emerged from behind a cloud and shone through the high windows of the temple, blazing off the golden sunburst symbols that decorated the room. Fathen almost hissed at the glare from those hated effigies. He would have them removed as soon as he completed the ceremony.

Perius had followed and stood next to him. The man's hands shook with hunger.

"Don't worry," Fathen whispered to him. "Your hunger will soon be a memory."

Perius offered a papery smile.

Fathen turned his attention back to the gathering. Their numbers had reduced significantly over the past days, between those Fathen had taken and those that fled. But there were enough to make a difference, enough to do what was necessary.

Fathen held up his hands to silence the nervous whispers. The gathering stared at him, and he basked in their uneasiness.

"Caros is a sham," he thundered.

The words echoed in the chamber. Several gasps greeted this proclamation, and many of the priests headed for the doors.

"Do not move!" Fathen shouted and threw his will across the room, touching every man in the chamber. His head pounded with the effort, and only the energy from the recently consumed heart allowed him the ability.

They all froze and turned back to face him.

That was the easy part, though it strained him. The next step would take every ounce of willpower he had, along with all the *elonsha* coursing through him. *Eligos help me*, he thought. "All of you, listen. The god you worship is a sham. He no longer has any power if, indeed, he ever did. He is a weak thing, no longer deserving of your worship or attendance."

All eyes were upon him now.

Fathen thought they would stay even if he released his hold. "You are under my control not because of any skill Caros has given me. I have you in thrall because my new master, Eligos, the Master of Shadows, patriarch of the *Inconnu,* has shown me what needs to occur, and your assistance is required for the great work to bring Zakerin under his sway. The Queen has sworn allegiance to him, and now all of you will do the same. You will serve Eligos."

Now came the difficult moment. Fathen stepped up behind Perius. A thrill ran through him as he drew the knife. *Elonsha* glittered along the edge of the blade, sparks of red like fireflies. He grabbed the old man by his newly darkened hair and jerked his head back. "I will now reveal the power of your new god, who you will come to revere as I have."

Perius grabbed Fathen's hands and tried to pull them away. Weakened by lack of food, the former Prelate had no strength. Fathen casually drew the knife edge across the man's throat. As he gave the Prelate rebirth, Fathen had the power to bring him death.

Blood poured. Fathen wrapped his hands around the wound. *Elonsha* filled Fathen as he took the corrupted blood over his hands. He sent his will toward all the priests. They didn't move as their former leader gurgled and thrashed. The once-dead Perius now slowly died again.

With the power flowing through him, it was easier for Fathen to send his thoughts as his master did. He felt the shock and surprise from two dozen minds and sent out his command. *Reach under the chairs and find the knife.*

Each man shuffled to a chair, feet dragging, and motions slow. They wanted to resist but Fathen pushed on them. His head pounded as the *elonsha* coursed through him. Scrapes of metal on wood whispered in the chamber as the clerics pulled knives from where Fathen had attached them with paste the previous night. Soon all of them had a knife in hand.

Speak the words, "for you, Eligos, my master in all."

Two dozen voices spoke the words, a small cascade of worship.

Fathen nodded. *Kill yourselves.*

His head screamed at the resistance from the pliable minds, but hands raised to throats or bellies or arms. Fathen realized he should have been more specific as each person chose their method of demise, some messier than others. Screams, groans, and gurgles filled the temple as the mass suicide occurred.

Fathen smiled as he imagined the impotent Caros weeping at the desecration.

Two priests had not taken blade to flesh. Fathen removed his hands from Perius's throat and the Prelate collapsed; all animation left the undead corpse.

Fathen walked toward the resisting men. As he passed those who died around him, more strength flowed into him, a cold biting power.

Yes, the voice of his master said in his head, faint but understandable. *You do well.*

Fathen smiled, pleased to return to his master's grace. He stopped in front of one of the resisting priests, a short man in his middle years with the blond hair and tan skin of an Amel.

"You are an abomination," the man said through clenched teeth.

Fathen didn't know his name. He realized he knew none of their names. "I wish I had killed you as soon as you stepped in this holy place."

"What would your family say if they heard such a threat?" Fathen asked. The Amels were a notoriously pacifistic people. "You are strong. I need some strength to lead. I will make you a lieutenant."

His broad face bunched in puzzlement. Fathen stabbed him in the throat. The priest grabbed his punctured larynx, gurgling as his eyes went wide.

The other man, a youngster no more than twenty, offered no such brave words. His brown eyes almost rolled white with terror as he kept his knife from his body. He whimpered. "Please," he said, his voice high with fright.

A flash of recall slapped Fathen.

The memory of a young boy pleading while—

Fathen snarled, forcing away the compassion that tried to weaken him. He grabbed the mewling boy's head and rammed the knife into his ear.

The light left the boy's eyes. He went silent and fell like a grain sack pushed off a wagon. The *elonsha* from the kill was not as powerful as that which flowed toward him from those who sacrificed themselves, but it all helped.

Fathen held his arms wide as men died around him. *Elonsha* energized his body.

As the last man died, the temple grew silent.

The perfume of death filled Fathen's nostrils.

Energy flitted over his nerves like lightning. He must use it or die again when it burst from his skin and consumed him.

"For you, my master," he said.

He recited words he had never learned yet knew anyway. The bastard Necromancer would know the words. But where he needed herbs and formulaic phrases and the permission of the Gods pretending to rule this world, Fathen needed nothing but his will, *elonsha*, and the power his master bestowed upon him. He had only to command and the corpses before him would obey.

"*Aaetpio de Eligos, golar amde omaos Inconnu odnay nonca mapsam.*"

393

Power drained from Fathen. It leached from his body like water down a drain and flowed toward the inert meat on the temple floor. He saw it, orbs of darkness crackling with red lightning riding on streams of black light. As the dark river touched a body, one of the orbs sank into the corpse, and the river surged to the next body.

In less than a minute, the stream of *elonsha* had run its course. Fatigue dragged on Fathen, and the headache returned. He thought he had left behind such afflictions when he died. It didn't matter. As the corpses stirred and stood, their gleaming eyes on him, their thoughts his, all of them proclaiming him their master, he forgot his aches.

He controlled the Temple of Caros, which he would refashion as the Seat of Eligos. The Queen had relinquished her authority in exchange for aid.

Zakerin was his for the taking.

39

Even the lands that fought against the Inconnu were not totally unanimous in their resistance. In Amelan, a group known as the Pratani (open wound) named after the volcano in that land, sought to execute both civic and military leaders, attempting to weaken the kingdom's efforts.

-Corberin of Draymed, *The Second Inconnu War*

Erick stood in a field he didn't recognize, barren except for a hundred-foot-tall, gray stone building. The sunburst emblem of Caros, painted in gold, covered half the structure's facade. The sigil gleamed, though no sun shone. Roiling gray clouds covered the sky.

Not knowing what else to do, Erick walked toward the temple. It didn't take long to realize that, though the ground moved, the building drew no closer.

He started running.

The ground moved faster, his heart pumped harder, and his breath grew short.

Still, the temple remained the same distance away.

He stopped and stared, now more uncertain.

The clouds darkened. Red lightning flitted across their surface. A chill wind reeking of rotten onions blew over Erick. He shivered.

The golden gleam of the sunburst grew dark. As it faded, the air turned frigid. Within seconds, the once brilliant symbol became the deep brown of river mud and oozed down the building's side. The stone it touched sizzled like water dropped on a hot pan.

A sound, somewhere between a large man's scream and the plop of boiling water, came from the building.

Horror roiled through Erick as he watched, helpless.

It was as if the temple itself screamed while it burned. The stone building melted and twisted, the facade disappearing as the brown emblem distorted and oozed. The lower half of the building soon crumbled

Erick covered his ears as the scream grew louder, but the agonized howl thrummed through his body.

With nothing to support it, the upper portion of the temple collapsed. It crashed to the ground in a rumble of rocks. Crimson lightning arced from the clouds and smashed into the falling boulders, pulverizing them into pebbles and dust.

Erick dropped to his knees, tears in his eyes, as a final, terrified wail smashed through him.

The building was dying. A cold wind blew the dust in whirlwinds and grit raced past Erick, stinging his skin.

When the dust cleared, the building no longer existed. No rubble, no broken pillars or outline of a foundation, just barren ground. It was as if the structure had never been. A group of people had replaced the building. At least twenty, Erick estimated, barely able to think. In their midst stood a tall man with long brown hair and eyes dancing with red sparks.

Erick recognized the man; a man they had killed over a month ago.

"Fathen," Erick said.

The priest didn't respond, only stood surrounded by his new acolytes, while the wind blew, and lightning bounded across the sky.

Fathen's fingers twitched, and bones sprouted from the ground in twisted formations, bleached white and extending as far as Erick could see.

They began to move.

Erick started awake at a bony claw on his shoulder. He rolled away, panicked, and tried to jump up. His blanket tangled his feet, and his head thudded into canvas above him. He dropped to the ground and let out a sob.

"It's me," Blink said as Elissia sat up.

"What's wrong?" she asked.

Erick's heart thudded. His breath came in gasps. "Another vision," he rasped as he leaned against the tent. It had been so long since he experienced one of the vivid dreams, he thought they had forsaken him. He had no idea if they were messages from the Gods or his imagination.

"What's happened?" Elissia asked. She pulled herself from under her blankets and crawled over to him. She had been there when his visions told him of the destruction of their hometown of Draymed. That event had almost destroyed their budding friendship.

"I'm not sure," he said, trying to sort out what he had seen. "I think Fathen has formed some sort of—"

"Fathen?" Elissia said. "He's dead, isn't he? You told me he was dead." Her voice trembled.

"He was," Erick said. "I don't know what's happened, but he was in the vision."

"He's created a group of undead," Blink said. Sharing his master's thoughts, he was as affected by the visions as Erick. "Somehow, he's come back and created *quana* to follow him. Eligos is growing in power again."

Erick nodded. Elissia wrapped her trembling arms around him. He shook as much as she did. "Time is short," Erick said. "We have to find this *wicaesir*, and soon. And pray to Caros and Denech she can help us."

~

They didn't sleep the rest of that night. Erick and Elissia lay curled together under a blanket while Blink sat nearby. They said nothing. The vision had drained Erick of all energy. Though they clung together in only their underclothing, they had no desire to do more than share warmth and closeness.

Hours later, the increasing visibility in the tent told them dawn approached. Elissia kissed Erick. He returned it and his desire returned with renewed vigor.

"I'll be outside," Blink said, a slight edge of disgust in his voice.

Ten minutes later, they lay in each other's arms, content, having chased the last of the vision's terror away as they joined together in love. Unease and a sense of urgency weighed upon Erick, but Elissia's tenderness and passion had removed the edge.

"We should get dressed," she said, running a hand over his head and sending tingles through his body.

His groin stirred again, but she was right. The rest of the camp would be rising soon, and they needed to be ready to travel.

They had walked with Anaran's company across the fields of Starrasen for eleven days. Recently, the terrain had changed from grasslands with the occasional gentle rise and dip to flatter ground dotted by brown tussocks and spindly flowers with large, milky white petals. The travel had been smooth, and Erick and Elissia had grown closer, taking every advantage of having their own tent. Erick passed the boredom of traveling by thinking about their nights.

Anaran also kept them entertained. He turned out to be almost as proficient a storyteller as Corby, regaling them with tales of Starrasen heroes and their bravery in the tribal wars, long before the time of the *Inconnu*, when the various factions of Starrasen families struggled for land, prestige, and herding rights. Those days passed after the war, when the tribes realized they needed to band together to keep their land from being stolen by the Straph invaders to the north. Now, the warriors participated in mock combats, and tribes that lived in the north occasionally skirmished with Straphan. They had never made a truce with their northern neighbors, and several frontier towns remained eternal fortresses, although conflict was seldom and nowhere near as savage as it had once been.

As they packed up camp, Anaran approached, a grin on his friendly face until he got close. His smile dropped away, and his brows furrowed. "You look as if swamp Gila bit ancestors," he said. "What's wrong?"

Erick didn't understand the analogy but assumed it was a bad thing. "Time is short. I need to find the person I seek soon."

Anaran nodded. "We reach the falls today. We can help you descend into the jungle, but we will go no further."

Erick nodded. "Thank you for what you've done."

They finished breaking camp and were traveling again within the half-hour. It was a beautiful mid-autumn day, although Erick wouldn't have known it if Corby didn't keep the days counted for them. Moisture filled the air, and although it wasn't hot, it was far warmer and more humid than home. Sweat clung to Erick. As soon as he wiped his brow with a cloth, more perspiration formed. Before long, his clothing stuck to him. He had no idea how Anaran's men moved in their leather jerkins without fainting.

"It's like walking through warm soup," Marcus said.

"Enjoy," Anaran told them. "Swamp is worse."

"That's wonderful."

Erick wondered how Anaran knew if he didn't go into the swamp. Then he realized that just because he refused to accompany them, didn't mean he hadn't been there before. Possibly he saw no obligation to take them further than the falls since that's all their seer demanded. "What can you tell us about the swamp?"

Corby translated the question.

Anaran's dark brows bunched thoughtfully for a moment and then spoke, with Corby acting in his role as translator. "It has been many years since I have been below the Nallis. I used to accompany raiding parties to gather the herbs for our weapons."

"The famous poisoned blades of Starrasen," Marcus said. "Used to great effect against the Straphs."

Anaran knew enough Zatrim to understand Marcus's words since he didn't wait for a translation. "Yes. The Northerners grew to fear our weapons, for if we did not kill them on the field, they suffered great agony and died many days later. We now only use these herbs for the hunting animals, so we send fewer men to find herbs." Even through the translation, sadness tinged his words, as if he missed the days of seeing his enemies poisoned.

Erick chose to think the warrior missed the treks into the jungle.

Anaran continued. "The swamp has grown more dangerous over the years. When I was a youth and hunting there, we feared the crocodiles and *baratas*, the large constricting snakes."

"Wonderful," Marcus said in a weak voice. Though he had overcome his fear of open spaces, snakes still rattled the thief. "This gets better and better."

"The clans who dare to hunt there speak of crocodiles that walk like men. They are savage and use our poisons against us. They attack with their teeth and claws, and rare is the party that ventures too deep without sustaining injury or the loss of a clansman."

"Why go there at all?" Elissia asked.

"And why the hell are *we* going there?" Mallow said.

"Many of the herbs we also use as medicines," Anaran said, "and we can find them no other place."

"And we're going because I must," Erick said. "Although only I have to go. No one here is bound to me in any way. You can break away anytime you want."

"I told my father I'd stick with you, so stick I will," Mallow said. "Besides, you need me. I'm the greatest tracker alive with an impeccable sense of direction. You'll need someone like that in a swamp."

"Is there anything you don't excel at?" Elissia asked.

Mallow put her hand on her chin and rubbed it as if giving the question serious consideration. "I'm not great at being modest," she said and winked.

Elissia glared for a moment, then laughed. "If I didn't like you so much, I think I'd want to kill you."

"You wouldn't be the first."

Erick chuckled in relief. Somehow the two women had come to terms with their disparate personalities. Erick didn't know how and didn't need to. It only made him happy they had.

"I hope the Gods watch after you," Anaran said. "There is a walled settlement at the bottom of the falls at the edge of the deep lands. It is called Fissis, and the *alasan*, the upright lizards, do not bother it. But few venture beyond without heavy guard."

"I have to trust in the will of Caros and Denech to guide me and keep me safe," Erick said.

The day grew warmer and muggier, and they walked with little talking. Erick's anxiousness grew. He already feared they were too late to do any good.

Calm down, Blink told him. *I saw it too. Having twenty servants is a long way from taking over the world.*

I know, Erick thought back. *I'm worried the vision means more. If Fathen is back and has powers, that can only mean Eligos is getting more powerful. It took all I had, and we barely inconvenienced him. How am I going to stop him a second time?*

Isn't that why we're doing this? To find someone who can answer that.

It was, but Erick couldn't help wondering if it was a waste of time.

No need borrowing trouble, Blink said.

Erick smiled. It was one of his mother's favorite sayings, and it rang true. This was the only course he had. His ancestors had put him upon it after conversing with the Gods. If it turned out to be wrong, if the Gods could be mistaken, what hope did any of them have?

Rather than making him gloomier, the thought lightened his mood. He was in the hands of fate at this point. All he could hope was that it worked in his favor. If not, at least he would die knowing he tried his best.

The sun had begun descending when a sound reached Erick. It was whispering, like leaves brushing over cobblestones. Erick shivered, wondering if the voice of Eligos had come to assault him like it had so many times before. But no smell of *elonsha* accompanied the shushing noise. It didn't fade; it only grew louder.

Erick was about to ask about it when he caught sight of water, the glimmer of sun on its surface catching his eye. Their slow north-western travel had finally brought them to the Upper Sterran, the river that crossed the entirety of Starrasen.

"The Nallis," Anaran said, pointing toward the lowering sun.

The river seemed to disappear, then he realized what the sound was, though he had never heard it before.

As they drew closer to where the river fell away, a mass of green came into view. The tops of trees. They stood overlooking the jungle.

"It's beautiful," Corby said, staring in wonder at the canopy of broad leaves, moss, and vines that made up the forest roof. Erick marveled at the greenery, like a carpet made of vegetation.

When they reached the edge, where the falls fell at least a hundred feet to thunder into a broad pool below, Marcus said, "I think I'm going to vomit." His olive skin did appear lighter, as if he were ill.

To Erick, the falls were amazing, something he never imagined he'd see and in its own way, as impressive as the vastness of Broken Mountain. Mist floated in the air, and birds rode the currents. The jungle stretched as far as he could see.

How are we ever going to find anyone in there? Erick thought.

I guess we start in town, Blink thought.

Erick hadn't noticed the cluster of buildings gathered at the far end of the lake, surrounded by a light brown wall. The buildings were difficult to see through the mist coming off the falls. Large pieces of olive-colored cloth rose in triangular shapes between several of the buildings, like large sails.

"How do we get down?" Mallow asked. "I'm good at a lot of things, but I haven't learned flying yet." She looked at Blink. "You going to carry us down?"

Blink shook his head. "I'm not a flying horse."

"It's too dangerous," Erick explained. The homunculus was strong for his size and could carry them one at a time, but Erick didn't want his familiar responsible for such a task. All it would take was one slip. And Erick agreed with Blink. He wasn't a beast of burden.

"Then how do we do it?" Marcus asked with a wary eye at the edge of the cliff.

In answer, three of Anaran's men came forward with thick hemp ropes.

Marcus's face paled further. "You've got to be kidding?"

~

R ather than having to climb down the rope, as Erick assumed when the warriors came forward, the men set about creating a sling that allowed people to sit and be lowered.

Erick went first. It was his job to do so, and he allowed no one to talk him out of it. Blink flew down, drifting on the currents. The birds saw him and flew away with angry squawks.

"Don't," Erick said, sensing Blink's desire to chase them.

"You're no fun."

Erick gripped the ropes tightly as the men above lowered him. To keep from staring at the ground below, he focused on the surrounding terrain until the mist from the falls obscured his view. The spray soon drenched him more than the humid air. The thunder of the falls filled his ears. He turned to look the other way, careful not to move too fast. He didn't want to cause the makeshift sling to swing any more than necessary.

A cliff face of dark fractured rocks jutting out in various spots extended as far as he could see. It was as if a giant or god had taken a mallet and pounded a deep dent into the world. Here and there, spindly trees clung to the cliff face, somehow finding enough soil to sustain them.

Instead of chasing the birds, Blink amused himself by flying near the falls, his left wingtip brushing the water. Erick smiled, the frightening drop to the bottom forgotten.

By the time he reached the ground, water dripped from the hair plastered to Erick's face, and he expected to squish when he walked. He stepped out of the sling and waved to the men above, hoping they could see him through the mist. He could barely see them.

He took a few steps away, the ground wet and mushy beneath his feet. Tufts of short grass grew up from a coating of moss. Every time he stepped, the moss broke apart, releasing an earthy smell with a rotted undertone, like old, dead trees. Water soaked into his shoes, making the last dry spot on him as wet as the rest.

Blink landed beside him and floundered for a moment. "That's weird," Blink said, raising his voice to be heard over the steady pounding of the falls. He poked a talon into the loam. "And smelly."

"Might take some getting used to," Erick agreed. The smell didn't bother him, but his companions probably wouldn't like it much. His tolerance for such scents was much higher than theirs.

They stepped aside and waited for the next person. It was Elissia, to no surprise.

She had the same reaction he did to the unstable ground. "This is like being drunk," she said, then blushed.

Erick suspected she was remembering what happened when they had been drunk and smiled as his cheeks heated up.

Elissia explored the area near them while the rope sling disappeared into the mist. She hadn't gone ten feet when she pointed at the moss and said, "Marcus is going to love this place."

Erick saw something black and long, slithering away. He stepped back and looked at his feet to make sure there wasn't a snake near him. He didn't dislike them as much as Marcus, but he also didn't want one crawling up his leg.

Corby came next, stepped off the sling, and almost fell. "So, this is what marshland is like," he said. "I've read about it but could never quite get the idea."

"Is the whole thing going to be like this?" Erick asked.

The scholar nodded. "It will probably get worse once we get into the true jungle and swamp."

Why not? Erick thought wryly. *No reason this shouldn't be difficult.*

While the others came down, Erick studied the town across the lake. All he could see from here was the wall and, rising above it in spots, the strange triangular cloth sails. They curled in at the bottom before disappearing behind the wall. They glistened with moisture.

"Clever," Corby said, noticing Erick's gaze. "Freshwater collectors."

"They have a whole lake of water," Erick said.

"Maybe there's something that contaminates it," Corby said. "The odoriferous flora certainly makes that a distinct possibility."

The others eventually made it down, though it took longer than Erick expected. Mallow didn't seem unduly bothered by the marsh. Sangay appeared uncomfortable; his dark eyes darted over the swamp. As he walked, he lifted his foot high before taking a step. *Almost like an ostrich*, Erick thought.

Other than the one snake, they saw no other animals. An occasional bird call sounded from above them.

Marcus came last, as Erick expected. He had his eyes shut tight, and he touched down on his butt before he opened them.

"Gods, it's wet," he said, jumping up and almost falling before Corby caught him. A sizable damp spot covered the back of his pants, although it was only slightly darker than the rest of his clothing. Elissia laughed.

"Not funny, 'Lissi," her brother said.

"Sure, it is," Elissia told him. "And it's only going to get funnier."

"That's what I was afraid of," Marcus said, face dour. "Anaran wished us strength of Sangara, although I think dexterity is going to be more important on this ground."

"Let's go to Fissis," Erick said, pointing at the town. "Hopefully, my ancestor was right and someone there can tell us where to find Alais."

The roar of the falls faded as the group walked away, replaced by squelching noises as they trudged over the springy terrain. Moisture covered every part of Erick, and he was now thankful for the unusual mid-autumn warmth.

They skirted the lake. Erick caught movement out of the corner of his eye—another snake slithering away from them. *At least they aren't aggressive.*

As they drew closer to the wooden wall, Erick got a rough idea of the size and shape of the town. The barrier extended from the edge of the lake to the jungle line but didn't drive into the trees, near as he could tell. Fissis was a sizable settlement, not as large as Draymed but bigger than many of the villages they had traveled through in Zakerin.

Soon, the smell of smoke, driven by the light breeze, reached through the overarching odor of vegetation.

He and his companions were still a hundred feet away when the soft, loamy surface suddenly turned into hard-packed earth. He stumbled, the jarring stop on the hard surface hurting his feet. "Ouch."

The others fared better. Erick had been so intent on studying the village he hadn't noticed the cleared land that circled the wall. His friends had.

A loud cawing echoed through the air. Part of the wall slid aside, revealing a square opening. Eight pale-skinned men emerged through the gap and trotted toward them, short-hafted spears in hand. The wall closed with a scraping sound.

The men held their spears low, not raised in a threatening manner. Nonetheless, Erick and his companions stopped and waited for the warriors to approach. They wore loose clothing of a muted green color; their shirts cinched to their waists by a tan cord. Hats the same drab color of their clothes crowned their black-haired heads. Except for one man—his shone bright green, like new summer grass. His belt also sparkled yellow against his shirt.

No one spoke as the villagers drew closer. They stopped about twenty feet away. The man with the vibrant hat stepped forward another five feet, spear lowered. "*Ando aklah tadik dialukan disni. Pergil.*"

Mallow stepped forward. "*Kama menwark tida mudra. Kama igin memsui hatun.*"

The man's pale face blanched, and he took a step back.

"What's going on?" Erick asked.

Mallow held up her hand; her eyes fixed on the man. "*Kit perlu apo, apo darida ando au oran, kama keberan untu.*"

Erick stepped over to Corby and spoke low so as not to disturb Mallow. "What are they saying?"

"They don't want us here. Mallow told him we want to go into the jungle." Corby continued to translate as he listened. "He's telling her the jungle is nothing but death, and he cannot allow it. Mallow is doing her best, but I don't think she's convincing him."

Erick listened for a few moments as Mallow and the man with the bright green hat continued speaking, their voices growing angered. The posture of the other villagers had changed, their spears higher, their faces grim. Erick couldn't believe they would get this far only to be stopped by eight men with spears and their stubborn leader. He walked up to Mallow and put a hand on her arm. She paused, her eyes fierce and face red.

"This jackass says he can't let us go into the jungle because we would die, and he won't have our deaths on his hands. I've tried to convince him we can take care of ourselves. He told me many of the people who came from 'up above' thought the same thing, and none of them have ever come back. He can't stop them because they are Sterrans, but he can stop us because we are foreigners with no rights here." Mallow looked as if she would happily throttle the man.

Erick found himself appreciating the small warrior and understood his need to protect others from their bad choices. Unfortunately, understanding didn't mean agreement. "Translate for me," he told Mallow. Then he turned to the man, straightened his back, and spoke. "My name is Erick Darvaul. I am a Necromancer."

"You sure about this?" Mallow asked.

"Yes."

"Okay. But be ready to run." Mallow spoke to the man in halting Sterran.

His eyes widened as she finished, but he didn't immediately launch himself at Erick or run screaming.

Erick continued. "I have traveled here at the direction of my ancestors. I am to go into this jungle to seek the *wicaesir* named Alais. I don't want to fight you, but I will not be delayed any further from my duty. I will get into that jungle, whatever it takes, even if it means conjuring undead to destroy your village."

Mallow hesitated again until a glare from Erick made her continue.

When she finished, the man, his eyes shadowed by the wide-brimmed hat, regarded Erick. He didn't seem concerned with the threat. His gaze drifted to each of Erick's companions before it finally returned to Erick. The silence grew unnerving, and Erick almost spoke again, though he had no idea what he would say.

"Alais?" the man finally asked.

"Yes," Erick said. "We seek Alais."

The man nodded, then spoke. Mallow translated. "We know of this witch and that some may come looking for her. You may venture into the deep land as you wish, but I advise you to wait until the day is light. To venture at night is to ensure you never reach her. You may stay with us this night."

He turned and dismissed his companions with a wave. The

warriors lowered their spears and walked toward the town wall, no longer concerned with the strangers.

A wave of relief passed through Erick. He had avoided a fight.

"Would you have destroyed the village?" Mallow asked as they walked toward the town, a hard edge to her voice.

Erick smiled. "You're not the only one who can tell bold lies."

Mallow returned the grin. "I never lie; I merely exaggerate."

Erick shook his head.

∼

T he wall slid open as they approached, again accompanied by the scraping sound. As they passed through, Erick glanced down and saw a groove coated with dark oil that smelled of meat. They used grease to slide the heavy wooden wall back and forth. It didn't explain how they concealed the door from the outside.

As they drew closer to the large cloths, Erick saw Corby was right. The giant cloths ended above large clay kegs. Drops of water turned into larger drops of water, which turned into rivulets running down the sails.

All the buildings were built of dark brown stone and wooden roofs. The smell of cook fires grew stronger and the scent of vegetation lessened. Some of the pale-skinned women tended fires, while others chopped vegetables and strips of bright red meat. Their clothing was the same dull green as the men, and looser, with no belts cinching the garments. They also wore drab hats. Black hair spilled from underneath them. Children ran between the buildings, their clothing as concealing as the adults.

The man in the bright green hat stopped next to one of the small dwellings, only a couple of buildings away from the wall. He pointed at it and spoke to Mallow.

"He says we can stay here," Mallow informed them. "Says dinner will be brought to us. There is a privy behind the building, and we can go there, but we shouldn't go anywhere else in the town. Strangers aren't welcome."

"If they don't have guests, why do they have an empty house set up for them?" Marcus asked.

Mallow asked, and the man answered.

"This house is for those from the 'upper land' when they come to hunt in the jungle. It's for Sterrans, not strangers. It's because we seek Alais that we're allowed to stay. He's not saying it, but it feels like she would be displeased if she found out they mistreated us."

"So, you're saying he knows her?" Erick asked.

"Knows her or knows more of her than he's letting on. It's just a hunch."

"Thank him for his hospitality, and tell him we will abide by his rules," Erick said.

Mallow relayed the message. The man nodded and left them.

Erick stepped into the home, which had no door. It was a one-room dwelling, twenty feet long and half again as wide. It was going to be tight with the seven of them inside. They removed their packs and set them against the wall.

"Now what?" Marcus asked.

"Now we wait until morning and head for the jungle," Erick told him.

"I know that much. Any idea yet how we're going to find one woman in such a large area?"

"Not a clue," Erick confessed.

Dinner arrived as the light disappeared from the doorway, and the room grew black.

Two women and two girls entered, their eyes gray and wide in their ghostly faces. None of them wore their hats, and their black hair hung to their waists. One of the girls carried a clay pot on which sat a flickering flame that gave enough light to illuminate the entire dwelling. The women brought a short-legged table on which sat seven bowls and cups, all made of clay. The other girl carried a clay pitcher.

The women said nothing as they walked to the center of the room and placed the table on the floor. The girl poured liquid from the pitcher into the cups while the women waited near the doorway, heads bowed. The girl with the lighted pot placed it in one corner of the room, warily watching Sangay until he backed away, hands held up in a gesture of peace.

None of Erick's companions spoke while they waited. Erick shifted uncomfortably. He thought he should say some word of thanks, though he knew they wouldn't understand.

As the girl finished and joined the older women, he finally spoke. "Thank you."

The quartet continued out the door without a word or sign of acknowledgment.

"I guess dinner is served," Elissia said.

"Yeah, but is it safe?" Marcus asked. "These are the people known for using poison on their enemies."

"They are not your enemies," a sibilant voice said from the doorway.

They all wheeled around. Marcus, Elissia, and Mallow drew their daggers.

A hideous, green-skinned monster filled the doorway.

40

I never believed that giants were real, but I saw giants walk that day.
  -Eyewitness account of the Battle of Osma

The creature made no move to attack, only stood in the door, a clay cup in its hand.

"Who are you?" Erick asked, overcoming his shock.

"What are you?" Elissia asked on his heels.

Erick had never seen an alligator, only read about them in one of his mother's books. This being was what he imagined, except it stood on two legs and wore a sleeveless shirt and a loincloth made of what appeared to be vines and moss. It had an elongated snout filled with crooked yellow teeth. A bony ridge above its neck held two ocher-colored eyes that regarded them all. Scaly skin the hue of leaves in summer covered its body. It wore no shoes, and its feet and hands ended in sharp talons, similar to Blink's.

"I am Sasesus," he said. Erick assumed it was a he because he saw no apparent breasts, although he wasn't sure. "Eat your dinner. It is not poisoned." His look and his soft, hissing voice were at complete odds with his gentle words.

"Tell us why you're here," Erick said.

"I can explain while you eat. And put away your weapons, there is no need. I am an ally. Or at least, I hope to be."

Elissia and Marcus looked to Erick, waiting for his okay. He nodded. He had no idea why this strange creature was here, but he had to assume if Sasesus meant to kill them, he wouldn't have announced himself.

The siblings put away their knives. Mallow was slower to do so.

The group sat on the floor beside the low table since they had no chairs. Sangay sat against the wall and removed his food from his pack. Erick didn't know where the desert man's meals came from or how he packed so much in his small bag.

The food smelled of meat and spices that promised to burn the throat and sear the tongue. They had no utensils or bread, so Erick picked up the bowl. Before he put it to his lips, he looked at Sasesus. "We seem to have an extra place if you would care to join us."

Sasesus opened his mouth slightly, then closed it. *A smile?* Erick wondered.

"I am not hungry, but do not let me stop you."

Erick nodded. *You want it?* He asked Blink.

I'll wait. I'm not convinced it isn't poisoned.

Erick smiled. If Blink thought there was a chance of such a thing, he wouldn't have let any of them eat. Erick put the bowl to his mouth and swallowed some of the rich broth. The rich, fiery spices set his mouth aflame. Erick almost choked. He grabbed the clay cup and drank the yellow liquid within. It tasted of blackberries. It cooled his mouth but did nothing to chase away the fire.

"This is delicious," Corby said.

Erick couldn't agree, although something enticing about the flavor made him want more.

"You were going to tell us who you were," Elissia reminded Sasesus. Her face was bright red, and her voice came out strangled as if the spicy food had nearly gagged her too.

The creature nodded. His long snout went up and down while his eyes didn't move. Erick found it disconcerting. "I am Sasesus, one of the *Aesirasai*, the chosen of Alais, from whom all comes."

Erick stopped eating as excitement ran through him. "You know Alais?"

Sasesus offered his strange nod again. "I am honored with the knowledge of her."

"So, you can take us to her?"

"That is my purpose."

Thank you, Denech, Erick thought. Until now, he hadn't fully realized how much the prospect of having to find the woman with no guidance weighed him down. Somehow, he had been able to keep the thought pushed down by his concerns of making it this far. To know he wouldn't have to spend precious months or years searching and possibly never finding her made tears of relief come to his eyes.

"That's wonderful," Elissia said. "You're the best news we've had in a long time."

"Yes, you are," Marcus agreed. "I knew there was more to green hat than he let on. You were here waiting for us, weren't you?"

"Alais knows much."

"She knew we were coming?" Erick asked.

"She knew there was a possibility. I have been here for many months."

Erick grinned. "I'm glad you waited."

The *Aesirasai* cocked his head to the side, then opened and closed his mouth again. Erick was more convinced it was the creature's way of smiling. "I am pleased you find my presence acceptable."

"More than acceptable," Elissia said as she held up her glass. "To Sasesus," she said, "and not having to stumble around a swamp like idiots wearing blindfolds."

They all held up their cups, except Sangay, who had not taken his from the table.

"To Sasesus," they all said and drank.

Erick slept well that night, better than in recent memory. Sasesus had informed them they would have three days travel through the swamp to reach Alais, where she secluded herself. Erick tried asking the strange creature about Alais, but Sasesus demurred, saying she would tell them what she wanted them to know, and it was not his place to do so.

The next morning, they arose early, packed, and left with Sasesus. The village inhabitants watched them go. Dark eyes glittered in somber faces, and none of them spoke.

"These people are unfriendly," Sangay said. "Living in such wet and stink must affect them."

It surprised Erick. The desert man had hardly spoken the past several days.

"Trust me," Elissia said, "compared to some of the receptions we've gotten, these people are like coming home to family."

They reached the wall. The village leader, the man in the bright green hat, waited there. When they drew near, he spoke, and Corby translated. "I hope you find what you seek and save us all, though I fear..." Corby stumbled for a moment, then finished the translation with a grave voice. "Though I fear your presence will bring our destruction."

"That would explain all the death stares," Marcus said.

"Tell him we thank him for letting us stay, and I will do my best to repay their kindness with something more than annihilation."

Corby translated.

The leader gave a grim nod, then tapped the wall. The carefully hidden door slid into its hole with the faint grinding sound, and the group passed through.

"This way," Sasesus said and started toward the jungle.

The next three days were a trial of wet, hot misery. Though the sun only shone fitfully through the dense jungle canopy, the vegetation trapped heat and moisture. Water dripped from the leaves and vines and sweat clung to all of them. Sangay seemed to suffer the worst, his flowing desert garb hanging from him in a soaked, shapeless blob. After the first day, he removed his head wrap to reveal a head of curly hair the color of sand. It gave him a much less foreboding appearance. As miserable as it was this time of year, Erick didn't want to think about what it would be like during high summer. It made him thirsty to consider it.

Each night, Erick praised Denech and Caros for sending them Sasesus. Without the *Aesirasai* guiding them, they would have never made it. If the numerous snakes and crocodiles hadn't killed them, eating a poisonous plant or drinking tainted water certainly would have. Sasesus had some power over the animals. At his presence, they either slithered away or watched from a distance, beady reptilian eyes following the group with undisguised hunger. Erick had never heard of any magic that allowed such talents. When Erick questioned Sasesus, he would say, "Alais gives many gifts."

Sasesus knew this swamp like Erick knew his lost manor house. He pointed out to the group what they could and couldn't eat, where to drink, and where to step and not sink any further than your ankles. That's the other thing that might have killed them. Loamy ground that looked firm could swallow a person. Sasesus demonstrated this with a dead tree branch once, and Erick shuddered to think of death by drowning in the fetid swamp water.

"It's one thing to read about a place like this," Corby said their first night of camp. "But it's quite another to experience it. I hope I can do the description justice when I write it down."

So, they were miserable and hot, but Erick reflected that it could have been so much worse.

On the third day, shortly after the House of Caros had begun its downward trek toward the horizon, twenty more creatures stepped from hidden places and surrounded them, bone weapons at the ready.

E rick hadn't seen or heard anything until the beings showed themselves. His heart jumped as they appeared, and his mind leapt back to a similar incident on the road, when swordsmen emerged from a field of grain. With as many times as this had happened since that ambush, he didn't think he would ever get used to it.

Before anyone could draw weapons, Sasesus held up his hand. "These are friends," he said.

"They have a funny way of showing it," Marcus said, hand on his dagger. "Scaring the hell out of someone and pointing weapons at them isn't friendly behavior."

Sasesus gave his open-mouthed reptilian smile. "My apologies, I forget you are jungle-blind. I saw them from far back. Had I remembered, I would have warned you."

Marcus nodded and pulled his hand away from the weapon. "You should visit my sewers sometime, and we'll see how you fare." Though the words were a challenge, the thief's tone made them a joke.

"He might do fine," Elissia said in a low voice. "This place smells about the same as the sewers."

Sasesus indicated the creatures around them. "These are more of my tribe, more *Aesirasai*. We should continue. The clearing is near."

"Yes, let's," Erick said with a nod. Now that he wasn't focused on the sharpened bones that approximated swords, he could see the resemblance between their guide and the newcomers. They followed the band of creatures deeper into the foliage.

"How much further?" Erick asked.

There was a pause as Sasesus considered the question. He gestured with his clawed hands. "Not far. Only—" he spoke a sibilant word Erick didn't understand. He cocked his head a moment and then continued. "One mile through the path."

"Thank you."

The "path" turned out to be barely a foot-wide break in the greenery. Several times Sasesus and the other *Aesirasai* had to slow down for Erick and his companions to catch up as they snagged on creeping vines or ducked low-hanging branches. Tight spaces had never particularly bothered Erick, but the closeness pressed in on him. The jungle had been challenging to navigate their whole journey, but this foliage seemed exceptionally dense and unyielding, despite the path. It was as if the land fought them, not wanting to let them through. Insect sounds echoed around them, and unseen creatures rustled through the undergrowth.

The whole situation unnerved Erick, despite the presence of Sasesus and the others. He never before understood Marcus's intense dislike, even fear, of open spaces. Now he began to have some inkling of how such feelings could exist. He broke out in a sweat, barely noticeable on his already slick skin. Cloying scents of flowers and vines clogged his nose. By the time they reached the promised clearing, he had to breathe through his mouth.

The growth ended so abruptly, Erick almost stumbled out into the clearing, a circular area large enough to hold his home village. Huts and open-air pavilions built from leaves, vines, and tree trunks filled the space. Crocodile-like *Aesirasai* moved about like any town, performing mundane tasks. The smell of roasting meat reached Erick's nose. He saw a haunch of some animal suspended over a stack of yellow stones. Juice dripped and sizzled against the rocks, although no fire was in evidence.

Many of the inhabitants stopped to watch as the group moved through the village. With their non-human eyes and impassive faces, it was hard to tell what they thought. This disturbed Erick as much as the close jungle had.

"People below the falls must make a living out of staring at strangers," Marcus said, his sarcasm defeated by his shaking voice.

The deeper into the village they went, the more nervous Erick grew. He wondered if they were being lured in to be killed and, if the rumors were true, eaten.

"I don't like this," Elissia said.

"That makes two of us," Erick told her.

They eventually reached the center, a circle formed by a cluster of huts. A large pit piled with yellow stones, similar to the one they had passed, occupied the middle. Although these gave off no heat, the charred sides and scattered bones provided evidence of frequent use.

"Wait here," Sasesus said, pointing a scaly hand at the ground. He then offered a curt nod and walked toward the largest hut at the edge of the circle. The armed contingent that followed them dispersed, leaving behind four of them to take up positions around the group, their sword-shaped bone weapons held loose and non-threatening.

"What do we think?" Elissia asked once Sasesus had disappeared into the hut.

"I think we may be main courses soon," Marcus said.

Corby shook his head. "I don't believe they would have taken the time to speak with us and bring us here if they were just going to kill us."

"You never heard of bringing cattle to slaughter?" Marcus asked.

Corby pointed at the pit. "None of those bones are human. I suspect the stories of the viciousness are exaggerated. Sasesus doesn't speak like a savage. If anything, he speaks better Zatrim than some born there."

"You may be right," Erick said. He noticed after the initial curiosity of their arrival, the *Aesirasai* went back to their chores, as if unconcerned by the interlopers.

Several long minutes passed in uncomfortable silence. The humidity made the sweat cling to Erick's face and arms. No one seemed inclined to talk.

Though Erick saw or heard nothing, a signal must have gone out from the tent. Their guards stiffened into an alert posture. Tension sprinted across the clearing until every inhabitant in sight stood erect and faced the tent.

Erick's skin prickled as nervousness infused him. He offered a prayer to Caros and Denech that this encounter turned out better than the disappointment of Broken Mountain.

Several charged seconds passed before anything else happened. Then the door to the hut swung open. Sasesus stepped out, his movements stiff and formal.

A woman followed.

A jolt passed through Erick as he thought the woman was Valarie, the gruff healer from the Procurer's lair in Kalador.

As she walked toward them, Erick realized the resemblance was superficial. Though both women had frizzy gray hair, this woman's visage shone with open friendliness where Valarie's had been bitter and contemptuous. The lines that creased her forehead and mouth gave her a regal look that spoke of wisdom and laughter, not pettiness and scowls.

She walked with a firm bearing, her apparent age no detriment to her ability to move. All eyes followed the woman as she advanced on Erick and his companions. When she passed a knot of the crocodile creatures, they offered a slight incline of their heads and made a sibilant sound deep in their throats.

She drew close to Erick, Sasesus behind her, all ease gone from his posture.

Erick didn't know if these beings acted this way out of fear or respect. The uncertainty knotted his stomach.

She stopped in front of Erick and stared into his eyes. A sensation of unknowable eons crept into his brain. However old this woman appeared, she was far older than anything Erick ever encountered. It dwarfed the impression of ancient time he had gotten from meeting the shades of the original Necromancers. Presence and power poured from her. Erick realized now his nervousness had not come from the jungle, but the aura emanating from the person before him. She was more than a woman, his mind told him. She was somehow the jungle come to life.

He dropped his gaze, unable to look long at the majesty behind the woman's countenance, fearful it would drive him mad. Only then did he notice her pale skin had a tinge of green beneath the pallor.

"Greetings, Erick of Draymed," she said, her voice rich and warm. "It is my understanding you have come a long way seeking me."

He forced himself to look up and meet her gaze. "We have." His voice sounded insignificant to his ears. "If you are the mistress known as Alais."

She offered a radiant smile. The last of his nervousness fled. He sensed she accepted his words, so the jungle now accepted him.

"I am. I suspect you knew that. It's not the average old woman who has a whole village of her children."

"Children?"

"Oh, yes. All you see around you are my children. I brought them up from the mud to become proper people."

Erick didn't fully understand the woman's words. Was she the queen of these primitive people? She obviously couldn't be the mother of one of these creatures, much less a whole village. Had he traveled all this way to meet someone deranged?

An amused sparkle filled her eyes, which Erick now realized were the deep, blue-black of the night sky. "I am not crazy. I am—"

"I know who you are," Elissia said, though it was not Elissia's voice. The bubbling, diseased voice belonged to the entity Erick had thought destroyed. Elissia's olive skin turned sickly green. Her eyes went glassy, and her mouth twisted into a snarl. "I know who you are," she repeated. "You think you can stop us, but you can't. Your power to defeat us disappeared when you fled from your lofty perch. You are nothing."

A dagger appeared in Elissia's hand. Before anyone could react, she lunged. The blade drove forward and slammed into the ancient woman's chest. Blood sprayed past Elissia's hand.

Alais let out a watery sigh and collapsed, the blade going with her.

No one moved for several seconds. Shocked, Erick stared at Elissia. The madness left her eyes, and the bilious green faded from her skin.

A deeply agitated hissing began, the sound coming from every village inhabitant. They drew their bone weapons.

Erick saw their death in every snouted face.

Terror filled Elissia's eyes. "What happened?" she asked. "What's going on?"

END OF BOOK TWO

ACKNOWLEDGMENTS

A shout out to Jill Lugar, who helped me make sure a difficult scene involving emotions and body parts read well. If it still doesn't, it's my fault. Also, to Josh, Kirk, Greg (and sometimes Damon), the guys I roll dice and move meeples with on Saturdays. They keep me laughing even when I'm losing horribly (which is often)

And as always, Tony. There for over twenty years with a promise of many more.

ABOUT THE AUTHOR

Paul Barrett has lived a varied life full of excitement and adventure. Not really, but it sounds good as an opening line.

Paul's multiple careers have included: rock and roll roadie, children's theater stage manager, television camera operator, mortgage banker, and support specialist for Microsoft Excel.

This eclectic mix allowed him to go into his true love: motion picture production. He has produced two motion pictures and two documentaries: His film *Night Feeders* released on DVD in 2007, and *Cold Storage* was released by Lionsgate in May 2010.

Amidst all this, Paul has worked on his writing, starting with his first short story, about Ziggy Stardust and the Spiders from Mars, at age 8. Paul has written and produced numerous commercial and industrial video scripts in his tenure with his former creative agency, Indievision.

Paul lives in North Carolina with three cats and his film director/graphic designer husband.

ALSO BY PAUL BARRETT

The Malaise Falchion (Book One of the Spade Case Files)

A Whisper of Death (Book One of The Necromancer Saga)

Knight Errant (Chronicles of the Knights of the Flaming Star Book One -
With Steve Murphy)

www.ingramcontent.com/pod-product-compliance
Lightning Source LLC
Chambersburg PA
CBHW020233110726
47898CB00004B/1243